STACY M. JONES

Midnight Judge

First published by Stacy M. Jones 2024

Copyright © 2024 by Stacy M. Jones

All rights reserved. No part of this publication may be reproduced, stored or transmitted in any form or by any means, electronic, mechanical, photocopying, recording, scanning, or otherwise without written permission from the publisher. It is illegal to copy this book, post it to a website, or distribute it by any other means without permission.

This novel is entirely a work of fiction. The names, characters and incidents portrayed in it are the work of the author's imagination. Any resemblance to actual persons, living or dead, events or localities is entirely coincidental.

Stacy M. Jones asserts the moral right to be identified as the author of this work.

Stacy M. Jones has no responsibility for the persistence or accuracy of URLs for external or third-party Internet Websites referred to in this publication and does not guarantee that any content on such Websites is, or will remain, accurate or appropriate.

Designations used by companies to distinguish their products are often claimed as trademarks. All brand names and product names used in this book and on its cover are trade names, service marks, trademarks and registered trademarks of their respective owners. The publishers and the book are not associated with any product or vendor mentioned in this book. None of the companies referenced within the book have endorsed the book.

First edition

ISBN: 979-8-218-51347-4

This book was professionally typeset on Reedsy.
Find out more at reedsy.com

For Nathan

Acknowledgments

Washington D.C. is one of my favorite cities and I've been wanting to set a series there. Connor Fitzgerald "Fitz" came to me via my FBI Agent Kate Walsh thriller series. He appeared in Dead Senate and the idea of him took hold. I wrote several other novels in between that one and this. Still, Fitz would hang around like a ghost in my office urging me to tell his stories. He didn't make it easy on me the way some of my characters do – he's a man with layers who doesn't want to give up his secrets easily. I know it sounds strange, but he and I are on this journey together.

Through that, I've been grateful for the support of my experts I use for my FBI Agent Kate Walsh series. It's given me a chance to reach out to old work colleagues, better understand the Supreme Court, and tie in a little history along with it. I am always grateful for the FBI agents, local detectives, forensic experts, and in this case, legal experts I've been able to lean on for information – those who responded to texts and late-night calls when I needed to problem solve or even when I couldn't find the information I needed online. Any mistakes are my own.

Special thanks as always to my incredible team without whom I would not be publishing novels. Thanks to 17 Studio Book Design for bringing my stories to life with incredible covers. Thank you to Dj Hendrickson for your insightful editing and Liza Wood for proofreading and revisions. I am so grateful to each of these incredible women who ensure my work is professional and interesting to the reader.

Thanks also to my advanced reader team who had first eyes on the finished product. I'm grateful for their feedback and interest in the new series. I'm also grateful for friends who are like family to me who keep nudging me along in this career. And to my mother who never fails to ask how book sales are going or what I'm writing and endlessly telling me to take breaks and days off and go have some fun.

I'm excited to start this new journey with all of you.

CHAPTER 1

Connor Fitzgerald groaned as the phone cut through the silence of his slumber, beckoning him awake. He rolled over and slapped the nightstand, refusing to open his eyes. He palmed the phone and brought it to his face. Only then did he crack one eyelid. 4:55 a.m.

He engaged the call still lying down. "Please tell me you're not heading out for a jog at this hour," he admonished the caller. "I've told you before you shouldn't jog in Rock Creek Park in the dark. All kinds of things can happen to you out there."

The woman on the other end of the line snickered. "There was a time when you would have beat me out the door on a run. You've gotten soft in your old age, Fitz."

"What do you want, Sutton? I know this isn't a social call." Fitz shoved himself upright, the sheet pooling around his middle and exposing his naked chest to the cool air. He had long ago determined that if he kept his bedroom colder than the rest of the house, he slept better. His guests didn't appreciate it quite as much.

"We need a favor," she said quickly, then didn't say anything else.

Fitz could only guess that the other part of the *we* in the equation was Sutton's fiancé, Judge Harvey Sinclair. Not that he had anything against the judge for dating his ex-wife. He just didn't want to get involved. Fitz had been married to Sutton for three years in their late twenties and divorced for more than two decades. He'd had many labels over his lifetime. Good husband wasn't one of them. He wasn't terrible, but he hadn't been what Sutton needed.

Against his better judgment, he asked, "What do you need?"

"Not on the phone."

"What time and where?"

Sutton rattled off the name of a coffee shop and the address. "It shouldn't take you long to get there. Only a few Metro stops."

Fitz hadn't told Sutton he had upgraded from his brownstone in Georgetown to a sprawling six-bedroom nearly five-thousand-foot house in Chevy Chase, Maryland. He had craved more land than his brownstone afforded. When his business took off, he invested in the house. He still had the proximity to Washington D.C. without being at the center of action after a long day.

Fitz had no idea how Sutton would feel about the purchase, not that her opinion should matter. He'd save the conversation about the house until they were sitting face-to-face. "I'll be there in thirty minutes."

"Make it twenty," she countered and hung up before he could argue.

Fitz dropped the phone into his lap and turned his head to look at the sleeping woman beside him. Her bare back was exposed and a leg snaked around the sheet. He hated to admit it to himself but he couldn't remember her name. Alicia. Amelia. Andrea...something like that. Given the amount they drank the night before, he wasn't surprised she hadn't been roused by the conversation.

Fitz slipped out of bed, jotted a note that he had to leave, and left her cab money – all the while fighting annoyance at himself for the choices he continued to make.

It wouldn't be morning if he wasn't chastising himself for something.

Twenty-three minutes later, Fitz sauntered into the coffee shop

CHAPTER 1

freshly showered and ready to take on the day. He had dark jeans cuffed with boots and a green Henley. He had two days scruff and his dark curly hair had a messy *I don't give a crap* quality about it that suited him fine. He didn't much care what anyone thought of his hair or anything relating to him. It was one of the reasons he was good at his job.

Fitz spotted Sutton sitting at a back corner table sipping coffee. When she locked her gaze on him, she pointed across the table to a cup she had already purchased for him. He stopped momentarily to look at the display case, craving something chocolate and sweet even at that hour of the morning. If he could get through the meeting without arguing, he'd allow himself a treat before he left.

Fitz moseyed to the back of the shop, not in any rush. When he reached the chair, he placed his hands on the back but didn't pull it out. He drank her in for the first time in months, maybe a year. They had spoken through text and occasional phone calls, but other than seeing her on the news or featured in the society pages, he hadn't laid eyes *or anything else* on her in a long time.

Sutton still looked beautiful and young, much younger than their forty-nine years. While time had its way with him, she had found the fountain of youth. Fitz ran a hand through his unruly hair and stared down at her, wondering if her emerald blouse, cream slacks, and matching purse had a designer label. Of course, they did. Her business as an interior designer had taken off right around the time they turned thirty. Long gone were the days of living in a one-bedroom apartment struggling to make the monthly bills with him.

Fitz dragged himself back to the present. "You woke me up early and dragged me out so it must be important. Besides, I haven't heard from you in a few months."

Sutton tucked her blonde bobbed hair behind her ears and trained her brown eyes on him. She pouted her pretty lips and batted her long, presumably fake, eyelashes at him, even though she didn't have to. Her looks weren't what had attracted Fitz in the first place. It was her brains and sheer ambition, which was on full display now.

"Harvey's son is in trouble at boarding school and I'm not sure who else can help him. A scandal of any kind is not going to look good for him, especially now in the middle of the Supreme Court confirmation hearing. I'm sure you've heard they started already. I need your investigative skills as much as I need your discretion."

Judge Sinclair had been nominated for the Supreme Court, even though almost no one supported it, even President Ellis Mitchell's party. He would be out of office in a few months but he was intent on ramming through his pick. There were backroom deals that had been made. Even with the president's party in the majority in the Senate, Fitz knew the confirmation wouldn't be a breeze. He'd be surprised if the votes were there at all.

"Say something, Fitz," Sutton barked as she folded her arms across herself.

"I don't know what you want me to say. This isn't what I do."

"I know what you do. Opposition research. I get it, Fitz," she said, dropping her voice low and seductive when she said his name. "That requires investigation, not to mention your years as a D.C. Metro detective. Who else can I ask for help?"

Fitz jerked the chair out and sat, his fist landing hard on the table. "Don't do that, Sutton. Don't pretend you're some damsel in distress when we both know that you aren't. Cut the act with me. What did the kid do?"

Sutton relaxed her posture and picked up her coffee, taking a sip and then lowering the cup to the table, cradling it in her hands. In all of that, Sutton never took her gaze off him. "There was a party and a girl was assaulted. One of her friends said it was Holden. He's denied it and so have his friends. It's a bit of a he said, she said. Law

CHAPTER 1

enforcement won't get involved but I want to know the truth."

Fitz didn't like what he was hearing. "I assume by assault you mean a *sexual* assault?"

Sutton frowned and nodded. "I don't know what the young woman has said. Her friend, who claims she was sober, is the one pointing the finger at Holden. I don't know if the girl who was assaulted has said much of anything."

"Women rarely lie about this sort of thing," Fitz challenged her. He watched her carefully to see if Sutton had any reaction to what he said. This wasn't the woman he had once married who would have defended a sexual assault survivor without even knowing the details. The allegation alone would have been enough for Sutton to throw support to the woman. Now, here she was seeming to question the veracity of a young girl's assault.

When she said nothing in response, Fitz extended an olive branch. "Is there something that makes you think she might not be telling the truth?" Even that question was met with silence. Fitz rested his forearms on the table. He cursed at her. "Answer me. You dragged me out here and are asking for my help. The least you can do is explain to me the sudden one-eighty in your personality."

"It's not the first allegation," she said softly and turned away from him. Sutton turned back to him with tears in her eyes.

Fitz didn't have much sympathy for her. "What happened the first time?"

"It was during summer break right before Holden's sophomore year of high school," Sutton started and then abruptly stopped. She pulled out her cellphone and clicked the side button to turn off the phone. When she was sure that it was off, she slipped it back into her bag that was hanging from the chair.

"What's that about?" Fitz asked, pointing to her bag. "Why do you need to make sure your phone is off to tell me this story?" He grew more suspicious as he sat there.

"Harvey wants me to be careful because people are out to get him. That's why he believes what happened at the school is related to him. He can't believe Holden would do something like that."

Fitz wasn't following. "You said Holden was accused of this before." He pulled the chair into the table a little more and leaned onto it. He dropped his voice. "Sutton, I need details and I need them now or I'm leaving."

"Fine," she said, relenting. "Holden and his friends were at Harvey's lake house in North Carolina and everyone was drinking. There were girls there and one of them claimed Holden had sex with her when she was drunk. Holden was just as drunk at the time. She didn't allege that he physically attacked her. She said that because she was so drunk, she couldn't consent. By that same argument, neither could Holden. She went to her father who wanted her to go to the cops. Harvey got involved before that could happen and convinced them to take a pay off. The young woman hadn't wanted to go to the cops anyway or sit through a long trial, so they took the money and kept it all quiet. To this day, no one knows what truly happened. I'm sure if this recent incident comes out, so will that one. He believes this time Holden is being framed. I'm not sure what to believe, but I need the truth."

Fitz didn't have enough of a grasp of the current situation for it to make any sense to him. "Why does the friend think Holden is the one who assaulted her?"

Sutton raised her eyes to him. "The victim woke up in Holden's bed."

Fitz could see how someone could question the first case. Even the victim hadn't wanted to go to the cops – right or wrong. "This is the second time an accusation has come up against Holden. While Sinclair may think he's been set up, don't you think your boyfriend should start taking this seriously?"

CHAPTER 1

Sutton cocked her head to the side the way she did when they were married. It was a sign of annoyance with him. "Fiancé, Fitz. We are getting married in a few months if all goes well."

"You mean if his confirmation hearing goes well." Fitz jutted his chin toward her. "How much has your father invested in Judge Sinclair?"

"Don't bring my father into this." Sutton frowned at his jealousy. They both knew it for what it was. Sutton's father, a big-time D.C. lobbyist, had hated Fitz on sight. He hadn't had the fancy boarding school education Sutton had nor was he an Ivy League graduate. Not that it mattered anymore, but today Fitz earned on par with Sutton's father. He had made good in the end.

"Tell me about the kid," he said, not apologizing for what he knew was a rude question.

Sutton expelled a frustrated breath. "Holden is a senior at a boarding school. They were all drinking at a party in Holden's dorm. A young woman said she was assaulted but she has no memory of who did it. She woke up the next morning in Holden's bed and claimed she couldn't remember anything from the night before. There is a rumor going around that there is a video of the assault and possibly photos. None of the boys are admitting to that. None of them will admit an assault even took place. One of the boys said she passed out in Holden's bed and that he slept on the couch in the common room. This was backed up by other students. There's a lot of speculation without much fact behind it."

Fitz couldn't deny that she was right. There wasn't much to go on. "How did the allegation come about? Did the young woman go seek medical help or go to the police?"

"No," Sutton said, her tone tight. "My understanding is she left his dorm without saying anything to anyone and when she got back to her room told her roommate she felt weird. It was her roommate who suggested she had been drugged and wanted her to go to the police because she said Holden might have assaulted her. The young woman refused the cops and the medical exam. She promised she'd go to the counseling center for support. Unsatisfied with that, it was the roommate who brought the story forward to her mother, who is a reporter for *The New York Times*. In turn, the mother brought it to the school's administration, which kicked off this whole thing."

"What exactly has been *kicked off?*" Fitz asked, confused by the situation. He understood now why Sutton had initially suggested there might not be an assault at all. He didn't see any evidence of one, only that a young woman woke up in a strange bed unsure of what happened the night before, which could mean anything. Fitz's main question surrounded kids at a boarding school without supervision. The *how* this was possible is what sat at the forefront of his mind.

"Brewster Academy has a zero-tolerance policy, as they should," Sutton said. "They have opened an investigation and have already tried to speak with everyone involved. The young woman only partially cooperated. Holden said he and his friends were completely cooperative, even letting school officials search their rooms for drugs. Harvey told them they could put up a fight on the search but the boys said they had nothing to hide. No drugs were found."

Fitz imagined that was because they had already been consumed. Dryly, he asked, "What is it you want me to do?"

Sutton pinned her gaze on him and they shared a look across the table. "Find out the truth for me. I need to know before I marry Harvey." She stared him dead in the eyes. "*If* I marry Harvey."

CHAPTER 2

Fitz rolled into the office around eight-thirty still replaying the events of the morning. He had turned his old brownstone into a comfortable office space. He passed through the empty reception area, which had once been the living room, and made his way up the stairs and down a short narrow hallway to his office – the former main bedroom suite.

He stopped and looked across the hall at the closed door. Fitz knocked once and opened it. "Charlie," he said to the woman behind the desk.

Charlotte Doyle, at least that's the name she had given him, was his only employee and she wasn't even that. She was more like a partner, but her secrets were vast and deep. Fitz learned at the start of their relationship not to ask too many questions.

Charlie, as she had told him to call her, had initially said she had worked for the Department of State. Fitz might have believed it but her investigative skills were better than his. Her shooting skills were too, even though he didn't like admitting that. She was whip-smart and had an eye for detail like no one he'd ever met. She sometimes talked to herself in different accents. The time Fitz caught her, she'd cracked a smile and laughed it off.

Finally, when Fitz pressed after seeing a deep scar that ran from her upper arm across her back, she admitted she'd been CIA. The pain in her eyes had been enough that Fitz left it alone.

Charlie gestured toward the chair in front of her desk. "You're late. You're usually here by seven-thirty."

Fitz laughed and sat down in front of her, resisting the urge to kick his long legs up on her desk. "Who's going to yell at me? It's just us."

Fitz owned the company. After he left the police department, he worked for John Huntly, who had a solid reputation for political opposition research. He could dig up dirt on anyone, even secrets people thought were long since buried. Huntly had a nose like a bloodhound for that kind of work. It was a chance meeting that brought the two of them together. The timing couldn't have been better for Fitz, who had been looking to make a change.

As a detective, Fitz had been talked into taking a high-profile serial homicide case in D.C. that no one else could solve. His former boss didn't want to turn it over to the FBI. Fitz had been baited with the promise of a promotion and a sizable raise if he could solve it. It was a tale as old as time. Fitz did it for the money. His Georgetown brownstone had been besieged by water leaks, growing mold, and was in desperate need of a new roof.

After Fitz solved the case, his boss made him run the circuit of news shows. The brass decided that with Fitz's attractiveness and charm, he might get the right kind of attention to get the department more funding.

What happened instead was Fitz's good looks whipped most of the press into a frenzy. A few interviews on CNN turned into a couple of interviews on late-night talk shows and the myth of the man became bigger than the truth. Everyone assumed Fitz lapped up the attention. In truth, they didn't see the panic in his eyes and the pool of sweat at his lower back before every interview.

Fitz hated the attention and his media fame became his undoing.

He never did get the promotion. The D.C. Metro Police Department

CHAPTER 2

brass decided Fitz was too much of a liability, too well known, and cases would suffer because of it. He got slapped with desk duty until they could figure out what to do with him. They were no longer happy with the monster they had created.

A few months later, when Fitz was living under blue tarps at the brownstone, he met Huntly in a bar one night while they were both drowning their sorrows. Huntly was getting old and there was no one to take over the business empire he had built. There wasn't anyone in D.C. who didn't know Huntly. He was a legend and had no qualms about the cases he took as long as the money rolled in. It was exactly what Fitz needed.

That beer turned into late-night dinners discussing Huntly's cases. That turned to some side work with hefty paychecks for Fitz. After about a year, Huntly made him a deal – pay him monthly for the business and take it over. It was an offer he couldn't refuse. Fitz's first year in business, even after expenses and paying Huntly, he made more than his last five years as a detective. Best of all, he loved the work.

Huntly stayed on taking a case here or there just to stay busy. The poor man died on the job a few months after Fitz took it over. Turned out, Huntly had willed Fitz the business. It was his free and clear. Everything had been left to Fitz including the man's rundown office, which was promptly sold.

With money flowing in, Fitz made the repairs to the old brownstone and hung his shingle there. The upgraded digs impressed clients and brought in even more, branching out beyond politics to businesses that wanted to vet upper management and partners. He couldn't have asked for a better location.

For a while, he slept in the bedroom on the third floor and worked on the lower floors. A few years of business growth raking in millions and another chance meeting brought him Charlie. He saw a lot of himself in her that night they met in a Georgetown dive bar only frequented by locals. While he was immediately attracted to her with her shoulder-length fiery red hair, crystal blue eyes, and ridge of freckles across her nose, he didn't want to hit on her. He didn't want her to be another one-night stand or a couple of months' fling. He had rightly sensed there was more to her that he wanted to get to know.

Bringing her on was probably the best decision Fitz made. The more he got to know her, the more impressed he was. She kept the office running smoothly and challenged him in the gym. The few times they had sparred together, Fitz was the one who walked away bruised and battered.

Charlie never talked about her past. Only that she'd been raised by a single mother and had won a full-ride scholarship to Georgetown University. Like him, she'd been married and divorced in her twenties and had chosen a government career over having children. They had the same Gen X temperament and knew how to steer clear of one another depending on their moods. What he liked more than anything was the easy way Charlie called him out on all his crap.

"You look tired." She smirked. "Was the woman you brought home last night a little young, too much for you? You have to leave those young ones alone, Fitz. They don't know the signs of a heart attack."

He laughed. "She was three years younger." Fitz knew that Charlie would zero in on him this morning. There was no hiding anything from her. He swore Charlie's intuition bordered on psychic. "Sutton called me this morning before dawn and asked to meet. When I got to the coffee shop, she asked me to look into something, off the books."

Charlie rolled her eyes. Although she had only crossed paths with Sutton a handful of times, the disdain they felt for each other was right on the surface. She leaned into the desk and scolded Fitz like a schoolboy. "You know no good will come of this. You've been divorced for two decades and yet she can still pull your strings. Haven't you

CHAPTER 2

punished yourself enough? People get divorced, Fitz. It happens."

"I know," he said absently. "I can't say no to her. I don't know why."

"You're still in love with her and hope she'll come to her senses and come back to you."

Charlie was wrong there. "That's not it. Sutton and I didn't work then and we wouldn't work now. I'm happy she's found someone."

Charlie wasn't convinced. "Come on, Fitz. There is a big *but* in that sentence."

Fitz wasn't sure he wanted to admit what he was feeling. He stared over at Charlie until her eyes grew narrow with knowing. "I don't think she's happy with Judge Sinclair. He's too old for her and too controlling. Sutton built a good business as a designer and now she's saddling herself with his poor reputation. Even if Sutton wasn't my ex, I'd be concerned for her. I wouldn't want you to take on something like that."

"That would never happen. I have better sense and far better taste in men."

Fitz broke into a wide grin. "That's debatable."

Charlie ignored the comment. "You know it doesn't matter what you do now you're not going to wipe the slate clean for all of your perceived marriage failures. It's noble of you to try, but it takes two people to make a marriage work and Sutton isn't blameless. What did you do that was so wrong? Not having the money Sutton's father has and working too much trying to give her the life you thought she deserved? That's hardly a poor husband."

It was true. Fitz hadn't cheated or even so much as flirted with another woman. He hadn't been a drinker or gambler or put the few friends he had above his time with her. He hadn't made her responsible for all the household chores. It was Fitz who cooked more than Sutton, even on nights he worked late. He knew he hadn't done anything terrible, but he hadn't been able to keep Sutton happy and for that he blamed himself.

"It doesn't matter why I'm taking this on. I'm taking it on," he said with finality in his voice, knowing Charlie wouldn't argue.

"So," she said with a shrug, "what happened to his kid?"

Fitz explained everything Sutton had told him about the first and recent accusations. "I've gone my whole life and never once have I been accused of being inappropriate with a woman. For him to be embroiled in something like this twice, all before he graduates high school, tells me something might be amiss with this kid. I want to find out what's going on with him and what other secrets Judge Sinclair is hiding."

Charlie flicked her eyes up to him. "We're investigating Judge Sinclair? I thought this was just about his kid?"

Fitz folded his arms across his chest. He had no reason to expand the investigation. "Call it a gut feeling. Judge Sinclair covered up the first incident. I want to know what else he might be covering up for his son or himself."

Charlie looked back down at the pad of paper in front of her. She made a note while she asked, "Are you going to tell Sutton about your expanded investigation?"

"I don't see any reason to disclose it." Fitz waited for a reaction that never came. He wasn't sure why but he felt a need to defend the decision. "If I'm going all the way to this kid's school outside of Boston, then I want to be sure I know what I'm walking into. We'd do this on any investigation."

Charlie cocked her head to the side. "I wasn't questioning you. But he's in the middle of the confirmation hearing. Don't you think the Senate dug up any dirt?"

Fitz laughed because he knew how poorly they did. "No one asked us and we're the best. I'm sure there is a lot more out there that hasn't been found."

CHAPTER 2

"What do you want me to tell Sutton if she calls?"

"She won't call here. What else is on the agenda?" Fitz asked, happy to push that aside for now.

"You have to meet Senator Graham Barnes. He wants opposition research done. I didn't get too many more details than that." Charlie checked the time. "He should be here in about twenty minutes, so you need to get yourself in the right head space. He's not easy to deal with from what I understand."

"They wouldn't be in politics if they were easy to deal with," Fitz said absently.

With Sutton's case underway and the schedule for the day mapped out, he left Charlie's office and headed for his own. Once inside, he grabbed a bottle of water out of his mini-fridge and sat at his desk. He had to finish writing a report for a business client and then call another potential client who had reached out about an investigation into his son's fiancée. Fitz still wasn't sure he was going to take that case.

Before Fitz got the chance to do anything, Charlie knocked on his office door. "You're going to want to see this."

Fitz raised his head. "What have you got?"

Charlie came in carrying her cellphone. "It's a video from the night of the assault. Someone shared it on social media with a link to a website for the full video. I assume the link isn't going to stay up for long. The website doesn't look sophisticated. The video label says this is Holden Sinclair assaulting a girl. Honestly, Fitz, I can't make out anything other than two people moving around in a bed."

Fitz reached for the cellphone then watched the short version of the video. When he was done, he clicked the link which brought him to a website aptly called StopHoldenSinclair.com. It was hard to tell from the grainy video what he was seeing. A girl's leg poked out from the covers and two people were moving underneath. All he could see was the back of the young man's head. It wasn't even clear the people were having sex and nothing was identifiable about either of the people. The bed itself, the only other thing in the frame, didn't have anything distinctive either. Fitz couldn't even tell the color of the comforter or sheets.

This wasn't a smoking gun. Another page on the website targeted Judge Harvey Sinclair with the message *Is this the kind of family we really want on the Supreme Court?*

For the first time, Fitz considered it was possible Sutton was right and this was all about Judge Sinclair. His son was just the sacrificial lamb.

CHAPTER 3

Brewster Academy was home to close to four hundred students in their freshman to senior years of high school. The boarding school catered to the rich and powerful. Unlike other prep schools, Brewster Academy did not offer scholarships and didn't bother with hardship students no matter their academic achievements.

It seemed to Fitz all that was required for admission was a family that had the right name and connections and the ability to pay the sixty-thousand dollar tuition. Fitz could afford it now, but even if he had a child, he'd certainly never send them here. He had received a solid public school education and it would be good enough for his kid. Not that he'd ever need to make the choice.

After his appointment with Senator Barnes, Fitz left the office. He made the nearly nine-hour drive only stopping once for gas. He had fueled up his SUV and himself and got back on the road again. On the drive, he called Sutton. After their meeting, it occurred to him he had never asked if Sinclair knew she had gone to him for help. Sutton informed him that she didn't want to bother Sinclair in the middle of the confirmation hearing. Fitz was to get the information as quickly and quietly as possible.

When Fitz asked if Holden would tell his father, Sutton assured him he wouldn't. None of it made Fitz comfortable. He had called ahead to the school and said he was investigating the incident for the Sinclairs and left it at that. The school headmaster assured him full access and said he'd meet with him as soon as he arrived. Fitz asked that he keep his presence under wraps for now as he didn't want to stir up any more gossip. He lied and said Judge Sinclair was embarrassed by the allegations as well as the online video and didn't wish to discuss it further unless legal action was being taken. Then, and only then, the school could speak to his lawyer. Fitz hoped it would buy him enough time to get in, sort out the incident, and have some resolution for Sutton before Sinclair was even aware he'd been to the school.

Fitz arrived late in the evening. His car clock glowed 9:25 p.m., but it was set ten minutes ahead. He hated being late for anything. Fitz drove down one narrow tree-lined road after another until he finally saw Brewster Academy in the distance. The school sat on more than seven hundred acres and was unlike any school Fitz had seen. Even the private prep schools where D.C. powerbrokers sent their children couldn't compare to the grandness of Brewster Academy.

Fitz hit the buzzer at the fifteen-foot-high iron gates, announced his presence, and then slowly pulled his SUV forward as the gates opened. The long road to the main building of Brewster Academy made Fitz feel like he was arriving to meet royalty in England. The grand edifice of the school was three stories of French Gothic style with a tall center tower and one on each side of the structure. The building had a steep sloping roof with soaring spires and turrets.

The sight of it knotted Fitz's stomach.

The paved road turned to crushed stone, crunching under his tires. Before Fitz even arrived at the building, a man stood ramrod straight outside the front door that was flanked by large lion sculptures on each side.

Fitz pulled to the side of the circular drive, put it in park, and cut the engine. He took his time getting out of the car, psyching himself

CHAPTER 3

up for this case. It was the first time in a long time Fitz was walking into a case feeling the dread of uncertainty. Nothing was adding up for him and that was problematic at best.

"Mr. Fitzgerald," the short bald man said with a stiff smile as he extended a hand. He had to crane his neck to look up at Fitz. "I'm Mr. Robins, the headmaster here at Brewster Academy. We spoke earlier."

"Please call me Fitz," he said as he shook the man's hand. Fitz's hand engulfed his and it was like shaking hands with a child.

The man squinted and shook his head. "We don't allow such informalities here."

"Okay, but I might not respond," Fitz said with a shrug. He didn't like Robins and wasn't going to address him by mister anything. The man wasn't *his* headmaster. "I'd like you to give me the lay of the land and what you know about the case. Then I'd like to see where all of this took place."

"You can't see that tonight. The children are in their dorms and it is nearly time for lights off. You can't disturb them tonight." Robins moved past Fitz and entered the building leaving no room for argument or negotiation.

Fitz followed right behind him. He swore the lions' eyes followed him as he entered. He didn't like being told no, especially by an arrogant little man like Robins. Once inside, Fitz stopped dead in his tracks. "Listen, Robins, I need to understand something before we go any further."

Robins turned on his heels to face Fitz. He tugged the bottom of his tweed sport coat down. "As I said, it's *Mr.* Robins."

Fitz took a few steps toward him until the man nearly had his face in Fitz's chest. He looked straight down at Robins. "Help me to understand something. If you're so strict on lights out and that children are not being disturbed, how did they pull off a party with alcohol? Seems to me if the kids were being monitored as they should be, none of this would have happened."

A groan of fear escaped Robin's mouth. He snapped his jaw shut and stepped back. "Is that why you're here? Is Judge Sinclair thinking of suing the school? Should I call our lawyer?"

Fitz put his meaty hand on the man's shoulder. "Calm down, buddy. This isn't a formal questioning. I need to understand the school's role in all of this. If there were supposed to be chaperones, I need to understand what they know and where they were while this took place."

Robins huffed in surprise and pulled out of Fitz's grasp. "Do not call me buddy, especially in front of the children. We have decorum to uphold."

Fitz tsked. "Drunken parties and sexual assault allegations aren't exactly decorum unless we've got different definitions. I didn't go to a fancy school like this, so we might not be speaking the same language." Fitz could tell he was wearing on the man. That was the point. Fitz needed to break through his stuffy demeanor and get down to the nitty-gritty. He needed to ruffle some feathers.

Robins wasn't going to be so easy to break. "Mr. Fitzgerald, what happened here was unfortunate and the staff responsible have been addressed. We don't routinely have incidences like this happen on our campus. We have a certain standard for our students and they are usually met."

Fitz shrugged it off. "I'm hearing words like *routinely* and *usually* and that tells me it's happened here more than you're letting on. I don't care about those other cases. I need to know what happened on this one and I need to know who was involved." Fitz stepped toward the man again, his face and tone stern. "I need to know that now."

Robins backed up holding his hand out to stop Fitz from coming forward. Had Fitz wanted he could have easily knocked the man on his backside. He wasn't looking for a fight. He simply wanted to make

CHAPTER 3

it clear to Robins that he wasn't going to deal with the usual red tape that hamstrung investigations at schools.

"Let's go to my office and I'll give you the details of what I know to date. We have been conducting an internal investigation. So far, not much has been discovered." Robins walked down a maze of hallways lined with large portraits of the school's headmasters. Robins, if he was lucky, would have his portrait among them. Fitz noticed the last headmaster had served from the mid-sixties until 2002.

"How long have you been headmaster here?"

Robins quickly realized why he asked it. He pointed to the last portrait. "I took over in 2002. I've been here since. It's a bit ostentatious to have all these portraits here. It's a board of directors' decision rather than my own."

Fitz followed him into a large, dark wood-paneled room that had a dark maroon carpet. The room had a desk in the middle of it, several chairs lining the walls, and another larger door off to the right. They passed by what Fitz assumed was a secretary's desk and then Robins opened the door leading to his office. "Please take a seat at the table and we can talk."

Robins went to a wide desk that seemed elevated from the rest of the room. The height of the desk might just have been taller than a normal size to give Robins the feeling of looking down at those who sat across from it.

Fitz pulled out the chair and sat. "When did you first become aware of the situation?"

Robins went to a filing cabinet and pulled out a file folder. He carried it over to the table and sat down. He flipped it open, pushed his glasses up his nose, and read. "The Monday after the incident which occurred on a Friday night. The young men and young women have separate boarding facilities. The young men are farther back on our campus while the girls' dormitories are in a cluster closer to the academic buildings. They are also separated by year, so we don't have freshmen bunking with seniors. There is quite a gap in maturity during that time, even if it's only a four-year difference."

"Tell me about the party," Fitz said, sitting back and folding his arms across his chest.

Robins didn't read from the file. He got straight to the point, finally. "The young men involved had a party on Friday night. They were celebrating a lacrosse win. They are allowed to have young women in the common room only. The same with the senior girls. Underclassmen are not allowed. There was a group of fifteen or so of them gathered together. They had prior approval and as such, the house parents gave them their space. They hadn't become loud or shown any signs they were out of control. There was no reason to check on them."

Fitz figured that made sense. "Were all of the students seniors?"

"Yes," Robins said. "Some of them have turned eighteen. Now that doesn't mean much here, they are still in our care. But they are technically adults. We give our seniors more freedom than the other students. At that point, we assume we have prepared them to go out into the world and make good decisions."

No one at eighteen was ready to make good decisions in Fitz's opinion. Sure, some of them did but far too many did not. "How'd they get the alcohol?"

Robins tsked. "That we don't know. None of the students have been willing to tattle on their friends. I can assure you it did not come from anywhere on campus and none of our staff would supply it. We assume one of the students was able to access it and brought it in."

"What about the drugs?"

"No drugs were found." Robins pulled a sheet of paper out of the file folder and slid it over to Fitz. "This is a report from the campus security. We searched the students' rooms and the whole dormitory

CHAPTER 3

building and found nothing. We even brought in a dog from the local police department. Nothing was found. I can't substantiate any drug use by any of our students."

That meant nothing to Fitz. He had pot in his room growing up and neither of his parents had any idea. "When did the search take place and did the kids know ahead of time that a search would be happening?"

Robins shifted his eyes away from Fitz. "Well, we didn't want to spring it on them. We aren't the police and we try to show our students the same respect that we require of them. We teach by example here." Robins smoothed down his tie. "We searched on Wednesday and the students knew late on Tuesday."

"Long enough to get rid of any drugs, assuming they hadn't used all of them over the weekend." Fitz pushed the page back to Robins. "This is useless. What else have you done to investigate?"

Robins flipped to another page in the file and read through a list of students they had spoken to about the party and the alleged sexual assault. No one saw anything. No one did anything. No one heard anything. "I don't know what more I can tell you. We have done our due diligence and we can't even substantiate that a sexual assault took place."

Fitz raised an eyebrow. "Did you see the video that surfaced today?"

"Yes, it was shown to me by one of the staff."

Fitz watched him carefully. "What did you think about it?"

"Honestly, it didn't look like an assault to me. It could have been casual sex. I also can't say that it happened in our dorm. Nothing was familiar to me."

"Good," Fitz said, surprising him. "That's what I thought too. Now, we need to get to the bottom of what really happened. To do that, I need access to your students and to conduct my investigation my way." He stood and stared down at Robins. "Understood?"

Robins gave a curt nod.

"Great. I'll be back in the morning." With that Fitz didn't wait for Robins to get up and escort him out. He found his way outside and aimed his SUV for the nearest hotel – already feeling like this was a waste of his time.

CHAPTER 4

Fitz slapped the bedside table for his cellphone and cursed his luck. This was the second morning he was jarred from his sleep by a ringing phone. He already regretted answering Sutton's call the morning before. Whoever this was Fitz was sure it wouldn't bring anything good.

"Hello," he grumbled then cleared his throat. "You better have a good reason for calling me this early." Fitz blinked open an eye and saw that it was nearing five a.m.

"Holden's been kidnapped. It's all over the news, Fitz," Charlie said and then had to repeat it. "You need to wake up. Judge Sinclair is going to be on CNN to give an update and interview. He said he called the FBI even though the kidnapper said not to call the cops. I don't know if he's trying to get his son killed or what he's doing."

Fitz shook his head as if he were trying to jar something loose. "How could he have been kidnapped? I was at the school last night."

"Did you speak with Holden?"

"No," Fitz said, sitting up in bed. He didn't bother turning on the light. His eyes adjusted to the darkness as he gave Charlie an overview. "Robins said that I could speak with Holden this morning because the students couldn't be disturbed last night. I didn't see any reason to press the issue. Are you sure Holden is missing?"

"Not *missing*, Fitz. Kidnapped," Charlie stressed and gave him the rundown of what she'd seen on the news. "The news report said Judge Sinclair received a call overnight that his son had been taken and that the kidnapper would call again in the morning with instructions. He was told not to call the cops. I'm surprised Sutton hasn't called you."

Fitz was surprised too. "I'll call her," he started to say. Three loud raps against his door cut him off. "I'll call you back."

"Connor Fitzgerald, this is the FBI," a man shouted. They banged their fist against the door one more time. "FBI!"

"I'm coming!" Fitz scrambled out of bed and grabbed a tee-shirt from the chair and tugged it over his head. He pulled jeans on, hopping on one foot and then the other until he had them around his hips. Fitz didn't even bother buttoning them as he unlatched the bolt lock and pulled the door open. He came face to face with two big angry men who flashed FBI badges in his face.

One shoved him back into the room before he had a chance to stop them.

"What are you doing? You can't come in here," he shouted to no avail. Fitz reached over and flipped on the overhead light and squinted as his eyes adjusted.

"Where's Judge Sinclair's son?" the darker haired agent who'd shoved him asked. When Fitz didn't respond, the man got up in his face. "Answer me. We know you were at the school last night asking about Holden Sinclair. The headmaster found out this morning that you weren't sent by Judge Sinclair, so where is the kid?"

Fitz held his hand up. "You've got this all wrong. Sutton, Judge Sinclair's fiancée, asked me to look into a recent incident at the school. I came up here to investigate it. I spoke to Headmaster Robins last night and he knew exactly why I was here. I even asked to speak to Holden last night and Robins blocked me from doing that."

The dark-haired agent shared a look with his buddy. "You're not authorized to investigate anything."

CHAPTER 4

"Just give me some time to explain." Fitz had worked as a detective long enough to know the FBI didn't play games. It would only help to be forthcoming with information and not hold anything back. They were on the same side after all – or they should be. "I've got my private investigator's badge and my business card in my wallet over there. I'm also a former D.C. Metro homicide detective. It's all legit and above board."

The dark-haired one barked, "You were a D.C. Metro detective? We weren't told that."

Fitz noted the slight mood change. If he hadn't been perceptive, he'd have missed it. Fitz extended his hand and introduced himself. "I run an investigative business out of D.C. now. I'm not sure how much you're around that area but people know me. I do a lot of opposition research for politicians and businesses."

The calmer of the two FBI agents extended his hand. "I'm Agent Josh Burrows. Go get your credentials."

Fitz crossed the room and retrieved his wallet from the bedside table. He carried it over and handed it to Agent Burrows, who examined it carefully.

"Do you want to call Sutton? I can make the call right now," Fitz offered again.

Agent Burrows handed the credentials back. "What is your relationship with her?"

Fitz wanted to ask why it mattered. He got the sense a question in response to a question wouldn't go over well. "Sutton is my ex-wife. We were married years ago but remained somewhat friendly. She called me early yesterday morning and wanted to meet, which we did. She wanted me to investigate an incident that happened here at the school with Holden. As you know, Judge Sinclair is in the middle of the Supreme Court confirmation hearing and this incident could impact that. I don't believe she told Judge Sinclair about the investigation."

"Why is that?"

Fitz felt a loyalty to Sutton, but he wasn't in the business of lying to the FBI. "She was concerned about marrying him because this was the second potential sexual assault connected to Holden. Sutton worried Judge Sinclair was helping his son to get out of trouble and that bothered her, especially given the seriousness of the accusations. She questioned whether this was the right relationship for her. I couldn't blame her if the allegations were true."

Agent Burrows didn't appear to understand as well as Fitz hoped. "I find it strange that your ex-wife would call on you to investigate her fiancé. Doesn't that seem strange to you?"

Fitz didn't have an answer other than the truth. "I don't know what to tell you. It's what happened. Sutton and I had a few rocky years after the divorce like most couples. Then we settled into a cordial and at times friendly relationship."

"How friendly?" Agent Burrows asked with an air of suspicion.

"Not like that," Fitz rushed to say. It wasn't the first time he had to squelch that kind of speculation. "I was happy Sutton moved on with her life. If she was happy with the judge, I was happy. Sutton and I learned a long time ago we didn't make a good couple."

"Why is that, Mr. Fitzgerald?"

Fitz didn't see the relevance and thought they were wasting time on this. "Sutton and I are from different backgrounds. She comes from money and wasn't happy with a lowly cop's salary. She made more than me even in the early years of her interior design business and her father hated me. Thought I was useless. As you know, life with a cop isn't always stable. The hours are as crappy as the paycheck. Sutton needed better than that." Fitz paused and admitted his truth. "Sutton *deserved* better than that."

Agent Burrows finally nodded along in understanding. "Is Sutton financially secure even without Judge Sinclair?"

CHAPTER 4

"Without question," Fitz responded with no hesitation in his voice. "She has a thriving business that's only grown over the years. She counts all the D.C. movers and shakers among her client list. If her money wasn't enough, her father is loaded. Do you know who he is?"

Agent Burrows shook his head. "Should I?"

Fitz wondered how Agent Burrows had missed the connection. "Sutton's father is Edward Barlow, one of the wealthiest and most powerful lobbyists in D.C. He's a powerbroker known for his backroom political deals. The guy is worth millions upon millions." There was something about the way the agent was absorbing the information that sparked Fitz's curiosity. "What does all of this have to do with Holden Sinclair's disappearance?"

"Holden isn't the only one missing," Agent Burrows said evenly.

Fitz wasn't sure what he was driving at. "Who else is missing? Is there another classmate missing? You just woke me up. I haven't even seen the news."

Agent Burrows shook his head. "Sutton has been missing since six last night. There's some question about whether she might have taken Holden."

Fitz absorbed the information like a punch to the gut. It physically knocked him back. "What do you mean Sutton is *missing*? That's not possible. She must be at her parents' house or maybe she had to travel to meet a client. *Missing* simply isn't possible."

"We've spoken to her father, her assistant, and several others. She hasn't been seen or heard from since she left Sinclair's house last night at six. Sinclair speculated she might have taken Holden."

Fitz couldn't even process the information. He couldn't believe it. "There's no way Sutton could have made it here from D.C. last night to kidnap him. Besides, what leverage did she use? Sutton is petite and the photos I saw of Holden were of a nearly grown man. How do you propose she pulled it off and, more importantly, why?"

"We don't know," Agent Burrows admitted. "We heard she sent you up here and we figured it was some kind of recon or distraction. Your response to Sutton's disappearance was genuine. You didn't know. We don't know how she pulled it off. Maybe she wasn't alone."

Fitz couldn't stand still. He paced a small circle as his mind spun with possibilities but nothing made sense. "Sutton wouldn't take off like this. I've never known her to do something like this and she wouldn't have involved me in something illegal. Your theory is all off. If someone took Holden, then they probably took Sutton too."

Agent Burrows shrugged. "We considered that. We have no reason to believe that Sutton didn't leave of her own accord."

Fitz turned to him, the anger building. "You have no reason to believe Sutton would have kidnapped Holden either. Furthermore, I'm telling you Sutton isn't someone who'd take off and she certainly wouldn't kidnap anyone. I'm sure her father told you the same." It occurred to Fitz then that the agent had lied to him. Agent Burrows had acted like he didn't know Sutton's father, but he just said he'd spoken to Sutton's parents.

Fitz narrowed his gaze. "What exactly did Sutton's father tell you?"

If Agent Burrows realized Fitz had caught the lie, he didn't show it. "He holds the same opinion as you. He is concerned something has happened to Sutton and doesn't believe that she could have had anything to do with Holden's disappearance."

"There you have it." The room seemed to be closing in on him. Fitz wanted them out of the room right now. More importantly, he wanted out of the room. "Can I leave or am I being held for something? I've been clear about why I'm here. Feel free to call my office. My business partner can tell you why I'm here."

When Agent Burrows didn't respond, Fitz lost all patience. He went over to the nightstand and grabbed his cellphone. He wasn't going to wait for Agent Burrows to decide. He punched in Charlie's contact.

CHAPTER 4

She answered on the second ring. "Charlie, I want you to speak to FBI Agent Burrows. I need you to tell him everything you know about why I'm here."

Agent Burrows didn't appear to want to speak to Charlie. Fitz wasn't going to give him the option. He thrust the phone toward him and held it there until the agent took the phone.

While he spoke to Charlie, Fitz walked into the bathroom. He stared at his reflection in the mirror cursing the circumstance. The deep line across his forehead seemed deeper than usual and his eyes were sleepy narrow slits. It was a good thing Fitz wasn't vain because he appeared haggard.

Fitz couldn't believe Sutton was missing. He simply couldn't get his mind around it. He bent at the waist and turned on the taps. He scooped cold water into his hands and splashed it on his face. It stung but he did it twice more, letting the pain of the cold water shock him into reality.

His ex-wife and her soon-to-be stepson were missing. Staring at his reflection, Fitz decided he wasn't going to head back to D.C. and leave the case in the hands of the FBI, especially because they thought Sutton was a person of interest rather than the victim Fitz knew her to be. No. He was going to find them both and clear Sutton's name. He needed to get out of the hotel as quickly as possible.

Fitz left the bathroom as Agent Burrows finished his call with Charlie. The other agent had left and he was alone with Burrows. He held out the phone. "Your story checks out if Charlie is to be believed."

"We have no reason to lie, Agent Burrows." Fitz walked over and took the phone from him.

"How was Sutton when you saw her last?"

Fitz knew what he was doing, asking about her state of mind. The agent was trying to see if Fitz sensed something was amiss. "She was fine but busy with work and wanted to get this squared away. Sutton doesn't like ambiguity. If she needed to end her relationship with Judge Sinclair, she would have done it directly. Sutton isn't the indecisive type, but she also wasn't going to go off half-cocked without all the information." Fitz tapped his chest. "That's why I'm here – to gather the information, so she can make an informed decision."

"It's fair to say then that Sutton wasn't too keen on marrying the judge," Agent Burrows said, not asking the question but stating it as fact. "Most women in love don't investigate their fiancé."

More women should was what Fitz wanted to say. Instead, he shook his head. "That's not what I said at all. I said she wanted to find out what was happening with Holden." He paused for a moment, trying to come up with the right words that would have convinced him had he been the investigator at the scene. He didn't fault the FBI agent for doing his job. It was frustrating for Fitz that he couldn't make his point.

After he thought he found the right angle, Fitz stressed, "Agent Burrows, you need to understand Sutton wasn't going to risk being involved with any kind of scandal. If Holden is sexually assaulting young women and the judge is bailing him out, he's helping to protect a predator. Sutton isn't going to stick around for that, no matter how much she loves him."

Agent Burrows didn't respond but his facial expression shifted ever so slightly around the eyes. They softened in understanding. "If your ex isn't involved in Holden's disappearance, then where could she have gone?"

If Fitz could have answered that then his blood pressure wouldn't be notching up as they stood there doing nothing. "She didn't take Holden. You're wasting time when you need to be out there finding her. I need to get out of here."

"I can't let you leave," Agent Burrows said with a tone that wasn't

CHAPTER 4

convincing at all.

"You can't keep me here unless you're detaining me," Fitz responded with the same level of dryness. "Am I being detained?"

Agent Burrows cocked his head to the side. "Not right now." He brushed past Fitz and headed for the door. As he gripped the handle, he turned back. "I'd suggest whatever you do, you don't cause any trouble for Judge Sinclair. I can't imagine what would happen to your career then."

"I've angered people with more power than him." Fitz said the words but couldn't help the sense of dread in his gut.

CHAPTER 5

After Agent Burrows left and Fitz was alone in the room, he made a call he'd hoped he'd never have to make.

"Fitz, this isn't a good time," Edward Barlow barked as he answered.

Fitz was surprised Sutton's father had his phone number. He hadn't spoken to him since the divorce. "The FBI showed up asking me if I've seen Sutton. What's going on?"

Edward didn't answer the question but asked one of his own. "Have you seen her?"

"Yesterday morning," he started and explained the nature of their interaction. "If I know Sutton as well as I think I do, she came to me looking for a way out. She doesn't want to marry Sinclair."

"You might be right," Edward admitted, lowering his tone. "I don't understand why she'd come to you. I have investigators on my staff if she wanted that kind of information."

The man took every opportunity to knock Fitz down a peg. "Discretion probably. Is there anywhere Sutton might have gone to hide out? I know you have several properties."

"I've inquired and she's not at any of them. I don't care what the FBI said, she didn't kidnap Holden Sinclair."

"That's a given." Fitz informed him that he didn't think the FBI would do much to find her. "I'm going to do this on my own. I need to know if you know anything that could help me."

He was met with silence. Fitz had to fight the urge to prod him. Finally, Edward said, "Sinclair called me last night and asked me if I'd heard from Sutton. He said they had an argument over dinner and she stormed off. He said he hadn't spoken to her after that and he was worried."

"That doesn't make any sense. Sinclair told the FBI she left around six. He said nothing about an argument or dinner. They also wouldn't have eaten dinner that early. What time did he call you?"

"Around nine."

The sinking feeling in his gut grew. "Has Sinclair ever called you before about an argument or Sutton storming off?"

"Well, no. That doesn't mean anything though, Fitz. You know Sutton."

Fitz did know Sutton. Most importantly, he knew Sutton didn't storm off. She stayed and fought it out, at least that's what she did in their relationship. "Sutton never liked leaving things unsettled. She didn't like sitting with the feeling of uncertainty after a fight. She'd worry what I was thinking or doing."

"Fitz," Edward said with an exasperated tone. "Sutton was young when you were together. Isn't it possible she had a different way of handling things as she got older?"

"Why are you defending him? He lied to the FBI and implicated Sutton in his son's disappearance." Fitz felt his anger bubble up and it had nothing to do with Judge Sinclair and everything to do with past complications with his father-in-law. He swallowed his pride and let the subject drop. "Did Sinclair say why they argued?"

"They argued about Sutton's relationship with you, Fitz," Edward finally admitted. "Sinclair knew you had met with Sutton and he demanded to know why. She wouldn't tell him and accused him of having her followed. Something Sinclair didn't deny. An argument followed. She probably took off to cool down. I'm not worried, Fitz."

Fitz let the weight of that wash over him. It seemed the judge didn't trust Sutton any more than she trusted him. He had nothing left to say. "You should be very worried, Edward," he said before hanging up.

Before leaving the hotel, Fitz tried calling Sutton but each call went straight to voicemail. He checked in with Charlie and he had two messages – one from the woman he'd shared his bed with the night before last and another from a current client wanting an update.

Both could stew.

Fitz drove to the gates of the school, which were now closed and locked with the FBI standing guard outside. He knew there was no way he'd be able to access Holden's friends. Fitz was left with few options. He parked his SUV at the side of the road and placed a call to a hacker he'd developed a relationship with on a previous case.

Ditch – Kevin Detrick on his birth certificate – was a hacker who had been arrested by the FBI. In addition to being wanted by the U.S. government, he was wanted by the Saudis, the Chinese, and the Russians for a swath of international espionage, money laundering, and insider trading. The FBI now used him as an asset, making him work off his crimes. He technically wasn't supposed to be moonlighting but Ditch never worried about the straight and narrow.

The phone rang a few times before it was answered. There was no need for formalities. "Can you get me some kids' cellphone numbers?"

"How young are the kids?"

"High school. I assume they might be on their parents' plans." Fitz didn't wait for a response. He rattled off a few names Sutton had provided. When Ditch had the information, Fitz added, "Are you able to triangulate the location of a cellphone for me?"

"If it's on," Ditch said through the staccato of clicking keys.

Fitz waited for Ditch to finish whatever he was typing. To his surprise, Ditch began rattling off phone numbers for each of the names

CHAPTER 5

provided.

"Are you sure these are the kids' phones and not the parents?" Fitz asked.

"Am I ever wrong?" Ditch paused for a moment and clicked a few more keys. "What number do you need a location search?"

Fitz gave him Sutton's phone number and her provider. "I'll take anything you can find – a current location or the last cell tower it pinged."

It took Ditch a few minutes to get the information. "The phone appears to be off. The last location I'm getting was at 9:55 p.m. last night. It pinged off a tower close to Charlottesville, Virginia. Before that, it pinged along Route 29. I'm not going to be able to quickly get the earlier data. I'd need time for that."

"That's good enough for now." There's no way Sutton could be in Virginia and be in Massachusetts kidnapping Holden. The cellphone ping confirmed that they were nowhere near each other. Fitz knew the FBI might argue she knew how cellphone data could be used in an investigation and she had someone take her phone to alibi her. That would indicate a level of criminal planning. None of it added up. He ended the call with Ditch and said he'd be in touch.

Fitz needed to get inside the school and start interviewing Holden's friends. Fitz called the first number on his list. The young man, Trevor, was one of Holden's best friends.

The phone rang three times before it was answered.

"Are you alone or is the FBI there with you?" Fitz asked even before introducing himself. He was using one of his burner phones and he was sure he was giving off kidnapper vibes.

"Who is this?" Trevor asked and waited for a response. When Fitz gave none, Trevor answered his question. "I'm alone in my dorm. The FBI was already here. Do you have Holden?"

Fitz introduced himself, stressing that he was someone safe. "I need to find Holden. I think the FBI is looking in the wrong direction. Can you help me?" Fitz knew he was taking a risk, but he also knew kids didn't trust cops. When Trevor didn't say anything, Fitz asked, "Do you know Sutton, Judge Sinclair's fiancée?"

"The FBI thinks she might have kidnapped Holden. I told them I only met her once when I was with Holden in D.C. on break. I don't think she could kidnap Holden even if she wanted to." Trevor spoke to someone close by, lying and telling them it was his father calling. When he got back on the line, he said, "I don't feel comfortable talking about this over the phone. Are you near the school? Can we meet somewhere?"

That had been Fitz's plan all along. He didn't think it was going to be this easy. It raised his suspicions, but he set that aside. "I'm about five minutes away. I'm not going to be able to get on campus. Is there a place you can meet me?"

"There's a coffee shop downtown." He gave Fitz the name of it and the street name. "I can be there in half an hour."

"Are you sure you're going to be able to get off campus without being followed?"

"That won't be a problem," Trevor reassured him and disconnected the call.

Fitz waited to try the other numbers. By all accounts, according to Sutton and the brief social media search he had done, Trevor was Holden's best friend. If anyone knew where Holden might be or the circumstances of his disappearance it would be Trevor. It also meant that he might be the one most watched by the school administration and the FBI.

Fitz waited at the school for a few more minutes. He tried Sutton's phone again and left a message when the voicemail picked up. He didn't think she'd get it but he hoped whoever had her would know that someone was looking for her. He got back in his SUV, glanced

CHAPTER 5

one more time at the school and the FBI milling around, and headed for downtown.

Fitz found a place to park down the block from the coffee shop and waited. He wasn't going to be the first one in the place in case it was a setup. He had driven by slowly and glanced in the windows and didn't see anyone suspicious. That didn't mean anything. There could be undercover cops anywhere. If this had been his case, he'd have a tail on himself. Agent Burrows didn't seem to be that focused on him though, no matter what he said.

Fitz waited until he saw a young man he assumed might be Trevor walking down the street toward the shop. He thought he recognized the young man from photos on social media. Trevor had a swath of blond hair that looked like it had been perfectly styled with a hairdryer, copious amounts of gel, and far too much time looking in a bathroom mirror. He wore a Polo shirt and pressed khakis.

Fitz looked the opposite in just about every way.

He opened the SUV door and stood there for a moment while Trevor looked around and then entered the coffee shop. Fitz scoped out the street waiting for the FBI or an unmarked car and saw none. When he felt it was safe, he walked down the street and entered the same door.

Fitz spotted him in the back of the shop at a two-seater table. He approached and introduced himself. Trevor stood and shook Fitz's hand. The young man didn't seem too concerned, which sparked Fitz's curiosity.

He pulled out the chair and sat. "Is there a reason you'd be willing to meet with a guy you don't know when your best friend has recently gone missing? That doesn't seem like the smartest move to make."

If Trevor thought better of his decision, he didn't show it. It was either steady resolve or pure arrogance. "My father is a senator and if whoever took Holden was going to take me, they would have done it last night. My father isn't as polarizing of a figure as Judge Sinclair, which I assume is why they took Holden."

That was an astute observation. "Do you know who took Holden?" Trevor shook his head. "I know it wasn't Sutton. It had to have been someone bigger than Holden. I assume you've seen photos of him. He's an athlete, muscular, and strong. I assume he would have put up a fight unless he was lured by someone he knew or by a convincing lie."

Fitz sat back and appraised him. He was smarter than the average eighteen-year-old. "When was the last time you saw him?"

"Last night after dinner. We all went to the common room to watch a movie and then went to sleep." Trevor watched Fitz carefully for a reaction. It made Fitz think he was lying about something. When Fitz didn't offer up any commentary, Trevor went on. "Holden has been stressed out lately given the accusations against him. He hadn't been sleeping well. I know he said he was going to bed but I can't confirm that's what he did."

Fitz confirmed he had heard about the allegations. He didn't go so far as to say that's why he was there. "Is there any truth to it? Did Holden assault that young woman?"

Trevor gestured with his hand, a wave of sorts to dismiss it all as not important. "I've known Holden since we met freshman year. He's never been someone who liked to hear the word no. He's like his father in that sense. Judge Sinclair always covered for Holden, even when he shouldn't. It only encouraged Holden to continue to behave erratically."

Fitz sat up a little straighter. "Erratically?" he asked with curiosity in his tone.

Trevor nodded. "It's not like I haven't done anything wrong. I'm at boarding school. We all push the boundaries. There have been a few times when we were drinking or scoring drugs and got caught by the school administration. The rest of us took our punishments because

CHAPTER 5

our parents weren't going to bail us out. Every time, Judge Sinclair called the school and Holden never faced the consequences."

"Did the same thing happen with the sexual assault?"

"That's why I wanted to meet with you," Trevor said with hesitation in his voice. "I think everything is tied together. The supposed assault and Holden's disappearance."

CHAPTER 6

It took Fitz a moment to process what Trevor said. Even then he wasn't sure he had heard correctly. "What do you mean you think they are connected? How?"

Trevor looked out into the shop again as if he were checking to make sure they were still alone. He turned back to Fitz. "Do you understand what happened the night they said Holden assaulted a girl?" He didn't wait for Fitz to respond. "I can see that you don't. You have to understand that night before you can understand what happened to Holden."

"I heard all of Holden's friends said there wasn't an assault. Was there one or not?" Fitz countered, wondering if this kid was winding him up or if he had real information. The kid may be smart but Fitz was smarter and more experienced. He leaned on the table. "Trevor, I need you to tell me the truth."

Trevor nervously licked his lips. "Holden had been accused of something like this before."

"I was informed there had been earlier allegations. What happened?"

"Holden put his hands up a girl's shirt and touched her. When he tried to go down her pants, she shoved him off and screamed for her friends. They were kissing and it got out of hand. Both of them were drinking. Holden was completely wasted. I don't think he even knew what he was doing."

CHAPTER 6

That was along the lines of what Sutton had described with the first. "What happened after that?"

"Someone told Robins and Holden got suspended. Before Holden was sent home, Judge Sinclair stepped in and said he'd handled it. My understanding is he spoke to the school's board director and the other family and it was swept under the rug as a miscommunication."

"You don't think it was miscommunication?" Fitz asked, his tone serious.

Trevor shook his head. "I know I'm supposed to be Holden's best friend and have his back and that whole bro code thing. I know you probably think I'm just ratting out my friends. I have sisters. I wouldn't want them around a guy like Holden."

Fitz could understand that. "What do you know firsthand? Not rumor or your speculation but what do you know?"

"It wasn't miscommunication. Before the party that night, Holden told all of us how far he was going to get. He told us in detail what he was going to do. There was anger behind what he was saying and entitlement – like he's owed sex whenever he wants. He doesn't care what the girl wants. That's why when it happened, none of us believed Holden when he said he didn't know what he was doing. He might have been drunk, but he knew what he was doing."

"I appreciate you telling me that, Trevor," Fitz said, making sure his tone of voice was supportive and firm. "There is no bro code when it comes to assaulting girls. I think you're more of a man because you're willing to come forward and stop your friend. Covering for him doesn't help anyone. When this situation happened, did anyone ask Holden's friends what went on?"

Trevor shook his head. "I think they were afraid to hear the truth. I tried to talk to Mr. Robins when we found out that nothing was being done. He didn't want to hear from me and said the matter was settled. We didn't go to him right away because it looked like Holden was going to face the consequences." Trevor pulled back and shook his head. "Why rat out a friend if there's no need? I didn't want to be on Holden's bad side."

Fitz understood that reasoning. "What happened after Holden got away with it?"

"Nothing at school. As I said, Mr. Robins didn't want to hear what I had to say. Holden got much worse." Trevor had a far-off look on his face. "The way he spoke about girls got much worse. It was like he was given license to behave however he wanted. He was taking more risks, drinking, and sneaking out."

"Was anyone aware of what was happening?"

"No one wanted to hear about it, so we had no one to tell."

"What about telling your parents?"

"It's a fine line," he said softly. "We've all been bailed out by our parents, usually for getting caught drinking on campus or sneaking off campus when we were younger. My father wouldn't have defended me if I was doing what Holden was doing and I didn't want to make him think I was. He made it clear he wasn't going to tolerate me getting in trouble. He was paying too much money to send me to school here and he wasn't going to jeopardize his reputation. He told me he could send me to a local high school and keep an eye on me at home. That threat kept me in line."

The way Trevor spoke with such conviction, Fitz believed him. "Did your father know anything?"

"He knew enough and he didn't want me to be around Holden. We argued about it often." Trevor sighed the way a teen does when he's frustrated with his parents not understanding. "Unless I was transferring to a different school, there was no way I was going to avoid Holden. The school campus isn't that big and we had all of our classes together. I'm not sure what my father expected. He doesn't like Judge Sinclair, so his hatred of Holden didn't surprise me."

CHAPTER 6

Fitz chuckled at that. "I'm not sure anyone likes Judge Sinclair."

"My father had a particular dislike for him. He didn't even like that Holden was in my class. The only thing my father told me the day he dropped me off freshman year was to stay away from the Sinclair boy." Trevor put his hands out wide. "I did the opposite of what he wanted. We ended up being in the same room with two others and we became fast friends."

"Do you know why your father didn't want you to be friends with Holden?"

Trevor shook his head. "My father never told me what went on between him and Judge Sinclair. I assumed it stemmed from that."

Fitz thought there might be more there to explore, but he didn't want to waste time. He didn't know how long Trevor was willing to talk. "What happened the night of the second assault? You said you believe that's what led to Holden's disappearance. I need to know about that party."

"It was held in our common room. The senior dorm is in the back of the property and we were able to sneak in some girls from a local high school."

Fitz held a finger up for him to wait. "The girls are from a local school? I thought you went to school with them at Brewster. Had you met them before?"

"Some of the girls were from a local school and others go to school with us. We have school dances and people from other local schools attend. That's how we've met most of them," Trevor explained. "Chloe goes to school with us. She's liked Holden for a while. He never paid much attention to her. The night of the party something was different about him. He said before the party that he was going to talk to her, so all of us needed to back off. One of our other friends had liked her and was hoping to hang out with her that night. Maybe because Holden knew he could win Chloe over, he did it on purpose. He was

45

like that. If he knew one of us liked a girl, Holden would try to have sex with her first. It was like some weird competition to him."

Fitz had known guys like that when he was younger. They weren't real friends and everything was a competition. "I know there was drinking at the party. Who bought the alcohol?"

"Does it matter?" Trevor asked with his brow furrowed.

"I'm not a cop. I can't arrest you but I need to understand how parties like this work. It's important for context." Fitz wasn't sure he wasn't being completely honest with that. He wanted to set the stage in his mind for the night and even the little details mattered. "This conversation doesn't go any further than us."

"Our roommate, Ned, got us alcohol. He has his brother's driver's license, and they look so much alike, it works every time," Trevor admitted and kept his focus on Fitz. "Ned is a good guy and I wouldn't want him to get in any trouble. He's not doing anything any of us wouldn't do if given the chance."

"Understood," Fitz said. He wasn't going to fault the guy for buying for his friends. He had done the same in his youth. He'd been the one to score the drugs too, which brought up the other question. "What about drug use? I heard Chloe didn't know what happened to her. She woke up and only knew she felt like something was strange. Was her memory loss from the drinking or was she drugged?"

Trevor nodded along with what Fitz said. "It was the local girls who brought the drugs. That's why I mentioned that. We aren't able to get drugs on campus and no one is going into town to buy them. Some alcohol with a fake ID is one thing, scoring drugs is another. Most of the people who go here have parents who are famous in some way. It's not worth the risk. The main reason we invited those other girls was because they could get us drugs, nothing too heavy. Just a little ecstasy and weed. I don't know if they brought anything else."

Fitz knew it wasn't weed or ecstasy that Chloe had taken. It was

CHAPTER 6

something stronger like ketamine or Rohypnol. He explained that to Trevor who wasn't able to offer anything further about the drugs. Fitz moved on to the meat of the story. "How many people were there that night?"

"Fifteen to twenty. I wasn't keeping track. The girls from the local school came over at ten-thirty after the last bed check for the night. Because we are seniors, we are allowed to stay up later in the common room on weekends. Our dorm mother goes to bed around eleven. She checked on us and turned in for the night." Guilt washed over Trevor's face. "It's not her fault that this happened. I know everyone is asking where the adults were. She couldn't have known what we had planned. We never had a party like that in our dorm before that night. We've had parties in the woods behind the dorm and we've snuck off campus to parties but we've never had a party in our common room. When she came to check on us, we were all watching television and hanging out. She reminded the girls that they had to be back in their dorms by midnight. We promised to walk them to the dorm."

"I assume after that you let in the local girls?"

"Yeah, right after that. It was supposed to be a fun night. That's all. A few of my friends liked some of the girls and they were hooking up. We watched as Holden made his move on Chloe and she seemed into it. As I said, she had liked him for a long time. But they stayed in the common room. Holden tried to get her to go into his bedroom but she wouldn't go, not right then."

"When did she go off with Holden?"

"I wasn't paying that close of attention," Trevor said, shrugging. "It was maybe a little more than an hour. Two at most. She seemed fine to me. She wanted to go with him. She wasn't trying to fight him off or say she didn't want to go. All of her friends were there. I didn't see Holden trying to convince her or take her against her will. It honestly seemed easy for him."

47

Even if Trevor didn't understand that wasn't all that constituted rape, Fitz did. "Isn't it possible she went to his room with him but didn't plan on having sex with him? It could have gotten out of hand and Holden forced himself on her. She had a right to say no at any point."

"Here's the thing though. Right after Chloe went with Holden, her friends left. Holden came out of his bedroom not even five minutes later. He said she passed out and he was going to sleep on the couch. He was visibly disappointed and complaining about how drunk she was."

"How long were they in the room alone?"

"Ten to fifteen minutes maybe. Holden said they were kissing and she just kind of passed out."

"Is there any chance that he assaulted her then?"

"No. He was angry. He asked us all why we gave her so much alcohol. He was annoyed about the previous allegation and said he wasn't going to risk something like that happening again. I don't think he had time to do anything."

Fitz could tell he was holding something back. "What are you not saying?"

Trevor bit at his bottom lip. "The way he was talking about Chloe before she even came over, I was worried about what had happened last time. I had set up a camera to record in his room. I have a video of exactly what happened in there and it was exactly like Holden said. They were kissing and then she passed out. He tried to wake her up and then got annoyed and left. He never returned to the room."

"How well-lit was the video?"

"They had the lights on."

That ruled out the video that had been posted online. "Are you sure he never went back in the room? Your video couldn't have recorded all night?"

CHAPTER 6

Trevor confirmed he went in and shut it off. "I slept on the other couch in the common room all night, keeping an eye on Holden. It was a setup."

"How do you know?"

"Because Chloe didn't have that much to drink. Someone drugged her and was trying to set up Holden. No one could have known I was recording in that room." Trevor glanced around the small café. "I wanted proof that he did something wrong. Instead, I got proof that cleared him."

"Have you told anyone about the video?"

"There's a few people that know. I didn't tell security or Robins about it. I didn't want them to think I was a creep. I wanted proof if Holden did something to her."

"Do you still have the video?"

"I have that and other evidence." Trevor didn't explain more. He pushed his chair back and stood. "You'll need to come with me."

"Let's go." Fitz was going to run down every lead until there were none left. He didn't think going back to campus was a good idea, but if it would get him closer to finding Sutton, he'd risk it.

CHAPTER 7

On the street outside the coffee shop, Fitz stood with Trevor while they hatched a plan to get onto campus without being detected. Trevor would drive his car and Fitz would hide in the back until they reached the dorm. Trevor assured him all the evidence was in his room and there were places to hide if the FBI or anyone from the administration showed up.

Fitz was considering if he was being set up when a large dark SUV slowed to a crawl in the middle of the street. Fitz only noticed it because it looked like a government vehicle with tinted windows. With the angle of the mid-day sun, Fitz wasn't able to see the driver or the passenger. He could tell that there were at least two people in the vehicle but couldn't pinpoint any distinguishing characteristics.

Trevor seemed unaware of it. Fitz didn't look away, worried the FBI was already tailing him. The hair on his neck stood up before Fitz registered alarm. As the SUV got parallel to them, the vehicle stopped, the passenger side window came down, and the barrel of a gun slipped out.

Pop. Pop. Pop

Fitz's hands were on Trevor's back pushing him to the ground as the first bullets struck the windows of the shop next to them. Glass shattered all around.

"Trevor, run!" Fitz shouted, dragging him up by the arm and pulling

CHAPTER 7

him forward. Luckily, he wasn't so bogged down in shock he couldn't react. As the gunman pulled the trigger again, Fitz and Trevor sprinted down the sidewalk and around the building. They kept running down the alleyway until they found a dumpster to hide behind.

Fitz watched from his crouched position as the SUV backed up, a pair of eyes covered in black sunglasses peered down the alley, and then the vehicle took off. Once it was gone, Fitz turned to Trevor. "Are you hurt? Did you get shot?"

Trevor checked himself over, the kid's hands shaking. "I think I'm okay. Your arm is bleeding," he added, pointing to Fitz's upper arm.

He turned his head to the side and saw the ripped fabric of his shirt. He shoved the sleeve up to reveal what looked like a graze. Fitz fingered the wound. "It's only a graze. Are you sure you're okay? Adrenaline will be blocking any pain you might be feeling."

Trevor patted himself down again and tugged at his clothing. "I'm okay," he said even though his voice creaked. He looked at Fitz with fear in his eyes. "What was that?"

Fitz didn't have an answer for him. He didn't know if the gunman was after him or Trevor or maybe both of them. "We have to get out of here. Where is your car?"

Trevor pointed down the alleyway.

As they sprinted toward the car, Fitz said, "You need to call your father and tell him what happened."

Trevor shook his head. "I don't want to involve him. They are probably after me for the video. We have to get to it before they do. Maybe they don't want me to tell the truth."

Fitz cursed whatever Sutton had gotten him into. When they reached Trevor's BMW, Fitz dropped to the ground on his belly and looked under the car. He was looking for a bomb and detonator device. When he saw nothing, he popped back to his feet. "It's clear."

If Trevor understood, he didn't say. They got into his car and quickly headed back toward campus. Fitz had more questions for him but needed a moment to process what had happened.

He sent Charlie a text, updating her about the events of the day and letting her know he'd call her soon. In the meantime, she needed to watch her back. Fitz had no idea if whatever was going on would reach his office door. She responded quickly expressing concern for him and assurance she'd watch her back. She asked him to call as soon as he found the time.

Fitz looked over at Trevor. "You need to pull over so I can hide in the back."

"If someone is after me, I'm not going in the front way. Just trust me."

Fitz didn't have any other choice.

Trevor drove back toward the school and when he turned down the road that ran to the side of the school campus, he bypassed the main entrance and kept driving. He turned off onto a dirt road that seemed to disappear into the heavily wooded area.

"There's a path," Trevor said, keeping his eyes on the road. "The only ones who use this back entrance are the people who maintain the grounds. There is a shed with equipment in the back, but otherwise, no one is ever back here."

"Have you driven this before?"

"A few times," Trevor responded without elaborating. The road became increasingly narrow and the tree cover denser the deeper they went. Trevor knew exactly where he was going and followed the dirt-rutted path with ease, knowing which forks in the road to take.

Fitz tried to record it all to memory in case he ever needed to take the path again. Trevor came to a stop. He put the car in park and jumped out. Fitz watched as he approached the tall wrought iron gate, pulled a key out of his pocket, and undid the bolt lock that held the chains that kept it secured. The lock opened and Trevor pulled the

CHAPTER 7

chains to the side and pushed open one half of the gate. He came back, got in, and pulled them onto the school property. They drove a little farther on the dirt road and parked on the side of the shed Trevor had mentioned.

"How did you get the key?"

"I didn't," Trevor said without elaborating. "We should walk the rest of the way." When Trevor got out, Fitz followed. Birds chirped off in the distance but their immediate surroundings were quiet. "We can go in the back door of the dorm. Classes are in session. I doubt anyone is around. Even the dorm mother isn't around this time of day."

Fitz hoped that was the case. He followed Trevor through the woods until the wide rolling-hilled campus came into view. The dorm sat in between the main part of campus and the woods. Seeing it firsthand, he understood why it had been so easy to sneak girls into the dorm and why no one on the main part of campus would have caught them partying. This was an out-of-the-way building.

Trevor used another key to unlock the back door of the dorm. As they stepped inside the beige stairwell, their feet squeaked and echoed off the steps as they climbed.

"What floor are you on?" Fitz asked as they passed the second floor and were still climbing.

"The top," Trevor said, looking back at Fitz. "There is only one big suite at the top."

"Has the FBI already searched your room? They might still be up there."

"They left before I did. After they left, they said they were going to search the rest of the campus. It didn't sound like they'd be back."

Fitz wasn't going to chance that. "I'll wait here in the stairwell while you go to your room and get the evidence you have."

"Don't you want to see the room like the FBI did?" Trevor asked when they got to the fourth floor. He had his hand on the door that led from the stairwell to the hall and was about to turn the knob but waited for Fitz's response.

Fitz wasn't going in. "Make sure we are alone and then bring the evidence out. Show it to me and then I'll determine if I need to search the room." Trevor left him standing on the landing. While he was waiting, Fitz pulled his phone out and tried Sutton again. The call went straight to voicemail. He texted Ditch and asked him to check the phone's location again.

After a few minutes, the stairwell door swung open and Trevor thrust a thumb drive toward Fitz. His face was flushed and beads of sweat formed at his brow. "Someone trashed my room. I think they were looking for that."

Fitz held it up. "You mean like the FBI was searching?" That wouldn't have surprised Fitz. They were looking for a judge's son. Robins seemed the type to grant permission to tear a place apart.

"I don't think it was that," Trevor said, glancing back at the door. "There's no one in there. I think you should see it."

Fitz couldn't do anything with the thumb drive. His laptop was back in his SUV. "Is there anything else on here other than the video you recorded that night?"

"Yeah, the real proof that Holden was set up."

"What does that mean?"

Trevor turned back to him. "It's a recording of a conversation about setting up Holden for sexual assault. You need to hear it for yourself to understand it all. I didn't want to tell you at the café because you just need to listen to it. I would have let you listen on my laptop but it's missing."

He had Fitz's full attention now. "Someone confessed to setting up Holden? Who?"

"Chloe's roommate." Trevor dropped his voice low and stepped closer. "Veronica, the roommate, explained to another friend of ours

CHAPTER 7

she was being paid off to set up Holden and then tell her mother, which is exactly what she did. The goal was for Veronica's mother to break the story in *The New York Times* and reference the other allegation. That isn't what Veronica's mother did though. She refused to write a story until facts could be established and she called the school."

Fitz couldn't believe what he was hearing. "Let me see your room." He followed Trevor into the hall and down to the door to the common room. There were several couches and chairs around a center coffee table. Off to the back was an entire kitchenette with a mini-stove, fridge, and sink. It was a nice setup for high school seniors.

Off the common room were four doors to bedrooms. Trevor opened one door off to the right and stepped inside. Fitz followed and stopped short when he saw the mess. It wasn't that the room had been searched. It had been ransacked. This wasn't the work of the FBI.

Clothes lay in heaps on the floor, ripped from the dresser and the closet. Books were upturned on the floor next to the clothes. Even the bed sheets had been pulled back and the mattress flipped.

"Where did you have it?" Fitz asked, holding up the thumb drive.

"Inside the grate." Trevor pointed to the rectangular air vent near the floor. "I kept it taped inside." He looked at Fitz for answers. "Who do you think is after me?"

Fitz didn't know. The only thing he knew for sure was Trevor wasn't safe here. "Pack a bag. You're coming with me."

CHAPTER 8

Once they were more than fifty miles away from the school, Fitz pulled his SUV off an exit, found a fast food place, and pulled into the parking lot. After realizing Trevor's room had been trashed and being shot at, Fitz wasn't taking any chances. He had Trevor pack a bag, leave his cellphone behind, and they left in his car. They drove the short distance back to where Fitz had parked his SUV outside of the coffee shop. He swept the car for bombs and tracking devices then Fitz drove them as far away from the school as possible. Fitz had shut off his cellphone and removed the battery, so no one, not even the cops, could track his location.

Once at the fast food place, Fitz got out of the SUV, popped open the trunk, and opened the bag he always kept in the back. It had extra cash, a change of clothes, and several burner phones. He powered one up and called Charlie.

When she answered, he said, "You're not going to be able to track me because my regular cellphone is off." Fitz gave her the rundown of everything that had happened in the short time he was at the school. "I don't know what I've stumbled into. I couldn't leave Trevor there to fend for himself. I don't think the gunmen were after me. I think they are after him for what he knows. I need to reach his father to let him know Trevor is with me and is in danger."

"Who's his father?" Charlie asked.

CHAPTER 8

"Senator Tom Wilson from New Jersey."

Charlie whistled. "You kidnapped a senator's son? Fitz," she dragged his name out with a tone of concern. "What are you doing?"

"I didn't kidnap him," he corrected her. "He came willingly and he's eighteen, so he's technically an adult. It was either take him or leave him to be murdered. They trashed his room and shot at him, Charlie. They didn't get anything, so who knows what they'd do next."

Charlie didn't buy the justification. "This isn't your battle to fight. Sutton got you sucked into her drama."

"It's more than drama," Fitz argued and hoped she understood. "I'm giving you the heads up before I call Senator Wilson. He might send in the FBI or the Secret Service if he's heard the rumors I might be responsible for Holden's disappearance. They might come to the office. I suggest clearing out and taking any private and sensitive information with you. They'll never get a search warrant for your house. I suggest working from home until this blows over."

"Got it," she responded dismissively. Sounds of shuffling papers and clicking keys buzzed through the phone. "I don't have much pending. Waiting for a few return calls. I'll set the office phones to forward to my cellphone until you're back. If I hear of anything, I'll let you know."

He was glad Charlie hadn't put up a fight. "Things will get back to normal soon," he promised even though he had no way to assure it.

"Keep me updated," Charlie said and when he didn't need anything else, she ended the call. She hadn't even asked him any questions about the case. That's how Fitz knew her anger had started to simmer, no matter what she said.

Fitz had too much else to worry about. He punched Sutton's phone number into the phone one more time. Surprised when it rang instead of going right to voicemail, he pulled the phone back and double-checked the number.

A gruff male voice answered. "We want five million if you ever want to see her alive. Tell the cops listening in you better bring the money alone."

Fitz's heart raced and he had a quick decision to make. The most important thing he needed to do was keep them on the line while he used another burner to text Ditch. Fitz took a big breath. "You're out of luck. I don't have five million dollars for you. Where is Sutton? Put her on the phone."

His demand was met with silence. A grunt followed. "Who is this?"

"Fitz," he said but didn't elaborate any more than that. "I'm coming for you. If you doubt that, let me tell you I have nothing to lose. Put Sutton on the phone. I want to know that she's okay." Fitz reached Ditch with the other phone and gave him the information. He worked to triangulate the coordinates of her cellphone but Fitz had to keep them on the line longer. The wait churned his gut.

Finally, muffled sounds echoed through the phone and then Sutton's voice, weak and scared. "Fitz, are you there?"

"Sutton, I'm here!" he shouted for no particular reason. "I'm coming for you. It's going to be okay."

"They want five million dollars. Call Harvey for me and tell him they need the money," Sutton sobbed into the phone. "If they don't get it, they are going to kill me. I believe them. Don't try to rescue me like you did when we were married and I fell into the river on that camping trip. You nearly died trying to save me. Don't be a hero, just get the money."

"Sutton, who took you?" Fitz asked, wondering why she was talking about a camping trip that he didn't remember taking. Shock could do that. Fitz had no memory of her falling in a river. His question was met with silence and then the gruff male voice got back on the line.

"You heard her. Don't be a hero. You have forty-eight hours to get the money."

"Where should I bring it?" Fitz asked but the call disconnected. He

CHAPTER 8

assumed now that they had his phone number, they'd use it to call back with more instructions. His heart thumped inside his chest as if it were ready to be free of his body. Fitz took a few deep breaths to calm himself down before he stroked out in the middle of the street. The mention of the camping trip stayed on his mind. It was such an odd reference to make, even if Sutton was in shock.

Then it hit him – Sutton was trying to send him a message.

Fitz texted Ditch to see if he was able to triangulate a location.

The response came back quickly. *Virginia but I couldn't get the specific coordinates. Need more time.*

Fitz didn't need more than that. The reason he couldn't remember having gone camping with Sutton is because they never went. He had told her a story on their first date of going camping with friends while he was in college. One of his best friends had gotten so drunk he fell into the lake and Fitz had to dive in and save him. Fitz had been drinking at the time and his friend had panicked in the water and nearly drowned them both. They had been at Lake Anna State Park in Virginia.

Fitz clicked the map icon on the phone and put Lake Anna into the search bar. It was close to Charlottesville, near where Sutton's phone last pinged. Lake Anna was one of the largest freshwater inland reservoirs in Virginia and one of the most popular recreational lakes in the state. The challenge was that Lake Anna covered an area of thirteen-hundred acres and had two-hundred miles of shoreline. There was a private and public part of the lake. It would narrow down some of the ground to cover, but Fitz could search for days and still not find Sutton.

He only had forty-eight hours before the ransom money had to be paid. But he didn't have five million in cash handy. Sutton's father would and so would Judge Sinclair.

"Trevor," Fitz called through the SUV from the open back hatch. He turned his head from the passenger seat to look at him. "We need to call your father and let him know you're safe. Should I make the call or do you want to do it?"

Trevor rubbed his eyes. "I don't want to talk to my dad."

Fitz wasn't going to debate this. "What's his phone number?"

Trevor gave it over without much of a fight. Fitz used a different burner phone than the one he used to call Sutton.

He had to go through the senator's assistant, but when Fitz finally got him on the phone, he got right to the point. "Senator Wilson, my name is Connor Fitzgerald. You might know me from D.C. as I run an investigative firm."

"I'm aware of you," Senator Wilson said, cutting off Fitz.

"I want you to know Trevor is safe. He's with me after someone shot at us." Fitz let the words hang in the air. When Senator Wilson didn't respond, Fitz asked, "Are you there, sir?"

"Why would my son be with you? He's supposed to be at school. Who'd shoot at him?"

"Holden Sinclair is missing and your son has information that may point to a broader conspiracy," Fitz started and waited for the senator to say something. He expected him to be shocked or angry or even express disbelief. Instead, Fitz was met with silence. "Were you aware Holden is missing?"

"I heard the news. My understanding is his soon-to-be stepmother took him."

"Sutton is missing as well," Fitz corrected him, trying to keep his anger in check. He hated to hear rumors spreading about Sutton already, especially when there was no proof to them. He had wanted to go into this call being reasonable and calm, but the senator needed to be shocked into reality. "As I said, Trevor was shot at today and his room was trashed. He's not safe at the school."

"Put Trevor on the phone right now," he demanded.

CHAPTER 8

Fitz finally had the man's attention. Before he put Trevor on the phone he asked if Senator Wilson had security. "We need a plan because he can't stay with me."

"Put him on the phone," Senator Wilson demanded again and Fitz walked up to the passenger side of the SUV and handed Trevor the phone. He looked like he wanted to do anything other than speak to his father.

The two spoke for a few minutes and it was decided Fitz would drop Trevor off to Senator Wilson back in D.C. His father's security team would take it from there.

Once they were on the road again and settled, Fitz asked, "How did they kidnap Holden from the school? The FBI wouldn't tell me and I never asked you. It didn't seem important until now."

"I don't know exactly. I saw Holden at dinner last night and he said he was going back to the room to study. The dining hall was the last place I saw him. His bedroom door was closed when I got back and I didn't bother him. I was woken up at around three this morning by Mr. Robins and the FBI asking me if I'd seen Holden because he was missing."

"What time did he leave the dining hall?"

"Around six-thirty, I think. I wasn't paying much attention. I got back to my room around seven-thirty. That's when his door was closed."

That left a lot of time for something to happen. "What about your common area? Was anything disturbed last night?"

"There was no sign that anything was wrong. I told the FBI that. His car is still in his parking spot in the lot and they found his cellphone on his nightstand. It didn't look like anything was missing from his room either." Trevor grew quiet for a moment and then said softly, "It's like he just vanished."

Fitz knew people didn't just vanish. "Did the FBI have a theory about where Holden was taken?"

"The dorm is what they suspect. His backpack and his cellphone were in his room. They think whoever took him, took him from there. He made it back from the dining hall and then something happened." Trevor looked over at Fitz. "I heard them speculating that Sutton had shown up to Holden's room and lured him outside to her car and took off with him."

Fitz still didn't understand how Sutton got into the mix. "Did anyone see Sutton do that?"

"No. It was just speculation since she was missing too. The FBI agent didn't think it made any sense but then another one said since there were no signs of a struggle it seemed like Holden knew who it was."

"Would Holden leave his cellphone if he left on his own?"

"No. He never went anywhere without it."

That's what Fitz had assumed. He agreed with whatever FBI agent speculated that Holden might have known the person, but he was sure it wasn't Sutton. "Is there anything else you think I should know?"

"I think you need to hear the recording and see the video I took."

"Why didn't you tell the FBI?"

Trevor looked up at Fitz with his eyes wide. "I don't trust them."

Fitz hitched his thumb over his shoulder. "Get my laptop out of the back and play it for me."

CHAPTER 9

As Trevor started the laptop, Fitz asked, "Before I listen to this, I need to know how you got this evidence. You seem to be real invested in getting evidence against Holden. While I understand the why, I need to know the how."

"I hoped you weren't going to ask that," Trevor said, clicking the keys on the laptop to queue up the recording. "When Chloe woke up that morning, she went back to her dorm. She didn't say much to any of us but I could tell she was feeling weird. She asked me what had happened the night before and I told her she had fallen asleep. When she asked about Holden, I told her he slept on the couch. He was in the shower that morning by the time she woke so she didn't see him before she left."

Fitz let him talk without interrupting him even as Trevor paused to collect his thoughts.

Trevor started and stopped a few times. "I don't know if she believed me. She seemed not to understand what I was saying. She left without saying much else. It was only after she went back to her dorm and told Veronica that she didn't feel good and had no memory of the night before that Veronica suggested she had been sexually assaulted. Chloe told Veronica what I told her about Holden sleeping on the couch. Veronica told her I wasn't to be trusted. Then without Chloe ever agreeing with her or confirming an assault took place, Veronica called her mother and told her Holden sexually assaulted Chloe."

At that point, Fitz didn't believe any assault had taken place. He didn't even need to see Trevor's video to know that much. "It was Veronica who was driving this whole thing. Why?"

Trevor gave Fitz a knowing look. "Looking back, after the fact, it was Veronica who kept pouring drinks for Chloe all night, telling her she needed to loosen up. When Holden started flirting with Chloe, it was Veronica who encouraged her to go with Holden back to his room. I'll never forget the look on Chloe's face."

"Was she scared?" Fitz remembered that Trevor initially told him she had gone willingly.

"It wasn't scared but surprise. Looking back now, I think it's because Chloe wasn't sure why Holden was flirting with her that night. He'd never shown any kind of interest in her. She went with him because Veronica encouraged her to go. As I said, another friend had been interested in her."

"Chloe went willingly though?"

"She seemed to. If she was drugged, she didn't really make her own decisions."

That much was true. "It sounds to me like Veronica set up this whole thing. It was easy enough given Holden's reputation and competitiveness."

"That's right," Trevor agreed. "Just no one was counting on the fact that we all knew what Holden was like and we were watching him."

Fitz understood now why Trevor had been suspicious of Veronica. "Play me the recording you have."

Trevor continued with the story. "Once Veronica started telling people that Holden had assaulted Chloe at the party, no one believed it. Everyone saw what I had. We all talked about it and decided we needed to do something about it. A few of us went to speak to Robins but he didn't want any part of the conversation. We had been drinking

CHAPTER 9

and snuck girls into our suite. He was only focused on liability for the school."

"He seems like a weasel."

"He is," Trevor said with a chuckle. "He's the worst. I didn't know what else to do. A girl I used to date, Emily, is friends with Chloe and Veronica. I went to her and asked if she believed Holden assaulted Chloe. She said she believed Holden was capable of it, but she didn't know. Chloe never once said that's what happened. She just had no memory of the night and Veronica was filling in the blanks. Emily and I decided to set a trap. We wanted the truth from Veronica."

"Whose plan was it to record Veronica?"

"Emily and I came up with a plan together," Trevor admitted, staring down at the laptop. "We didn't know what she was going to tell us. But we didn't want to give her any chance to change her story once she told the truth. The goal was to bring it to Chloe. It was more about Chloe knowing the truth than clearing Holden's name."

"That's the conversation on the drive?" Fitz asked, looking at Trevor with newfound respect. He had to give it to the kid, he had balls. More so than most eighteen-year-olds he had encountered. What Trevor probably didn't know was he had committed a crime by doing so. Massachusetts was a two-party consent state when it came to recording a conversation. He didn't want to dampen his triumph so he let it go. "Play the recording for me."

"Let me set the stage for you first," Trevor said as he clicked a few buttons on the keyboard. "Emily was going to record the conversation on the phone when she could get Veronica alone. That took some doing because Chloe was always there. The one thing neither of us wanted to do was traumatize Chloe more, and we didn't think Veronica would tell the truth with her around. Emily finally was able to get Veronica alone about a week after the party. She turned on the recording on her phone, set it on the table, and sat down for lunch. That's when the confrontation happened." Trevor clicked the play button and a hum of background noise filled the truck. A young woman's voice saying they needed to talk cut above the rest. Fitz assumed the voice belonged to Emily. He leaned in closer to the laptop and listened.

"I want to know what happened with Chloe and Holden," Emily said with a kind of confidence Fitz rarely heard in a young woman's voice. "Trevor told me nothing happened. He showed me a video that proved nothing happened."

"Don't be so naïve, Emily. Trevor is lying. We all know Holden is capable of something like that. He was the only one who could have drugged and assaulted her." Veronica had an air of indifference in her voice. She changed the subject to an English report the two had due.

Emily wasn't going to let the subject drop. "You're lying to me, Veronica. You were the one pouring Chloe's drinks all night." When Veronica didn't respond, she pushed harder. "All of us know you're lying. You were the one who was trying to get Chloe drunk and encouraged her to hook up with Holden. You're more to blame than he is."

Veronica sighed loudly. "I'm not to blame. We all know how Holden can be. Things got out of hand. He drugged Chloe at some point that night."

"No," Emily said loudly. "You were the one giving her drinks. If anyone drugged her, it was you. We both know you bear some responsibility for what happened that night and I want to know why. I don't care about Holden. I don't even care if he gets in trouble. What I want to know is how you can do that to your best friend." There was so much passion and conviction in her voice that Fitz forgot for a moment she was a high school senior and not a homicide detective.

"She's not my best friend," Veronica said, not denying the accusation.

Emily picked up on that too. "So, you admit you're the one who

CHAPTER 9

drugged her?"

There was silence on the recording for several beats. Fitz wondered if that was all until Veronica finally spoke. "Can you keep a secret?"

"Yes," Emily said, lying convincingly. "All I want is to understand what happened that night."

"Holden is not a good guy. He's been accused of this before and you've witnessed the way he treats women. He thinks he's better than all of us. It was time for some payback."

"I don't understand. You're hurting Chloe in the process."

"Collateral damage," Veronica responded flippantly as if her friends didn't matter at all. "When I was promised thousands of dollars to set up Holden, I jumped at the chance. My mom is a reporter and all I had to do was set him up and tell her like the guy asked me to do and Holden would be done. He'd get kicked out of the school and get justice like he deserves."

There were words Fitz didn't understand. Then Emily's voice came through clearer. "That's messed up, Veronica. Who asked you to do something like that?"

"I can't tell you. I was told I had to keep it a secret. My mom doesn't even know." Veronica groaned loudly. "She's the one who messed up the whole thing by not breaking the story. That's what she was supposed to do and then wouldn't. The guy nearly didn't pay me. I had to convince my mom she had to do something. That's when she called the school."

The anger in Emily's voice bubbled up. "I can't believe you'd do something like that. Chloe could have been assaulted. Holden wouldn't have known she was drugged and couldn't consent. The only reason it didn't happen is because she passed out and Holden's friends made sure he didn't go near her the rest of the night. You have to tell me who asked you to do it."

"I won't tell you."

Emily pushed harder. "Veronica, do you think you're safe? Whoever this is could be after you because you know their secret. What if they come after you?"

"What do you mean?" Veronica asked with confusion in her voice. "You don't think they will come after me. I did what they told me to do."

Fitz thought she was being naïve but what did he expect from a high school senior who was willing to drug her friend. The recording was hard to stomach. He turned to Trevor and his face had paled as he listened. Fitz wondered how many times the recording had been played. He focused his attention back on the two girls talking.

Emily said, "Veronica, you have to tell me who asked you to do this. Did they contact you here at school?"

"Online. I never met him. We set a place for him to leave me the cash and the drugs. I was supposed to get paid more when my mom ran the story. That's why I need her to run that story."

"How much did you get paid so far?"

"Twenty grand. I'll get another payment of thirty if she runs the story," she said with annoyance as if she couldn't believe her mother had messed up her plan.

Emily yelled at her friend. "I can't believe you did something like that. Why would you do that?"

"Chloe will get over it. It's not like she was even sexually assaulted," Veronica said flippantly. "She doesn't remember what happened. How can she be traumatized if she can't remember?"

"You're disgusting," Emily said with rage in her voice. "Tell me who asked you to do this."

"No." The girls didn't speak for several beats and then Veronica said, "All he said was he was planning to take down the whole Sinclair family and this was the first step in the process."

"Does he have a name?" Emily asked again. She was relentless in her

CHAPTER 9

pursuit and had garnered Fitz's respect and admiration. She'd make a good journalist or homicide detective.

"He went by Blaze. It's what he told me to call him."

"How did he contact you?"

"First on social media and then we started texting."

"Do you still have the messages?"

"No. He told me to delete them and I did."

Emily wouldn't let it go. "How did he pick you?"

"I don't know," Veronica responded, growing weary of the questioning.

"Why Chloe?"

"Chloe was just collateral damage for the greater good, Em. You need to lighten up and don't worry about it."

Emily wasn't taking her foot off the gas. "When was the last time you heard from him?"

"This morning. He asked me if my mom was going to write the story. He wanted to know when it was going to be published. He said he might need my help again. I told him my mom was already angry with me and I couldn't risk getting in any trouble. I had to lay low for a while."

"What did he say?"

"That he'd be in touch." There was the sound of a bell ringing and shuffling books. The audio cut off.

Fitz turned to Trevor. "Please tell me you got Blaze's phone number."

"Emily went through Veronica's phone that night and got it. I guess she hadn't had the chance to delete the contact information like he told her to." Trevor provided Fitz with the phone number. "It's a Michigan area code. I wasn't able to find anything online. The number doesn't come back to anything."

"I'm going to need to speak to Veronica." Fitz got into the slow lane and turned off the next exit. He pulled his car into the first parking lot of a fast food joint and put it in park. He looked over at Trevor. "I think we are far enough away from school. No one has been following us. Do you want me to put you on a train back to your father in D.C. or take you to a safe house until I speak to Veronica? I have to go back to Brewster Academy."

"I can't come with you?" Trevor asked.

"It's too dangerous." Fitz also wanted to get Veronica alone. "Which do you want?"

Trevor shrugged, obviously disappointed. "I'll take the train."

Fitz assumed Trevor would be safe on the train.

After Fitz searched for the nearest Amtrak station, he pulled up directions on his phone and navigated back to the road.

Trevor remained pensive. "I don't think Veronica will talk to you. She's been difficult to deal with and you heard what kind of person she is on the recording."

Fitz knew what he was in for and the risk he'd be taking. "Don't worry about me, Trevor. I'm not planning on giving her much of a choice. Play me the video you took in Holden's room."

Trevor held up his phone so Fitz could see the screen out of the corner of his eye as he drove. It wasn't a long video, less than five minutes. It was exactly as Trevor had described.

Holden and Chloe entered the room. They were flirting and kissing. Then as they sat down on the bed, Chloe stumbled. Holden asked how much she had been drinking and before she could even respond, she passed out. Holden shook her arm a few times then cursed his luck. He stood from the bed, looked down at her for a moment, and then threw the comforter over her. He left the room without looking back.

Fitz turned his head to Trevor. "Send me both the audio and video files." The young man had gathered better evidence than he'd had on some of his old police cases.

CHAPTER 10

Before Fitz tried to track down Veronica, he had a call to make. He'd been putting it off long enough. The phone rang a few times before Edward picked up. "Fitz, did you find something?" he said instead of hello. This wasn't a social call and Edward wasn't going to waste any time.

Fitz appreciated that. He quickly explained the call from Sutton's kidnappers and tracking her cellphone. He finished by explaining, "It seems Judge Sinclair lied to you, Edward. Sutton never took his son. There's something fishy about his whole story."

"Jealousy is a devilish thing, Fitz. You and Sutton have been over for a long time. Let her be happy."

"Did you hear what I said? Sutton has been kidnapped." Fitz punched the SUV's roof in frustration. He'd just told the man his daughter had been taken and was being held for ransom and his only response was that Fitz was jealous of Sutton's relationship with Sinclair.

"I heard you," Edward said evenly. "What do you think we should do? I can wire the money to you and you can take it to the kidnappers to get Sutton back." Edward didn't seem to bat an eye at the cost. Of course, his daughter's life was worth a lot more. "Do you think we need to call the FBI for the exchange?"

"I don't think it's going to be that simple. All of this started when

Judge Sinclair's son was set up for sexual assault. It seemed to spiral out of control when things didn't go according to plan. Now Holden and Sutton are missing and another student, who uncovered the truth, was shot at and his room trashed. They went after a senator's son, Edward. This can't be as simple as paying a ransom and getting Sutton back."

After several beats of silence, Edward asked, "What do you think this is all about then?"

"I don't know." Fitz wished he had a better answer. "I just know it's bigger than a ransom payment. If all they were after was ransom, they would have kidnapped someone with more power than Sutton."

"Do you think they are coming after me?" Edward asked a legitimate question. His politics were as questionable as Judge Sinclair's. He was a rich powerful lobbyist who had angered more people than Fitz could count.

"I don't think they are coming after you," Fitz said after a few beats. "I think it ties back to Judge Sinclair. Even if you think I'm jealous, you have to accept a few things don't add up."

They talked over their theories, neither offering up anything solid. When the conversation ran dry, Edward asked, "Do we tell the FBI?"

Fitz knew the FBI had a process for when families wanted to pay the ransom, particularly keeping track of the serial numbers of the bills and often putting a tracking device in the bag. Fitz was hoping to get Sutton back without paying any ransom at all. Still, he couldn't tell his ex-father-in-law not to call the feds. "I'll leave the FBI involvement up to you. It's not the direction I'd go, but I can't tell you what to do."

Edward was quiet for several moments and Fitz thought he might end the call there. He was surprised by the response. "I'd rather not get the FBI involved either. If I get the cash, will you pick it up?"

"Sounds like a plan." Fitz was surprised Edward was putting that kind of trust in him. There was a time when Edward wouldn't have

CHAPTER 10

trusted him to take out the trash. Now, he was entrusting Fitz with his daughter's life. "I need some time, but I'll be there."

They arranged a pick-up time. It would give Fitz time to go to his house and get a few weapons as well as check in with Charlie. If he was going alone, Fitz might as well make sure his affairs were in order.

There was a lot of ground to cover and he still didn't feel like he was on firm footing. He needed answers from Judge Sinclair first and foremost before speaking to Veronica. He had no idea if he was in chambers for the confirmation hearing.

The judge's administrative assistant answered Fitz's call sounding rushed and frantic. When Fitz asked to speak to Judge Sinclair, she paused and asked what it was about. He had no choice but to explain who he was and his relationship to Sutton. She put him on hold and Fitz assumed the FBI was getting ready to listen in or trace the call.

"Connor," Judge Sinclair said with the air of power and arrogance he was known for in D.C. circles. No one called Fitz by his first name or anything other than the nickname he'd had since grade school. His first name sounded foreign to his ear. "I'm sure you know by now Sutton and Holden are missing. Do you know where they are?"

"You say it as if they'd be together. We both know Sutton did not kidnap your son." Fitz said it with more anger in his voice than he had meant.

"It's the prevailing FBI theory and one that makes the most sense."

If Fitz could have crawled through the phone, he would have knocked the man on his backside. "In what world does it make sense that Sutton would kidnap your son? I was told she was with you last night. That you had dinner and fought. You told her father she left angry. That's not what you told the FBI. You said she stopped by briefly early in the evening and left by six." Fitz didn't want to give away that he had tracked her phone. "What went on between you?"

"That's none of your business. I will not discuss my relationship

MIDNIGHT JUDGE

with Sutton with you now or ever." Judge Sinclair spoke to someone on the other end of the phone, a muffled dialogue Fitz couldn't hear. When he got back on the line, he said, "Where are you right now? The FBI would like to speak to you again."

"I'll check in with them," Fitz assured. He debated for only a moment letting him know about the information he'd gathered about Holden. He figured letting Sinclair know might garner him some goodwill with the FBI. "Sutton wasn't the only reason I was calling. I found out some information about Holden."

"I'm listening."

So is the FBI. "I've come into some evidence that clears Holden from any sexual assault on Chloe. It's my understanding he was set up by someone at the school."

"That doesn't surprise me. I thought all along Holden was innocent."

Fitz screwed up his face in disgust. "How can you treat a sexual assault so casually?"

"You just told me Holden was set up. I assumed the young woman was lying about Holden and now she's come to her senses."

Fitz realized the way he had said it could have been misconstrued. "Chloe was drugged. He was not aware she was drugged and she passed out in his bed. His roommates made sure that Holden slept on the couch in the common room. If it wasn't for one astute young man, there'd be no evidence. The bigger question is why someone out there wants to set up your son."

Fitz let the information sit with him for a moment before he continued. He was fully expecting the FBI to be behind him on the road at any moment. He was sure they were listening in and tracing the call. "Do you know a man by the name of Blaze?"

Judge Sinclair didn't react to the information Fitz provided. "Is Blaze a first or last name?"

"I'm not sure. All I was told is he is the one who paid for Holden

CHAPTER 10

to be set up. I was curious if you were familiar or had received previous threats." When Judge Sinclair didn't respond, Fitz continued. "Someone tried to set up Holden for an assault and now he's missing. Blaze is going to a lot of trouble to take down Holden and you might want to ask yourself why. The two must be connected."

"Do you have evidence Holden was set up or just some story being told by other students?"

"I have evidence," was all Fitz said. He wasn't going to let Sinclair know what he had.

"I need you to hand over the evidence to the FBI." He spoke to someone on the other end who Fitz assumed was an agent. "Did you hear me, Connor? I need you to go to the FBI immediately and turn over this evidence."

"I'll share it with them. I have a few things to take care of first." Fitz waited for an argument that never came. "Has there been any ransom request for Holden?"

"No," Judge Sinclair said, his voice stiff. "I was hoping Sutton was doing this to test me. Our relationship has been a struggle lately."

It seemed Sinclair glossed over the information about Blaze and was still stuck on Sutton. There was a thread there Fitz needed to pull. "Why would Sutton commit a felony to test you? What is it you're not telling me?"

"Nothing you need to be concerned about. I don't understand why you're still in contact with her. You and Sutton have been divorced for more than twenty years."

Fitz smirked. "Nothing you need to be concerned about."

"Then I have nothing left to say." With that, Judge Sinclair hung up.

After he dropped Trevor off at the train station and waited for the train to pull out of the station, he called Senator Tom Wilson and told him about the change in plan. He assured Fitz he'd pick his son up at the train station in D.C.

Before leaving, Fitz did a quick search of *The New York Times* website. It didn't take him more than a few minutes to locate Veronica's mother, Morgan Williams. He found Morgan's profile under her most recent article and clicked on her name. Her full bio came up with her email address but no phone number. He clicked around on the website and found a number for the newspaper tipline desk. If he had more time, he could have asked Ditch or Charlie to track down her cellphone number. He didn't want to waste his time waiting for it.

He punched in the tipline number and when it was answered by a young woman, he asked for Morgan Williams. He said he had a story for her and refused to speak to anyone else. He was patched through immediately.

"This is Morgan Williams. Can I help you?"

Fitz made a quick introduction. "I'm calling about your daughter Veronica," he said and waited.

"Is she okay? I heard there was some trouble at Brewster Academy."

Fitz confirmed. "I don't know how to tell you this. I have evidence your daughter was working with an unknown individual, who goes by the name Blaze, to set up Holden Sinclair for sexual assault. I have audio evidence of Veronica admitting she drugged Chloe. She concocted the story about the sexual assault and was supposed to get you to cover the story. For the record, through some fortunate events in the dorm that night, no assault took place. Your daughter set up Chloe and then concocted a story on the backend."

Before Morgan could argue with him or tell him he had to be mistaken and her daughter would never do something like that, he played the audio clip. He turned up the volume so she could hear better. When it was done, he said, "I figured it was best to come to you first. I'd like to speak to her, but I assume she won't talk to me."

Morgan remained quiet for so long Fitz wasn't sure if she was still on the line. He said her name once and she coughed. "I don't even

CHAPTER 10

know what to say. I can't believe Veronica would do something like this. She was so insistent I write the story I should have suspected. What are you going to do with the recording?"

Fitz hadn't been prepared for the question. "I'm not releasing it if that's what you're asking. It's evidence."

She sighed heavily. "Are you at Brewster Academy now? Have they found Holden?"

Fitz didn't hold anything back. "Holden is still missing as is his father's fiancée, who happens to be my ex-wife. The FBI doesn't have a good grasp on the situation yet. I can't stress this enough, Morgan. Veronica is not safe. I was with one of her classmates, Trevor Wilson, who obtained the recording and he was shot at by an unknown assailant and someone trashed his room. I can't do anything to protect Veronica." Fitz gave Morgan the phone number for Agent Burrows. "He's difficult but he's a solid agent and seemingly a good guy. You can trust him."

Morgan considered what Fitz said but came back with her own plan. "Have you given the FBI the evidence?"

"No." He thought back to his call with Sinclair. "They might be aware of it. Time is of the essence."

Morgan said she didn't want to call the FBI yet. "I need to speak to Veronica first."

It sounded to Fitz like she was willing to meet with him. "How long until you can get to the school?"

"Give me three hours." They planned where they'd meet then hung up.

It was a delay Fitz hoped would prove useful later. He had one last call to make. When the kidnapper answered, Fitz said, "I got your money."

He reiterated, "Good. You're paying attention. I'll call you back with a time and place to meet. If you're not there on time, Sutton is dead.

Come alone."

Kidnapping 101 was leverage. Fitz knew the kidnapper wouldn't do anything to Sutton until they got their money even if it was past the deadline.

If Sutton was dead, they had no more bargaining chip.

CHAPTER 11

Fitz sat in the back of the nondescript main street café in a city several miles from Brewster Academy. It was in a small town where no one but locals would visit. Fitz wasn't even sure how Morgan had heard of the place, but it was perfect for the meeting.

Fitz had surveilled the establishment before he went in to be sure he hadn't been followed. He ordered a small coffee and a sandwich even though he wasn't hungry. He didn't know the next time he'd get to eat, and he needed to keep his energy up.

Fitz had arrived thirty minutes before the meeting to scope out the place and get settled before they arrived. It was enough time for him to eat the sandwich, drink his coffee, and even order another.

When he was finished, Fitz checked his watch and noted Morgan and Veronica were fifteen minutes late. He assumed Morgan might have had a hard time getting Veronica to go with her or maybe Robins or the FBI stopped them.

The minutes ticked by and Fitz was ready to give up. He finished his second coffee and was about to get up when Morgan and Veronica walked in. Veronica had her blonde hair twisted into a bun at the top of her head. She wore low-rise jeans and a shirt short enough to show a trim of skin across her abdomen.

"Morgan," he said and extended his hand to the woman with shoulder-length blonde hair the same shade as her daughter's. She had the handshake of a journalist used to dealing with powerful people.

Morgan handed her daughter a crisp twenty and sent her to the counter before Fitz could offer to buy them something. Morgan sat down and looked over at Veronica at the counter. "It took me some time to convince her to come with me. I tried bringing up the subject, but she refused to speak to me."

"I expected nothing less." Fitz tapped his pocket where he had his phone. "I think once she hears the recording of herself, she might be singing another tune."

Morgan leaned her arms on the table. "Do you really think she's in danger?"

"I do." He dropped his voice. "I don't know exactly how all of this ties together. I need this to be off the record too. I should have said that before when we spoke on the phone."

Morgan waved him off. "I'm not looking to write a story. When the time comes, if there is a story to write, I'll seek a quote from you if you're willing to go on the record. For now, consider me a concerned mother who wants to keep her child safe."

Fitz believed her and it allowed him to be candid. "We still don't know who took Holden and there's been a ransom demand for Sutton. Someone figured out Trevor has evidence linking Veronica to Holden the night of the incident."

"Trevor's father is Senator Tom Wilson, correct?" Morgan asked and Fitz confirmed. "Could the shooting have something to do with his work in Congress?"

"I don't think so. Not with everything else that's happening. It would be too much of a coincidence."

Morgan seemed to understand. "I know what Veronica did was wrong. Illegal. I don't understand why she did it. She's never been in serious trouble before now." She shook her head as if she couldn't believe it.

CHAPTER 11

Fitz was glad she was taking it seriously. "What do you want to see happen?"

"This goes beyond anything I ever anticipated. I expected underage drinking, maybe drugs, or trouble with boys. I never expected this kind of criminal activity." Morgan looked down at the table. "Veronica needs some kind of psychological help. More than anything, she needs to be held accountable for her actions. She lied to me and harmed a young woman who did nothing to her."

"You didn't mention Holden."

Morgan smiled ruefully. "That young man has problems of his own. It's not that I don't care if he was harmed, but he's got quite the reputation. It made believing this story much easier. I'm sure if he's not guilty now, he was guilty before. There was another allegation."

"I know. That's actually why Trevor was watching so carefully that night." Fitz couldn't blame her for how she felt. He felt much the same way. It didn't even bother him that Holden was missing. He wasn't here for him. He was only here to find Blaze, who may have had a hand in Sutton's kidnapping. They chatted for a few more minutes until Veronica carried over their drinks. She sat down at the table looking sullen and annoyed.

"Why am I here?" she asked as she took a sip of her large Frappuccino. She licked the drink off her lips and looked at Fitz. "My mother wouldn't tell me anything on the way other than to pack a bag because I wasn't going back to school anytime soon. If this is about Holden, I don't know where he is. I'm sure he ran off someplace. He does things for attention."

"Do you know for sure he ran off?" Fitz asked, interested in her take on the situation.

Veronica focused on her drink. "I don't know anything for sure. I know Holden is trouble. Look what he did to Chloe." She had an indignant look on her face that didn't deserve to be there after what she had done.

It was the opening Fitz wanted. "That's why you're here talking to me. I want to better understand what happened with Chloe and Holden."

Veronica cast her eyes at her mother. "I already told my mom everything. She should have written a story about it. I guess she's one more person protecting Holden."

Fitz was glad to see Morgan not taking the bait. "I heard the official story, Veronica. What I'm looking for now is your role in what happened that night."

"My role?" she asked, coughing on the sip she had taken. "I didn't have a role in what happened. This was all Holden. I was there for Chloe the next day."

He wasn't surprised by her denial. "Would you like to hear a recording of you admitting your role in what happened to Chloe or do you want to skip the embarrassment and tell me the truth?"

Veronica pulled back and looked at her mother with concern. "What's he talking about? What recording?"

"You need to answer the question," Morgan said, deferring to Fitz. "I'm here to support you. The only thing you need to do right now is tell the truth."

"What truth?" she demanded but Morgan simply pointed to Fitz. Without her mother bailing her out, Veronica turned to Fitz. "What are you talking about? I don't know who is telling lies about me. Anything you have on that recording is made up. It's all lies from people who don't like me."

That was a lot of protest for a young girl who had done nothing wrong. Fitz leaned forward and rested his arms on the table. "I have a recording of *you* admitting you drugged Chloe and tried to set up Holden. Then the next day it was you who told Chloe she had been sexually assaulted by Holden. Because you drugged her, Chloe doesn't

CHAPTER 11

know what happened. Do you remember doing that?"

"This is crazy. I'd never do something like that." Veronica's voice squeaked and her eyes were wild with fear. She turned her head to her mother and pleaded. "Mom, you have to believe me. This guy is trying to blame me for something I didn't do."

Morgan did nothing but shake her head. "I can't help you, Veronica. You made your choices. The only thing that will help you is the truth."

Veronica turned back to him. "Who are you?"

Fitz wasn't going to debate this. He rested his phone on the table, pulled up the app with the recording, and hit play. Veronica's voice came through loud and clear. She was confident and arrogant as she described what she did. There was no sign of fear or remorse. Even though it was the third time Fitz heard the recording, it didn't stop the sickening feeling that filled his gut. He wouldn't be surprised if Veronica was a budding sociopath.

He looked across the table at Morgan and his heart broke for her. It was one thing to be the mother of a victim, it was entirely another to be faced with the horrendous crime your child committed, especially when they were admitting it so brazenly.

Veronica listened and was rendered speechless. It was clear to Fitz she had no idea anyone had recorded the conversation. She had fully trusted her friend, Emily, and had no reason to suspect she'd been set up. She raised her eyes to Fitz. "Emily wouldn't do that to me. Who recorded this? Isn't it illegal? Can't they get in trouble?"

Morgan slammed her fist down on the table, making both of them jump. "You're worried about who recorded you, Veronica? Listen to what you said. You admitted to committing a crime against a friend of yours. You were complicit in this from the start. Not only did you hurt Chloe, but you tried to jeopardize my career with a fake story."

Veronica stuttered and stammered, not able to get out a full sentence in her defense.

"I want to help you, Veronica," Fitz said after giving her a few moments to stew in her mess. "This isn't something you came up with on your own. You were used by someone. That person tried to kill me and another student from Brewster Academy earlier today. Blaze may be the one who kidnapped Holden and my ex-wife."

Her eyelashes fluttered as if she were trying to make sense of it all. "A student was almost killed today. Who?"

"I can't tell you that. You have to trust me that you're in danger." He locked his gaze on her. "All you have to do is tell us the truth."

Veronica's eyes got wide and she looked at her mother and then back at Fitz. Her bottom lip quivered and tears formed in her eyes. "He told me if I told anyone, he'd kill me."

Fitz wanted to believe her. He was sure the threat was made, but the tears and the quivering lip were fake. She was giving him the emotion she assumed he expected. He didn't want to call her out on it. Not yet. "I know you're scared. I need to know who made you do this."

Veronica turned to her mother. "Am I in trouble for this?"

Morgan caught the look on Fitz's face. "We can talk about that later, Veronica. It all depends on your willingness to help. You did a terrible thing. As Fitz said, this is your time to start redeeming yourself."

"But, I—" Veronica started to argue and her mother's stern look shut her up. She turned back to Fitz. "What do you want to know?"

"Who contacted you?"

"His name was Blaze like I said in the recording. I don't know if that's a first name or last."

"Did you ever meet him in person?" Fitz knew she had denied that to Emily. He wasn't sure though. He caught the look on Morgan's face. She was hoping her daughter had not met this person.

Veronica took a breath and nodded. "Only once when he gave me the money. We mostly texted." Veronica stared down at the table. "Holden deserves everything he got. He's mean to most of us and can get away with anything because of who his father is. Last year, he bullied two freshmen so badly that they left school. He sexually assaulted that other girl. He told us he was untouchable and everyone believed him. When Blaze reached out to me, I thought maybe this was a chance at revenge."

"You hurt your friend in the process," Morgan countered, disgusted. "How could you do something like that to her?"

Veronica wouldn't meet her mother's eyes. "Chloe isn't as nice as you think she is. We were friends, but she was mean to me a lot. I didn't think…" She stopped talking and wouldn't raise her head to look at either of them.

"You didn't think. That's exactly right," Morgan said, scolding her again.

Fitz worried Veronica might shut down on them if Morgan continued. "Veronica, please tell me more about your interaction with Blaze. How long ago did he first contact you?"

"About a month ago. When I first got the message on social media, I thought it was someone at school. That's why I gave him my phone number. I figured as soon as I saw their number, I'd know who it was. The profile on social media was blank – no friends, no photo. I figured it was someone I knew and who knew how much we all hated Holden. Then I realized once he was texting that I didn't know who it was and that he was older. I could tell that by how he texted. He said if I didn't want to help him, he'd find someone else. He was willing to pay me and I needed the money. My mom doesn't have the kind of money other parents have at the school."

Morgan winced. "You've never wanted for anything, Veronica. I may not make as much as other families do, but I've rarely said no to you."

"What about the Chanel purse I wanted last month?" Veronica said, her tone snotty. "I wanted one like my friend and you told me no. I knew you couldn't afford it."

"Whether I could afford it or not wasn't the issue. You are in high school and don't need a designer purse." Morgan looked over at Fitz with her cheeks red. "It's true I can't afford designer purses. I may be a respected journalist but the salary is what it is."

Fitz sympathized with her. She was a hard-working person just like he had been his whole life. "You don't need to justify to me. Money or not, my kid wouldn't be getting designer anything." He turned his attention back to Veronica. "Are you telling me you did all this for the money and to get back at Holden?"

She nodded and sat back in the chair. "Holden deserves it."

"Where did he meet you when he gave you the money?"

"In the back of campus behind the senior boys' dorm. I met him in the woods one night."

Morgan's mouth fell open at the danger her daughter had faced, still faced.

"Where did you get the roofies?"

"He gave them to me with the cash." Veronica nodded and turned to her mother. "I want to leave. I've said enough."

"Describe him for me first. Then you can go."

Veronica sighed. "He was like five-foot-ten, had dark hair. Not muscular. Kind of a normal-looking guy. I'm not even sure that I'd know him if I saw him again. It was dark in the woods that night."

"Weren't you scared he might hurt you?"

Veronica shook her head. "I was there to help him." She turned to her mother again. "I'm ready to go."

Morgan looked at Fitz. "Is there more you need?"

Fitz knew his time was running thin. "Do you have any idea who kidnapped Holden?"

Veronica shook her head. "All he wanted me to do was what I did. He's angry with me now that my mom won't write the story and it got

CHAPTER 11

all messed up that night." She stood from the table before signaling to Fitz she wasn't going to say more.

"I hope you get the information you need and get your ex-wife back safely," Morgan said before going. "I'm going to call Agent Burrows when I get Veronica back home."

"Thank you for your help," Fitz said, frustrated that he still didn't know more.

CHAPTER 12

Nearly an hour into his drive back toward Washington D.C., Fitz knew he was being tailed. He hadn't noticed the four-door black Honda sedan initially. As he started down the interstate, the tail became obvious weaving in and out of traffic to keep up with him. The first thing Fitz did when he noticed the car was pull into the far-right lane and slow down, forcing the car to pass him.

He stared straight ahead as if he didn't notice and focused on the two men in the car in his peripheral vision. He didn't get a clear look at them, definitely not enough of a look to call in a description to anyone.

What he did get was the Maryland license plate number. He kept his slow steady pace in the right lane and called Charlie. "I need you to run a license plate for me."

"Are you okay?" she asked, hearing the stress in his tone.

"I'm on my way back and being tailed." Fitz gave her the plate number then described the events of the day and went into detail about the case. "I didn't get a good look at the guys. I pulled over to the slow lane and forced them to pass. If they had pulled over too it would have been obvious they were tailing me. Now they are in front of me and probably trying to figure out what to do. There's not another exit for a few miles."

CHAPTER 12

"Hold on, I'm running the plate number right now."

Fitz heard her clicking away at her laptop while he kept his eyes on the road. He was sure the car was going to turn off the next exit and then reenter the interstate. Then they'd be in the perfect position to keep tailing him. He needed to figure out quickly what he was going to do. He wanted to shake the tail for good.

Fitz got a lucky break. Up ahead was a wooded rest area. There were two small buildings Fitz assumed were bathrooms and several large trucks pulled over. He slowed his speed and turned off the ramp while keeping his eyes on the car trailing him. If they noticed him pull off, they didn't react.

Fitz drove up the road and found a place to park in the back in between two big trucks. His SUV would be shielded from the road by other trucks parked in front of him and shaded by the low-hanging branches. It would buy him some time. How long was anyone's guess.

He cut the engine and lifted his phone to his ear. "I'm pulled over for now. I don't think I'll have much time."

"It's okay," Charlie said absently. She clicked a few more keys. "The car belongs to Clancy Corporation. They are based out of Michigan and they are a holding company with several businesses, most of them I can't access here." She rattled off names of the few businesses she could see but none of them were familiar to Fitz. She checked the records for CEO and board members but that information wasn't public record either.

"Are they a dummy corporation?"

"It could be," she said and then clicked a few more keys. "What I'm seeing here doesn't make a lot of sense. I can't access who owns this corporation. It's not even listed in the public filing which it should be. Is there any other search you want me to run?"

Fitz stared ahead trying to figure out his best move. "I don't think so. If you can't access the names of anyone, that's not going to help me. I don't know what Sutton has gotten herself into."

"This isn't your fight, Fitz," she reminded him even though he was sure she knew he didn't care. He was in this now. "What do you need me to do to help you?"

Fitz didn't know if anyone could help him. "I met with Morgan and Veronica. She was a real piece of work. She made a deal with a guy and set up her friend for sexual assault. It didn't happen because Holden didn't have sex with a passed-out girl. I guess we can be thankful for something."

Charlie whistled. "They are growing sociopaths younger and younger these days. Did Veronica care at all that she hurt this young woman?"

"She didn't even seem to care that her life might be at risk. I've never seen someone who's supposed to be smart be so detached from her actions and the consequences. I don't know, Charlie. The bottom line is I didn't get any helpful information. All I got was a basic description that could be anyone. There was a phone number out of Michigan but when I tried to call it, it had been disconnected."

"Do you have any more information on Blaze?"

"I don't even know if it's a real name. I'm sure it's made up, something to call him to humanize him. He reached out via social media and then text. When she agreed to meet, he dropped off cash and roofies for her at the school."

"Even sounds risky. How'd he know she'd be willing in the first place?"

That was the question Fitz kept coming back to. Whoever was behind this had to know Veronica would be willing. "That's the question I've been tossing around. Maybe he'd been watching them. He could have picked at random. For all we know, Veronica wasn't the first one he contacted. Just the first one who said yes."

Charlie groaned loudly. "This is a mess, Fitz. What are you going to

CHAPTER 12

do about the tail?"

Fitz leaned to the side and looked out the front window around one of the trucks parked in a space in front of him. "I don't know if they figured out where I went. Maybe I can get back on the interstate and see if they are there. I'm going to have to try to lose them because I'm headed to Sutton's father's house to pick up some cash for the kidnappers. Do me a favor and give Ditch a call. See if he can come up with anything on Clancy Corporation."

Charlie said she'd call him right after she hung up with Fitz. "Level with me. Are you doing okay?"

"I'm as good as I'm going to get."

"I'm here if you need me," she said with an exasperated tone and ended the call before Fitz could say anything else. She should know by now Fitz wasn't going to talk about his feelings.

Fitz waited in the parking lot a few more minutes and let a large rig pull out in front of him. He followed right behind and got back on the interstate. He kept his eyes focused on the road and kept a steady pace in the middle lane while he passed slower traffic.

He didn't see the car anywhere in sight. It didn't mean they weren't there or they hadn't sent another tail. For now, he figured he was safe. Fitz turned on the radio to a classic rock station and distracted his racing mind. Music was the only stress relief he was going to get.

The drive went without a hitch back to D.C. Fitz stopped for gas and food a few times and never spotted the tail again. He assumed he shook them loose when he pulled over at that rest stop. Its placement was fortunate and he'd had luck on his side. Fitz also assumed the goons tailing him probably weren't that adept at mobile surveillance because if he had been tailing someone, Fitz would have found them easily enough.

He made it to Sutton's father's house just after midnight. He pulled into the driveway and took notice of the downstairs lights. Edward was expecting him. Fitz was never sure how the man was going to react. He could be as mean as a rattlesnake or as docile as a rabbit. Fitz was never sure which he was going to get. The one constant that always remained true was Edward looking down his nose at Fitz who was never and would never be good enough for his daughter.

Fitz locked his SUV and took long strides up to the house. He rang the bell and the housekeeper let him in. He figured the staff would be off for the night, so he was surprised to see someone other than Edward answer the door. Sutton's mother had passed a few years ago.

The young woman directed Fitz into Edward's private sitting room in the back of the house and told him to wait there. She closed the door behind her, leaving Fitz on his own. He'd been in the sitting room only once and that was when he'd come to ask Edward for Sutton's hand in marriage. The conversation ended with cursing, slamming doors, and Fitz telling the man he was going to marry her with or without his blessing.

Suffice it to say, Fitz didn't have any good feelings about the room.

The door creaked open and Fitz turned to see Edward with a highball glass in his hand. The old man's eyes were squinted in either drunkenness or pain. Fitz wasn't sure and it might have been a mix of both. "Edward, I'm sorry I arrived so late. I got here as quickly as I could."

"Have you heard from her?" Edward asked, walking to the brown leather couch. He stumbled, sloshing the brown liquid out of the glass onto the rug below. He dropped down onto the couch, spilling more of his drink.

Fitz wasn't going to bother asking if he was okay. Neither of them were. "I got proof of life, as I said on the phone. I'm hoping to get her out without making an exchange. I have some idea where she is. I need to bring the money with me in case all else fails."

Edward swished the dark liquid around in his glass. "Do you think

CHAPTER 12

you're going to fail, Fitz? Am I going to lose my daughter?"

Fitz knew the man was drunk – obliterated was probably a more apt description. "Edward, I've never let anything happen to Sutton on my watch. I'm not going to start now. If all goes to plan, I'll be back with your daughter and your money."

Edward hitched his jaw toward the briefcase sitting next to his desk. "I don't care about the money. If you bring her back, it's yours."

Money had been the primary contention between the two of them when he'd been dating Sutton. Edward didn't like his lack of earning potential and he often made snide remarks that he was with his daughter for the money. Fitz's face burned hot with even the suggestion he'd keep it.

Fitz propped his hands on his hips and looked down at the pathetic mess in front of him. "Believe it or not, Edward, I make a good living now. I bought a house in Chevy Chase and I run a multi-million-dollar business. I've come a long way from being the beat cop I was when Sutton and I first got together. I don't have to be here right now. The least you could do is show me some respect."

Edward laughed. "Respect." He swilled back a gulp of his drink. "What do you know about respect?"

"Is there a reason you're trying to goad me into a fight? I didn't do this to Sutton. It's the new man in her life – Judge Sinclair." Fitz held his arms out wide and looked dramatically around the room. "I don't see him here to clean up his mess. He's the one lying to the FBI. I'm here though, as I've always been."

Edward looked up at him through bloodshot eyes. "Do you know I told Sutton not to marry him? The man is a disgrace and she shouldn't have to take on his rotten kid. The pair of them are trouble – old money, entitled trouble."

That was rich coming from him. "What's your beef with the judge?"

Edward turned his head away and took another large gulp. When he was done, he rested his near-empty glass in his lap. "He tried to buy me off, Fitz. That man had the audacity to come here and offer me cash for an endorsement of him – a public endorsement. He wanted me to go to senators and tell them how they should vote too. I told him no way that was going to happen. Do you know what he did?"

Fitz didn't have any idea.

Edward pushed himself to a standing position. He swayed one way and then the other. Fitz fought the desire to hold him upright. He looked over at Fitz. "He told me he'd ruin me if he didn't get what he wanted. Well, here I am, ruined." Edward gestured toward the briefcase. "Take the money, kill the judge, and bring my daughter back alive."

Fitz didn't take the threat seriously. It was the ramblings of an angry drunk. "I'll bring her back as soon as I can."

Edward left Fitz standing there as he stumbled out into the hallway and shouted for his housekeeper to bring him another drink.

CHAPTER 13

Fitz walked the perimeter of his house making sure there were no broken windows or other signs of forced entry while he'd been gone. Given he had been shot at and then tailed, he wasn't taking any chances. He needed sleep, a shower, and guns before he'd head back out on the road to rescue Sutton. There was no way he'd be able to get through the dense woods near Lake Anna at this time of night. He'd do more damage to himself and his flashlight would alert them he was out there. He needed the element of surprise.

Fitz didn't like leaving her with her captors and it didn't seem like anyone else was coming to her rescue. While he wanted to rush to Sutton's aid, his law enforcement training told him gathering as much information as possible first would be more beneficial.

When it appeared the house was fine, Fitz unlocked the side door and unloaded his SUV including the briefcase with the money. He was still shaken by Edward's behavior. He'd never seen the old man quite that drunk before and certainly not a rambling mess.

There was an undercurrent to all of this that still baffled Fitz. He wasn't getting the full story and he knew it. He suspected Sutton could have told him more but chose to keep him in the dark. He was sure Edward hadn't told him the full story either. Judge Sinclair lied to him. Even the FBI didn't seem to have a clue.

Fitz dropped his bags in the tiled foyer and turned on the small table lamp. He was still getting settled and the living room was a mix of a few favorite furniture items mixed with boxes that still needed to be unpacked. He was waiting for a furniture delivery that would be there in three days. He'd have to ask Charlie to let them in if he wasn't back yet.

Fitz moved through the living room to the kitchen in the back of the house. He pulled open the fridge, grabbed a can of Coke, and popped the top. He took a long sip and leaned against the counter. He pulled his cellphone from his pocket and noticed a few missed text messages from women he'd recently dated. He didn't have time to engage in conversation tonight. They'd have to wait, which he was sure was going to lead to some drama.

Fitz finished the rest of the soda in a few sips, tossed the can in the green recycling bin, and headed for the back stairs. The house was so large he had a front and back staircase. He climbed to the top and made a right down the hall to his office. Fitz flipped on the light, went to the framed reprint of the Lincoln Memorial, and swung the photo out from the wall to reveal a wall safe behind it.

He turned the nob, getting the right combination, and it clicked open. Fitz pulled out two handguns and a stack of cash. He had a locked gun safe in the basement too but this was enough for now. Fitz placed the items on his desk then locked the safe, moving the photo back into place over it. He was just about to sit down when a rattle came from the floor below.

Fitz reached for one of the guns, checked to make sure it was fully loaded, and headed back into the hall. He stopped when he heard the noise again.

Scratching coming from the front door.

Fitz moved slowly down the hallway, past the back stairs to the open landing where he could see over the railing to the first floor. The top of someone's head bobbed up and down through the square window

CHAPTER 13

at the top of the front door.

"Who's there?" Fitz shouted.

The person stared up. "It's me, Fitz. My key won't work."

Fitz relaxed against the banister. "Charlie, I'll be right there." He jogged down the front staircase and unlocked the front door. When he pulled it open, he said, "I thought you were coming to kill me."

She entered the house and closed the door behind her. "I'd like to kill you. You told me to work on the recent case we got but then you never left me the case file. I was coming over here to see if you left it in your office. I didn't realize you were home." She told him the name of the case and held up her keys. "It's not working."

He took the keys from her and went to the door. He hadn't changed the locks. Fitz opened the door and tried them. They seemed to work fine for him. "Maybe it was sticky," he said, tossing them back to her. "I have the file you need in my office."

Charlie followed right behind him up the front stairs to his office. She had seen the gun in his hand and then the one on his desk. "How dangerous is this, Fitz?" she asked, leaning against the doorjamb.

He ignored the question and went to the filing cabinet, unlocked it, and pulled out the requested file. It was a simple case, just doing an educational and background check on an upcoming candidate for a local school board. The client wanted the person thoroughly vetted before backing them. It was one of those clients who didn't believe the already available information and wanted Fitz to double-check it all. He got those cases sometimes and, more times than not, it turned out the client was the one with a lot to hide, which is why they assumed everyone else did.

He handed the file to Charlie and apologized again for not bringing it to the office the previous morning. Fitz went to his desk and sat down, stretching his arms overhead.

"What's the plan now?"

"I'm going to get some sleep and then try to rescue Sutton."

Charlie didn't look convinced. She left her post in the doorway and sat down on the edge of his desk. She angled her body so she was looking at him. "Is it safe for you to go alone?"

"I don't know," he said honestly. Fitz blew out a frustrated breath and shrugged. "I don't know what she's gotten herself into." He recounted the conversation he had with Sutton's father and then the brief one he had with Judge Sinclair. "Sinclair lied to me but more importantly, he lied to the FBI. I don't understand why. Her phone was at Sinclair's and then she left heading deeper into Virginia, the opposite way from her house."

"How do you know Sutton left Judge Sinclair's on her own?"

Fitz's head snapped up. "What do you mean?"

Charlie grabbed a chair and sat. "Fitz, you said Sutton left Judge Sinclair's house after a fight. Then she was tracked in Virginia. How do you know she was the one driving when you were tracking her cellphone?"

"Are you saying you think Sutton was kidnapped from Judge Sinclair's house?"

"From the house or outside of it when she was walking to her car. Did you consider *when* she was kidnapped?" Charlie was looking at him with a mix of sympathy and annoyance.

"I didn't," Fitz admitted. "I was there to find Holden and when the FBI woke me up this morning asking about Sutton, I didn't know what was happening. Once I found out she was in Virginia and got the ransom request, I didn't stop to consider where she was when she'd been kidnapped. Those details didn't seem as relevant as the fact that she had been taken."

"Maybe Sinclair was covering his tracks."

Fitz didn't understand. "You think he did something to her? That he's involved with her kidnapping? He's the one who told the FBI he

CHAPTER 13

thought she kidnapped Holden." He sat back in the chair, annoyed with himself now for having tunnel vision.

"It might be why he's lying to you and the FBI."

If that were true, Fitz needed to know immediately. He got up and reached for his keys on his desk.

Charlie narrowed her eyes at him. "I thought you needed sleep?"

"I do," he said. "This is more important."

"Where are we going?" Charlie asked standing with him.

"I'm going to Judge Sinclair's house to see if Sutton's car is there. If she was kidnapped from his house, then her car has to be there, right? You're not coming with me."

"Unless they ditched it," Charlie said as she followed Fitz out into the hallway and down the front stairs. She trailed behind him out the front door, ignoring the rest of what he had said. Fitz stopped long enough to lock the door behind them. She waited until they were in the driveway to add, "I don't think if Judge Sinclair was involved in kidnapping Sutton he'd leave her car there to be found. Don't you think they would have taken it with them?"

"I don't know," Fitz said, climbing into his SUV. "It's not a good idea for you to come. You need plausible deniability for when I kill him."

Charlie pulled open the passenger door. "I'm coming with you to make sure you don't do anything stupid."

Fitz turned the SUV on and put it in reverse. He allowed her to come without an argument. She was right that her presence might temper his stupidity. "I have a general idea of where I can find Sutton. What I don't know is what I'm going to face when I find her. If I can figure out what Sinclair is doing, then maybe I..." He didn't finish his thought because he just didn't know. All he knew was he wanted to search Sinclair's for any sign of Sutton.

Charlie sat quietly in the passenger side as Fitz drove the distance from his house to Judge Sinclair's. The streets were dark this time of night. The lamps cast shadows that would catch Fitz's attention. He was still on high alert.

Fitz glanced over at Charlie. "Now you're too quiet."

She turned back to him. "I'm not sure what to say. I don't understand what you've got yourself ensnarled in. I'm worried it's going to impact business. Should I be looking for a new job?"

"Charlie. Stop." Fitz said the words but he forced himself to see it from her perspective. He was going far outside the scope of his business and going up against powerful forces and had no stake in the game. There was no paying client. The FBI had even shown up at his door. "I concede from the outside this doesn't look good. I was doing Sutton a favor and now I'm completely caught up in something. It's not like I can walk away now."

She arched an eyebrow. "Exactly what I thought. I guess I'll get my résumé ready."

Fitz caught the dramatic tone in her voice. She was half-serious with him. She wasn't going to get her résumé ready, but she was concerned about how this would impact the firm. For as much as Fitz had built the business, Charlie had been right there at his side making sure everything worked smoothly. The business was as much her face as it was his, at least in the eyes of many of their clients.

Fitz tapped his finger against the steering wheel. "I promise you I'll find Sutton and then drop the whole thing. I'll let it go completely. I'll get Sutton back and call it a day."

"Do you promise?" Charlie asked, her voice sounding younger than her years.

Fitz didn't want to promise because he had no idea what was going to happen once he found Sutton. But he couldn't resist the look on Charlie's face. "I promise you I'll find Sutton and let the rest go. The FBI can sort out what happened with Holden."

Charlie seemed satisfied with that answer. "Did Sutton have any

CHAPTER 13

tracking in her car? Sometimes cars will come with a tracking service."

Fitz had no idea. It wasn't like he was keeping close tabs on his ex. "Even if I knew, I wouldn't know how to access it. It's been a long time since she shared information with me like that."

"How do you know where Sinclair lives?" Charlie asked the question Fitz hoped she wouldn't.

"Sutton told me," he lied. In truth, when he first found out Sutton started seeing Sinclair, he had followed her to his house once. Only once. He knew Sinclair's reputation and had been concerned. He had no good reason for following her. Even at the time he had chastised himself and never did it again.

Fitz parked a few houses down from Judge Sinclair's and scoped the street for any FBI who might be watching the home. There wasn't a police presence that he could see. The home had a security gate and cameras that Sutton said sometimes worked. Fitz knew he'd have to climb a fence and risk getting arrested for trespassing.

"Wait here and I'll be right back. If the cops come, take off. I don't want you getting mixed up in this." Charlie started to protest but Fitz shut her down. "We can't both go to jail."

"I'm not paying your bail."

Fitz laughed as he shut the door. He walked the short distance to Judge Sinclair's sprawling estate and found an area of the fence he could climb. There was always a place to breach security. He just hoped the risk came with a reward.

CHAPTER 14

The estate had three garages – a three-car garage attached to the house, a two-car garage attached to the smaller guest house, and another garage in the back of the property that housed the judge's vast car collection. While Fitz had admired certain cars from afar over the years, he'd never seen the point of collecting. He was far too pragmatic.

Fitz bypassed the main house and then the guest house. He figured if Sinclair was going to hide Sutton's car it would be in the back out of sight where no one would think to look for it. Two lights on the second floor of the home shone brightly. Fitz assumed it might be Sinclair's bedroom. While Sutton had talked about the grounds, she hadn't given him a layout of the house.

Fitz jogged slowly past the main part of the property to the back garage. Sutton had once told him the tree covering made it impossible to see the garage from the house. She had said in jest that she could forget all the money Sinclair had wasted on cars because it was out of sight and out of mind for her. She was right. The dense tree coverage shaded the property and gave Fitz the coverage he needed.

The front of the garage had solid thick doors. He moved around to the side where he assumed there'd be a window. As Fitz hoped, there were two unobstructed side windows. He tried the first and then had to step back and engage the flashlight app on his phone. He shone it in

CHAPTER 14

the window and looked for Sutton's BMW. The only cars he saw were Judge Sinclair's. He moved to the next and shone the light around the garage.

There, in the back half under a tarp, was Sutton's BMW. The only reason Fitz recognized it was because her front headlight had a crack. She'd mentioned it to him months ago. She was terrible at getting that kind of work done, so he wasn't surprised the crack was still there.

He texted Charlie he had found the car and was going to confront Judge Sinclair. He walked around to the front of the garage and past the door but he stopped himself on the side lawn as he faced the house.

He wanted more proof.

Fitz doubled back, turned the handle on the side door of the garage, and pushed it open without any loud alarm going off. He walked past the row of cars, counting six in all with Sutton's in the back. Fitz lifted off the beige cover and threw it to the floor. He went to the driver's side and pulled open the door. A stack of her business cards sat in the center console.

He noticed something else too. Something that couldn't be missed on the console, floor, and buckle of the seatbelt – blood.

Anger rose in Fitz's chest. He didn't care who saw him out there now. He went in search of a light and found the switch near the door where he had entered. He flipped the light and headed straight back to the car. He snapped a photo of the license plate and several more around the exterior of the car. Then he focused on the blood spatter in the front seat. He got photos of different angles and then stepped back wishing he hadn't opened the car door with his hand. If there had been prints, they'd be smudged and contaminated by his own.

Fitz felt around under the seats but found nothing. He used his shirt to open the back doors. When he was done, he went around to the other side and did the same with the passenger door. He wasn't sure what he was looking for, but he didn't find anything else of value.

As Fitz went back to the driver's side, that's when he noticed the seat position. It was far enough back he could have driven the car. Sutton would have it pulled closer given her short frame. Someone other than Sutton had parked the car in the garage. He snapped a few photos, left through the side door, and marched straight toward the house.

Fitz moved like a man with a purpose. He cut across the grass and, as he turned the corner to head to the front of the house, he walked right into Charlie on the front walkway.

He reached out and grabbed her arms, steadying her. "What are you doing? I told you to wait in my SUV," he scolded her, his voice rising.

Charlie stepped back out of his grasp. "No, Fitz. I'm not going to let you do something stupid. You're too angry to be thinking straight." When he started to protest, she told him to shut up and listen. "You're not going to help anyone by going in there and shaking the truth out of Sinclair. You're going to get yourself arrested and that's not going to get you to Sutton before the ransom is due."

Fitz pointed back to the garage. "Her car is there and there's blood all over the front seat. Someone else drove it too. The seat is pushed back too far for Sutton. If I'm going to rescue her, then I need to understand what's going on."

"Call the FBI, Fitz. Let them come out and explain it to you." He brushed past her, not listening. The way Charlie wanted to do it might be the appropriate way and it might even be the best way, but it wasn't the way it was going to get him the answers he needed.

If confronted, Sinclair would spin a tale for the FBI, and the only question they'd have is why Fitz had trespassed. They'd turn the whole thing around on him.

Charlie called after him but he marched forward without looking back. She was well-intentioned. He'd give her that much. "I have to do it this way. Just trust me."

CHAPTER 14

She followed after him. "I'm worried you're going to make things worse."

Fitz didn't have time to argue with her. He was focused on only one thing. He took the porch steps two at a time and banged his fist on the door so hard it shook. Charlie calmly walked up behind him and pushed the doorbell. She raised her eyes to him and shook her head.

"I didn't see it," Fitz said, feeling like she might be right. He was feeling out of control.

"Of course, you didn't. You're not in your right mind."

When no one came to the door moments later, he rang the bell again. His temper got the better of him and he pounded his fist against the door for good measure. The upstairs light was still bright, so he knew someone was home. A moment later, Fitz heard the shuffling of feet on hardwoods and a man with a deep voice telling him to stop pounding on the door.

"What do you want?" Judge Sinclair barked as he pulled the door open. He stopped short when he saw the two of them. "What are you doing here, Connor? You have no right to be here."

Fitz shoved him back from the doorway and forced his way into the house. Sinclair had about thirty pounds on him, all fat, and Fitz towered over him. He grabbed Sinclair by the front of his bathrobe, slamming him into the wall. "What did you do to Sutton?"

Sinclair's arms flailed at his sides as his chest rose and fell. He heaved in breath after breath. "I didn't do anything to Sutton. Get off me. I'm calling the FBI."

"How did you know we weren't the FBI? Your son is missing. If you were so worried about him, pounding on your front door at this hour could have meant anything. You should have been running to the door. Not yelling about the noise." Fitz pushed his fist right under the man's chin, careful not to press down and cut off his oxygen. He wanted to scare the man into submission, not actually kill him, which didn't seem like it would take all that much.

Sinclair tried to pull Fitz's hand away but it didn't budge. "I heard from the FBI earlier tonight. They said they'd call me."

Fitz didn't want to hear his excuses. "Where is Sutton?"

"I don't know. I haven't seen her."

"That's a lie and we both know it." Fitz leaned down inches from the man's face. "Edward said she had dinner here and you argued. He said you called, worried because Sutton had stormed out and left. That you haven't heard from her. You told the FBI she left at six. Far too early for dinner and a fight. Which is it?"

Sinclair sucked in a frustrated breath. "That's none of your business."

Fitz gripped him tighter by the bathrobe nearly pulling the man up on tiptoes. "Her car is in the garage and there is blood on the driver's seat. I'm going to ask you one more time. What did you do to Sutton?"

"Nothing!" Sinclair shouted. He looked past Fitz at Charlie. "You're just going to let him manhandle a Supreme Court Justice like this? Help me!"

"Fitz does what he does, Sinclair," Charlie said, her voice calm and steady. She moved to join them. "Besides, you're not confirmed yet. Don't get ahead of yourself. What did you do to Sutton?"

Sinclair expelled a nervous breath and his body deflated, making it even harder for Fitz to hold up his girth. "All right. All right. Let me go and I'll tell you." Fitz dropped him and Sinclair stumbled to stand upright. He fixed his bathrobe, pulling it tighter around him. "We got into a fight and she went out to her car. I don't know what happened after that. Later in the evening, after I had spoken to Edward, I saw her car sitting in the driveway. It was still running when I went out there, but Sutton was nowhere to be seen. I swear to you!"

Fitz didn't believe him even though the story could be plausible. "What did you do then?"

"I went outside. I called for her but she wasn't around. I figured she

CHAPTER 14

walked off. I got in the car and put it in the garage. I swear I didn't see the blood until after I moved the car."

"Did you tell the FBI?"

Sinclair shook his head. "I wanted them focused on my son; not whatever Sutton was doing."

"Why did you tell them you suspect her of taking Holden?"

"I figured then they'd be looking for them both."

"Did you tell them about her car?"

Sinclair didn't respond.

It was clear to Fitz he had left out that information. Fitz breathed through his nose like a bull ready to charge. He forced himself to step back as Sinclair cowered. "It didn't occur to you that Sutton might have been kidnapped too and right out of your driveway?"

Sinclair angrily pulled at the belt on his robe. "Who would have taken Sutton? She's a grown woman. She wasn't acting like herself the last time I saw her. Maybe she staged her kidnapping."

Fitz balled up his fists and wanted nothing more than to drive one right into Sinclair's face. He held his temper in check. "There's been a ransom demand. It's clear to me now she was taken from your driveway and you potentially destroyed evidence in the process."

Sinclair stared at Fitz and didn't say another word. "If you don't leave, I'm calling the FBI."

Fitz pulled the phone from his pocket. "You don't need to worry about calling them because I'm going to do it right now."

Worry lines creased the judge's forehead. "Fitz, come on. Let's not get the FBI involved in this. It will take time away from looking for Holden. We can work this out. I don't need a scandal. I swear to you I didn't realize when I moved her car that anything was wrong."

Ignoring him, Fitz turned around and left the house with Sinclair calling after him. Fitz wasn't going to give him the satisfaction or engage with him. All he cared about now was getting a crime scene tech to Sutton's car and sweeping it for evidence. On the chance that anything happened to her during the ransom drop or Fitz wasn't able to rescue her and catch her kidnappers, whatever evidence was left was critical.

Despite Sinclair's protests, Fitz called Agent Burrows. When the agent answered, Fitz said, "I think you can safely rule out Sutton as your kidnapper. I found her car with blood in the driver's seat in Judge Sinclair's garage. He said he found it running in his driveway and then moved it, destroying evidence in the process. He's been hiding it from you. They had dinner last night before Sutton disappeared."

Agent Burrows absorbed the information. "Was this before or after Holden went missing?"

"Before." Fitz walked off the porch and away from the house to the middle of the driveway. "That means Sinclair knew about Sutton well before Holden ever went missing. If he's the one who speculated that Sutton might have him, then he lied to you. I don't want to tell you how to do your job but something doesn't smell right to me."

"I'll send an agent over immediately," Agent Burrows said but he wasn't done. "I have other questions about your time at the school. It seems you stirred up quite the hornet's nest."

"Not me, Agent Burrows. It's got nothing to do with me. Just do your job and sort it out." Fitz disconnected the call. He was tired of doing the FBI's job for them.

He notified them of Sutton's innocence and that's all he was going to do. Why they hadn't searched the house when they went there about Holden, Fitz didn't know. Nothing about any of this made sense.

CHAPTER 15

Fitz left Sinclair's property and went back to his SUV.
Charlie was a few steps behind him. "What are you going to do now?"

He glanced back at her. "Wait for the FBI agent to arrive and make sure they do their job. I'm afraid Sinclair is going to convince them that they don't need to take any evidence."

"Don't you think you should wait for them *at the garage?*" Charlie looked back at the property. She tugged on the back of his shirt. "Aren't you worried he's going to get rid of evidence?"

Fitz shook his head. "He won't." He made it to his SUV and leaned against it, expelling a breath. What he didn't tell Charlie was that he couldn't stand there a minute longer with Sinclair because he didn't trust himself not to cause the judge bodily harm. Sinclair was a disgusting entitled man who thought he was above the law and that consequences didn't apply to him.

Fitz pushed himself off his SUV and turned to look at the house. "He's probably in there calling his lawyer to protect himself. That's what men like him do. He doesn't care Sutton is missing."

"What's his end game, Fitz? Why hide what happened to Sutton?"

Fitz had spent hours trying to make sense of it all. "I have no idea. He's protecting himself for some reason. But your guess is as good as mine."

Charlie wasn't going to let it go. "What do you think he did?"

Fitz didn't know because the evidence in front of him wasn't adding up. If it had been a domestic incident, there'd be no ransom. Sutton might not still have been alive to give him a clue to her location. He found it hard to believe Sinclair was involved in Sutton's kidnapping, but his actions didn't make any sense either. "Maybe he was so angered by their fight that he didn't care."

"What was the fight about?"

"Edward said it was about me. He told me Sutton found out that Sinclair had her tailed and caught her meeting with me. Sinclair didn't say anything about that."

Charlie looked between the house and Fitz. "He's got something to hide."

As much as Fitz tried to control his anger, he couldn't stand there. He marched back towards the house, took the porch steps two at a time, and didn't bother knocking. "Sinclair!" Fitz yelled as he entered the foyer. "We need to talk!"

Sinclair rounded the corner of the foyer fully dressed this time. "You need to get out of my house."

"FBI is on the way." Fitz stood with his hands on his hips, staring the man down. "I want to know why you lied to the FBI. When you told them Sutton left, you already knew her bloodied car was sitting in your garage. Your response to all of this was to tell the FBI that Sutton took Holden."

Sinclair looked away from Fitz. "As I said, I had to keep the focus on my son. I figured if I told the FBI Sutton took him, they'd be looking for them both. I didn't know what happened to her. I couldn't be caught up in another scandal, not during the confirmation hearing." Sinclair leaned back against the wall and sat down on the stairs with a thud. "I don't know what will become of it all. I need to find my son."

"Holden isn't the only one at risk. Another student was shot at

CHAPTER 15

yesterday. There was the accusation about the assault and now a kidnapping. Who would want to hurt you like this?"

Sinclair laughed. "Who *wouldn't* want to hurt me like this? I'm not a friend to either side of the aisle. Even my judicial colleagues hate me. I haven't made a lot of friends in politics. It could be anyone." He looked over with the first sincere look on his face that Fitz had seen. "Do you think they are going to kill him?"

"No," Fitz said and meant it. "First, trying to set him up for sexual assault. When that didn't work, now they have taken him. Have you considered they want you to drop out of consideration for the Supreme Court?"

Sinclair shook his head. "I'm not doing that."

There was something Fitz didn't understand. "How'd you get the nomination when everyone hates you?"

With defiance in his voice, he said, "President Mitchell chose me out of the five he vetted. I'm not dropping out."

Fitz looked down at the pathetic man who still seemed to only care about his career. He didn't know how it felt to reach the level the judge was facing. Fitz had only ever been a detective. "We need to find Sutton," Fitz said to no one but himself.

"Holden is the priority," Sinclair said, looking up at him.

"The FBI is on it."

Sinclair shook his head. "Forget about Sutton. Help me find my son. I'll pay you."

"I don't want your dirty money," Fitz spat. "I run an ethical business."

"Digging up all of our dirt," Sinclair said, scoffing at him.

"Someone has to keep the checks and balances. The American people have a right to know who's governing them – good or bad. There shouldn't be any skeletons left in the closet."

By his expression, it didn't seem like Sinclair agreed with that. "I don't see how decisions I would have made twenty or thirty years ago should impact my ability to do my job today."

"If you killed someone and got away with it. If you were a member of a hate group. If you funneled money to America's enemies. All of these things matter to the American people, so they matter to me. It doesn't matter how long ago these things took place. What matters is they happened."

Sinclair didn't seem to be persuaded. "People change, Fitz."

He shook his head. "They don't change. If there's something in your past you're ashamed of, you should lead with it and clear the air."

"Not in this climate. They'd stone you for a candy bar you stole when you were five."

Fitz didn't fully disagree with him. He often thought the kind of stoning Sinclair mentioned might be what kept good people out of politics and left those who were ruthless and conniving. He aimed to level the playing field. "It's still better than hiding and being someone you're not."

Sinclair turned his head away and wouldn't meet his eye. "Why did Sutton meet with you?"

Fitz assumed he meant yesterday at the coffee shop. "Sutton called me and asked me to look into what happened with Holden. She wanted to know if it was true. She's having a hard time, Sinclair, knowing just how far you'd go to protect your son. Sutton wanted to know what she was up against and if the relationship was worth saving. She had doubts. Was that what your fight was about? Edward said you had her tailed."

"I did." Sinclair still wouldn't look at him. "The fight was about that and the same one we've been having for months. I want her to stop working. If I'm going to be a Supreme Court Justice and we are married, I don't want a wife who works. She doesn't need to work and it would look bad for me, like I couldn't support our family."

Fitz didn't understand that attitude. Everyone deserves to have a

CHAPTER 15

purpose. "It's not the 1950s, Sinclair. I can tell you right now there's no way Sutton is going to give up her job. She spent years building a successful business. It's not just work for her, it's her passion. Sutton has never and would never be the kind of woman who sat around all day or who lunched with the society circuit. You are asking the impossible from her."

Sinclair grimaced and cursed. "You know her too well, Fitz. That's exactly what she said to me before she stormed out of here. I demanded she give it up and she said she'd rather call off the engagement."

"That sounds like Sutton. How'd you respond to that?"

"Not well." Sinclair dropped his head into his hands. Fitz wasn't sure if it was real emotion or if he was putting on an act. "I told her if she didn't abide by what I said, then we wouldn't be married. Either she got on board or we should cut our losses."

Fitz thought it was stupid of the man to make such a demand. "I assume Sutton told you to shove it."

"That's exactly what she did after she called me a few choice names and threw her engagement ring at me." Sinclair whistled then chuckled lightly. "I had no idea she had such a vocabulary."

Fitz did and had seen the same side of Sutton many times. She was headstrong, determined, and had a hot temper when she wanted. She wasn't used to being told what to do by anyone. Her father had tried and had told Fitz he wasn't strong enough to tame his daughter. That had been another argument. Fitz hadn't wanted to tame her. He had liked Sutton exactly as she was.

Before Fitz could respond to him, a car pulled into the driveway. Fitz looked down at him. "This is the time, Sinclair. If you know anything else about Sutton, tell me now. If there's something I should know that you don't want the FBI to know, it's now or never."

Sinclair pushed himself up. "Kevin Bauer. You should look into him if you want to find Sutton."

"Who is Kevin Bauer?" Fitz asked. It was not a name he was familiar with at all.

Sinclair moved to the front door, took a step outside then turned back to Fitz. "A few months ago, I thought Sutton was cheating on me. She started acting strangely and didn't respond to calls and texts at certain times. I caught her in a few lies. I used the same private investigator to tail her yesterday as I did then. She was seen in the company of Kevin Bauer, a well-known property developer. I asked Sutton about him once and she denied being involved with him. I never caught them being intimate in public. Of course, you know that's not Sutton's style. She went to his apartment in Adams Morgan more than once. I've not mentioned his name to the FBI because I don't know what they were doing together and there's no point ruining his reputation over nothing. Except, I don't feel like it's nothing. If you're looking for her, I'd start there."

Now that Sinclair had mentioned Kevin Bauer was a property developer, Fitz had a vague recollection of the man from the news. He had no idea of his connection to Sutton. "I don't think Kevin is going to kidnap Sutton for ransom."

"Maybe not but they could both be in it for the money."

"Did the kidnapper call you to pay the ransom?" Fitz asked, curious why Sinclair was just mentioning the money now.

"No. I wouldn't pay even if they did. I don't pay ransom for anyone, Fitz. Not even if it was for my son. Just as the United States has a policy, I don't negotiate with terrorists. If I were you, I'd consider Sutton's kidnapping might have been staged."

Fitz watched as Sinclair left the house and walked out to the FBI. He hadn't considered it had been staged. He also hadn't been able to shake the feeling in his gut that the whole situation still wasn't adding up somehow.

CHAPTER 16

Early the next morning, before the clock struck six, Fitz made his way through D.C. to pay Kevin Bauer a surprise visit at his apartment. Before leaving Sinclair's the night before, Fitz had spoken to the FBI agent, showed them Sutton's car, avoided any conversation about a ransom, and asked Sinclair for Kevin's address before leaving.

Charlie had been unusually calm about the whole thing. She promised she'd continue to keep an eye on the business as Fitz left to find Sutton. He hadn't disclosed to her the full details of his conversation with Sinclair, only that Sutton might have been having an affair. Fitz had a restless night of sleep wondering if Sutton was capable of such a thing. When he finally got honest with himself, he admitted that he once suspected Sutton of the same thing.

Fitz had never gone looking for evidence. He didn't make a habit of looking for information or asking questions he didn't want answered. Instead, he had stuffed those feelings deep down and let the marriage play out as it had. In the end, affair or not, Fitz had lost her and he never did find out if his suspicions were more than insecurity.

As early as it was, Fitz had to circle the block four times before he found a place to park that wasn't by permit only. After walking the few blocks to the building, he was fortunate to catch someone coming out as he approached. The last thing he wanted was to have to be buzzed in.

Fitz took the elevator to the third floor and found only two apartments – one to the right and Kevin's to the left of the elevator. He knocked twice then stepped back. He heard grumbling on the other side of the door about the hour.

"Who is it?" a man shouted from inside.

"Connor Fitzgerald. I'm Sutton's ex-husband. I need to speak with you. She's missing."

"Oh goodness," the man gasped as he pulled open the door. He stood about five-ten with sandy hair and day-old stubble. He knotted the belt of his blue bathrobe around his trim body. "What do you mean she's missing? I just saw her a few days ago."

Fitz didn't want to do this standing in the hallway. He gestured past the man. "Can I come in to speak with you, please?"

Once inside the doorway, Kevin stood with his hands on his hips blocking Fitz's further path inside. "What do you mean she's missing?" he asked again, more insistent this time.

Fitz saw no reason to dance around it. He explained what had been happening and for good measure, added, "There's been some speculation you might be involved in her disappearance." Seeing the man now, Fitz didn't think there was any way Sutton was involved with him. Not that she had a type, but if she did – Kevin wasn't it.

Kevin stepped back as his hand went to his chest. "I adore Sutton. I'm most certainly not involved in anything bad happening to her. I'll do anything I can to help you. Please give me a moment to get dressed."

Fitz stepped into the spacious living room. Sutton's design choices were all over the space. From the art on the walls to the modern style of the furniture and decorations. A framed photo on the fireplace mantel caught Fitz's eye. He lifted the silver frame to get a better look. Kevin and a man stood together in front of what looked to Fitz like a

CHAPTER 16

castle in Ireland or maybe Scotland. They had their arms around each other and beamed smiles of love and affection. He put the photo back when Kevin cleared his throat from the other side of the room.

"I'm sorry I don't remember your name." Kevin had changed from his bathrobe to pressed jeans and a tucked-in blue button-down shirt.

Fitz turned and extended his hand. "It's Connor Fitzgerald. You can call me Fitz. I'm Sutton's ex-husband and a former D.C. Metro homicide detective. I run an investigation firm of sorts. Sutton asked me to look into a few things. Judge Sinclair suggested I speak to you."

A mocking smile spread across his face. "Sinclair believed Sutton and I were having an affair."

"He suggested that. I'm assuming that's not the case." Fitz pointed to the photo. "I assume your boyfriend or husband."

"Husband," Kevin said with tension in his voice. When he saw that Fitz did not react, his shoulders released. "Sutton helped me plan the wedding. She also helped me with interior design here and in my office. I've hired her to design my new building that's three months from finished. We had reason to be spending time together. Not that Judge Sinclair would listen to her. She tried telling him but he wouldn't hear of it. We had a private investigator following us for months."

"Does Judge Sinclair know you're gay?"

"She said she told him, but he said he didn't believe her." Kevin walked to the mantel and picked up the photo. He raised his eyes to Fitz. "My husband is an emergency room physician. I work primarily in construction and development. I never make it a point to tell people I'm gay. I don't shy away if anyone asks. When there are rumors, I address them head-on. Maybe I wasn't out enough for some people. I never hide who I am. If Sinclair chose not to believe Sutton, that's on him."

Fitz said he understood. "Did Sutton confide in you much about

Sinclair?"

Kevin put the photo back and gestured toward the couch. When they were seated, Kevin explained, "When Sutton and I first met, it was purely professional. She is one of the most sought-after interior designers in the D.C. Metro area. Everyone who's anyone wants to hire her and she's picky about what clients she takes. She accepted my offer and we started working together. It wasn't more than a month into that professional relationship that we became fast friends. We have a lot in common and share similar interests. Sutton has a wicked sense of humor too." Kevin clicked his tongue and cursed Sinclair. "That man was trying everything in his power to make sure Sutton felt small and diminished. He tried to get her to close her business and wanted her to rely on him completely for everything. It might not have been my place, but I told her more than once to end things. I was concerned for her."

Fitz didn't want to ask the question because a part of him was afraid of knowing. He couldn't shy away from the truth now. "Was there any domestic violence in the relationship? Did he ever hit her?"

Relief washed over Fitz when Kevin shook his head. "Not that she ever told me. I think she would have mentioned it. She told me everything else. You must know not all domestic abuse is physical."

"I do know that."

"That said, I do think the relationship was emotionally abusive and it might have led to physical or financial abuse if she married him. That was my concern. All the hallmarks were there."

Fitz swallowed hard and inched closer to the end of the couch. "What do you mean?"

"He was controlling with everything Sutton did. Where she went, what she wore, who she talked to. He even tried to tell her what clients she could take on. If he couldn't get her to give up the business, he was going to try to control the business. He put her down constantly.

CHAPTER 16

She wasn't smart enough or pretty enough. He tried to break her in many different ways." Kevin shook his head in disgust. "When Sinclair couldn't control her, he iced her out. He'd go between arguing with her and belittling her or icing her out completely. Some of the things he said to her, it pains me to even think about."

Fitz ran his palms down his thighs, trying to control the anger starting to bubble up. "What did he say?"

"It was disgusting," Kevin said with anger in his voice. "One Sunday, we were supposed to have dinner and discuss design choices for my office. Sutton showed up to the meeting and it was obvious she had been crying. After urging her to tell me, she admitted she had been at Sinclair's house before meeting me. He told her she looked fat and sloppy and that she couldn't go out looking like that. When she asserted herself and told him she looked perfectly fine, he called her stupid and uncouth. He said her family was old money and she should have known better. He did everything he could to knock her down a peg."

Fitz had never known Sutton to look fat or sloppy a day in her life. During the whole time he'd known her, she had ranged in size from four to eight. Not that it mattered even if she had gained some weight, it was no way to speak to someone. She was one of the smartest people he knew. Nothing Sinclair said had any merit. Even if there was, he shouldn't have said it.

Still, though, it made little sense to him Sutton would stand for that treatment. "I'm frankly surprised Sutton would put up with it. When I saw her, she was looking for justification to leave him. It sounds to me like she had more than enough reason."

Kevin agreed with that. "She had every reason in the world not to be with him. Does Sinclair have any room to talk about weight? I'm not going to criticize him, but of all people to be throwing around insults like that, he should look in the mirror. Sutton never argued with him because he'd only get louder and more aggressive. Then the next day he'd act like he never said any of those things and she was making it all up. If she tried to talk about it, he'd say she was being overly sensitive then buy her a gift to shut her up."

"There had to have been something that made her stay." Sutton wasn't shy or one to hide from problems. None of this sounded like her.

"He threatened her business and to destroy her reputation."

Fitz didn't believe that could be the only reason. "I know Sutton and she'd overcome any of that. Besides, her reputation was solid. It wouldn't matter what Sinclair said, he wasn't going to be able to make much of a dent. There had to be more." Kevin didn't respond. It was clear to Fitz he had more to say. "If there's something else, please tell me. My only goal here is to rescue Sutton."

"Could Sutton be in hiding? Maybe they fought and she took off?"

Fitz wished that had been the case. "I received a ransom call. Someone has her," he said, giving weight to each word. "I need to find her. The only way to do that is to figure out why this is happening. I'm running out of time."

Kevin raised an eyebrow. "Do you have any suspects?"

If Sutton trusted Kevin, then Fitz did as well. "I believe Sinclair is involved somehow. I need to understand why and what this might be all about. Sinclair's son is missing too." Fitz went on to tell Kevin about Sinclair's son and the school. "It's a confusing mess right now of things that don't add up. I'm trying to have it all make sense."

"I might be able to help." Kevin got up from the couch and walked out of the room, leaving Fitz sitting there. While Kevin was gone, Fitz checked his phone and saw two missed calls from Agent Burrows.

Kevin returned with a thick manilla eight-by-eleven envelope. He extended his hand to Fitz. "Sutton gave me this to hold onto. While I don't want to break her trust, if she's in trouble then maybe there is

CHAPTER 16

something in here that can help. If we weren't in dire circumstances, I wouldn't be giving this to you. No one knows I have it. Sutton gave it to me about six weeks ago and asked me to put it in my safe and not to give it to anyone under any circumstances."

Fitz took the envelope. "What is it?"

"I don't know. I never looked inside. Sutton said I'd be safer if I didn't know and I believed her." Kevin sat down on the edge of the chair across from Fitz. He clasped his hands at his knees. "As you know, no matter what Sinclair said about her, Sutton isn't stupid. She's cunning and smart and I think had a plan to get out. Between you and me, I think she was scared to leave. She said she found out some things that scared her. She wouldn't tell me what. I asked Sutton if he knew she had found out whatever the secret was and she confirmed he had indeed. That made it riskier for her."

Fitz felt the weight of the envelope in his hands. He wanted to open it there, but if Sutton didn't think Kevin should know, he wasn't going to expose her secret. "Did Sutton give you any idea what she was planning to do with this information?"

Kevin shook his head. "She came here one night very bothered. Sutton had another fight with Sinclair where he put her down, called her names, and threatened to destroy her business. When she showed up, she had that envelope with her. Sutton said she'd been holding onto this information for a while. She said it wasn't complete, whatever that meant. Sutton said she had more information to find. I told her she should drop the whole thing and leave him. I told her she could stay here and we would protect her. Sutton refused and said there were still things to be done before she could leave him. She said it was insurance and for her protection."

Fitz thanked him for the information. "Is there anything else you think I should know?"

He pursed his lips and then shook his head. "I'll do anything I can to help you find her. Whatever you need, money or anything, call me. Sutton is an amazing woman and deserves to be happy. I hope whatever that is helps you figure things out." Kevin got up and walked Fitz to the door. He glanced down at the envelope, his eyebrows drawing together. "Do you think Sutton will be angry I shared that with you?"

"Sutton gave this to you because she trusted you and knew you'd keep it safe. Therefore, she'd trust your judgment." Fitz held up the envelope. "If Sutton thought this was important, then I'm sure it is. It might be the key to unraveling this whole mess."

Kevin thanked him for helping Sutton and for relieving him of his guilt for breaking her trust. "When you find her, please call me and let me know. If there's anything else you need, call me. I'll help in any way I can."

Fitz left and headed straight out of the building to his SUV. All he wanted to do was open the envelope and figure out what Sutton had discovered about Sinclair.

CHAPTER 17

The first thing Fitz did when he got into his SUV was lock the door and pull open the tab on the envelope. He tugged out a stack of paper and laid it on his lap. As he peered down at the top page with interest, Fitz realized quickly he wasn't sure what he was looking at.

He flipped through the pages and discovered Sutton had records of offshore bank accounts in Sinclair's name. There were four accounts in all totaling tens of millions of dollars. The bank transfers were from a host of names Fitz didn't know.

All except for one.

Danny Martin was a well-known gangster in the D.C. Metro area. He had run with the Romano crime family in New York and then moved his operation to D.C. He specialized in high-priced escorts. Fitz was sure he had more than one politician in his pocket. Now, maybe a federal judge too. Sinclair was the chief judge in the United States District Court for the District of Virginia. He held a lot of power and oversaw many federal cases. Fitz knew Danny Martin had been before that particular federal court more than a few times.

Danny Martin was well-known, even to Fitz. Back when he was a detective, he and his partner worked with the FBI to wiretap Martin on several occasions because, in addition to his escort ring, he was accused of extorting money from local businesses, involved in the gambling racket, and running drugs.

Fitz counted the deposits that came from Martin to Sinclair. There were six payments in all, totaling close to ten million. Fitz noted the businesses that had paid Sinclair, one of them an investment firm currently in legal trouble for mishandling more than twenty million dollars of their client's money. The company had paid Sinclair more than three million dollars.

What exactly Sinclair was doing wasn't clear from the records. There was a lot of money in offshore accounts from payments by questionable people. He was up to no good but doing what exactly wasn't clear. Fitz assumed that is what Sutton meant when she told Kevin she needed to dig a little more. Fitz had no idea what Sutton was going to do with these records or how she had managed to get them. All Fitz knew was that having them put her at risk.

Fitz put the records on his passenger seat and called a familiar number. His old partner, Ellis Smith, answered on the second ring. After a little small talk, Fitz said, "What's the skinny on Danny Martin? Any open investigations?"

"Danny connect to one of your *fancy* D.C. cases?"

Fitz let that slide. "Let's call it a side project. I'm looking at some financial records of Martin paying millions to someone high up in government and I need to know why."

Ellis whistled. "That can't be good. We don't have any open investigations on Martin. You know how it all went south. About a year after our investigation went bust, we started pursuing him again but it was shut down quickly. We haven't gotten the go-ahead to pursue him again. That doesn't mean he's out there living the straight and narrow. A leopard doesn't change his spots."

Fitz agreed with that. "What do you think about this money?"

"Depends on who it went to. We have long suspected someone is protecting Martin. There was no reason to shut down the last

CHAPTER 17

investigation. We were making serious inroads. Then bam. We were told to close the case. You know it takes some time to bring down organized crime. Even the higher-ups here couldn't seem to get a straight answer as to why we were being shut down. All I know is the order was direct and unwavering. We were hands-off Danny Martin. I know several big-wigs who seek out Danny's girls, but it's more than that, Fitz. We weren't even after him for that."

"Any chance he turned to the FBI and was working as an informant?"

"Not that we saw." Ellis spoke to someone on the other end, telling them he was going outside. "Give me a minute, Fitz."

While Fitz waited for Ellis to get to a place where he could speak freely, Fitz picked up the stack of papers again, thumbing through them.

When Ellis said he was in a better place to talk, Fitz asked again about the FBI.

Ellis blew out a frustrated breath. "That's the thing, Fitz. The FBI was told to shut it down too. I have a buddy over there and we talked outside of official channels. Their directive came down an hour before ours. We spoke that afternoon. No one has been able to figure it out. This is more than just Metro impacted."

It means that it had to have come from high up in the Department of Justice. "Has anyone looked into it, followed the chain of command up?"

"My buddy is trying. He's not getting far."

Fitz wanted to ask about his FBI contact. He knew Ellis wouldn't tell him. If he'd been comfortable saying the agent's name, he would have already said it. "Where did you leave off in the case against Danny? Was he back working with the Romano family?"

"He's an equal opportunity offender, Fitz. Anything he can get his grubby little fingers into, he's been doing. Drugs, guns, gambling, prostitution, and the usual shake-downs of construction and garbage.

Whatever he can do to earn the cash, he's going to do it."

That's what Fitz had suspected. "Where did you leave the case?"

"We were finally getting someplace, Fitz. We had witnesses who were willing to testify and we had some solid wiretapped evidence of his operation. Then poof, overnight everything was shut down." Ellis dropped his voice lower than it had been. "Look, Fitz, I don't get it. My boss doesn't get it and his boss didn't give him much information other than the order came from the top. What I can tell you is whoever decided Danny Martin is untouchable came from higher up than the D.C. Metro Police Department. He's been a priority for us for years. You don't just all of a sudden decide that a case the department has put so much manpower and resources into suddenly isn't worth it. And especially not when we were finally getting some traction."

That traction, Fitz suspected, was the reason the rug had been pulled. That was more telling than any evidence Ellis might have uncovered. Fitz was so lost in his thoughts that he missed what Ellis said. "I'm sorry, what?"

Ellis repeated himself. "What's your interest in Danny Martin?"

Fitz hadn't wanted to involve the cops, not yet and not officially anyway. Ellis had been his partner though and more than that, his friend. "Sutton is missing under some interesting circumstances. There's been a ransom call. The FBI believes she might have taken Sinclair's son who is also missing. We both know Sutton didn't kidnap anyone." The only thing Fitz held back was the information burning a hole in his passenger seat and his suspicions about Sinclair.

Ellis cursed a streak. "You should have led with that. What can I do to help?"

"Nothing much you can do that I'm not already doing." Ellis wanted to know the whole thing, so Fitz started with an abridged version. "It started because Sutton was concerned about Sinclair's son. The kid has been trouble and Sinclair has been bailing him out. This time the

CHAPTER 17

kid was set up. In the process, both are missing."

"I saw on the news Holden Sinclair was missing. I didn't connect it to Sutton. When did you find out?"

"The FBI showed up at my hotel room while I was up in Massachusetts at Brewster Academy, trying to get a sense of what was going on. I had no idea the kid was missing at that point. I didn't know about Sutton either until the FBI showed up and suspected my involvement."

"What did she get you into, Fitz?" Ellis had never loved Sutton. He always told Fitz she had been too high-class for the likes of a lowly homicide detective. He wasn't surprised when the marriage had ended. He took Fitz out to a bar the Friday the divorce papers were finalized and they got wasted on whiskey.

"Whatever she got me into, it's bigger than Sutton. Much bigger than Sutton."

"What's it about then, Fitz?"

"Sinclair is into something. I don't know what yet. I can't even give you a theory right now. There's something here though." Fitz ran down the entire story about the fight Sutton had with Sinclair the night she went missing and finding her car. He also mentioned Sinclair's lies to the FBI. "He also told me Sutton was having an affair. I went to the guy's house and he's got a husband. He was working with Sutton and they had become friends."

"Maybe Sinclair got some bad intel," Ellis said evenly. "There was a time you suspected Sutton of cheating. I don't think you can rule it out."

Fitz wished he had never confided that bit of information. It's what had been the final nail for Ellis. "I don't think so. The guy had some interesting things to say about Sinclair. There was abuse in that relationship, Ellis. It doesn't sound like it had turned physical yet. But it was emotional and he degraded Sutton frequently."

"That doesn't sound like her, man. Are you sure? Is the guy credible?"

Fitz couldn't fault him for asking that. He was having trouble with the same thing. "It sounds complicated to me."

"Complicated means you're not telling me something."

"I will. Just not now. I need to figure out what it means."

"What do you need from me?"

Fitz knew by even asking the question, he was admitting to some of the evidence Sutton had uncovered. "Was there anything in your investigation tying Danny Martin to Judge Sinclair or anyone high up in government?"

"You think the two are connected?" Ellis asked, his tone tinged with surprise.

"I don't know if the two are connected," Fitz lied with ease. "I need to know if there was a connection. I don't think if Sinclair was involved with him directly, he'd have handled the dirty work on his own. I assume there'd be an intermediary. What I'm asking is if the man's name came up in your wiretap."

"No, Fitz. Never. No one else in government either other than the politicians hiring escorts and that's about everyone in D.C. Do you think Sinclair is the reason our investigation got shut down?"

Fitz told him to slow down. "Go through your evidence again and see if there's anything you missed."

"Evidence is locked in the evidence room, Fitz. You know I can't sign it out without everyone knowing."

"You know there are ways." If Fitz could have gotten his hands on the evidence, he would take the time after rescuing Sutton to go through all of it. He didn't want Ellis to get in trouble though. "Don't do anything you don't want to do. It's not worth risking your career."

Ellis didn't confirm either way. "You said the FBI showed up at your door. Who is the agent?"

"Agent Josh Burrows. Not someone I'd ever met before. I can't get

CHAPTER 17

a good read on the guy. He didn't seem to believe that Sutton was involved. Then again, he kept calling her a suspect."

"That's not a name I know. What field office is he out of?"

"I didn't even ask," Fitz admitted. He had been assuming that if it was related to Judge Sinclair they'd have been out of the main FBI building in D.C. Burrows could have been from the local Massachusetts field office for all he knew. "If you hear anything about him, let me know. He's called me twice in the last couple of hours and I need to return the call."

"There has to be more I can do for you, Fitz. You said there was a ransom call for Sutton. Are you going to pay it?"

Fitz hesitated to tell him the plan. He didn't want his friend involved and definitely not in any official capacity. "I have the money from Sutton's father. I'm going to do everything I can not to turn it over. I believe I know where they are holding Sutton. I asked for proof of life and she gave me a clue on the phone. I'm going after her myself."

"I'll come with you."

"No," Fitz said, nearly yelling the word. "I didn't want to tell you for this reason, Ellis. You can't come with me. I don't want the cops involved and I'm not going to tell Agent Burrows this information, so you can't be involved either. I know Sutton doesn't have Holden Sinclair. I need to protect her as much as I need to find her."

Ellis cursed again. "She's going to be the death of you, man. You're not even married anymore. I'd turn this over to the FBI and let them handle it. Let the chips fall where they may. If Sutton doesn't have anything to do with the kid's disappearance, the FBI will figure that out."

"You and I both know I can't do that."

"Tell me you're not still in love with her."

Fitz chuckled at that. "Nothing like that. She's in trouble and I'm going to help her. It's as simple as that."

"It's never simple with her," Ellis said before asking one more time if there was anything he could do to help. When Fitz declined, Ellis promised he'd be there if he needed anything. "I mean it. Call me if you need anything, even if it's bail money for when the FBI arrests you for obstructing their case."

"I hope it doesn't come to that." Fitz didn't want to get on the FBI's bad side. He relied on them for other facets of his work. He ended the call and sat back in his SUV, resting his head and closing his eyes for a few seconds.

Ellis was right about one thing – it was never simple with Sutton.

CHAPTER 18

Before Fitz had a chance to call Agent Burrows, the ringing phone cut through the momentary silence in his SUV. Fitz opened his eyes and turned his head to look at the screen even though he already assumed the caller. Three calls in less than ninety minutes. He lifted it to his ear. "I was about to call you back, Agent Burrows. I've been busy—"

"You are supposed to be staying out of my investigation." The agent punctuated his words for emphasis. If he was trying to come across angry, he had failed. It was akin to Agent Burrows acting angry when the real reason for the call was under the subtext.

Fitz ignored the man's attempt at ire. "If you want to ask me how *my* investigation is going, you could have called for that reason alone. Did your team make any headway at Sinclair's? The judge is lying to you."

"Don't play games with me, Fitzgerald."

"Just Fitz," he reminded him. "I don't understand why you're getting angry with me. I figured out Sutton was kidnapped from Sinclair's and called you. I told the mother of the young woman who set up Holden to call you. I'm finding all sorts of evidence the FBI is missing. If you're angry with me for showing you up, just say that. By the way, I never asked you, what field office are you connected to?"

"Headquarters," Burrows said, relaxing his tone slightly. "You were right about Sutton's car. It came back as her blood. Judge Sinclair said that he didn't see the blood and moved her car from the driveway back to the garage where you found it. He wants to press charges, Fitz, for trespassing. I told him there was no way anyone was doing that. You riled him up."

Fitz ran a hand down his stubbled face, glad that Burrows was coming around to his side. He wasn't going to put his full trust into Burrows yet though. "If I were you, I'd start to question Sinclair's involvement in all of this. He told me Sutton was having an affair and that proved to be untrue. I spoke to the guy and he has a husband. He was Sutton's business partner. I also found out there was some abusive behavior on Sinclair's part. Nothing physical that I can confirm. Whatever went down in that house the other night, Sutton didn't leave by her own accord and she certainly didn't kidnap Holden. Have you come to that realization yet? I'm not going to work with you until you realize Sutton isn't a suspect."

"Fitz, we aren't working together. I was serious when I told you to stay out of my investigation." Burrows paused for a few beats too long, maybe expecting Fitz to argue with him. Fitz knew how to play the game and offered up nothing. He wasn't going to debate him. When the silence ticked on for an uncomfortable period, Burrows relented. "Sutton is officially no longer a suspect. She's been listed as a missing person. That said, Sinclair didn't offer up anything else. He's sticking to his story that she left at six and he found her car later. He put it in the garage for her. As I said, he claims he didn't see the blood. When he found out Holden was missing, he thought she was trying to get him back."

Fitz rolled his eyes. "None of that sounds strange to you?"

"All of it sounds strange to me," Burrows admitted. "The whole thing from start to finish sounds strange."

"Why are you calling me?"

CHAPTER 18

"You're going to make me say it."

Fitz had no idea what the man was going to say. If Burrows thought he was transparent, he wasn't. Conversations with him were like walking through a foggy night, only able to see about a foot in front. "You're not easy to read, Burrows. And mind reading has never been my skillset."

Burrows blew out an audible breath. "You seem to have a better handle on this case than my team. People also are willing to speak to you when they are avoiding my agents."

"I'm a charming guy," Fitz said and waited for a laugh that never came. "I don't know what to tell you. I connect with people. I gave you what I know."

"Where are you now?"

"On the street in my SUV in Adams Morgan. I won't be here for long."

"Where you headed?"

Fitz wasn't going to tell him about going after Sutton, even if she wasn't a suspect. He answered a question with a question. "Did Morgan Williams call you? She's Veronica Williams's mother."

"Not yet."

"I didn't get into this fully with you before," Fitz started, figuring he'd tell him everything he knew about Holden. "There's something strange going on with Holden Sinclair besides the fact that he's missing. Someone wanted him to take the fall for a sexual assault. They paid off another student to set him up. If that has anything to do with him being missing, I can't say for sure. It seems to have started with that and we have to ask ourselves why." Fitz described in detail the information he had garnered from Veronica, including the audio and video evidence from Trevor. "That young lady is a piece of work. She knowingly set up another girl to be assaulted. You need to explore all of that more." Fitz provided him with Morgan's phone number. "She was easy to speak with and was amenable to helping. Trevor is the son of Senator Tom Wilson." Fitz provided that phone number too.

"You've covered a lot of ground, Fitz. For a mostly one-man operation, you're good."

Fitz had a lot more ground to cover. Even waiting for the ransom, the kidnappers weren't going to hold off for long. He wasn't going to outright tell Burrows what Sutton had been hiding, but he'd point the agent in a direction. "Do you know the name Danny Martin?"

"Everyone knows the name. What does he have to do with anything?"

"A joint FBI and D.C. Metro case was going on for some time. The agents and detectives involved were told to back off. Det. Ellis Smith with D.C. Metro was on the case. He was my partner. I suspect there might be a connection between Danny Martin and Judge Sinclair."

"You suspect or you know, Fitz?"

Fitz's non-response answered the question. "I believe Sutton suspected the judge of some kind of wrongdoing, but she didn't get to finish looking into things before this happened."

Agent Burrows growled into the phone. "Fitz, if you know something you have to tell me."

"I told you everything I know. The rest is speculation and we both know you don't deal in speculation." Fitz ended the call before Agent Burrows could argue further. He reached over into the passenger seat and pulled the file of documents onto his lap. He stared down at it, wondering what it all could mean and how Sutton had found it all. What bothered him the most was she had found the information and had her suspicions about Judge Sinclair long before she had come to Fitz for help.

Ellis was right, she was going to be the death of him. Charlie was right too – he should have told her no. Some relationships just don't die, no matter how much time passes.

CHAPTER 18

With nothing more Fitz could do in D.C., he tossed the file back to its place next to him and started his SUV. He headed south out of D.C. He checked the time. It was about a seventy-mile drive and he'd arrive at dusk with just enough light to see. Fitz had a loose plan about how he'd handle the search for Sutton. There was no telling what he'd face when he arrived. He'd have to be prepared for anything.

Fitz had been hoping to have more information before attempting the rescue alone. He could have told the FBI or Ellis and had a full force of law enforcement behind him. Something itched in his gut that if he did that, it might cause more harm to Sutton than good.

Fitz stretched out one arm and then the other as he turned onto the interstate and headed south. He stretched his back on his left side and then his left leg. His body had grown tense over the last couple of days and his muscles had started to tighten, knotting in areas that made movement painful. It was more than stress. The reality was his body wasn't what it had been in his twenties or even thirties. Dodging bullets and holding the tension of the last few days had already taken its toll.

Sitting in the office day after day had softened him in a way he didn't like. Fitz made himself a promise that when this case was over, he'd make sure to get back to the gym and eat right. Charlie had been on him about that and he had brushed it off far too many times. Now, he was paying for it.

One long interstate turned into another. Fitz kept hitting the button on the radio until he found a classic rock station that came in without static. He hummed along to one song after another trying to keep his mind focused on the task.

Just as he was getting tired of the drive, his burner phone rang bringing him out of the mental haze he'd slipped into. The number that flashed on the screen was unfamiliar to him. He engaged the call. "Hello," he said and waited.

"Tonight at midnight at the Jefferson Memorial near the Tidal Basin," the kidnapper barked.

Fitz worried they had moved Sutton and this drive to Lake Anna was nothing. "I can be there for the exchange."

"As soon as you give me the money, I'll take you to Sutton."

"No. That's not the plan and you know it. You won't get one dollar of this money until I see Sutton and confirm she's fine. You'll hand her over and then you'll get the cash." Fitz wasn't sure what they were trying to pull but he wasn't having it. He glanced at the exit sign and knew his was coming up next. Once he turned off and headed into a more wooded area of Virginia his cell signal would drop and it would be a dead giveaway to the kidnapper that he was traveling. "Do we still have a deal? You're testing my patience and I have a lot to do."

"Sutton's life is at risk if you don't do exactly what we say."

"Listen," Fitz said, his voice ratcheting up the anger. "If you harm one hair on her head, I'm going to kill every last one of you. My reach goes far and wide. I've been patient with you so far. I've played your game and got you the money. I'll be there alone. No cops as you asked. But that's about as far as I'm willing to go. No Sutton, no money. Do you understand me? You're going to have to decide which is more important."

Again he was met with silence. Fitz wasn't sure if the kidnapper was checking with someone else or trying to figure out how serious he was. He listened closely to hear any back chatter or static on the line and heard none. "Are you there, Blaze?" Fitz asked, trying to goad the man and test a theory.

"Be there or Sutton dies." The line went dead without any confirmation or reaction.

Fitz got into the right lane and pulled off the next exit. He took a right at the light and headed down a one-lane road toward Lake Anna State Park. Before getting to the official park entrance there was a lake

CHAPTER 18

road that went around the perimeter of the lake that provided access to the houses on the water's edge. The park had areas for camping and smaller cabins. Fitz didn't think they'd be keeping Sutton there. There'd be too many people and the park rangers keeping an eye out. No, they'd want privacy and somewhere out of the way so as not to arouse suspicion.

Lake Anna was one of the largest freshwater inland lakes in Virginia, covering an area of thirteen thousand acres and two hundred miles of shoreline. There's no way he could do a blanket search of the area himself. He was counting on Sutton's information to point him in the right direction.

That would give him plenty of time to hit the spots where he thought Sutton might be held. He knew the exact area of the lake where he had stayed with his friend. It was smack in the middle of the east side of the lake, near the old Victorian house that had long since been demolished. The property had never been sold so there was an open plot of land where the house had once stood. Fitz had looked it up online before he left to make sure the plot of land was still empty. It was and that was where he'd pull off and stash his SUV. He'd go by foot from there.

If Sutton's information proved fruitless – then he was out of luck and she might be out of time.

CHAPTER 19

Fitz turned into the open driveway that turned into a wide expanse of lawn that had grown up through the broken gravel. He aimed his SUV to the right side of the property under the tree cover. The sun slowly dipped below the horizon casting off the last shimmer of light across the water. He stepped out and breathed the fresh air deep into his lungs.

Fitz had brought a vest, flashlight, ammo, guns, and two holsters – one for around his waist and the other on his ankle. He'd head into the search as armed as he could but not weighed down so much that he couldn't be agile and run. As Fitz fastened his vest in place, car lights bounced off the trees, making him freeze in place. He glanced out toward the road and waited as the car passed, seemingly no wiser that he was there. Three more cars followed in the time he stood there preparing.

Fitz walked across the property and down to the tree line that hugged the start of the shore. It was as close as he could get to the water's edge without being seen. He wasn't sure what exactly he was going to do. It's not like he could walk up to each house to look inside. He hoped that the kidnappers would give something away.

Fitz clung to the statements Sutton had said on the phone about his friend. *Don't be a hero and try to save me. You nearly drowned.* Sutton wouldn't have told him that if she hadn't been near the spot where it

CHAPTER 19

had happened. She was smart enough to know that just saying she was at Lake Anna would be useless for any searcher.

He walked up from the lake toward the first house, his guns and vest hidden by his clothing. A man stood in the back of the home near a grill. He raised his head to Fitz and waved a hand overhead.

"Sir," Fitz called out as he approached. "I was hoping you'd be able to help me. I'm looking for a friend. I thought she might have come this way. It's gotten dark and she might be lost." It was a good enough ruse that wouldn't make most people suspicious.

The man waved him up the property. "People are walking the shoreline all the time. Do you have a photo of her?"

It never failed to surprise Fitz how easily people fell for a simple lie. If he'd been there to do the man harm, he'd already be dead. Fitz didn't wish for a world where everyone was always suspicious, but he wondered if people knew how often they put themselves in harm's way.

He pulled a phone from his pocket and scrolled to a photo of Sutton. "I haven't seen her in a few hours. I know she has some friends down this part of the lake. I thought she might have walked there. She's not answering her phone."

The man leaned over from his grill and looked at the photo. "Pretty," was the first thing he said. "Haven't seen her. There's an older man, John, next door. He sits in his chair at the shoreline all day with his grandsons while they play in the water. Then he stays out there until the sun sets. He'd know if she was by this way. He talks to everyone and seems to know what's going on in our little section of the lake better than anybody." The man winked at Fitz. "John is retired and I don't think he's enjoying it. He's got to keep himself busy."

Fitz got the message loud and clear. John was a busybody. "Thanks for the tip," he said as he backed off the property with a wave.

Fitz walked down to the shore to John's property. Sure enough, there was an older man, probably mid-seventies, sitting in a bright red Adirondack chair with the lake lapping at his feet.

Fitz approached him slowly to not startle him. "Excuse me," he said as he got close enough for the man to hear him. The man turned his head to look up at Fitz and offered him a friendly wave. "Your neighbor told me you might have seen my friend. He said if anyone knows what's going on at the lake, it would be John."

He beamed a smile and nodded. "I've been coming to this lake since I was five years old." He hitched his thumb over his shoulder. "My family has owned that house for generations. First came here when my grandfather owned it. I try to keep a watch on things. What do you need?"

Fitz squatted down beside him and handed over his phone. "I've been looking for a friend of mine. I think she might be staying with some friends. It's been a few days since I was able to get in touch with her and I'm a little worried."

The man squinted at the phone and then back over at Fitz. "You a creep or a pervert?"

This man wasn't as trusting as the last. "No, sir. I assure you I'm not. I used to be a D.C. Metro homicide detective." Fitz wasn't sure he should tell him that Sutton was his ex-wife. That might make him look all the more suspicious. "I'm worried she might have fallen in with the wrong people and they aren't letting her leave. All I want to do is check in on her and make sure she's safe."

John wasn't buying the story. "You said you used to be a detective. What happened?"

"Remember that serial killer case a few years back?"

John bobbed his head up and down. "It took the detective six months to solve it. Even the FBI couldn't figure it out."

Fitz extended his hand to him. "I'm the detective who figured it out. You might have seen me on the news a few times. Let's just say

CHAPTER 19

my commander thought I got too big for my britches and they didn't quite know what to do with me. I've been working for myself."

John shifted in his chair. He reached out his hand and shook Fitz's, still squinting at his face. "It is you." He released Fitz's hand and gestured toward the phone. "Tell me the real story about the woman. Did she commit some terrible crime? Old girlfriend here with her new love?"

Fitz laughed and shook his head. "Nothing quite that dramatic. I swear to you. She has not done anything criminal. I'm worried she might be in danger. The situation is sensitive and I don't want to drag the local cops in. If she's fine, I'll be on my way. If she's not, then I'll drive her back to D.C. where she lives. It's as simple as that."

John watched him for a few seconds and relaxed his shoulders. "She's down three houses from here. I saw her standing along the shoreline with another guy two nights ago. She looked a bit disheveled and didn't seem so happy with the guy. I thought it might be a lover's quarrel but something didn't seem right with it. I've been trying to keep my eye out for her, maybe catch her alone and ask if she's okay. I haven't had a chance. She's never alone." John gave him a knowing look. More passed between them with the look than the words he spoke.

"Did you only see the one man with her?"

"No. There are three that I've seen. I walked down there a couple of times a day. Took my grandkids with me. Waved hello to one of the men who's always on the back porch. He didn't wave back. I assume he thinks I'm a nosy neighbor out for a stroll with the kids. I was trying to check out the place. Looks like one front entrance, one back. A row of windows across the lakeside, a big porch, and a sprawling lawn. The house went up for sale last year. I don't know who bought it."

Fitz stood up to his full height. "What made you watch them so closely?"

"Strangers who didn't look like they were here to enjoy the lake." The man pushed himself up from the Adirondack chair. He looked over his shoulder and turned back to Fitz, leaning in. "Before you ask me what I mean, I'll tell you. They weren't dressed right. They are all wearing jeans and boots. There was a mud streak on the woman's arm and she had a broken heel on her shoe. They all appeared to be tense and not enjoying their time. Not lake people by a long mile. I've been trying to figure it out. Now you come along and start asking questions, that makes me suspicious too. I don't buy your story, but I figure you got a reason for keeping the details to yourself."

Fitz trusted the man and it wouldn't hurt to have an ally. "Her name is Sutton Barlow and she's my ex-wife. She called me a few days ago to look into something for her. A day later, she was abducted by those men and they are holding her for ransom. They think we are meeting tonight in D.C. for the exchange. I figured out they were holding her here on Lake Anna. I need to get her out of there before they hurt her."

John had been watching him carefully while he spoke, probably assessing for any deception. It seems he found none. He gave a curt nod of his head. "You should have said that right off. What can I do to help you?"

"Nothing to help me. I need to go in alone." Fitz reached into his pocket and pulled out the card for Agent Burrows. He handed it to John. "If things don't go my way or you don't see us come by here again in a few minutes, you call him and tell him what I was doing. You tell him where Sutton was being held."

John held the card in his hand. "Why not bring in the whole SWAT team?"

"It's too delicate for that." Fitz gestured toward the card. "Can you do that for me if everything goes south?"

CHAPTER 19

John flicked his gaze up. "You're going to take on three of them? I haven't seen if they are armed but I assume they must be."

Fitz raised the hem of his shirt to show his gun holstered to his hip. "I'll be fine. I've encountered worse in D.C."

"Your funeral, buddy." John gestured back toward his house. "I'm going to take cover inside. While I wish you the best and I'll call this FBI agent if things go south, I'm going to have to request you don't bring trouble to my door. I have a wife and little kids inside."

"I'd never dream of it. I appreciate all your help." Fitz waited in the shadows as John trudged up the hill to his house. He lingered until John was safely indoors, the door clicking shut behind him.

Moving swiftly, Fitz moved three houses down and positioned himself at the edge of the tree line. From there, he cautiously observed the back of the two-story A-frame house, bathed in bright light from both upstairs and down. Just as John had warned, a figure lounged on the back porch, cigarette glowing like a fiery eye in the darkness. The man's feet were propped on the railing, attention fixed on a device in his hands—likely a phone, Fitz guessed. Confronting him directly would only arouse suspicion.

Fitz crept up the side of the property hidden by the neighbor's tall trees. He stopped once when he got parallel with the man but he didn't notice Fitz at all. He continued around to the front of the house, clocked the truck in the driveway, and took note of the Virginia license plate number. He said it to himself several times to commit it to memory then surveyed the front of the home. There were no signs of Sutton or the other two men. He crouched down beside the truck and pulled out a knife. He jammed it into the rubber of each tire and let them deflate. Fitz wasn't giving them any chance to follow if any were left alive.

Fitz made his way across the front of the home and down the other side, stepping into the grass to soften his footfalls. Returning to the back of the home, he hoisted himself up onto the porch with the agility of a cat, all the while watching the man absorbed in his phone, oblivious to Fitz's approach.

With his heart pounding, Fitz edged closer. A loose board creaked under his step, snapping the man's attention toward him. Fitz felt his breath catch in his throat and he lunged toward him. Before the man could draw a weapon or even call out for help, Fitz caught the side of his temple with the butt of his gun. One strike and then another brought the man to the ground. Fitz grabbed him by the arms and dragged him off the porch to the soft grass below.

Once back on the porch, Fitz positioned himself on the blind side of the door, emitting a soft groan in hopes of alerting anyone inside. Holding his breath, he waited, then tried again with a louder noise, hoping to provoke a response.

Finally, someone took notice.

"What are you doing out here?" a man barked as he stepped out onto the porch. "Where are you?" He took a few steps from the door and stopped, looking around. Before he could react to his absent partner, Fitz was on him, throwing several crashing blows to the back of the man's head. The man careened onto the porch floor, not even able to put up a fight. Fitz got him on his back and slammed his fists into his face with frightening fury, bloodying his knuckles in the process.

The man moaned as his consciousness slipped away.

Fitz dragged him off the porch and tossed him beside his partner. Two down – one to go. Likely the one armed and holding Sutton.

CHAPTER 20

Fitz had no idea how much time he'd be afforded before the two men he had attacked and rendered unconscious would wake and come for him. He had to move strategically and swiftly. Fitz nudged open the downstairs door with the toe of his boot and waited for gunshots that never came.

He entered the open doorway, gun raised, alert to every detail. The lingering scent of a recent meal drifted from the kitchen – a pot of rice on a cold burner, chicken legs half-covered in foil, and a sink strewn with dirty dishes submerged in dirty water.

The house was eerily quiet except for the distant murmur of a television.

Fitz resisted the impulse to call out Sutton's name. Moving through the kitchen and into the living room, he noticed a closed door to his right. Pressing his ear against it, he strained to detect any sound, but there was none.

Taking a deep breath to steady himself, Fitz advanced. Opposite the closed front door, a staircase beckoned. He tested the first step, expecting a creak that never came. He ascended quickly, his heart pounding. Reaching the second-floor landing, he swiftly checked left and then right—no sign of anyone. He exhaled in relief. *Where was Sutton?*

Creeping down the hallway towards three closed doors, Fitz

approached the one where the murmur of noise could be heard. Hand on the knob, he turned it, but it resisted. He stepped back, then threw his shoulder against the wooden barrier. With a splintering crash, the door burst open, and a woman's scream pierced the air.

Sutton screamed at the sight of Fitz. Her hand flew to her heart and she jumped from her chair. "What are you doing here?"

"Where's the other guy?" Fitz demanded, sweeping the room as he ignored her question. His senses were on high alert, he expected any moment for their assailant to appear, drawn by the noise of the shattered door and Sutton's scream.

"He's gone, Fitz. Left for D.C. an hour ago," Sutton replied, her voice shaky with fear. "There were two others who were waiting for his signal. They were going to kill me after they got the money."

Fitz tightened his grip on Sutton's arm, his fear palpable as he locked eyes with her. "We have to get out of here now. I knocked out the other two, but they're not dead. We need to move. Now!"

Sutton stumbled forward, her thoughts still catching up. "But… what…"

"There's no time," Fitz cut her off, positioning himself protectively in front of her as he moved toward the hallway. "Is the front door unlocked? Can we get out?"

"I don't know," Sutton stammered, glancing back towards the bed. "My purse—"

Fitz pulled her forcefully towards him, cutting her off. "It doesn't matter. We need to go."

She clung to him as they hurried down the stairs. "I don't even understand how you found me."

"Later," Fitz said tersely, his arm around her waist as they descended quickly. "Were there only three men?"

"Yes, just three," Sutton confirmed, regaining her composure. "They kept me locked up. I didn't cause any trouble, so I had time alone.

CHAPTER 20

There was no phone and the window in the room was nailed shut. I tried to wave for help but I don't think anyone could see me."

Reaching the ground floor, Sutton shook free from Fitz's grasp, her shock dissipating. She grasped the front door handle and pulled—it swung open unexpectedly. "They said this door was locked. I didn't bother trying it."

Fitz guided her outside and down the steps. He scanned their surroundings, making a split-second decision. "We'll cut through the neighbor's property to the shoreline. Keep up."

"You don't have to be so angry," Sutton snapped back, offended. "I didn't ask to be kidnapped."

Fitz muttered a retort under his breath, frustration boiling over. "If you hadn't gotten involved with that…" He didn't call Sinclair the name on his lips. He sprinted across the driveway with Sutton struggling to match his pace. With one hand on her arm and the other on his gun, he urged, "We need to move faster."

They darted through trees and down a grassy slope. Fitz wanted to check if the two men were still unconscious where he left them, but in the darkness, it was impossible to tell. He noted Sutton's shoes slowing her down—a broken heel. "Take those off and throw them in the trees."

She hesitated.

"Take them off now!" he demanded, pointing to her shoes.

She kicked them off into the grass and picked up speed, outpacing him now. She turned back to him. "You said we have to move quickly. You're just standing there."

Fitz picked up his pace without hesitation, heading back towards his SUV. As they passed John's house, he glanced briefly towards the windows, wondering if their ordeal had been witnessed. He'd thank the man another time.

They raced together down the shoreline back to his SUV. He

unlocked it and helped her inside, locking the door behind her. He hesitated at the back, considering disarming himself but thinking better of it. He had no idea what they'd encounter on the way back.

He slid into the driver's seat, turned the engine over, and put the SUV in reverse. Fitz kept the lights off for now, giving them a last few minutes of cover. He was surprised that no one had come for them. Fitz hadn't thought it would be as easy as it had been.

Backing out as quickly as he could he swung around so he could drive forward out of the driveway. He didn't turn the lights on until they were out on the road. They rode in silence until they reached the interstate and the adrenaline that had fueled Fitz's body subsided. He couldn't have a rational conversation with her until he was feeling back to normal.

Sutton stared out the window in silence. Fitz had once known her so well – knew every mood, expression, the way her body stretched and contorted, the way her anger might flare when she felt scared or insecure, how she thought she wasn't as smart as some of her friends. He knew it all. There had been a time when they had been in sync with each other.

Now, it was a bit like sitting next to a stranger. There was a divide between them that went much farther than the distance from the driver's seat to the passenger. They weren't each other's people anymore. Fitz swallowed the pang of regret and stared straight ahead at the road. He relaxed his grip on the steering wheel as he tried to imagine what Sutton was thinking about and feeling. Her body language gave away nothing. She sat still with her hands simply folded in her lap and her head turned to look out the window.

He resisted the urge to ask what had happened and how she ended up with those men. He wanted to know if they had hurt her in any way or taken any liberties with her. Fitz had worked those kinds of crimes and knew better than to push a victim to tell their story. There'd be

CHAPTER 20

time enough for that. For now, he'd let her sit and process, if that's what she was doing. Everything in him wanted to reach over and offer her some kind of affection, a touch or caress to let her know he was there for her and his earlier anger had dissipated as soon as they were in the safety of his SUV.

What he wasn't going to do was apologize. That he wasn't going to do. Sutton had gotten him into a mess for reasons yet unknown and he had put his life on the line for her. She owed him an explanation. Fitz was simply biding his time. He reached for the radio and turned it on, letting the music fill the void.

Fitz drove back to D.C., passing by the exit for Sutton's house and heading north on the beltway to his home in Chevy Chase.

It was only after he had missed her exit that Sutton turned to him. "Where are we going, Fitz? I want a shower and a fresh change of clothing. I have to decide what I'm going to do."

Fitz glanced over at her and tensed his fingers on the steering wheel. "What you're going to do is shower at my house. I'll find you some clothes and then we are calling Agent Burrows so he can interview you about what happened. I've been quiet this whole time allowing you to work through whatever you need to work through, but the FBI needs to know you're safe and they need to know what's going on with Judge Sinclair."

"No," Sutton said nearly in a whine. "I want to go home."

"It's not safe for you there. Those men know where you live and they will come for you. I'm sure they are already regrouping. The ones at the lake house aren't going anywhere for a while. I deflated all four tires. When they reach the one who went to D.C. and he figures out you're gone, he's going to come for you again. You can't be stupid enough to think they won't."

The biting remark made her wince. "I'm not stupid." Fitz didn't respond, let her stew on what he said. After several long minutes of silence, she said, "If we are going to your house, you missed your exit too."

"I don't live in Georgetown anymore. The rowhouse is only for work now." That was all he said. He didn't owe Sutton any further explanation. He gestured toward the glove box. "Open that up and explain that to me. I spoke with Kevin."

Sutton swallowed hard and licked her lips as she stared at him. "You spoke to Kevin." She said the words slowly, dragging them out as if she couldn't believe that Fitz had done that. "Why would you need to speak to Kevin? How do you even know about him?"

"Sinclair told me you were having an affair with him. In the interest of finding you, I thought for a moment you might be hiding out there," Fitz responded without missing a beat. "I knew right away there was no affair. As I said, open up the glove box and explain."

Sutton seemed poised to ask more questions. She chose instead to do as he asked. She opened the glove box and saw the familiar manilla envelope. Her voice lowered and her hand shook as she reached for them. "He gave you these? He broke my confidence?"

"He thought you were in trouble, Sutton. He was willing to do whatever he could to help you. Besides, he gave them to me, not the FBI. I don't see why that would upset you. You're the one who got me involved in this mess." Fitz got off the exit and took the side streets until he reached his driveway. He pulled his SUV up the drive while Sutton kept her eyes focused on the documents.

It was only after he pulled to a stop that she raised her head and took in her surroundings. "You can afford to live here?"

Fitz jerked the gear shift into park. "Business is good. I've upgraded." He didn't mean for that to sound like he had upgraded his life *since her*, but that's exactly how it came across. He didn't correct himself. "It's not any of your business where I live. We've been divorced for decades. I moved in recently so it's not fully furnished and a bit of a

CHAPTER 20

mess. But what you need is inside."

Fitz got out and grabbed the briefcase with the five million. He had stashed it behind the driver's seat. He started toward the house with Sutton still in the car. He didn't wait for her. She could catch up.

After trailing behind him, she caught up to him at the door. "What's that in your hand?"

Fitz held it out to her. "You need to take this back to your father. It's the ransom he was willing to pay for you."

"Oh," Sutton said her eyes wide. She tucked the papers under her arm and took the briefcase from him. "I don't know that we should involve the FBI, Fitz. There's a lot you don't understand."

Fitz looked over his shoulder at her, his scowl returning. "That's part of the problem, Sutton. I was only supposed to be looking into Holden and rumors about him. So far, I've been shot at, Sinclair has threatened to arrest me for assault and harassment, and I had to rescue you from being kidnapped. I'd say that there's a lot I don't understand. We are not calling the FBI until you come clean with me."

He turned his body all the way until he was toe-to-toe with her. "Let me remind you that even though I'm no longer wearing the badge, it doesn't mean I don't still have the same skills for detecting lies. So before we get in there and you start concocting some story, you have one chance to come clean. I can't help you if I don't know what's happening. It's what I should have had from the start."

Sutton searched his face and her features softened. "Someone shot at you? Are you hurt?"

Fitz pulled the sleeve of his shirt up to show her the makeshift bandage wrapped around his upper arm. "It was a graze, thankfully. I don't think I was the intended target. There's a mess up there at Brewster Academy. I was with one of Holden's friends when we were shot at. He's safe with his father now."

Sutton lowered her eyes and focused her attention on the ground. "I assume Holden is still missing. They let me watch the news and they said he was missing and that the FBI thought I might have taken him." She flicked her gaze up through her thick eyelashes. "I swear, Fitz. I didn't have anything to do with that."

She was giving him a look she had used when they were married – the shy, submissive wife, pulling his strings to gain favor. Fitz was pleased that it didn't work any longer. "Cut the crap, Sutton. I'm not your doting husband who is going to buy it anymore. You know a lot more than you're saying and significantly more than you told me in that coffee shop. Take a shower and think about getting your mind right. I'll make you something to eat and we can talk."

Sutton looked away from him, caught in her deception. "Fine," she said and moved to brush past him into the house.

He reached for her then and touched her arm, drawing her attention. "They didn't hurt you, did they? Take any liberties?"

"No. For being kidnapped the experience wasn't that bad, except for the threat of impending death."

Fitz relaxed his shoulders and unclenched his fists he hadn't realized were balled until they unfurled. "I'm glad for that. Do you know anything about them?"

"After a shower, I'll tell you everything," she promised and turned to face the door.

Fitz would have to wait, but her tone was at least resolute enough that he believed her.

CHAPTER 21

Even with the late hour, Fitz needed a substantial meal and he assumed Sutton did as well. He fired up the grill in the backyard, laid down two steaks seasoned the way he liked them, and had vegetables cooking in the kitchen. He moved between the back of the house watching the steaks to the small kitchen table where he laid two place settings. He poured Sutton iced tea, grabbed himself a beer, and put a mixture of cauliflower and Brussel sprouts on plates.

Fitz was standing near the table when Sutton walked in. One of his favorite gray tee-shirts slipped off her shoulder exposing her freckled skin. It enveloped her body coming down to the middle of her thighs. Fitz had given her a pair of his shorts with a drawstring. If they were under the tee-shirt, he couldn't see them. Her damp hair lay in messy tendrils at her shoulders. He had not seen Sutton looking quite so…delicious was the only word that came to his mind…in a long, long time. He was not prepared for the feeling of it.

"I'll go get the steaks," he said through a mouth filled with cotton. Fitz left the kitchen without looking back. He shook off the warmth that spread through his midsection as he stepped out into the cooler air. Fitz took longer than necessary to get the steaks off the grill, giving himself a moment and chastising himself for his silly schoolboy response.

MIDNIGHT JUDGE

He carried the steaks back into the house, avoided making eye contact with her, and slid into the chair across the table from where she sat. He pointed to the steaks on the platter in between them. "The one on the right is medium-well as you like it."

The corners of Sutton's mouth turned up in an appreciative smile. "You always made the best steak. That is one thing I miss about us being together. You were never afraid to get into the kitchen."

"Sinclair doesn't cook?"

Sutton chuckled softly. "Sinclair doesn't do much of anything about the house. He has a cook and a housekeeper. Not unlike how I grew up." She lowered her eyes to her plate as she cut into her steak. "I guess with you, I got used to doing things myself. Making a nice home for both of us. It feels weird to have people wait on me all the time."

"Glad I could break you of the habit," Fitz said without any animosity in his tone. If anything, he was teasing her, hoping to draw her out. He wasn't going to wait until they were done eating. He'd already delayed long enough calling Agent Burrows. "Tell me about what happened, Sutton. I went to Sinclair and he told me you two had a fight and you left. Then I found your car with blood in it hidden away in his garage. The whole scene smelled of something foul."

Sutton took a few more bites and wiped her mouth on her napkin. She stared over at him but didn't meet his eyes. "Sinclair and I did fight over dinner. Much like we have been fighting for months now."

"What was it about?" Fitz thought back to what Kevin had told him.

"Everything," she said and her shoulders hung low. "It got to a point where I couldn't do anything right. I didn't dress well enough for him. I didn't wear my hair right. I wasn't moving out of my condo fast enough and in with him." Sutton rested her arms on the table and locked her gaze on him. "Fitz, he wanted me to give up my business. He said no wife of his was ever going to work. His ex-wife doesn't work. She never has and it would look bad for him if I continued.

CHAPTER 21

He said there was no way that he was going to marry me if I kept my business. For a while now, I've thought he's been trying to sabotage me. I've heard rumors someone has been bad-mouthing me. You know how hard I worked at building this business and my reputation. It was disheartening at best."

"At worst?"

Sutton seemed at a loss for words. She stared at him with a blank expression on her face.

"Abusive," Fitz said, answering his question. "It's abusive, Sutton, to sabotage your partner in that way. He knows how hard you work. He knows how much your clients love you. You've been featured in national magazines. You've won awards for your work. No man worth anything should have been doing anything other than encouraging you, supporting you, and building you up."

"That's something I've always loved about you, Fitz. My success was never a problem for you."

"It was our success. When I succeeded at my job, it benefited us until it didn't. The same with you." Fitz had never understood men who didn't celebrate women in all of their accomplishments. The ones who tried to minimize the value they brought to the family. He had never wanted to hold Sutton back even if it meant losing her in the process. Fitz had never been one of those men who simply wanted a woman to look pretty on his arm or to make a home for him. He'd have been bored to tears in minutes. "Did you know for sure Sinclair was talking trash about you?"

Sutton gave a slight nod. "A former client told me. Sinclair had no idea I had done work for her in the past. She was considering me for a new project and mentioned my name to him. He came right out and told her I'd had so many complaints about my work I was closing up shop."

Fitz wanted to put his fist through Sinclair's face. "That's libelous,

Sutton. You must know that. He can't do that to you." His voice had risen to such an octave that Sutton pulled back in her seat. "It's not okay to treat anyone like this, especially someone you're planning to marry. You cannot marry him." Fitz didn't feel like the words even needed to be said at that point, but he still had no idea where her head was on the subject.

Sutton let him stew for a minute. "I'm not going to marry him, Fitz. Once all of this started I had no intention of going through with the marriage. I was trying to carry this through."

"Carry *what* through?" Fitz asked, confused by the statement. When she didn't respond right away, he set his fork down and leaned on the table. "Sutton, tell me what is going on. There is something critical you're holding back and I want to know."

Sutton tipped her head back. "I'm working with a journalist from *The Washington Post* to bring Sinclair down. He's a criminal, Fitz. He's been taking bribes and favors from people for as far back as I can find. Well before he was ever installed on the federal bench. Now with him on the eve of becoming a Supreme Court Justice, he must be stopped."

Fitz hadn't been prepared for the heaviness hung over him when she finally revealed what she had been doing. It was incredibly dangerous as she had quickly found out. There was no surprise learning that Sinclair was a criminal. That much he already surmised "How did you get roped into this? A journalist came to you? Who?" Fitz asked the question but he could guess the answer. "Tim?"

Sutton remained stone-faced and silent.

"Answer me, Sutton. Did Tim come to you and ask you to spy on Judge Sinclair and dig up dirt about him? Is he the one who put you in danger?" Timothy Dalton was an investigative journalist for *The Washington Post*. He also happened to be Sutton's ex – the man she had been dating right before Fitz started dating her. Tim had also been involved in Fitz's demise at the police department, calling him a

CHAPTER 21

liability seeking fame and fortune for routine police work. The man had never figured out that it was the D.C. Metro brass that had been whoring Fitz out to the media, not the other way around.

"I knew you'd be angry, Fitz. You've never liked him. I knew if I came to you and told you how I was working with Timothy you wouldn't get involved."

It hit him then, the implication of what she said. His jaw stiffened. "You're telling me you used me as part of this investigation. My looking into Holden had nothing to do with you wanting information to decide your relationship with Sinclair, but rather I was on a fishing expedition for Tim?" Fitz hated saying the man's name.

Sutton shifted her eyes away. "I genuinely wanted to know what was happening with Holden."

Fitz's nostrils flared. "You're lying to me, Sutton. You got me involved in this whole thing under false pretenses. You used me. I thought we meant more to each other than that."

Sutton released an exaggerated sigh. "I've never known you to be so dramatic."

Fitz couldn't believe what he was hearing. He'd dropped his cases to head up to Brewster Academy to help Sutton, was accused by the FBI of being an accomplice to a kidnapping, got shot at, and then rescued Sutton from kidnappers, risking his whole life in the process. She had the gall to sit there like it wasn't a big deal she had lied to him. Fitz couldn't speak. He scraped the chair back against the floor, the legs creaking under his weight. "I can't even look at you right now."

Fitz charged out the back door without looking back. He stood near the grill with his hands on his hips, sucking in deep breaths of air, trying to calm down. Over and over again Fitz chastised himself for his stupidity in trying to help her. Charlie had been right – Sutton didn't care about him. She'd use him as long as he allowed himself to be used. She knew he had a soft spot for her and she took advantage of it.

Fitz couldn't shake the image of Tim and Sutton meeting together, conspiring about how easy it would be to con him into helping them – all the while never knowing the truth. Neither of them had counted on the fact Sutton might be in real danger. Where was Tim when Sutton was being kidnapped? Fitz didn't see him risking his life to find her and bring her back safely.

Fitz was so lost in ruminating about how he'd been made a fool he didn't feel the small hand snake around his back. He didn't notice Sutton standing next to him until she had firmly invaded his space.

"No," he snipped when he finally felt her presence next to him. He shrugged away from her touch, not looking down at her at all. He stared off into the darkness of the backyard. "I want the truth and I want it now. What does Tim have on Sinclair and how did all of this come about? You owe me the truth even if it's days too late."

When Sutton didn't immediately respond, Fitz stepped in front of her and wrenched his phone free from his pocket. He held it up in her face. "I can call Agent Burrows right now and you can tell him what you've done. I'm done playing this game with you."

Sutton reached for him and he swatted her hand away. "You're being impossible. Let me explain then we can decide together what to tell Agent Burrows." She wasn't going to give in to the tantrum and he knew it. Fitz also knew no matter how angry he was he wasn't going to stay angry for long. What he wasn't going to do was keep playing the game.

"If we walk back into that house, you're telling me everything. If you leave out one detail that I later find out, I'm going to tell Agent Burrows to arrest you for obstruction of justice, and don't think I'm kidding. You have wasted police resources already on this little game of yours." Fitz didn't know if that was technically true. He still had no idea how the kidnappers factored in. He sounded serious enough that

CHAPTER 21

Sutton conceded the point. It didn't escape Fitz's attention that she still hadn't apologized.

Once they were seated back at the table, Fitz crossed his arms and stared over at her with a steady gaze. "Go on."

Sutton relaxed into the chair. "I went to Timothy. He didn't come to me. If there was anyone who started this whole thing it was me. I was in Sinclair's home office one day and I saw a ledger on his desk. I took a peek thinking it was household bills. Much to my surprise it was for an account I'd never heard anything about. The information didn't make any sense to me. I stepped back away from his desk as he entered the room. His eyes went right to it and he asked me if I saw what was in it. I lied somewhat convincingly and told him no, that I was just leaving him some coffee."

"Did he believe you?"

Sutton shrugged. "I don't know. Sinclair didn't ask me again. He took the coffee and kissed me. As I was leaving, I noticed he went to the desk and closed the book. He thanked me again for the coffee and I left the room. I saw from the corner of my eye as I was leaving that he went to a wall safe he has behind a photo and put it in there. We never talked about it again."

Fitz still didn't understand. "That was enough to make you suspicious?"

"Danny Martin's name was in the ledger, Fitz. There isn't anyone in D.C. who doesn't know who that is and the crimes he has been accused of committing. I saw a payment from him to Sinclair. If you recall, Sinclair was the one who overturned Danny's conviction on an appeal. The payment occurred two weeks before Sinclair's ruling."

Fitz hadn't remembered that case but he should have. "You can't be serious."

"Dead serious, Fitz."

"Do you have proof?"

Sutton chewed on her bottom lip. "No. I've never seen the ledger again. We have the proof in the offshore accounts but not from that one. The dates don't match up. I must be missing some accounts. But I know what I saw and that got me looking for more." She leaned into the table. "I found a lot more. Enough to send Sinclair to prison for the rest of his life." Sutton let that sink in and then dropped another bomb. "I believe it was Sinclair who had me kidnapped to keep me from coming forward with the information during his confirmation hearing. I don't think they were supposed to ask for ransom. They were just supposed to kill me. They went rogue."

CHAPTER 22

"Slow down, Sutton," Fitz said, releasing his arms from the coil on his chest. He rested them on the table. While what she said about Sinclair having her killed made a lot of sense, there were huge gaps in the story. "After you found that initial information, what did you do?"

"That's when I called Timothy. I didn't know who else to call. I wasn't even sure what I was looking at." She must have seen the flicker of hurt in his eyes that he tried to hide. "I would have called you, Fitz, but with your law enforcement connections, I didn't want to put you in an awkward situation. I swear I didn't want to get you mixed up in this. When I came to you about Holden, I needed to understand what was happening with Sinclair's son. Was he involved somehow? Did Sinclair cover up his crimes? I didn't think you'd ever be connected to the rest. I know you don't believe me, but we weren't using you."

Fitz put his feelings aside. "You called Tim and what? Said you think Sinclair was taking bribes?"

"That's exactly what I did," Sutton said without a trace of regret. If anything, she seemed still enthusiastic about her decision even after being kidnapped, much to Fitz's surprise. "You have to remember I didn't have any proof. I had seen the ledger but didn't have a copy and I couldn't access his safe. I had nothing tangible to show anyone. Even if I had chosen to go to the cops, what was I going to give them?

No one was going to believe me. Sinclair is a well-respected federal judge. His name was already being tossed around for the Supreme Court."

"He isn't well-liked. I'm sure someone might have believed you."

"Well-liked and respected are two different things."

Fitz couldn't argue with that. "Okay, so you call Tim and tell him what you found but have no proof. Did you ask him to start digging?"

"That's exactly what I asked him to do. He has the know-how and it was potentially a huge story. Pulitzer Prize-winning stuff to bring down a federal judge and Supreme Court nominee. My goal was to stop him from being nominated. It's taken much longer than anticipated."

"When did you initially find the ledger?" Fitz asked, assuming this must have gone back much further than he thought. If so, it meant she had stayed with him the whole time working to bring him down.

"More than a year ago," Sutton admitted. "I know what you're thinking. Yes, it was nearly impossible to stay with him that whole time. It's also why I was willing to put up with his abuse. Then again, the abuse didn't start until after I found the ledger. That's when Sinclair started to get controlling and asked me not to work. All of it, finding the ledger, the abuse, and his name being mentioned for Supreme Court Justice happened around the same time. It was his way of controlling things that started to get out of control for him."

That at least was put into context for Fitz. Sutton went on to explain how she and Timothy worked together for more than a year to dig up dirt on Sinclair. The records she found that she had given to Kevin to hold were copies of what she had already provided to Timothy.

"I needed a backup, Fitz. I trusted Timothy but he was focused on the story. I didn't trust anyone at that point."

"How does Holden fit in?"

"I don't know," Sutton admitted with hesitancy in her voice. "I was

CHAPTER 22

serious when I said I wanted to know what had happened. I know Sinclair made the last incident go away. He was protecting his son when he should have let the kid face the consequences of his actions. I needed to know what was happening at the school." Sutton licked her lips nervously and lowered her gaze. "I swear, Fitz. I didn't know all of this was going to happen. I didn't know he'd be kidnapped or that I would be too. I didn't know you'd ever find out about what I was doing with Timothy. He didn't have anything to do with you investigating Holden. It was all my idea. He said he wasn't interested in what Sinclair was doing with Holden. That people wouldn't care or see it as anything more than a father protecting his son. Maybe he's right in that nobody would care. I cared because he was hurting young women and getting away with it. I wanted to know because I wanted to do something about it. I didn't want Holden to turn out like Sinclair. I thought there might still be time for the young man to get the help he needed."

For all of Sutton's delays, lying, and bluster, Fitz believed her. "There's one big glaring problem, Sutton. This time Holden didn't do anything wrong. He was drunk with his friends and they were having a party, which they shouldn't have been doing. As far as I can tell that's about all he did wrong. He didn't assault that girl. They were both set up. It was only because of his friends that there's proof of that."

Sutton's features tightened. "Are you sure?"

"Veronica Williams admitted it to me. I met with her and her mother, Morgan, who is a reporter for *The New York Times*. Veronica not only slipped the drug into Chloe's drink, but she also told her the next morning that she had been sexually assaulted by Holden. Then she called her mother and told her she had to run the story. Morgan, thankfully, had better sense. She refused and called the school."

Sutton pursed her lips and her brow constricted. Fitz knew she was having trouble making sense of it in the same way he had. "Why would they set up Holden? What would they have to gain from it?"

"Money," Fitz responded evenly. He explained what Veronica had told him about being paid for her part in the setup. "I have indisputable proof of what she did. Two of her classmates recorded her confession. There was no denying what she had done. She didn't even have a good reason for doing it other than the money. Rightly, Morgan is concerned about who approached her daughter. They paid her and provided her with the drugs to use. It was diabolical, Sutton. Someone infiltrated those students to set up Holden and Chloe. Then they went after the student who disclosed everything to me."

Sutton took a moment to absorb the information. "The one who recorded it?"

Fitz confirmed.

"What's his name?"

"I'm not providing that information. We were shot at by these people. The kid is with his parents. The FBI has the information. This isn't going to be fodder for Tim's story. Did any of the kidnappers go by the name Blaze?"

"No," Sutton said with a shake of her head. "They used nicknames if they used names at all and none of them were Blaze. Who is that?"

"The person who set up Holden."

It was taking Sutton time to understand. "I can't comprehend why someone would want to set up Holden. What purpose would that serve?"

"I've been asking myself the same question. I assume whoever did that kidnapped him when the setup didn't play out like they planned. I thought you were kidnapped by the same people, but it doesn't seem connected." All Fitz knew for sure was Judge Sinclair was at the center of it all. "Could Tim have been involved in any of this? Maybe to make his story bigger? Grander?"

Sutton cocked her head to the side. "Fitz, you may not like him

CHAPTER 22

but you know he's a respectable journalist. He didn't want me going after Holden. He was adamant it wasn't pertinent to the story about Sinclair and the bribes he was taking. That was Timothy's focus. He said anything else would be gossip and get in the way of the real story." She locked her gaze on him. "Besides, Timothy didn't want you anywhere near this story. He said if you got involved, you'd blow the whole thing wide open before he could bring it to press. The goal was an irrefutable story big enough that law enforcement and the public couldn't avoid. We wanted to ensure there was no nomination. Now we have to ensure there is no confirmation."

Fitz kept going back to the fact Sinclair was so unlikeable. He didn't understand why he was nominated. It made Fitz wonder what Sinclair might have had on the president or someone high up in politics that his name would even be a contender.

Sutton watched him. "Fitz," she said slowly, "you're thinking about something. What did you pick up on that I'm missing?"

She had become too good over the years at reading his every expression. He answered her question with a question. "Given Sinclair is taking bribes, is it too much of a jump to wonder if he might have something on the president, which is why his name is even up for consideration for the Supreme Court? It's not like anyone likes him. He's problematic without all of this."

Sutton hadn't considered that.

Fitz pressed on. "You've gone to events and dinners with him around D.C. Did you get the feeling people wanted him for the Supreme Court?" Sutton had the inside track, more so than anyone Fitz knew.

"People paid him lip service, but that's how the D.C. circuit is. It's all fake, you know that. People say what they think they are supposed to say and wait to get into their little cliques to say what they are really thinking. Then hope that no one discloses it publicly."

"So, no one wanted him. Is that what you're saying?" Fitz wanted the bottom line.

Sutton agreed with his statement. "While I said he was respected, you're right that he isn't well-liked. No one could stand him. I found that out fairly quickly when we started dating. I was concerned because I didn't want people to not like me as an extension of him." Sutton took a sip of her tea. "Part of me wondered if they would think I had questionable taste for having a relationship with him."

Fitz was one of those people. "Do you believe Judge Sinclair may be blackmailing President Mitchell or someone else who has influence over the president for the nomination?"

Sutton thought about that for a moment. She didn't refute it. "I never saw any sign of that and neither did Timothy. He would have told me. It would have been a topic for discussion. You're the first one, Fitz, who has ever raised that possibility. I think it's more than possible given how much disdain there is for Sinclair."

If anything was the story that was it. "What is the focus of his article so far?"

Sutton's mouth drew in a firm line. "I can't tell you that. You're talking to the FBI and I don't trust them."

"Why not?" he demanded.

"Sinclair has reach. As I said, I don't know who to trust. While there are people who hate the man, he seems to have a lot of influence in this city. If he is blackmailing someone and it goes all the way to the top, there is no telling what kind of revenge Sinclair can take." She held her arms open wide as if to say *see, it already happened*. "I was kidnapped. I'm not going to risk that again. I'm also not going to risk handing over all the evidence to the FBI so they can shut down the case. It's not going to happen, Fitz. It's why I left evidence with Kevin in case something happened to me."

Fitz wanted to argue but the logic was sound. In her position, he might be doing the same thing. He corrected himself on further

CHAPTER 22

consideration – he was doing the same thing by going after Sutton alone and not telling the FBI. Fitz sat back and watched her expression for any cracks, any sign that Sutton wasn't dead set on the direction she was headed. He found nothing but steely resolve. Fitz decided right then and there he was in – not that he had much choice.

"Let me help you both." The last thing Fitz wanted was to help Tim, but he wasn't going to walk away from it all now.

Sutton eyed him. "You're willing to lie to Agent Burrows?"

"Lie by omission." Fitz sat back and thought the whole thing through. "You don't know who kidnapped you. You fought with Sinclair and were kidnapped outside of his home. You don't know why or anything after that. I rescued you. You can't tell him what you don't know." It occurred to Fitz he hadn't heard the details of the actual kidnapping yet. He'd wait until Agent Burrows heard it so Sutton didn't sound rehearsed. "Do you think you can handle that?"

Sutton didn't even need to think about it. Most importantly, she didn't say she wanted to ask Timothy which would have enraged Fitz to no end. She extended her hand across the table. "You have a deal."

Fitz took her delicate hand in his. "Since I cooked, you can do dishes while I call Agent Burrows."

"I see nothing has changed. You always hated doing dishes."

Fitz pushed back from the table and stood. "A lot has changed, Sutton. More than you realize."

CHAPTER 23

The next morning at nine, Fitz and Sutton arrived at his office. Fitz would pay for it once the agent knew, but he wanted to make sure Sutton was ready.

She had spent the night in Fitz's spare bedroom and he had taken her to her condo early that morning so she could grab a change of clothing for the day and pack an overnight bag. Fitz wasn't going to let her live alone until the whole situation was over as much for her safety as his. He wanted to keep an eye on her. As much as Sutton said she had no one to trust, Fitz didn't trust her. She hadn't even put up a fight when he had mentioned it that morning. He sensed she was relieved to know she'd be safe with him.

Agent Burrows hadn't been half as angry as Fitz thought he'd be when he had called him with the news Sutton had been rescued. He provided Burrows with the details of where to find the kidnappers, although he suspected they might be long gone by now. Burrows wasn't happy Fitz had hidden the ransom call and had gone after Sutton alone. There wasn't much he could do about it at that point. Fitz also let Burrows know that since rescuing Sutton, the kidnappers had been calling him nonstop, threatening him. They told him he was as good as dead for disrupting their plan. The last call came in at two that morning. Fitz provided Burrows with the phone number.

Fitz had also called Charlie to let her know he had successfully

CHAPTER 23

rescued Sutton. He left out that he had invited Agent Burrows to the office that morning to interview Sutton there. The mistake he made was encouraging her to continue working from home. Now that he was at the office and found the downstairs lights on, he knew Charlie had come to work.

Fitz leaned against the doorjamb to her office and gave her a wry smile. "I told you that you didn't need to come in this morning. I appreciate the coffee though."

Charlie pointed toward the floor. "There are pastries in the conference room for the meeting I assume you're having with the FBI." She cocked one of her perfectly arched eyebrows. "I thought I told you to stay out of this. It's not good for you and it's certainly not good for business."

"Charlie, come on," Fitz said, trying to smooth it over. "You knew when I went to rescue her that I was fully involved until the end. She's staying with me until I can be sure she's safe." He walked over to her desk and leaned down. "I'll tell you more about what's going on after Burrows leaves. It's a big case and it's not going to hurt us in the end to have our name attached to it."

"Your name," she corrected and flicked her eyes up to his. "I don't trust her, Fitz. I know she's your ex-wife and you've got a sweet spot for her a mile wide. I think you've got a blind spot for her too. I don't see anything good coming from this."

Fitz pulled up a chair and sat so he'd be eye level with her. "I admit I've been carrying a sweet spot for her. I can't even deny that. Last night, when Sutton was trying to manipulate me and it was clear she used me, I realized I didn't feel anything. The anger came and went so fast because Sutton doesn't have the same hold over me that she once did."

Charlie let out a light chuckle, a breath through her nose in short bursts while maintaining a stealthy level of eye contact. Fitz looked away first and the slow smile spread across her face. "I might actually believe you if I thought one little wiggle of her hips wouldn't have you naked in her bed."

Fitz shook his head back and forth so hard it dizzied him. "I swear, Charlie, I'm a changed man. She's hot. I think you can even see Sutton is a beautiful woman, and I did react to her last night when she came down from a shower wearing my tee-shirt. It was a reaction, that's all. Nothing any other red-blooded man wouldn't have had. But it was fleeting."

Charlie scrunched up her nose like she smelled something foul.

"I didn't do anything at all. I swear to you. I didn't even have the desire." Fitz sat back, rather proud of himself. "I'm unbiased and thinking about this clearly. I can't say that I was at the start, but I promise you I am now."

Charlie tilted her head to the side and paused, not quick with a reaction like she might have had another time. She watched him carefully, the way he had watched Sutton the night before. "I don't know if I believe that. I want to believe it. What's your plan?"

Fitz shifted his eyes toward the door. Agent Burrows should have arrived by now. "Do you want to sit in the meeting with us?"

"Who's the agent?"

"Agent Josh Burrows. The same guy I've been telling you about. You spoke to him briefly on the phone."

"I know Josh Burrows," Charlie admitted, not saying more than that. Fitz wasn't surprised. Her long career at the CIA put her in touch with most people in the security and criminal justice world. "He's not someone who is going to believe things easily, Fitz. He's a good agent and can smell a rat from a distance. If you're thinking about playing him, you better be ready."

"Neither of you said anything about knowing each other."

Charlie shrugged but didn't offer more.

CHAPTER 23

He pivoted. "I'm not going to play him, but I'm not going to tell him everything."

"He's going to walk away knowing that, Fitz. Then he's going to wonder why you're lying because a lie of omission is still a lie." Charlie moved some papers and leaned her arms on her desk. "Be brief and to the point and answer his questions. If that's where you start, later when you're being evasive, he might not notice."

Fitz thanked her for the information. "I have it under control. Are you sure you don't want to sit in?"

Charlie shook her head. "I have enough going on with our other cases. Besides, when this thing goes south, and it will, I don't want my name front and center with the FBI. Someone is going to have to be around to bail you out." She smiled up through her long eyelashes. "Just you though. I'm not bailing *her* out."

Fitz broke into a wide smile and stood, shaking down his pant legs. "You have to stop with the hate. It's all going to work out. I promise you."

Charlie went back to reading from the file flipped open on her desk. She muttered, "Famous last words. John Wilkes Booth thought that too before he was hunted down in that barn and shot."

Fitz didn't hold back the laugh. She had some wild references sometimes and the things she pulled out of the air were one of the reasons he kept her around. "I haven't shot the president."

"Not yet. But you're about to take down a potential Supreme Court Justice." She raised her head ever so slightly. "Just as dangerous, and your co-conspirator is about as reliable as the ones with Booth. Don't be the one holding the gun at the end of this."

Fitz waved her off as he exited the office and went down the hall to the stairs. He couldn't shake off the feeling that her words might be prophetic. He wasn't lying when he told Charlie he was over Sutton. It was the first time since meeting his ex-wife that he didn't have any feelings for her other than wanting to ensure her safety. Something he'd do for just about anyone.

By the time Fitz reached the middle of the staircase, Agent Burrows's voice reached him. He was greeting Sutton and asked where they could speak. "I have the conference room all set up for you," Fitz shouted from the stairs, taking them two at a time down to the living room turned waiting room. He rounded the corner and came face to face with Burrows. "I'm going to sit in the interview with you."

"I don't think so, Fitz. I need to interview you separately."

"I don't have much to say other than what I already told you. Sutton wanted me to sit in with her. She's been through an ordeal and needs the support." When Burrows didn't move or change his stance, Fitz stepped toward him. "Do you want to traumatize her more? She's been so scared she's staying with me, her ex-husband. I don't even know the details of her kidnapping. If you want to get to the bottom of anything, allow the poor woman some support. I can bring Charlie Doyle down here if you're more amenable to that. She said the two of you know each other."

Burrows cast his eyes up toward the ceiling. "She's here now?"

Fitz stepped back and made a motion toward the stairs. "I can go get her if you want me to."

Burrows changed his mind quickly. "It's fine. Sit in on the interview. There's no reason to bother Charlie. I'm sure she has better things to do."

Fitz couldn't help but notice the constrained tone of his voice. He couldn't tell if it was fear or if maybe Charlie and Burrows had something a little more than professional between the two of them. "How well do you know Charlie?"

Burrows ignored the question but wouldn't meet Fitz's eyes. He marched back toward the conference room where Sutton was sitting flipping through a magazine. She had already poured herself a cup of coffee and had a half-eaten croissant sitting in front of her. Sutton looked up at Fitz as he entered. "It feels weird to be sitting in your dining room."

Burrows raised his eyebrows in a question.

"This used to be our house," Fitz explained, offering him some coffee which he declined. Fitz went to the counter and poured himself a cup, adding more cream and sugar than actual coffee. He carried it back to the table and sat. "I live elsewhere now and converted this to an office. This is the first time Sutton is seeing it like this." She didn't appear to be too shaken up. She looked instead to be as comfortable as possible with her coffee and magazine. She was making a liar out of him already.

Agent Burrows didn't waste any time getting down to business. "Sutton, did the kidnappers hurt you in any way?"

"They roughed me up a little when they took me. But otherwise, once we got to the house, they left me alone. I had a bedroom with a bathroom. They cooked for me."

"I'm glad Fitz was able to rescue you unharmed." He glanced at Fitz then back to Sutton. "Let's start from the beginning when you were at Judge Sinclair's house. That was the last place I was told you were seen. Is that where they kidnapped you?"

Sutton reached for her coffee and took a sip. She cradled the cup in her hand. "Sinclair and I argued and I rushed out of the house, not able to deal with him any longer. He can be caustic and cruel when he wants to be. There's only so much I can handle in one evening. I got to my car and headed down the driveway. There was a black SUV blocking the end of the driveway. It pulled up as I was trying to leave and blocked my way out. Before I even knew what was happening, two men were out running toward my car. I didn't know what was going on. At first, I wondered if they were Secret Service. They were wearing all black and one of them had an earpiece in. They stormed me, one going to the driver's side and the other to the passenger side. I didn't even get the chance to lock the door before the one man on my side yanked open the door and tried to pull me out. He didn't say anything to me other than to come with him. I didn't even know what was happening. I fought back then, slapping and punching him. I think I caught him but ripped a nail in the process. I knew I was bleeding when he pulled me out of there. I hit my leg on the steering wheel and have a bruise on my thigh."

"The blood was from your nail?" Burrows asked with an air of curiosity. "There was quite a bit of blood."

Sutton held her hand up to show him the bandage around her middle finger. "Did you ever have a nail ripped clean off, Agent Burrows? It bleeds more than you'd think." She didn't wait for his response, she tilted her chin down to the table and looked up at him through her lush eyelashes. "It was terrifying, especially when they kept telling me they were going to kill me. Once they got me to the house, they said there was a change of plans and they were going to ask for ransom. I assumed they meant from Sinclair. When I said that they just laughed and said they were going to try but he wanted me dead."

"They told you Sinclair was the reason they kidnapped you?" Fitz asked, interrupting her. She had not told him that.

Sutton turned her body so she was facing him. "Not in so many words. That's why I assumed at the time Sinclair was behind my kidnapping."

"Did they call him for a ransom?"

Sutton nodded. "They made the call probably ninety minutes after I was taken. I heard one of the kidnappers arguing with him on the phone. He knew right away that I was gone. The conversation though made it seem like Sinclair was involved and they were asking for more money, not to give me back but to kill me. When they talked to you, I figured they'd kill me anyway but they were stuck on the ransom

CHAPTER 23

idea."

Fitz turned to Burrows and the implications of what Sutton said sunk in for both of them. Not only had Sinclair lied to Fitz, but he had also lied to the FBI, which was a crime.

Burrows gave nothing away in his expression. He gestured toward Sutton. "I need to hear the rest of this story and then we need to talk about your relationship with Sinclair."

CHAPTER 24

By the time Sutton was done disclosing everything that had happened during the kidnapping and describing the kidnappers in detail, Burrows had lost his indifferent, unreadable demeanor.

"Do you realize Sinclair told the FBI he thought you kidnapped Holden?" he asked her when she was done describing what her days were like with the kidnappers.

"I had no idea initially. I came to learn later that the FBI suspected I was involved. It was Fitz who told me that Sinclair was the one who suggested it."

Burrows shifted in his seat. "We weren't aware until later that you were missing. Sinclair indicated he thought you might have taken Holden. We did not want to make a public statement in that regard until we had some proof. It was Fitz who notified us when he found your car hidden in Sinclair's garage."

"I see," she said, her tone stiff. "What was his explanation?"

"He didn't offer one. Sinclair denied knowing it was there and suggested to me Fitz put it there to make you look less guilty." Burrows glanced in Fitz's direction. "There was a confrontation at the house. Sinclair ended up a bit bloodied by it. I talked him out of pressing charges given the circumstances. I'm not sure I fully understand how Fitz got involved in all of this."

CHAPTER 24

Fitz knew he was lying. He had explained the whole thing to him. This was a test for Sutton and he remained quiet to see how it would play out. Her credibility was on the line now.

Sutton took a deep breath, her chest rising and falling. "I had asked Fitz to go look into a situation on campus that concerned me. Holden had been in trouble before and it sounded like it was happening again. That was in part the fight between Sinclair and me that night. I thought he needed to allow Holden to face the consequences of his actions. Sinclair reminded me I wasn't Holden's mother and never would be. He suggested since I have no children I had no right to tell a father how to parent. Maybe he's right, but Holden was trouble. I was concerned about my reputation being connected to it all. I thought Fitz might be able to look into the situation and find out the truth and how dangerous Holden might be."

Burrows sat upright with interest. "You think Holden might be dangerous? Do you have proof of that?"

Fitz saw what Sutton was doing. She was taking the heat off herself and redirecting it. It was a good play, but he wasn't sure Burrows would buy it for long.

Sutton kept her gaze focused on Burrows. "He had been accused of sexual assault before and Sinclair paid off the family. He was being accused again. I know Fitz uncovered that this time he was being set up. He'd also been accused of disruption in classes, drinking on campus, and an array of other infractions."

"I'd say the last part is fairly common with kids at boarding school," Burrows said evenly. "The assaults are more concerning. You said Sinclair knew about this?"

Sutton nodded. "And paid off the family."

"Do you have any idea where Holden might be?"

"No." Sutton looked between the both of them. "I swear to you. I wanted Fitz to get me some information about what Holden was doing. That's all. I haven't seen him in months since his last school break and that was a short family dinner."

"I believe you," Burrows said and cocked his head toward Fitz. "We still need to discuss how you managed to find Sutton and why you went alone."

Sutton cleared her throat. "Fitz called my phone in one of the rare instances the kidnappers had turned it on. They asked him for ransom and he demanded proof of life. I got on the phone and slipped in a hint only he would know about where I was being held. Luckily, it was a place I knew Fitz was familiar with and had some history there." The corners of Sutton's lips turned up in a soft smile. "Please don't be angry with Fitz that he came for me alone. I'm sure he didn't want to waste the FBI's time when they were looking for Holden. For all he knew, he couldn't find the right spot."

Burrows kept his back straight and his expression neutral. "Is there anything else you think I should know? We'd like to have you both work with a sketch artist to get some composites of these men. Do you believe you can do that, Sutton?" When Sutton agreed to it, Burrows asked if he could send the artist to the office.

Fitz readily agreed to that. "I only saw two of the men and I didn't get the best look at them. I'll do what I can to help."

Burrows gave a stiff nod and thanked Sutton for the interview. He said he'd be in touch if he needed anything else. Before getting up, he told Fitz he needed to speak to him alone. "Let's take a walk outside." The meaning was clear – Burrows didn't want Sutton or anyone else in the office to overhear them.

Fitz didn't know if he was being taken to task or if Burrows had other concerns. He left Sutton sitting in the conference room and followed Burrows out the front door.

Once they were on the sidewalk and about a block away, Burrows stopped and turned to Fitz. "I think she's lying about something.

CHAPTER 24

Maybe not lying but holding back. Did you get that sense?"

Charlie was right, Burrows wasn't someone easily fooled. Fitz remembered the advice Charlie had given him. He looked Burrows right in the eye and stood toe-to-toe with him. "I don't believe Sutton fully told me the truth either. It sounds to me like Sinclair has been up to no good for a long time. He blamed Sutton for a kidnapping he knew she couldn't have committed and hid her car. The only excuse he gave me was he didn't know what she was doing and didn't want the focus taken off Holden. It was plausible but not believable."

Burrows turned his head to look back at the office. "What do you think is *really* going on?"

"I don't know," Fitz said with a trace of honesty. He knew what Sutton had told him and he had seen the documents, but he didn't know fact from fiction – not yet. "If you want my opinion on this, and I have nothing substantial to give you, no real evidence to speak of, I believe Sinclair is dirty. There's more he's not telling you, and I suspect he is into a lot more behind the scenes than we might ever guess."

Burrows wasn't stupid. He cocked an eyebrow up. "You have evidence to back this up?"

"None. It's pure speculation based on what Sutton said about her kidnapping and what I saw up at the school." Fitz wanted to give him something else. "I don't know if this has anything to do with anything, but I was talking to my old partner Ellis Smith at D.C. Metro. He told me his case against Danny Martin was blocked from going forward and the FBI case was shut down as well. I mentioned the name to you when we spoke before. What I didn't know was Judge Sinclair overturned the last conviction Danny Martin faced a couple of years back. It came up on appeal in front of Sinclair and he threw out the whole case. Now the other cases have been shut down."

Burrows furrowed his brow. "For someone who claims he has no evidence, that's a pretty big accusation."

Fitz held his hands up in surrender. "All I'm saying is that it's a big coincidence. Either someone is out to get Sinclair by kidnapping his fiancée and his son or Sinclair has some part in it. I'll be honest with you – this feels like we are dealing with two different things. The people who were trying to set up Holden and possibly kidnapped him and then the other group kidnapped Sutton. Again, I have no proof. Just a feeling. What we do know is Sinclair lied to us both. My money is on him being more involved in something…anything. This whole situation stinks. But if you start looking into it, I'd suggest you don't trust anyone."

Agent Burrows chuckled. "Have you always been this cynical?"

"It's D.C. You can't live here and not be cynical. There's an undercurrent of crime, backstabbing, and underhanded deals." Fitz was being straight-up honest about that. Since he'd given up his badge and gone into the private sector where people no longer feared he'd arrest them, the sheer volume of underhanded dealings he'd been witness to was impossible to quantify. "There's only one person I trust completely and that's Charlie. It's why I'm in business with her."

Burrows absorbed the information, nodding his head. He didn't ask anything else about Sinclair or Sutton. He surprised Fitz with what he said next. "You can trust me. How is Charlie doing?"

Fitz turned his head to the side like a dog whose ears had perked up at the mention of dinner. "How do you know Charlie?"

"We…um…dated, I guess you could say." Burrows's hand went up to his face and he held it there against his chin. "As much as anyone can date Charlie. She's a tough nut to crack. When she was working for the State Department. I came to learn later that it was the CIA. I figured it out and she didn't deny it."

"What happened between you two?" Fitz didn't normally ask people about their relationships, but it seemed like Burrows wanted to talk.

CHAPTER 24

"She broke up with me more than a year ago and we hadn't spoken until you forced me to speak to her the other morning. She was living in my house one minute and gone the next. I know she quit the CIA about the same time. I don't know if her quitting came before or after the breakup. When I realized she had left the agency, I thought she might be going through something and I reached out to her to see how she was doing. She never returned the call. I still don't know what I might have done wrong. It's good to know she's landed on her feet." There was a question embedded in there that Burrows didn't speak aloud.

Fitz put him out of his misery. "Charlie landed on her feet workwise. There's no one else that I'm aware of. If anything, she seems to relish being single. At least, that's what she says. I can't speak for her, but in the time she's been here, she's grown to be one of my best friends. She might have gotten too close to you too fast. If you didn't do anything, and you seem like a nice enough guy, I suspect she scared herself with how she felt about you."

"We did move a little fast," Burrows said with a chuckle. "You know how it is in this line of work. Things are intense day to day with work and the caseload and that can carry over to other parts of life. She didn't say anything about moving too fast. I thought we were on the same page until we weren't. I guess it is what it is."

Fitz felt for the guy. He seemed to be still carrying a torch. "Now that you know where she is, maybe you can ease back in. I can tell her you were asking for her."

Burrows looked back at the office. "I don't know, Fitz."

Fitz put his hand on the man's shoulder. "Whatever you want to do just let me know."

Burrows let the subject drop. He refocused his attention on Fitz. "If Sutton tells you anything of value, please let me know. I believe she's up to something, possibly in over her head. She seems like a nice woman, too nice to be with Judge Sinclair. He didn't even seem to care she was missing. He was too quick to place the blame on her. I hope she stays away. If she's involved in something illegal, Fitz, I'm not going to go easy on her. I've given her ample opportunity to be straight with me."

He'd given Fitz ample opportunity too. The underlying message was clear. "If there's something actionable I come across and you're willing to investigate Sinclair, trust me, I'll share it with you." Fitz hoped his meaning was just as clear.

Burrows thanked him and headed down the road. He got into a government SUV parked at the curb and sped off. Burrows waved at Fitz as he passed, leaving him with a sinking feeling in his gut. He had to find out what Sutton and Tim were doing and get the information to the FBI. He'd have to play double agent for now.

While Sutton was right that it was dangerous to turn over the information, it was just as dangerous for them to be going after Sinclair alone. A newspaper story could only do so much – the evidence had to be handed over before it was destroyed.

Resolute about what he needed to do, Fitz headed back to the office, called Sutton's name as he entered, and closed the door behind him. He found her sitting at the conference table where he left her. It didn't appear she had moved at all.

"I thought that went well," she said, not raising her head to look at him. She was engrossed in the same magazine she had been reading when the meeting first started. When Fitz didn't respond, Sutton flicked her eyes up to him. "Did you hear me? I thought that went well. What did Agent Burrows say when he was outside with you?"

Fitz eased himself back into the chair across from her. "Burrows thinks you're hiding something about Sinclair. I covered for you as best I could. He's not buying it, Sutton. I trust him and I think he can help us."

CHAPTER 24

Sutton sighed and closed the magazine. She pushed it away from her on the table. "Fitz, we talked about this. We can't go to the FBI with this information. Not until Timothy breaks the story."

"What then, Sutton? What happens if he breaks the story and Sinclair destroys all the evidence before the FBI can get to it or worse he starts taking out witnesses? Have you considered any of that? You think you're building this big case, but if Sinclair starts destroying evidence when the story is published, what then? Your whole case goes out the window and I suspect Timothy will be in serious trouble with his editors."

Sutton sat back and watched him as he went on, making the case for why Agent Burrows should be involved. While Fitz thought he was making a good case, it didn't seem to sway her. "None of this is up to me at this point. We need to speak to Timothy. It's his investigation now and I'll do whatever he thinks is best."

If that was how she was going to play it, Fitz had no problem betraying them both. "Call him and get him down here now."

CHAPTER 25

Timothy Dalton wasn't used to being summoned anywhere. He'd been working for *The Washington Post* as an investigative journalist since he graduated with a master's degree from Colombia School of Journalism in the mid-nineties. He was a few years older than Fitz, stood a few inches shorter than him, and had an arrogance about him that made most people fear him. Not Fitz. He couldn't stand looking at his smug mug.

"What is the meaning of this?" Timothy yelled as he slammed the front door to the office, swaying the chandelier and rattling the photos on the wall. He had left Fitz and Sutton waiting for more than an hour after she had called him requesting a meeting. He had initially refused to come to Fitz's office and had chastised Sutton for sharing any information. Fitz had taken the phone and told him in no uncertain terms that if he wasn't at the office within thirty minutes, he'd be calling Agent Burrows back and disclosing the whole scheme.

Hence why he left them waiting for more than an hour.

It was a power play Fitz didn't care for and wasn't going to entertain. It didn't escape his notice that at no point since rescuing Sutton had she called Timothy to tell him she was safe. There were many reasons why Fitz disliked the man – how he treated Sutton was at the top of the list.

At the slam of the door, Fitz stepped out of the conference room

CHAPTER 25

into the hallway. He pointed a finger at the pinched-faced man. "Don't slam my door again. You're late and I've already texted Agent Burrows that I might be following up with more information this afternoon."

That stopped Timothy cold. "You wouldn't dare. That would destroy the entire investigation, sending more than a year of work up in smoke."

"Not my problem," Fitz said, rocking on his heels. "Guess you should have thought of that before you were late and then dared to come into another man's office shouting and slamming doors. I'm not sure how you're used to working but that's not going to happen here. Sutton is in the conference room. If you'd like to drop the attitude and join us for a civil conversation, you're welcome. If not, get out and I'll call Agent Burrows."

Timothy's back stiffened and his eyes got wide. He stepped back toward the door as if contemplating the decision. Fitz didn't stick around to see what he decided. He left Timothy there in the foyer and sat down at the table with Sutton.

"Your boyfriend is deciding if he should stay or go."

Sutton shot him a warning look. She dropped her voice to a whisper. "You didn't have to start it out like that."

"He didn't have to come into a business slamming doors. For all he knows I had clients in the office." Fitz folded his arms across his chest and waited. It wasn't a minute later when Timothy walked in. He avoided Fitz's eyes and sat next to Sutton. He offered her a stiff hello.

Fitz jutted his chin toward her. "I thought you two were friends. You're not even going to ask if she was harmed during the kidnapping. Geez, Sutton, I guess you had more than a few reasons for dumping him." Fitz bit the inside of his cheek to stop himself from chuckling. If he was going to be forced to work with this idiot he was going to have some fun with it.

Ignoring Fitz's dig, Timothy turned to Sutton. "Of course, I've been worried about you. I didn't know what to do. I didn't even realize until the next day that you were gone. I tried texting you several times when I heard the news about Holden. You hadn't responded to the meeting request. Forgive me for being so abrupt. Just the notion that *he's* involved and knows what we have been doing is concerning."

Sutton offered him a pleasing smile as if all was forgiven so easily. "It's okay. I know how busy you have been with everything. There was nothing you could have done. Fitz rescued me. I had no choice but to tell him. He found information that I had hidden."

"I see." Timothy turned to face Fitz then. "What is it that you think you know?"

To get the ball rolling, Fitz explained his involvement from the moment Sutton had contacted him until the meeting with Agent Burrows. He left nothing out. There was no reason to. If they were going to work together, he'd give them both the respect of honesty. He couldn't say he expected to receive the same in return.

As Fitz detailed everything he knew, Timothy went from surprised to concerned to even paler than his natural skin tone. Fitz didn't stop there. He kept right on going, detailing all of the concerns he had expressed to Sutton about their investigation. "That is why I demanded the meeting. I can appreciate you're a good investigative journalist, Tim. I was a detective and I know what suspects do when they are outed. Now a piece in *The Washington Post* may well destroy Sinclair's chances for the Supreme Court. Maybe even the rest of his career. I'm more concerned about what it will do to any potential criminal case. As soon as he is outed, Sinclair and anyone connected to this case will destroy the evidence. You two are going to be left holding the bag so to speak."

"I'll have copies of all the evidence I find."

"Copies, Tim. It's not the same as actual evidence." Fitz knew that

CHAPTER 25

wasn't technically true. But as soon as the FBI showed up at Sinclair's the actual evidence and any other corroborating evidence that they hadn't uncovered would be gone. The case wouldn't be nearly as strong.

Timothy thankfully didn't argue with him and didn't correct him about the name. Fitz knew he didn't like the shortened form of it and it was precisely why he used it. "What do you suggest then? My understanding is Sinclair is untouchable and people have been trying for years to bring him down. His reach goes to the highest levels and someone is protecting him. If we turn this over to the wrong FBI agent, then all hope could be lost. You might have laid out all the evidence of what you've seen and what we currently have but you've not made the overall connection."

Fitz would get back to what Timothy knew in a moment. "I haven't heard anyone trying to bring Sinclair down. I know he's not well-liked. It's never been apparent to me that anyone was trying to suggest he was a criminal. I think I would have heard about that by now."

Timothy glanced over at Sutton as if she would be able to answer the question better. When Sutton didn't have anything to say, he shrugged. "It's possible I misspoke. No one I've spoken to since the start of this investigation has anything nice to say about Sinclair. I guess I assumed it would only be natural, given everything we found, that someone would be suspicious of him before I got involved."

It was a reasonable enough explanation for Fitz. The evidence was most important to him, far more so than the reason why the investigation was taking place. If they were going to do this, they had to do it right. "The evidence is most important in this investigation. Everything you're gathering must be turned over to law enforcement rather than writing a story."

"I'm writing a story, Fitz," Timothy said with force. "I didn't do all of this not to break the story. It will be the biggest one of my career.

There's no way I'm doing this to help the cops. If they wanted in on this then they could do their own investigation. The story is a non-negotiable."

Fitz had a feeling that was going to be the case. He hadn't thought for one second he was going to be able to talk Timothy out of it. He had asked the question mostly to test the man's commitment and focus. He offered a compromise. "Then wait and coordinate with law enforcement. Once you feel like your investigation has gone as far as it can go, turn everything over to them. Let them get their ducks in a row before publishing. You can have the story ready to go. If the FBI doesn't raid Sinclair's place or for some reason the investigation gets shut down, run it and you'll be no worse off than when you started. At least, you'll have given it a legal chance before you blow the whole case wide open and Sinclair and his associates have a chance to hide evidence, particularly any evidence you didn't find."

"Coordinate," Sutton said almost to herself. She shifted in her seat until her body was turned to face her friend. "It's not a bad idea, Timothy. You can write the story and before publication hand it over to the FBI with a forty-eight-hour deadline to do something with it or you're going to print."

A deadline wasn't quite what Fitz had in mind. It wasn't the worst suggestion. He could agree to those terms. "I don't know if forty-eight hours is enough time, but you can certainly tell them if they don't move quickly, you're going to run the story. I think your editors would agree law enforcement should at least have a crack at it. You can include quotes from them as well if they are willing to go on the record. That would only bolster the story."

When Timothy still didn't look convinced, Sutton added, "If you don't go to law enforcement, I believe both of us could be considered an accessory to a crime. I know my reputation would be in jeopardy. Yours too. Your readership might also question why a story was more

CHAPTER 25

important than a legal case. This could be a win-win for your career." Timothy screwed up his mouth in consideration. He took short shallow breaths through his narrow pointed nose but remained silent. Fitz took his silence as an opportunity to drive home another point. "Here's the other thing to consider. If Sinclair is as powerful as we all believe and we know he can get investigations shut down, then he can come after you too. As I said, when I was up at Brewster Academy someone shot at me. Someone is using kids to set up Holden. Three men took Sutton hostage. You aren't safe and you might just need the FBI's help. I wouldn't alienate them too quickly. I believe Agent Burrows can be trusted."

Fitz knew that if Timothy wasn't convinced by everything he and Sutton had said, then nothing would convince him. He sat there in silence watching Timothy digest all the information. He was thoughtful in his decision-making. Fitz could give him that.

"Point taken," Timothy said after several moments. He sat back in his chair. "Given how we collected the evidence, do you think any of it can be used in court?"

It was a question to which Fitz didn't have an answer. "Ideally, the FBI is going to want to gather the evidence to ensure search warrants were issued properly and it stays within a legal chain of command. That said, I'm sure whatever you provide them would be an essential jumping-off place. They will determine what they can use. Did you break the law while gathering any evidence?"

While Timothy shook his head, Sutton appeared less sure. "I riffled through Sinclair's desk and broke into his safe, Fitz. I'm sure given I don't live there and he didn't permit me, that could be considered a crime."

Fitz was sure Sinclair would bring that up if the case ever went to court. "How did you manage to break into the safe?"

"The combination was Holden's birthday. I tried a few different combinations until I cracked it."

That didn't surprise Fitz. "Where was Sinclair while you were doing that?"

Sutton chewed her bottom lip and wouldn't meet his eyes. "I drugged him."

Fitz leaned on the table not sure he had heard correctly. At least, he hoped he hadn't heard her correctly. "What do you mean?"

"I slipped a sleeping pill into food I made him, had sex with him, and waited until he fell asleep. When I was sure he was out cold, I went into his office."

Fitz tried to keep his expression neutral, but he knew he wasn't succeeding. "Is this something you've done before with Sinclair?" He paused for a moment, thinking of their marriage. "Or anyone else?"

"That was the first time. Ever. But after I found evidence, I tried it twice more with him. I think he caught on the last time I tried it because he forced me to cuddle with him and I wasn't able to get out of his grasp."

Fitz sat back trying to keep his mouth from hanging wide open. The sheer audacity Sutton had in doing that. She risked her safety, her reputation, and ultimately her livelihood. He wasn't surprised now she'd been hesitant to go to the FBI. "How do you think that's going to play out in court?"

"I wasn't planning on ever telling anyone that's what I did."

"I see," Fitz said even though he didn't. He looked over at Timothy. "Did you know that's how Sutton obtained the evidence?"

"You do whatever you have to do, Fitz, for the good of the investigation. Sometimes things get messy. We are trying to take down a tyrant here before he ends up on the Supreme Court." Timothy folded his hands on the table. "I hate to say it but the ends have to justify the means. If Sutton didn't do that, we wouldn't have half the information we have now. There'd be no investigation. We cannot let this man end

CHAPTER 25

up on the highest, most powerful court in the nation."

Fitz wanted to argue with the reasoning. He didn't want Sinclair on the Supreme Court either. He didn't think in the way that Timothy or Sutton did though. "How did you plan to explain this to the cops?"

"Well that's the point, Fitz," Sutton said slowly, dragging out her words. "Until your involvement, we didn't need the cops. I had no intention of ever involving them."

Fitz had assumed as much. "Do you believe Sinclair had you kidnapped to keep you from sharing the evidence you found?"

Sutton nodded slowly. "That's exactly what I think. The phone call the kidnappers made all but proves it."

Fitz sighed and turned to Timothy. "Tell me the rest of the evidence. The real evidence. I want to know your case start to finish."

CHAPTER 26

When Timothy made no move to tell him, Sutton nudged him in the side. "Fitz is a part of this now whether you want him to be or not. He was honest with you about what he knows and now we need to be honest with him." When Timothy started to argue with her, Sutton pushed back. "He risked his life to save me. I'm going to tell him if you're not." She only gave him a few seconds to decide. Then she got up from the table, went to the end of the room, and pulled open the cover of the whiteboard. She reached for one of the markers and started to write.

"Stop!" Timothy said, jumping up from his chair. He took the marker out of her hand and asked her to sit. "I'll explain it to him." He turned back to the board, erased what Sutton had started writing, put Sinclair's name at the top, and drew a map with arrows down from him connecting to lobbying firms, corporations, and mobsters alike. Next, he drew arrows out from Sinclair's name to the side. He wrote down a series of senators' names with question marks next to it. He drew lines from their names to some of the lobbying firms and companies.

When Timothy was done, he turned back to Fitz. "This is everything we have found so far. It goes much deeper than this. There are still many unanswered questions. We have connected Sinclair to these lobbying firms, corporations, and criminals through payments he received from them. We didn't initially understand the reason for the payments. After researching we found there's a record of court cases each of them won even when the evidence was stacked against them. The lobbyists were pushing for specific legislation and you guessed it, it was pushed through Congress shortly after the payments were made."

Fitz let the information sink in. While Sinclair might have been hated by most, if this was true he held more power than Fitz realized. It might well be the reason he was so hated. "How far back do the records go?"

"Fifteen years," Timothy said without missing a beat. "Sinclair has been doing this since he was appointed to the federal bench, possibly longer. The records we were able to find only go back that far. We can assume he started it before then. One doesn't rise to the level of a federal judge and then start committing crimes. Plus, he must have significant influence because some of these happened far outside his jurisdiction. Few, if any, were brought before him. What we have not been able to understand yet is how he was able to sway the cases to go in a favorable direction. Some of the criminal cases had juries."

Jury tampering was a felony in all states. Sinclair must have had powerful people in his pocket to be able to accomplish this if it's true. "Have you looked into Sinclair's background?"

"We were working on that when Sutton was kidnapped."

Sutton had been dating the man for more than two years. Fitz didn't understand how they weren't starting with a leg up. "You must know something about his background that can help the investigation. What have you been doing for two years?" The edge in his tone didn't go unnoticed.

She yelled back at him. "What do you expect me to do? I've been doing the best that I can. When I drugged him, you had a problem. When I stuck around to keep up the ruse of the relationship, you had a problem with that. When I asked for your help to investigate Holden, you gave me a hard time. What is it you want from me, Fitz? I'm not the great Connor Fitzgerald, national hero bringing down a serial killer on my own." Her cheeks flared red and Fitz knew he'd gone too far.

Fitz apologized. "I'm just surprised. That's all, Sutton. I never understood why you were with Sinclair. After you saw that ledger, I don't understand why you didn't just leave him."

Sutton didn't acknowledge his apology. Her nostrils flared. "I overheard Sinclair on the phone with what sounded like him taking a bribe. Asking about the money and promising a favorable outcome in a civil trial. That was shortly after finding the ledger. I couldn't walk away. I had to know."

"Do you know who it was on the other end of the phone?"

"Cisto Electric," Sutton said evenly. "They had been accused of polluting drinking water in rural Virginia. They dumped contaminated wastewater in a nearby water stream that ended up in the drinking water basin. That's the summation of it anyway. I don't know the ins and outs. The case was in front of another judge who ended up recusing himself because of a conflict of interest. Sinclair was brought into the case. I thought the whole conversation about the case was highly unethical and unusual. It sparked my interest. You'll see in the record that soon after he took the case, he became much tougher on the plaintiff's side, even blocking potential evidence that should have made it in. Now if that's what tipped the case to the defense or if the jury had been tampered with, Sinclair didn't say. He promised Cisto Electric a win and that's what he delivered."

"You garnered all that from the phone conversation?"

"I gathered most of it from the call," Sutton said to start. Then she dropped the bomb. "The rest I figured out when I saw the payment from a Cisto Electric lawyer that was made right before the jury came

CHAPTER 26

back. Sinclair made more than three million off the deal. It was a bargain for Cisto Electric who could have lost in the hundreds of millions."

Fitz whistled loudly and shook his head. "If what you're saying is true – and I'm not doubting you. But if this is what happened, this is incredible. It's surely to be the largest scandal in American history tied to a Supreme Court nominee, far beyond even the sexual harassment claims that have been leveled in the past."

Timothy offered him a smug smile and an *I told you so*. "You understand the gravity of the situation then, Fitz. There is still a lot of work to be done. We don't even know how people have come to realize that Sinclair would be open to being approached like this or how he is jury tampering if that's what's occurring. We also don't know if he's making payments to other people. We assume he must be but we have no paper trail for that. Sinclair must have a separate account that we haven't found."

"He must also have a network of people working with him or at least aware of what he's doing."

Timothy shook his head in confusion. "How do you figure that?"

Fitz wasn't sure how Timothy didn't assume that. "He's a busy man with a full case schedule. He must have someone working with him to put feelers around to see who'd be amenable to this and broker the deal. I can guarantee you that Sinclair isn't putting his neck out that far. If he was, we'd have heard about this a lot sooner. He might feel safe to have a conversation with an executive of Cisto Electric in the privacy of his home, but he's not going to meet with anyone in public." Fitz gestured toward Sutton. "Have you ever seen anyone come to his home?"

"No," Sutton responded with emphasis. "He never has anyone there outside of a handful of close friends. He didn't even want me to bring people I know to his house. He said it was a private respite away from the world for him."

"A respite to commit crime," Fitz said mostly to himself. He looked between them. "Does anyone else know about your investigation?"

"Other than Sinclair possibly suspecting Sutton of snooping around, I don't believe so," Timothy said. "I haven't even told my editor. He knows I'm working on a big political scandal investigation but that's as far as I've told him. I've been at the job long enough that he trusts me to do my job. He won't question me until I lay out the evidence and then he'll tell me what we need to do from there."

Fitz raised an eyebrow. "You haven't been ready to disclose anything yet?"

"Not yet. I felt given the holes in the investigation and the fact that we don't have a lot on Sinclair's background we have more work to do."

"I'd agree with that." Fitz zeroed in on Sutton, questions about how she had obtained the evidence still plaguing him. "How did you get the evidence out of Sinclair's house without him knowing?"

Sutton remained matter-of-fact. "He has a copier in his office I used. For records I couldn't copy or didn't have time to copy, I took photos with my cellphone and printed them out at home. I didn't have enough time though. I only wish I could have kept going."

Timothy laid a hand on top of Sutton's. It was the first sign of affection between them Fitz had witnessed. He looked away as Timothy spoke. "It's good you didn't try. If Sinclair had caught you in the act, there's no telling what he might have done."

The kidnapping was starting to make more sense for Fitz. Sinclair had to be worried about what Sutton would do. Even if he didn't know the full extent of what she had found, he must have suspected she was a risk for him. She had career-ending secrets, ones that could land him in prison for a long time.

"Something on your mind, Fitz?" Sutton asked, pulling him back to the conversation at hand.

Fitz shook off his internal thoughts and recovered quickly. "Your kidnapping makes sense in the broader context. What doesn't make sense to me is Holden's kidnapping. I don't think Sinclair is going to kidnap his son. We also need to figure out who tried to set up Holden. There's more at play here than what Sinclair was doing. It's like we are caught in the middle of two factions at war. Could anyone else know what Sinclair is doing?"

While Sutton readily agreed with that, Timothy didn't appear so sure.

Fitz persisted. "I think we need to consider that someone else found out Sinclair's secret and might be blackmailing him. Having his son publicly accused of sexual assault right before his confirmation hearing and then kidnapped during it when nothing came of those accusations is next-level evil. In all my years of police work, I've seen some crazy things. This one…I'm not even sure I have words for it. We'd be fools not to consider how what's happened to Holden factors into this."

Sutton put her other hand on top of Timothy's, still resting on hers. "Sinclair is dangerous. If we figured out that he is taking bribes, then someone else had to have found out. Sinclair is scared. If Fitz hadn't gotten there in time, they would have killed me. I think that was the plan all along. The only reason the kidnappers resorted to ransom was to make some extra money before they killed me. I don't even know if Sinclair realizes I'm still alive."

Fitz hitched his chin toward her. "Have you heard from him at all?"

Sutton shook her head and frowned. "Not once. Not one call. I don't know if the kidnappers would admit to him that I got away. For all I know they were supposed to have killed me right there in his driveway that night. Maybe make it look like a carjacking."

It didn't seem that far out of the range of possibilities. "If you died right there, Sutton, there could have been many explanations, even a bad business deal gone wrong. Maybe everything went off script for him that night."

Timothy released Sutton's hands, the reality of the situation finally settling in for him. "You can't be involved in this anymore, Sutton. We have to find a way to keep you safe. If Sinclair came after you once, then we can't be sure he's not going to come after you again." He turned his head sharply to implore Fitz. "What can we do?"

Fitz set his strong desire to protect Sutton aside. She had been brave enough to start this, he knew nothing he said was going to make her walk away from it now. The determined look on her face told Fitz all he needed to know. She implored him with her eyes to make the case for her. "Sutton will be fine. She can stay with me for the time being. That address isn't listed anywhere. She'll be safe. I think we need to press forward with the investigation. The sooner we can get Sinclair behind bars, the safer we will all be."

Timothy asked Sutton if she was sure. When she confirmed everything that Fitz said was right, he didn't argue with her. "Fitz, you're good at digging into people's backgrounds. Could you work with Sutton to figure out Sinclair's past and how he might have started down this path? I'm going to see if I can get any of the sources I've been developing to go on the record. We can take a few days to work and then meet back here to discuss."

Fitz thought it was as good a plan as any. He didn't fully trust Timothy, but he was stuck with him for now. Fitz reached his hand across the table. "The only way this will work is full transparency between us. If you can agree to that, I agree to the plan."

Timothy extended his hand to Fitz and shook it. "You have a deal."

CHAPTER 27

Fitz left Sutton sitting in the conference room while he went to speak to Charlie. He'd need her help on the background investigation into Sinclair. He should have spoken to her first given her reticence for the whole thing. Fitz could do the work without her help. Charlie would just be more efficient.

He knocked once on the half-closed door, leaned in to check if she was on the phone, then nudged the door open wider. He found Charlie hunched over her laptop with earbuds in. Fitz knocked louder, drawing her attention, then stepped inside the office.

"I need to talk to you," he said as she took the earbuds out.

Charlie raised her chin slightly to acknowledge him. "Meeting over?"

"That's what I want to talk to you about." Fitz crossed the room and sat down in the chair across from her desk. He tried to take a casual approach to the request, but he knew no matter how he framed it, Charlie's initial response would be no. "I promised Tim I'd help him with the rest of the investigation into Sinclair. He still hasn't been able to get a lot of background on the man and the allegations are worse than I anticipated. I was hoping—"

"I'll help you," she said, surprising them both. Charlie pulled back in her chair as if she was surprised she had said the words. She shifted her eyes to the right, thinking. "I don't know why I said yes so quickly."

Charlie chuckled to herself. "I overheard part of the conversation and it sounds to me like this is more than gossip. Sinclair is dangerous, and we can't have that on the Supreme Court. When I joined the CIA, I took an oath to protect the United States. I might not work for them anymore, but the drive to serve is still in me."

Fitz knew she had more to say and he wasn't going to stop her now.

Charlie furrowed her brow. "When you first started this, I assumed, wrongly I'll add, that you were only doing this to help her."

"You weren't wrong," Fitz admitted, interrupting her. He gestured for her to continue.

"I thought it was unfair for her ex-husband, whose heart she broke, to investigate her fiancé to see if she should marry him. It sounds to me like Sutton overheard things that rightly gave her pause. She was brave enough to investigate further and it's opened up a whole can of worms that probably needed to be opened up a while ago." Charlie softened her gaze at Fitz. "I don't think she'll be able to help you much as you go forward. It's not her skill set and she's still in danger. You're going to need someone to have your back. I don't trust Tim or Sutton to be able to do that for you."

Fitz knew this was Charlie's long-winded way of apologizing for being difficult earlier and giving him a hard time. "You're off the hook. If you're willing to help me that's all I needed to hear. How much of Tim's information did you hear?"

"The whole thing," she admitted. "I wanted to see if you two could get past your nonsense and accomplish anything. That nearly didn't happen. I also wanted to see what Sutton was dragging you into. I can't say I wasn't shocked by the information. Sinclair must have a network helping him. His reach sounds wide."

Fitz agreed with that assessment. "How do you think this first got started?"

"If he hasn't been dirty since the start of his career, it started soon

CHAPTER 27

after."

"You think it started that early?"

"I've seen men like him, Fitz. Mostly in other countries. They lay the groundwork early on. Either he's been bad since his early college days, probably cheating on tests and so forth, or he learned early on when he was a lawyer about the power he had. He was a prosecutor for a time, right?"

It seemed everyone including Charlie knew more about Sinclair than him. "I don't know anything about the man, other than what I've learned recently. I had heard the rumors that he wasn't well-liked and so didn't understand why Sutton would have a relationship with him. Other than that, I never looked into his background."

Charlie sat in silent contemplative thought. "Huh," she said finally as Fitz tried to figure out what was on her mind. "You might have been telling the truth. If my ex moved on and I wasn't over him, I would have run a full background check on the woman he was currently with."

A short, surprised laugh escaped Fitz. He believed her. "I did that with the first guy she dated after the divorce. It's been years. I am over it."

"I guess so," Charlie said with wonder in her voice. "Anyway, I read Sinclair's bio when I heard his name first being tossed around for the Supreme Court. He went to Georgetown Law and clerked for a judge on the U.S. Court of Appeals. After that, he clerked for Supreme Court Justice John Paul Stevens. That was his first real taste of power. I wonder about his time there."

"How long did he clerk for Stevens?"

"A year, which is somewhat common. After that, Sinclair went to work for the Fairfax County Commonwealth Attorney's Office. He spent three years as a prosecutor before being picked up by a criminal defense firm where he spent the bulk of his career before being appointed a district court judge in Virginia and most recently a federal judge. He's wielded a lot of power in nearly every position. I'm sure he's built a powerful network as well."

A feeling of being overwhelmed settled over Fitz. It was a lot of ground to cover. "Do you think he could shut down an FBI investigation?"

"Depends on who Sinclair was able to access and what threats were made."

That had been Fitz's concern. "He's had all these years to develop a solid network. Who knows what information he's been collecting on people too."

"If he's been collecting information on people, he's using someone."

If that were true it had to be someone Sinclair trusted. More than a few times, people had confused Fitz's job with being a private investigator for hire. He had the license. It was the first thing he did when he was let go from the police force. It's not what he did though – he didn't go after cheating spouses and insurance fraud. He didn't handle criminal defense cases and he surely didn't dig up dirt on victims of crime to slander them and impeach their credibility in court. Most people understood. He had found that the more powerful the person, the more they expected Fitz to compromise his ethics and his business for their wants and needs. He knew a handful of the private investigators in the D.C. Metro area, but he only knew of one shady enough to do the kind of work Sinclair would require.

"Peter Campanella," Fitz and Charlie said at the same time. They both broke into laughter. "You thought of him too?"

Charlie nodded. "The way I figure it, Sinclair has held positions of power for a long time. Maybe he started taking small bribes and saw the power he held. He could have justified it like it wasn't hurting anyone. Those smaller bribes turned bigger and bigger over time. Sinclair would need to protect himself. He'd need to have dirt on

CHAPTER 27

people to keep them quiet."

"Do you think he approached anyone about offering bribes or do you think people came to him?"

Charlie wasn't sure. There was no way she could be. "He'd have to have a middleman, I assume. Sinclair isn't going to do that kind of thing himself."

"Could he have been using Pete for more than a few things?"

"Pete's shady enough to do that."

They had one more potential lead than they had earlier in the day. Fitz gestured with his hand toward Charlie's laptop. "I assume after the meeting with Tim you came up here and started running some background on Sinclair?"

Charlie pointed to the computer. "It's running reports now. I have parameters set up for background information on him and any businesses he's connected to. It will also run real estate reports. I'm checking his credit as well."

They needed a social security number for that. Fitz raised an eyebrow in a question. "That's not information that's just out there."

Charlie shrugged it off. "I have ways of getting what I need. This isn't going to end up in court, Fitz. We don't have to be careful how we are collecting the information."

"It could end up in court," Fitz argued. He saw the dismissive look on her face and realized what she was saying – their investigation wasn't going to end up in court. What they found was going to be turned over to law enforcement, not necessarily how they came by it. That would be up to the cops to figure out how to access it. "I get what you're saying, but let's not do anything too out there in case the FBI asks. We don't want to do anything illegal."

"I didn't do anything illegal," Charlie assured him.

Fitz didn't know if she was telling the truth or not. When she didn't want him to know, she could be impossible to read. It was her CIA skills that she was never without. It was one of a few things that made their friendship and working partnership so interesting. Unless Charlie wanted him to know something, he'd be left in the dark. "Let's go talk to Sutton and see if she ever met Pete and then pay him a visit."

They found Sutton sipping tea in the conference room flipping through the same magazine she had been reading earlier. She barely glanced up from the article when they walked into the room. It was only after Fitz told her they needed to talk that she acknowledged them. She closed the magazine and tossed it to the side of the table.

"What's going on, Sutton?" Fitz asked as they sat. When he left the room to speak to Charlie, she'd been fine. Now she appeared sullen and angry. Charlie sat next to him and watched their interaction closely.

"Timothy texted me after the meeting. He was harsh in his response about involving you. While he's going to do things your way, I broke the trust between us."

"Does it matter?" Charlie asked with a tone that indicated nobody should care what Timothy thought. She reminded Sutton. "He didn't do anything to try to rescue you. If there is anyone between the two of them you can trust, it's Fitz."

Sutton didn't even look in her direction. The tension between them was thicker than Fitz would have expected. "What's the plan, Fitz?" The undertone in that was, *What is she doing here?*

"I asked Charlie if she'd be willing to help and she agreed. This isn't something we can do on our own, Sutton." He wasn't going to argue with her. "I can take you back to my place later. Right now, you can spend the day upstairs in my living quarters. It's quiet and clean and there is a television up there. You can order food or work. Whatever you want."

"It's fine."

Fitz was grateful for the lack of argument about that. It was time to

CHAPTER 27

get down to business. "Have you ever met a man by the name of Peter Campanella? He's a private investigator."

"I've met him a few times. He's worked for Sinclair for a while. I believe that's who Sinclair was using to follow me around."

"You've met him?" Fitz asked, not hiding the surprise in his voice. When Sutton confirmed, he went on. "We believe Sinclair might be using Peter to dig up information on people. If Sinclair has been taking bribes and doing this for some time, he's going to need collateral to make sure no one turns on him. Do you know what he's done for Sinclair besides tail you?"

"He's done a few things. I know he got involved when Holden was accused of sexual assault the first time. He's the one who dug into the family of the victim. I tried not to be at the house when he was there. I didn't get the best feeling from him. He's not very smart if he reported back I was involved with Kevin. I didn't realize you knew him, Fitz."

"I wouldn't say I know him," Fitz responded. "I've met him a handful of times. He's a shady guy and is known for doing some underhanded investigations, going after victims and their families is no surprise. Neither is Sinclair using him to go after you."

"Do you think you'll get him to talk?"

"I don't know." Fitz glanced over at Charlie, knowing she had the skills to get anyone to talk if that's what they needed. He turned back to Sutton. "You stay here while Charlie and I visit Peter. If you need anything, call me."

"What can I do to help? I want to be useful."

"Background research on Sinclair," Charlie directed, finally drawing Sutton's gaze. "Use the internet and social media. Every and any accessible piece of public information you can find."

"Consider it done." Sutton watched them leave.

Fitz stopped in the hallway and glanced in Sutton's direction, hoping that she wouldn't cause too much trouble here on her own.

CHAPTER 28

Peter Campanella's office was a ramshackle row house in the city's northeast quadrant. Split into four quadrants, the northeast had a diverse population and a mix of architecture with many of the residents renting rather than owning homes. It had less crime than the city's southeast quadrant but not quite the same appeal as the northwest.

After circling the block a few times, they found a place to park and walked back three blocks to the office. The front door didn't hold any signage. If one didn't know it was the office of a private investigator, no one walking by would have suspected. It looked like it could be a low-rent accountant's office or a down-and-out lawyer who didn't have many cases.

Fitz was surprised to find the door unlocked and easily pulled open. The musty stench of cigarettes hit them as soon as they entered the place. Four brown chairs pushed up against the far wall created a makeshift waiting area. The room featured 1970s brown paneling on the walls and a reddish shag carpet that had seen better days.

"I can't imagine coming in here and hiring anyone for anything," Charlie said, rubbing her nose.

The small front room, sans a desk or any signs of a receptionist, connected to a small narrow unlit hallway which led to the back of the building. Fitz could hear the rumble of a television or radio off in the distance. He was sure Pete knew they were there. He didn't believe the private investigator remained this unsecured given his reputation and work. There were cameras hidden someplace that had announced their arrival. He glanced around trying to find it and finally settled on the overhead light fixture. It was the only place a camera could have been hidden.

Fitz tipped his head back and spoke directly to the camera. "Peter, I'm Connor Fitzgerald and this is Charlie Doyle. I need to speak to you about an ongoing case."

After a few beats, Charlie asked, "You sure he's here?"

"He's here," Fitz said, fairly certain. "Neither of us are armed. We only want to talk." That wasn't true. Both of them were armed.

Charlie started to take a few steps toward the hallway. Fitz reached for her arm and pulled her back. She tipped her head back to look at him. "You think something's wrong?"

"I think…" Fitz never got the words out because Peter showed himself at the end of the hallway. As he walked toward them, the bruises on his face and caked blood above his eye and under his nose became apparent. As he got closer, Fitz realized that Pete wasn't so much walking as he was limping. "Are you okay? What's happened to you?"

"I got the snot beat out of me. What does it look like?" Pete held onto the wall for support. When Fitz asked him if they were alone, Pete nodded. "It didn't happen here. Not that they couldn't have found me here. My assistant is out for the day. I just came in the back way. Didn't even realize until you walked in that the front door was unlocked. What do you want? As you can see I'm in no condition to help you." Peter swayed on his feet, even the wall not offering him enough support.

Fitz rushed to the man's side and helped prop him up. "We should get you to the hospital."

CHAPTER 28

"Not doing that. I can't explain what happened to me. It would trigger a call to the cops and that's the last thing I'm doing." Pete tried to shrug off Fitz but he wasn't strong enough.

"Let me walk you back to your office and we can talk."

Charlie went to the front door and flipped the lock. She turned back to Pete. "Did Judge Sinclair do this to you?"

Pete's head snapped to attention. "How'd you know?"

"I didn't until you just told me," Charlie admitted. She walked over to them and put her shoulder under Pete's arm to help Fitz walk him back to his office. He didn't resist the help from her. Pete winced and groaned with every step.

As they got to the office and eased Pete down in his desk chair, Fitz said, "You're going to need the hospital whether you want it or not. Just tell them you got mugged and you don't know who did it. The cops can't get anything out of you if you don't know. You've probably got a concussion and the way you're moving, I suspect some broken ribs."

Fitz stepped back from him and surveyed the office. The room was a match for the small waiting area in the front from the wood paneling on the walls to the red shag carpet. "What's with this office, Pete? Your private investigation business is doing well. You've got famous clients and you're bringing them to this dump?"

"Hey," Pete said, turning his head up to give Fitz a dirty look. "Don't insult a man's space. I don't bring those clients to this office. I get stop-ins off the street here. I don't need them to know how much money I'm making. I downplay it and it's worked well so far."

All that amounted to was Pete telling him that he was cheating on his taxes. Fitz held back the judgment. "We're here to talk to you about Judge Sinclair. It seems that maybe your relationship with him has soured."

Pete snorted. "You think?" He gestured for them to sit down. It seemed he was going to speak to them after all. Once they were seated, Charlie on the couch on the far wall and Fitz in the chair at the side of his desk, Pete took as deep a breath as he could, groaning in response. His hand went to his ribs. "You're right. They're broken. What do you want to know?"

Fitz clasped his hands together, his knees splayed wide. He leaned forward slightly and locked his gaze on Pete. "First, I want to know who did this to you. You said Sinclair, but I can't imagine him doing that himself."

"Yeah, he didn't. He sent some goons after me. But his message was loud and clear."

"What's the message?" Charlie asked.

Pete smirked over at her. "Not to talk about what I know. How do I know you're not here to test me?" He shifted his eyes between the two of them. "Either one of you could kill me and it wouldn't take much."

"You know I'm not here to kill you." Pete knew Fitz had been a homicide detective. That alone had to give him some comfort. "I can't account for the timing other than to say I rescued Sutton Barlow from some men who took her from Sinclair's house. We believe Sinclair was involved in that kidnapping. I suspect the men who came after you might be the same." Fitz described the two men from the cabin that he had attacked while rescuing Sutton. He saw the look of recognition on Pete's face. It was confirmation enough.

"Sounds like them. I didn't know Sutton was missing. Sinclair didn't say anything to me. He called me the other night to tell me his boy was gone and asked if he could pay me to help find him. I spoke briefly to the FBI agent in charge who told me in no uncertain terms that I would not be welcome in the middle of their investigation. They told me that if I got in their way they'd slap an obstruction charge. Sinclair told me he'd have my back and to do what I could."

It sounded like Sinclair. "Did you get involved?"

CHAPTER 28

"I'm not stupid. The FBI told me to stand down and that's what I did. I didn't take any money from Sinclair. I told him I'd snoop around a little. I told him if I found Holden he could pay me then." Pete blew out a frustrated breath. "I made a few calls. That's about all I could do without getting in the FBI's way. I may do a little shady stuff to get information, but I'm not stepping on the toes of the FBI. They will yank my license so fast that my head will spin. I'm not looking to throw my whole business away for Sinclair, even if he claims he could help me."

"I don't understand," Charlie said, drawing his attention. "He beat you up over not helping to find Holden?"

Pete screwed up his lips and shook his head. "He had other reasons to want me out of commission."

"What are those reasons?" Charlie asked directly.

Pete stared at Charlie with a look that Fitz couldn't read. He was either deciding if he could trust her or he was coming up with a good story. Charlie didn't let it bother her. She watched him carefully, waiting out his silence. As the stalemate between them dragged on for so long, Fitz nearly spoke to break the tension.

"I did some bad things for Judge Sinclair. I dug up dirt on some people I shouldn't have," Pete responded finally as his shoulders relaxed. His whole body deflated in the chair as he tipped his head back and stared up at the ceiling as he spoke, confirming exactly what they had believed. Hearing it firsthand brought a new perspective to the case. Pete went on. "Sinclair needed dirt on people so that he could blackmail them or maybe to hold over their heads so they couldn't blackmail him."

Charlie didn't let up. "Why would anyone want to blackmail Judge Sinclair?"

Pete lowered his chin and turned back to Charlie. "That I don't know and I didn't ask. I don't always ask my clients the *whys* of their situation. Sinclair wanted me to dig up dirt on people and that's what I did. I'd argue that it's not unlike what the two of you do. The only different thing is I wasn't handing what I found over to a political campaign to use against their rivals. I was handing it over to one man."

"If you were doing the job as Sinclair asked, then why would he have you attacked like this? It doesn't make a whole lot of sense to me."

"There are some things even I won't do."

Charlie gestured at him to move it along. She was growing tired of the way he was parsing out information. "What was it you wouldn't do?"

Pete remained tightlipped.

Fitz held his hand up to stop whatever was about to come out of Charlie's mouth. "Pete," he said slowly, "we are here to help you. Sinclair was behind Sutton's kidnapping. He tried to take her out to silence her based on what she knows about his business dealings." That was about all Fitz was willing to tell the man. "It sounds like you know too many things about Sinclair and he's coming after you now. We can help protect you. We want to bring Sinclair down."

Pete closed his eyes. "You think that's possible? You have no idea how connected he is."

"I know, Pete," Fitz said, hoping the undercurrent of what he was saying got the message across. "I know far more than you think. I know you were helping Sinclair dig up dirt on people. That's why we're here. I want to know exactly what you found. I need to know who Sinclair is connected to and what he's doing with the information."

Pete sat up straight and pointed to a filing cabinet pushed up against the window at the end of the couch. "Everything I've ever dug up for Sinclair is in the bottom drawer. He doesn't know I kept records of everything. He told me to hand over everything and destroy the rest. I've worked for him for so long that I assume he believed me. No one

CHAPTER 28

has come to this office to ransack it for information yet. I guess they believe this beating would be enough to silence me." Pete grew quiet for a moment. With resolution in his tone, he added, "Take all of it. If it can help you take down Sinclair, use it. Someone has to stop him. He's gotten out of control."

Fitz studied the filing cabinet and signaled for Charlie to take the files. He wasn't done with Pete. "What is it Sinclair wanted you to do that you refused?"

"You sure you want to know? Once you know it you can't unknow it."

It made Fitz all the more interested in knowing. "I'm sure," he said with conviction.

"President Ellis Mitchell has a college-aged daughter," Pete said after a moment. "He wanted me to go to the college and take some risqué photos of her. Sinclair wanted me to stalk her on campus and get the photos. If I wasn't able to get them by spying on her, then he suggested that I get someone to sleep with her and either record it or convince them to take some photos. If neither of those things worked, he wanted me to plant some drugs on her and call the cops."

All Fitz heard was Sinclair was willing to blackmail the President of the United States. His stomach dropped at the implications of that. "Do you know why he wanted you to do this?"

"This was back before he was nominated. He's been holding it over my head ever since. When he was nominated, I knew he had gotten someone else to do it. There's no way President Mitchell would have nominated him otherwise. He wanted on the Supreme Court and it didn't matter what he had to do to get that nomination, even if he had to blackmail the president. I threatened to go public with the information."

Fitz and Charlie shared a worried look. This did go all the way to the top. "Why did you refuse?"

"Not only would it not be possible – the young lady has the Secret Service all around her, and it's illegal to do something like that with anyone let alone the president's daughter – I'm not insane. I'm not going to be involved in blackmailing the president. Absolutely not. Sinclair tried to convince me and I shut it down. When the threats started, I should have walked away."

"What did you do?" Charlie asked what was on the tip of Fitz's tongue.

"I did what I had to do. I reminded Sinclair about all the dirt I had on him." Pete held his arms open wide. "This was the result. I'm as good as dead, so take those files and do what you have to do."

CHAPTER 29

The information Sinclair had hired Pete to find took up three file boxes that were now in the back of Fitz's SUV. Pete explained Sinclair had been so paranoid by any record of the investigation and the ability of hackers to gain digital information he demanded Pete go old school and keep paper files of everything. How that was going to be safer or keep the man out of prison eventually Fitz didn't understand.

He was grateful for the wealth of information Pete was willing to share. Fitz and Charlie offered to go to the hospital with him, but he declined, saying he'd call a friend to help him.

Fitz shifted his eyes to look at Charlie on her phone in the passenger seat. "What do you think about what Pete said about setting up the president's daughter? That seemed like an impossible ask."

Without looking up from her phone, Charlie responded, "Reckless. Stupid. Ill-conceived. There was no way he was going to pull it off. His daughter, Hailey, is a junior at Georgetown. She lives in a condo in an upscale area of Adams Morgan. Not where I'd have my kid if she was going to college."

Fitz took his eyes off the road to glance over at her. "There's nothing wrong with Adams Morgan. There's good nightlife over there – eclectic restaurants, clubs, and things I'd assume a twenty-year-old college-aged woman would enjoy."

Charlie dropped the phone and shifted to look at him. "That's my point. She's the president's kid. I know she has Secret Service protection, but there are lots of ways to get herself in trouble in that neighborhood. The crime isn't bad but…" Charlie didn't finish her thought.

"I think that could be possible anywhere she lived."

Charlie conceded the point. "Do we alert the president to the fact Sinclair hired someone to go after his daughter?"

A decision like that was a weighty one. Fitz had always known that about his job. The information he found for clients had a direct impact on who was elected or not. Sometimes it even stopped people from running for elected office altogether.

Fitz had been debating telling President Mitchell since leaving Pete's office. It wasn't only a matter of telling him. It was also a matter of how to gain access. "I don't know that he'd believe us. Since Pete refused, we have no idea if Sinclair went through with it or who he might have used. It's all speculation right now. All we have is Pete's word that the request was made. Then again, if someone set up Hailey, and Sinclair used the information to get Mitchell to nominate him, the point is moot. It's a done deal." Fitz glanced across the SUV to look at her as he stopped for a red light. "What do you think?"

Charlie gave him a knowing look. "I think we assume it happened and the president knows. Let's focus on what we can control."

With that tabled, Fitz asked, "What did you think about Pete overall? If this goes to court, do you think Pete would be credible on the stand?"

"He's credible enough. He had a longstanding relationship with Sinclair. He knows the man fairly well from what I can tell. He has a long track record of being a private investigator for some well-known clients. His business relationships alone lend him some credibility." Charlie grew quiet for a moment, then added, "It doesn't help Pete's got a chip on his shoulder. Of course, someone just beat him to a pulp.

CHAPTER 29

He's identified the men who did it as the same men who attacked Sutton, which means they are around. I'd say we are safe trusting Pete."

Fitz puffed out his chest. "I knew I made a good decision when I hired you. You are one of the most logical people I know."

"Some men think that's a bad quality."

Fitz turned his head sharply to look at her. "What men? Are you out there dating and haven't told me?" He wanted to ask about Burrows but held his tongue.

Charlie didn't meet his eyes. She stared straight ahead. "What does it matter if I date? When are you not screwing random women? When I was with the agency, relationships were nearly impossible. Now..." Charlie's voice drifted off and she sighed. "They just seem ridiculous."

"I can attest to ridiculous," Fitz said with a laugh. He navigated down one street and then another before pulling down an alleyway to the back of his row house. The house had come with a small carriage house in the back that had long ago been converted to a garage. He hit the button to open the door, pulled in, and cut the engine. He had detected the noticeable shift in Charlie's energy. She didn't give much away but when she was sad or contemplative, her whole mood shifted and Fitz recognized it.

He reached over and touched her arm, letting his fingertips graze her skin. "I'm here if you ever want to talk. I hope you know that. Dating sucks. I'm not good at it. I don't know what I'm doing half the time. At our age, all of it seems like a wasted effort. Half the dates I go on, I'd rather be at home drinking a beer and watching a game. Still, I'm masochistic enough to try."

That got a smile out of her. She rested her head back and turned her head slightly to look over at him. "That's what it feels like – masochistic."

Fitz started to ask a question but stopped.

"Ask it," Charlie insisted, sensing he had more to say.

"I was going to ask if you regretted not having kids."

Charlie sat up straight and kept her eye contact steady. "I don't regret it. I never had a strong desire to be a mother, so I didn't. Not that there was much occasion in my line of work. Even if that hadn't been my occupation of choice, I don't believe it's a path I would have gone down. What about you?"

Fitz had two brothers and five nieces and nephews between them. He had never talked about this with anyone but his siblings and parents. There was a catch in his voice as he spoke. "Sutton and I tried for a while but it didn't happen. We sought help from a specialist and both went through a battery of tests. I was hoping I was the issue. It turned out it was Sutton. We considered an egg donor and surrogate. The marriage was on the rocks at that point and it didn't seem like the time to try. If I'm being honest with myself, trying to get pregnant was putting a strain on us that we didn't recover from. I wanted to stop. I was fine not having kids, but Sutton kept pushing. It was too heartbreaking for her. I tried to be supportive as best I could. Nothing made it better."

Charlie reached out her hand and slipped her fingers through his, squeezing hard. "I didn't know you went through all of that. That must have been difficult for both of you. I'm sorry I've given you such a hard time about that relationship. You seem like such an odd pairing. There's a lot between you I didn't know. I rushed to judgment."

The ironic part was that Charlie hadn't rushed to the wrong judgment. What she saw between Sutton and him was exactly why the relationship hadn't worked. He didn't admit it to Charlie, but Fitz knew the relationship with Sutton had been doomed from the start. He had nearly backed out of the wedding. He squeezed Charlie's hand and thanked her for being supportive.

"It is what it is at this point. I want to make sure she's safe. Get her through this situation then put some distance between us again. You're right where Sutton is concerned, I take on too much." That was all Fitz was going to say about that. He released Charlie's hand and turned around to look in the backseat. "Could you bring these in while I keep Sutton distracted? Put them in your office for now. I don't want Sutton to know we have them. I promised Tim transparency, but I want to go through all of this first and decide what we will hand over to him."

"I assumed you weren't going with full transparency."

"I'm not," Fitz agreed with conviction. "It might be the detective still lurking in me or maybe it's some weird patriotic need to protect some people before it goes to press. I have no idea what kind of dirt Pete found and on whom he found it. For all we know, these are secrets that go back to their youth. You know the kind of dirt we dig up. I'm not going to randomly turn that over to a journalist without vetting the information first. It will be too much of a temptation for him."

"You'll get no argument from me." Charlie reached for the door handle and opened it. Before getting out, she asked, "What are you going to do with Sutton? Do you think it's safe to leave her at the house?"

Fitz got out of the SUV, opening the back door after closing the driver's door. "She's safe here and no one knows my new home address. She didn't even know I had moved, so there's no way she had told anyone about the house. I'll have a friend watch over her while I'm here." He flipped open the lid of one of the boxes and counted the files up to fifty. Some were thick, dense files and others appeared to only have a few pages in them.

"Sutton," he called after he shut off the security system and entered through the backdoor. He didn't know if she'd hear him up on the third floor. He waited until he was on the top floor before Fitz called her name again. He navigated down the hallway toward the door that separated one part of the building from the other. He knocked once on the door then turned the handle and opened it, stepping into the sitting room.

Sutton shook as she held her cellphone in her hands and tears ran down her face. Fitz resisted the urge to rush to her side. He was going to ask if everything was okay but it was evident it wasn't.

He took a few steps into the room. "What's going on, Sutton?" he asked, trying to keep his tone steady and straightforward. He didn't want to give in to whatever drama she was about to unleash on him.

Sutton raised her eyes to him. "Sinclair called me and ended the engagement."

Fitz held back what he wanted to say, which was *why would that make her sad.* "Yeah. He tried to have you killed. I would have assumed the relationship was over at that point. I don't understand the tears. You told me you were only in the relationship over the last year to build a case against him. I would think you'd be happy to be rid of him." Sutton stared at him blankly. "What am I missing here, Sutton? You're either happy to be out of an abusive relationship or you're not. If you're not, I suggest some therapy."

Sutton took three sharp breaths in and out through her nose, her nostrils flaring. "When did you get to be so cold, Connor?" She never used his first name unless she was angry. More than angry, boiling over with rage. Sutton wiped the tears from her eyes and pushed herself up. "You may not have any emotion, but I thought I was going to marry Sinclair before I realized how truly terrible he is. It was hard enough learning he was a criminal but now having this confirmation that it was him trying to have me killed. I'm sorry if my emotions are too much for you."

"Did he admit to trying to have you killed?"

"No. He tried to see me and I refused. He got angry, screaming and yelling at me. Then told me to never contact him again. I assume he

CHAPTER 29

did it to make me look like a scorned woman if I say anything now. That's probably why he suggested to the FBI that I took Holden. He was working to attack my credibility." More tears ran down her face.

There was a time when Fitz would have tried to smooth over the fight and make it better for them both. He didn't bother now. "I have some work I have to do tonight. I'm going to drop you off at the house. There's food in the fridge or we can stop on the way and pick you up some dinner." He didn't wait for her response.

Fitz turned on his heels and headed for the door, knowing when she got ready she'd follow.

The tide had turned in their relationship and it was about time.

CHAPTER 30

After getting Sutton situated at his house and showing her how to engage the alarm system, Fitz called one of his friends, Dave Shank, to ask him to swing by the house to check on her if he could. Dave had worked patrol with Fitz while the two were coming up in the police force. They had become fast friends and remained friends during their careers at D.C. Metro. Both had moved on to greener pastures.

Dave ran a million-dollar security firm that had contracts with the government, celebrities, and all the who's who in the country. His reach was vast and the position suited him. Why Dave remained living in D.C. when the man was better suited for Hollywood, Fitz didn't know. But they got together for beers a few times a month and he was glad for their continued friendship. It also didn't hurt to have someone with that kind of firepower and connections in his pocket. It was rare Fitz needed extra security – his work wasn't usually dangerous – but Dave was always there willing to lend a hand. In turn, Fitz did what he could to help Dave when the need arose. Fitz trusted Dave with his life and there was no one better suited to keep an eye on Sutton.

On the way back to the office he picked up pasta carbonara and salad for Charlie from her favorite restaurant. If he was going to make her burn the midnight oil on an unofficial, unpaid case, the least he could do was make sure she was well-fed. Charlie had texted him

CHAPTER 30

earlier that there were some wild names in the case files. She hadn't provided him with the specifics. It was enough of a tease to hurry him back to the office as quickly as possible.

Fitz stood in the doorway watching Charlie work. She had moved the files to the conference room and was deep into a file. He knew that she had heard him come in but had yet to raise her head. She was intent on finishing whatever had grabbed her attention. The smell of the pasta was making that difficult.

Charlie sniffed the air as a smile spread across her face, raising her high cheekbones ever farther up her face making her eyes narrow. She finally looked up at him. "If this is your idea of a bribe, you can influence me any day of the week," Charlie said with a wink. "Is it from Bertolucci's?"

Fitz turned the brown bag around so she could see the name and logo. "Would I get you pasta carbonara from anywhere else? They have the best chicken parm too, which is what I got. If you make some room on the table, I'll grab some plates and we can eat while you tell me what you've found so far."

Charlie went about gathering up all the files she had laid out while Fitz set the table and unpacked the bag. Once they were seated and a few bites in, she explained that she had only gone through one file box and already had the names of D.C.'s most prominent lobbyists, attorneys of all kinds from D.C.'s most well-known law firms, and other movers and shakers. "If that isn't enough, there is an entire file box just labeled *Congress*."

Fitz finished chewing what was in his mouth, not able to get it down fast enough. "Sinclair was digging up dirt on all those people? He couldn't have been taking bribes from all of them."

Charlie reasoned that was an accurate assessment. "I don't know what he was doing. Whether he was building an arsenal to blackmail them into supporting his nomination or what he had planned, it's clear he had a purpose."

"What kinds of things did Pete find?"

Charlie twirled the pasta on her fork. "Past drug convictions. Current affairs. Gambling and other debts. General misdeeds that most wouldn't want public. There's evidence that two of the married men are having same-sex affairs. It runs the gamut."

The deeper they got into the information about Sinclair the more sinister it became. There were still things that weren't making sense to Fitz. "Is there anything that stood out as particularly egregious?"

"All of it, Fitz." Charlie took a few more bites and sat back in the chair. "There's a criminal defense attorney named Nancy Gibbons. Her son, Tyler, has addiction issues. He's been in and out of rehab for the last several years. Over the last year, he's gotten himself clean and sober and back in school. Sinclair wanted Pete to buy drugs and offer it to him to get him to relapse again."

"Why?" Fitz asked his voice rising with his disgust.

"There's a note from Pete that Sinclair needed something on Nancy. He'd been insistent that Pete had to find something but no reason was given, at least not in the file. Pete noted that he tried – he dug into everything including her financials, her background, marriage, friends, business associates, former clients he could find and there wasn't anything. Her Achilles was her son's drug habit. Pete indicated in the file Sinclair wanted him to buy cocaine and try to sell it to Nancy's son and film it. The goal was to get documentation that not only had Tyler relapsed but to catch him committing a crime while doing it. Sinclair was adamant he needed something to hold over Nancy's head."

"I assume Pete said no."

Charlie shook her head. "Not exactly. Pete indicated he didn't refuse. He told Sinclair he would do it and film it if Tyler said yes. Pete never did it though. Now whether he initially was going to do it

CHAPTER 30

and something caused him to stop or maybe he couldn't get the drugs."

"You can get cocaine anywhere in D.C.," Fitz countered, gesturing toward the door. "I can walk outside to the street or make one phone call and get cocaine like that." He snapped his fingers to drive home the point. "That wasn't what held Pete up. He might not have wanted to commit a crime for the sake of helping Sinclair. It might be where he drew the line."

"I'm surprised he ever had a line."

"President Mitchell's daughter," Fitz reminded her. Charlie dismissed him with a wave of her hand. "There's a theme here, going after people's kids. I find it curious someone went after Sinclair's son in the same way. I would assume it's possible someone knew what Sinclair was up to and targeted his son for revenge."

Charlie leaned forward and took another heaping bite of pasta. "It would make sense. It seemed as if Pete was discreet in his work. He never indicated, at least in the files I read, that anyone caught him or confronted him during an investigation. I did a few internet searches to see if any of the details Pete uncovered had ever made the news. I saw a few articles here and there. For all we know Sinclair employed one of the D.C. public relations firms to plant stories on his rivals."

That was what Fitz had been expecting. There were three other judges whose names had been tossed around in political spheres about other possible Supreme Court nominations. "I expected to see Sinclair going after his rivals."

Charlie hitched a thumb over her shoulder. "The third box is full of that information. Maybe I should have started with the most relevant, but I wanted to get through these other people first. I was leaving the Congress box for you. I was going to dig into the rivals while you were doing that."

Fitz and Charlie finished dinner talking about the rest of the information she found. He cleaned up the plates, rinsing them and stacking them in the sink. He put the leftovers in the fridge and refreshed their drinks. He pulled back the tab on a Coke can and took a long sip. He looked over at the boxes. "Which one is Congress?"

"The one on top of the two boxes. Hand me the one on the bottom. That's Sinclair's rivals."

Fitz put the Coke can on the table and lifted the two file boxes, still surprised at the heft of them. The one question he hadn't asked Pete was just how long he'd been working with Sinclair. It had to have taken considerable time to gather this much information. He also should have asked Pete for an accounting of how much Sinclair paid for all of this. Fitz wasn't sure Pete would have answered the question, but he should have asked.

Fitz had to admit to himself he'd been a little thrown because of Pete's physical condition. He normally would have gone harder on him. He couldn't summon up the rage when he looked at Pete's battered and broken face.

Fitz rested the boxes on the table, pulling off the top box and sliding the other over to Charlie. He tugged off the lid and counted the files it contained – thirty-six in all. It meant Sinclair had gone after thirty-six members of Congress in this little scheme. Fitz looked down at the table feeling like he was missing something. It hit him at once. "Did you bring down any paper to take notes? I want to pull out the most relevant information. When we're done, I want to go interview some of these people. I think we should start with Nancy."

"I didn't bring anything down with me," Charlie said, tapping the side of her head. "I locked away all the pertinent information in here. You know I'm a terrible notetaker."

That was true. She had learned a long time ago when working for the CIA not to keep any notes. Anything written or recorded could be found by the enemy. The only way they'd get the information from her was torture. Charlie said she had ways of avoiding that – first and

CHAPTER 30

foremost not getting caught.

Fitz headed for the stairs and made his way to his second floor office. As he reached for the pad of paper in the top drawer, the phone rang. He checked his watch before letting it go to voicemail. At nearly nine, no one should have been in the office. His clients or possibly a new prospective client could wait until morning.

Fitz snagged a pen from the holder and had his hand on the light switch when the phone rang again. He looked back over his shoulder, giving in to the instinct to answer the call. He scooped up the receiver. "Fitz Associates," he said with a casualness as if it were mid-workday.

"Fitz, it's Senator Reed Lane. Do you have a moment?"

Fitz had done some work for Lane on his last reelection bid two years ago. The man had wanted Fitz to dig up dirt on himself to see what another oppo research could have found. Outside of a few paid parking tickets, the man was squeaky clean. The senator from Maine had run one of the more positive-minded campaigns Fitz had witnessed.

"I'm not normally in the office this late, Senator Lane. I'm in the middle of an investigation." Before Fitz asked if he could call him back tomorrow, the senator sighed loudly enough that Fitz told him to go on.

"I don't like speaking out of turn or accusing anyone of anything, but…" Lane trailed off leaving Fitz to wonder.

He eased down into his desk chair. "Go on. Please speak freely."

Lane hesitated for only a moment longer. "I received a call tonight from one of my staffers who received an anonymous tip you weren't someone anyone should associate with going forward. I was told that you had lied to the FBI and attacked Judge Sinclair. Is there any truth to these rumors?"

Fitz winced his eyes shut and cursed under his breath. Sinclair was going to try to destroy his business. He probably thought a threat like that would put Fitz out of commission, scrambling to distance himself from Sutton to save his hide. Instead, it only emboldened him. "I assure you I did not lie to the FBI. You can call Agent Josh Burrows and speak to him directly about my interactions with the FBI. I'm in the middle of a complicated case, in which the FBI is the lead. As you may have heard Judge Sinclair's son is missing and so was his former fiancée, who happens to be my ex-wife. I was merely going to Sinclair to try to find her. We had a brief confrontation, given her bloodied car was found hidden away in his garage. I'm sure Sinclair didn't tell you that though."

"I don't know who called me, Fitz."

"I do – probably one of the men I attacked in order to rescue Sutton, my ex. I'm not going to get into the specifics, Senator Lane, but if you value your reputation, you'll put some distance between yourself and Judge Sinclair. There will be some things coming out about him that you're not going to want to be associated with. You can feel free to pass that along to your colleagues who I'm sure received the same call as you did this evening."

"I see." There was a stiffness to Lane's tone that hadn't been there before. "How is the investigation coming along?"

Fitz smiled at the phone. "You know I won't disclose that information. What I find will go directly to the FBI."

"I've always trusted you, Fitz," Senator Lane said after a moment. "You were a straightshooter with me and others you worked for, not to mention your reputation at D.C. Metro. We sure appreciate that you're one of the good ones. Can you say anything about your investigation? Should we be worried?"

Fitz threw him a bone. "All I'll say is I'm looking at an extensive blackmailing operation that could rock the halls of Congress. All those with secrets might want to prepare themselves."

Senator Lane gasped. "Who is responsible for this?"

CHAPTER 30

"You might want to consider who is trying to ruin my reputation and put a stop to my investigation. The confirmation hearing is still going on and someone might have a lot to lose."

Lane grew quiet as the meaning was clear. "Please get in touch with me when you know more."

Fitz ended the call knowing he just put a bullseye right on Judge Sinclair. He didn't feel like he had an option – it was time to fight fire with fire.

CHAPTER 31

Charlie got one look at Fitz when he returned to the conference room and knew something was wrong. "What happened?" she asked as she laid the file on the table.

Fitz stood in the doorway still formulating the best course of action. He ran a hand down his stubbled face. "That was Senator Reed Lane calling to let me know Sinclair has started a smear campaign to destroy my reputation." Fitz paused and walked the short distance to the table, pulling out the chair and sitting. "Actually, he wasn't sure who called. I don't suppose it was Sinclair directly. One of Lane's staffers received an anonymous tip telling him that he should no longer associate with me going forward. He was told I lied to the FBI and attacked Judge Sinclair. He called to let me know because we had such a good working relationship. He didn't say it outright, but it sounded to me like he had trouble believing what he'd been told."

Charlie pinched the bridge of her nose. "I don't think anyone who knows you, Fitz, would believe that about you. Then again, you did attack Sinclair and lie to the FBI – all with good reason."

The corner of Fitz's mouth turned up in a wry half-smile. "You can't blame me for attacking Sinclair now that we know all of this." He gestured toward the stack of Congress files. "Is there anything on Senator Lane in there? I wouldn't think so given our investigation turned up nothing. You never know though."

CHAPTER 31

"I flipped through the files and there wasn't one on him."

That reminded Fitz of a question he'd had earlier. "Do we know if Sinclair has used any of the public relations firms here in D.C.? You know the ones that have foreign governments for clients and the shadiest of individuals." That kind of dark money was all over Washington D.C. The Saudis had hired a U.S. public relations firm to help their image after 9/11. The Libyans had hired one when Abdelbaset al-Megrahi, a Libyan intelligence officer who had been convicted of the Lockerbie Pan Am Flight 103 bombing, was up for compassionate release. While seemingly impossible to believe, there had been a short media article about the U.S. backing off their hate of Libya – or something to that effect. Fitz couldn't recall all the details. He had heard of a PR guy who had worked for Libya's Gaddafi family and even edited an article that ended up being an anti-western, anti-NATO diatribe that was sanitized down enough to make it palatable.

That kind of business alone in D.C. was one of the reasons Fitz continued the good fight. If he could shine a little light into the darkness and root out the bad, he figured he was doing some good. He'd never win the fight – that wasn't even a thought in his head. There was too much to uncover. Still, it wouldn't surprise Fitz if Sinclair had hired one of those firms.

"How would we find out if Sinclair hired one of those firms?" Charlie asked.

Fitz knew the primary six firms in D.C. that did that kind of work. None of them were close friends of his. In fact, most of the public relations folks hated Fitz for the work he did. "I don't think I'd get the information even if I wanted it. If they are trying to sanitize Sinclair's reputation, the last thing they are going to do is give me the ammunition needed to bring him down. I assume that's also how he got the idea to go after Sutton's business in the way he did."

Charlie didn't disagree with that. She didn't have any sources in the public relations firms either. People in D.C. knew what they did but most of the public was clueless. She pointed to the file box. "While I didn't see anything on Senator Lane, there is a file on Senator Austin Ford. He's been one of the most outspoken critics of Sinclair. He's also in the same party as Senator Lane, and I'm sure they have a close working relationship. You might want to start there. Given Sinclair is attacking you, we should probably follow up with all of our clients to let them know they might be getting a similar call."

Fitz knew that would have to be done. He didn't have the energy to focus on it now. "It's too late to start those calls. Let's see what Pete found on Senator Ford and go from there. He is not someone who has used our services in the past." A heavy tired feeling fell over Fitz making his shoulders slump and his arms feel like there were weights attached to them. It was either the pasta or the overwhelming feeling of how far this scandal went.

Charlie read the air change in the room. "We have to fight, Fitz. We can't give up now. I know it seems like we are up against the impossible. Too many bad guys doing too many terrible things. This is when we need to dig in the hardest and fight for what's right. Do you really want Sinclair on the Supreme Court?"

The only place Fitz wanted Sinclair was behind bars. He tried to shrug off the sense of impossibility and got down to work, pulling out the file on Senator Ford and opening it. The file wasn't as thick as some of the others. It contained some black and white photos of Ford on the right side of the file and narrative content from Pete's investigation on the left. Fitz started with the content.

Pete had started the investigation nearly eight months ago. He had received a tip from Sinclair that Ford was dating a young assistant in his office. Pete had followed Ford for several months and had captured evidence of this affair. There were photos of Ford, who was thirty-nine years old, with a young woman who looked no more than twenty-

CHAPTER 31

five. The pair were seen at restaurants, a music venue, the movie theater, and seeing a Broadway show at the Kennedy Center. Ford was unmarried and had no children. There was no reason he couldn't have been dating. The only question was, who was this woman and did she, in fact, work for Ford?

In the back of the file was a note from Pete. He had interviewed the young woman, Serena Hartly, and she admitted she and Ford were involved. She had gone to work for Ford as an administrative assistant and the two quickly got involved not long after she started working there. When pressed, Serena admitted that she had come on to Ford and that the relationship was consensual and he had not pressured her in any way. In fact, Ford had been hesitant to pursue the relationship at all and had her sign some legal document that it was a consensual relationship. Fitz didn't know what kind of legal document that would be. It was foolish of Ford, even with the legal document of consent, to be involved with a staffer.

Fitz didn't know if everything Pete had collected amounted to much, given the glowing interview Serena had given. If she didn't feel like there had been sexual harassment, and Ford went out of his way to legally state the relationship was consensual, then what was anyone going to do legally? Now the public perception of it might be something different. That might tank the man's career, which ultimately might be the point.

There was a power imbalance and that rarely led to anything good. While the relationship might be sunshine and roses now, there was no telling where it could end up. It would be Serena's reputation that would suffer more than Ford's. Possibly her job prospects as well.

Fitz flipped through page after page looking for any nugget of information that might help. He didn't find anything of value until the last page. It was a simple handwritten note from Pete that stated: *There's something bothering me about the interview with Serena. She was* lying to me about something and I don't think it was her feelings for Senator Ford. She begged me not to interview him or ask him any questions about their relationship. I didn't interview him because there was no need. She seemed almost afraid that I might question him. She showed me the legal document Ford had drawn up, so I know that's real. I can't account for the nagging in my gut. There's something I've missed.

Fitz went back to the photographs Pete had taken from the shadows. He had successfully conducted surveillance several times. All of the photos were black and white, candid shots where the couple remained oblivious to Pete's presence. Fitz wondered what it was that had him stumped.

Fitz glanced up at Charlie with her head bent over another file, strands of her hair shaken loose from her ponytail and trailing across her face. When the light hit her hair just right, it was like a glow of fire framing her face. She told him her hair was so distinct that the time she spent in the CIA, she had shaved her head because it was too hard to conceal under wigs. He understood why but it was a shame. It was her most distinctive feature. He started to ask her a question but stopped. He'd move on to another file for now.

Fitz grabbed one more file from the box and went through it start to finish. Then another and another. Some of the files amounted to nothing, others had damning information about senators and those in the House of Representatives. There was nothing too scandalous. It was run of the mill information Fitz and Charlie had uncovered about many they had investigated.

Charlie had gone through file after file as well. Not stopping until she was done. She had taken a few notes here or there but nothing that made her sit back and alert Fitz to the content. When he was done with the files in his box, he went back to the Senator Ford file, still wondering what Pete could have meant by the note.

Fitz checked the time – eleven-forty-eight. He reached for his

CHAPTER 31

cellphone. "I'm calling Pete," he said to Charlie, who seemed to be in a world of her own, engrossed in the file she was reading. The phone rang several times before a groggy voice barked that someone better be dead to be calling so late. Fitz identified himself. "I know it's late. We are going through your files and I have a question. First, did you get the medical care you needed?"

Pete sighed and asked Fitz to hold on. Rustling of blankets echoed through the phone. Pete groaned once and then twice more before getting back on the phone. "The ER doc fixed me up as best he could. Just going to take time to heal. He wanted me to make a police report but I declined. He gave me some pain pills, which is why I sound so out of it. I'm surprised the phone even woke me. This stuff knocked me out cold."

"No concussion?" Fitz had been sure that with the blows to the head Pete would have one.

"Doc said no. I guess I have a hard head in more ways than one. What's your question?"

Fitz explained the files he went through and even noted the call from Senator Lane. "Sinclair is going after me now, so we need to stop him. You said that you had a weird feeling about Serena Hartly. Tell me about that."

"Yeah that one had me stumped," Pete said and coughed twice. "I don't know, there was something off about the chick. She seemed smart enough for the job, maybe a little too smart."

"What does that mean? She was young, just out of college."

"Right, so why was she taking a job as administrative assistant when there were lots of jobs available with her communications degree? There are always job postings for communications staff. At the time of the investigation, there were at least six available in other senators' offices. I looked."

Fitz hadn't even considered that. Pete hadn't provided Serena's background in the file. "What are you suggesting?"

Pete paused and breathed heavily into the phone. "I thought you would have caught on. A honeytrap, Fitz. Someone paid Serena to seduce Ford. The only complication is she fell for him in the process and wasn't willing to turn against him."

"You don't have any proof of that," Fitz said calmly, even though he didn't think it was out of the realm of possibilities. He'd seen crazier things happen with political rivals. If Sinclair needed Ford on his side, then having something on the man was a way to do it.

"You're right, I don't have any proof." Pete coughed again and groaned how tired he was and how he needed to get back to sleep. "I'll say this and then I'm hanging up. About three weeks after I spoke to her, Ford broke up with her. Serena quit and now she's working for Dunn & Foster Agency. You know what they do, right?"

Not only was it one of the public relations firms that fronted foreign adversaries, but they were also the biggest public relations firm behind most of the scandals in D.C. Not all of the stories that came from them were true but were true enough to get coverage in some shady rags and gossip papers and websites.

"How do you know all this?"

"I went looking for more information after the fact and that's what I heard. She won't take any of my calls, so I could never confirm my suspicions. Her actions are enough to warrant further investigation." With that Pete said he had to go and hung up before Fitz could say anything else.

Fitz put his cellphone on the table and stretched his arms overhead. Knots had formed in the back of his neck and shoulders. "I need to call it a night. Did you find anything?"

Charlie raised her head and flipped the file folder closed. "Run of the mill information. Nothing too scandalous. I didn't see anything that would end anyone's career. It might be enough for Sinclair to use

CHAPTER 31

to keep someone quiet."

That amounted to what Fitz had found in his files. He explained the information he found in Senator Ford's file. "I want to speak to Serena. She's working at Dunn & Foster. Pete had his suspicions before but found it even stranger they had broken up right after he interviewed her. Then to find out where she's working now. None of it added up for Pete and I tend to agree. Pete said she wouldn't speak to him, but she might speak to us – with the right leverage."

Charlie looked over at him through her thick eyelashes. "What leverage is that? You know I can't use any of my tricks."

Fitz shook his head. He didn't expect her to pull out any of her CIA interrogation tricks on a young woman. "There's no reason why we can't lie to her. You are one of the most convincing liars I know. I say we go in there telling her what we already know. We only need her to confirm it. Otherwise, she might be facing serious legal implications."

"Let's come up with a workable plan."

Fitz didn't know why but he felt like they were finally making some progress.

CHAPTER 32

The next morning Fitz met Charlie in front of an eight-story neo-Gothic office building with a concrete French limestone exterior and punched black windows on D.C.'s famous K Street. The street was home to lobbyists, advocacy groups, and public relations firms. K Street was a major thoroughfare in Washington, D.C., and some would argue the real center of power in the district.

Fitz held two coffees in his hand – a basic black coffee with a little milk for him and a salted caramel mocha with whipped cream and a caramel drizzle for Charlie. How she could consume that many calories and sugar in a drink and still stay in fighting shape he didn't understand. Either she had the metabolism of a hundred men or she restricted her calories when he wasn't around.

Fitz hated to admit it, but Charlie remained in better physical shape than he could ever dream of being. She ran at least five miles a day and hit the weights four to five times a week.

At a few minutes to seven, just as the street started to fill up with people getting to their offices, Charlie rounded the corner. She had black pants and a scooped neck shirt on with her Army green utility jacket over the top. Charlie rarely worried about formality. It was one of the many things Fitz liked about her.

He held the coffee out to her and she took it, knocking back a long sip. "I don't know how you can consume that much sugar."

CHAPTER 32

Charlie eyed him over the rim, having heard this from him more times than either of them could count. "I missed you on my run this morning," she said giving him a knowing glance. Charlie reached out and patted his stomach, which wasn't as taut as it used to be. "I think if either of us needs to watch our sugar it's you."

"Fair enough," Fitz said dryly, the message having been received. "Are you ready for this interview?"

"Born ready."

"I haven't seen her come in yet. There might be another entrance. Do you want to head up to the office and wait outside or down here?" Fitz watched down one side of the street and then turned to look at the other.

"There she is," Charlie said, tugging on Fitz's sleeve. She pointed down K Street to the woman with a mane of blonde hair walking toward them. She had on high heels, a tight skirt and blouse that strained the front buttons. Her hips popped with every step. It was an unnatural gait practiced over time to draw attention.

Fitz raised his eyes from her hips back to her face. "She certainly wants people to notice her." He lowered his gaze to Charlie who was also watching Serena walk towards them. "Is it me or does she look older than twenty-something?"

"That's exactly what I was thinking," Charlie said as she sipped more of her coffee. "She has that young appearance where she might be in her twenties if you don't look too closely at her neck and her hands. I've met women like her before. She could easily get away with looking like an older twenty-five-year-old while being well into her thirties."

Fitz noticed the lines creasing Serena's neck at her open collar shirt. "You think this was a setup?"

"It's looking like that," Charlie said wryly. "Men aren't that smart when they see something they want. They say women are the emotional ones. Put a hot woman they want to screw in front of them and most will fall for just about anything."

"Ms. Hartly," Fitz said, moving to stand in front of her and half blocking her path to the front door. He didn't want to appear to be too intimidating but wanted to get the point across.

Serena stopped cold and eyed him. "Can I help you?" She turned her attention to Charlie who stood a few feet from Fitz. "Are you with him?"

Charlie stepped closer to her, keeping her posture more casual. She introduced them both. "We were hoping to catch you before going into the office, Serena. We don't want to cause any trouble with your boss. This is a sensitive matter."

Serena's eyes darted back and forth, assessing both of them carefully. "What's this in reference to? Who did you say you're with again?"

Charlie hadn't. She had only mentioned their names. Fitz extended his hand and she tentatively shook it. "I'm with Fitz Associates. We are a political opposition research firm, among other things."

"What are those other things?"

"Investigations. Bringing information out of the dark and into the public eye. Uncovering the truth," Fitz said with an air of casualness. "I like to right wrongs, Serena. I think you've been hiding a few things." He leaned into her then. "Like the real reason for your relationship with Senator Ford, for instance."

Serena started to shake her head and deny the relationship.

Charlie stopped her before she dug herself too deep. "We saw the photos. We know the relationship happened and we suspect we know why. The information is going to come out one way or another. Your best bet is to talk to us directly and let us help protect you. If the wrong people get hold of this information, you're risking everything. I assume that's one of the lessons you learned working in public relations. It's better to be in front of the story instead of on the back end of it. Things might get complicated for you."

CHAPTER 32

Serena tipped her head back and looked up at the building. "I need to call my boss and tell him I'm going to be late." She pulled the phone out of her Chanel purse and made the call, telling the person on the other end that she was detained this morning in an off-site meeting and that she'd be into the office as soon as she could. Serena assured the person she didn't have anything pending. When the call ended, she dropped the phone back into her purse. "There's a coffee shop around the corner. We can speak there."

Once they were seated in the farthest available four-table in the back of the coffee shop, Serena asked, "How do you know I was involved with Austin?"

It didn't escape Fitz's attention she had used his first name instead of the more formal Senator Ford. "We are investigating a case and your relationship with him came to our attention. I'm here to get your side of it because from where I'm sitting something doesn't add up."

"It wasn't sexual harassment if that's what you're thinking." When Fitz told her it wasn't, she drew her features into a question. "Then why does the relationship matter to you?"

Fitz turned to Charlie, knowing they were going to get into the meat of it sooner than planned. Serena needed less warming up than they had speculated.

"Was it supposed to look like sexual harassment?" Charlie asked directly, not mincing her words.

Serena's eyes grew wide with understanding. "Why would you ask me that?"

"You're not twenty-five and you're not a first-time staffer at Dunn & Foster."

The lines in Serena's forehead creased. "Why would you say that?"

Fitz didn't know if she was trying to buy time or was honestly surprised that they had picked it up accurately. Before he could respond, Charlie continued. "For one thing, the lines on your neck and forehead. You've taken great care of your skin but the early signs of aging are obvious." If that stung, Serena didn't show it. "If I was suspicious after I got a better look at you, the way you spoke to the person in your office was a dead giveaway. You lied about where you were going with ease. You were letting them know instead of asking for permission. No first-time staffers at a firm like Dunn & Foster would have carried off the conversation with that level of confidence." Charlie rested her coffee cup on the table. "Let's cut through all of this, Serena. You're wasting our time. I want to know who hired you to seduce Austin Ford and why?"

Serena released a breath that it seemed like she had been holding for a long time. Her shoulders slumped forward. She answered the second part of the question first. "I failed in what I set out to do. Austin was far too smart to fall for it and too kind to entrap. I fell in love in the process and when he learned the truth, he rightly ended things with me."

"What is the truth?"

Serena folded her hands on the table. "Exactly what you said. I was hired to seduce him and make it look like sexual harassment. I was also hired to spy on his office and see who he wanted for Supreme Court nominee. As you know a lot of names were being thrown around and our client wanted the insider track."

"Might your client have also wanted you to sway his thoughts on the matter?" Charlie suggested and while she hesitated, Serena nodded. "Who did your client want as the Supreme Court nominee?"

"Was it Judge Sinclair?" he finally asked when Serena didn't respond.

"How did you know that?" Her voice had risen an octave. She quieted quickly realizing how loud she had been. Serena ducked her head low and whispered, "I was told no one knew. I never even told Austin. I refused to tell him who hired me. I only told him that I had been hired to entrap him into a sexual harassment case. Given the

CHAPTER 32

document he made me sign and the fact that I had fallen in love with him, I told him there was no way I could do that to him. I think he broke up with me more because I wouldn't tell him who had hired me rather than because of what I was there to do. I think he might have forgiven that."

She still hadn't answered their question or confirmed what Fitz had said. He wasn't going to let it go. "Was it Judge Sinclair who hired you?"

A worried look fell over her face. "I could get fired if anyone found out."

Some would have taken that as confirmation. Fitz needed her to say the words. "Did Judge Sinclair hire you or Dunn & Foster?" When she didn't respond, Fitz raised his voice and pushed her harder. "If you can't tell me the truth, then maybe we call a friend of mine at the D.C. Metro police station and we can get to the bottom of it. What you did was a crime. Do you understand that?"

Serena froze, her eyes as big as saucers. "I didn't know it was criminal."

"What did you think would become of the information? It was going to be used to blackmail someone, a senator no less. It's a federal offense." Fitz didn't know if it would rise to that level. It would take a whole lot to bring those to justice. The threat was enough to shake Serena into action.

"Judge Sinclair hired Dunn & Foster. He's been a long time client. Longer than I've been employed there. I was supposed to seduce Austin and sway him into being supportive of Judge Sinclair's nomination, giving him an easier confirmation hearing. The sexual harassment was just back-up in case things didn't go his way."

"Whose idea was this?" Charlie asked.

"My boss came to me with the plan and had greased some wheels for me to be hired. I don't know the process. All I know is I was supposed

243

to be twenty-five, fresh out of college, and had a new driver's license with my new age. I didn't think I had much choice in the matter. It was take the gig or get fired," Serena said and Fitz wasn't sure he believed that. "Look, I didn't know what I was doing was illegal. We were trying to get the best outcome for our client. That's about it. I fell in love in the process. I got burned and have to live with the result of that."

Fitz didn't care all that much about her feelings. "Why did you end up telling Senator Ford?"

"I was in love with him and he asked me to move in with him," Serena said with sadness in her voice. "He knew all along I was older than I said. He questioned why with my college degree I'd be seeking a job there. I said I was trying to get into politics and had to work my way up. I talked to him about his image and such. He knew he could use me differently. We had a real plan for the future. I knew I couldn't go forward in the relationship without telling him the truth."

Fitz had to give her credit for that. "He ended it right after?"

"Immediately." She lowered her eyes to the table. "He said he couldn't trust me and I understood. As hard as it was, I understood. He hasn't taken my calls since."

"What did you tell your boss? Sinclair?"

Serena raised her head and looked Fitz right in the eyes. "I told them Senator Ford wouldn't take the bait. I said we had developed a friendship but he wouldn't cross the line. I assume the photos you saw were taken by a private investigator." Fitz confirmed they were. "He never told me who he was working for and I didn't give him much information."

Fitz had no idea if she was in danger. "I'm going to give you a piece of advice. Judge Sinclair isn't to be trusted. His people can't be trusted. If I were you, I'd take some vacation time and get out of D.C. for a while. The photos I saw showed a close relationship. If I know you're

CHAPTER 32

lying, so does he."

Serena paled at the information. "You think I'm in danger."

"We know you're in danger. You're one pawn among many in this game," Charlie said and urged her to leave. "Call in sick. Work from someplace else. Tell your bosses you have a sick relative. Do whatever you have to do to ensure your safety."

Fitz and Charlie left Serena sitting at the table on her phone coming up with a plan with her sister to get her out of D.C. If they had accomplished anything, it was to confirm what they already knew – Sinclair was going to buy his Supreme Court seat and he didn't care who got in his way.

CHAPTER 33

After securing the story from Serena, Fitz wasn't quite so ready to go back to his office. They had a mid-day meeting with Nancy Gibbons and a few hours to spare. Once they were back outside, Fitz shielded his eyes from the sun. "I want to speak to Senator Ford and see what he *really* knows. I want to tell him who set him up."

"I think that's a good idea," Charlie said with some slight hesitation in her voice, drawing his attention to her. When Fitz pressed her she added, "Do you think he already received a call from Sinclair's people alerting them to the fact that you are causing trouble?"

Fitz had already considered that. "I'd rather meet the man in person and address it head on than hide."

"This is why I love working with you." Charlie was already on her phone searching for Senator Ford's office address.

While she was doing that Fitz was stuck on one thing about their interview with Serena – she never asked Fitz who had hired them. It was possible she already knew or had been so stunned that they had found out about the plan that she hadn't questioned it. Fitz didn't believe she was as naïve as she had come across.

Once Charlie found Ford's address in Russell Senate Office Building, they were on their way. It was a little less than a two mile walk that took longer than usual as they had to dodge foot traffic at that hour

CHAPTER 33

of the morning.

They arrived at the building and approached the front desk manned by a United States Capitol Police officer. Fitz flashed both his driver's license and his investigative credentials. "Butch working this morning?" he asked as the officer handed the identification back.

"You know Butch?"

"I used to be a homicide detective with D.C. Metro before branching out on my own."

The young officer snapped his fingers. "That's why you look familiar. No, Butch isn't working this morning. He's started taking afternoon shifts here. He's over at the Hart building in the morning. Who you here to see?"

"Senator Ford." Fitz leaned down on the counter. "Listen, I know I technically need an appointment. I uncovered some personal information about Senator Ford and rushed right over." Fitz winked at the young man, hoping the meaning was implied. "It's information the senator wouldn't want public. I'm trying to prevent that from happening and there was no one answering his phone when I tried calling. I assume I beat his staff here."

The young officer pointed toward the ceiling. "They are up there. Not sure why they aren't answering their phones."

"I don't know." Fitz shrugged. "If I don't get up there and get them this information and it goes public, all our heads are going to roll, especially if Senator Ford finds out I was here and could have prevented it."

The officer didn't respond to Fitz, he gestured toward Charlie. "I need to see your identification." After she slipped it over to him, she reiterated Fitz's earlier point. The officer hesitated for only a moment and then let them go. "I'm only saying yes because I know you from television. You're the one who stopped that serial killer. If you say you have something for Senator Ford, I believe you."

Fitz rapped his knuckles on the desk and thanked him. He knew the young officer could lose his job, but Fitz wasn't going to do anything that could make that a possibility. With his badges in hand, they jogged up the stairs and found Ford's office with ease.

Fitz took the lead with Charlie bringing up the rear as they entered the office. A young staffer sat at a reception desk. She smiled up at them as they entered. "Can I help you?"

Fitz had kept his credentials out and showed them to the young woman who barely glanced at them. "I don't have an appointment, but it's important I speak to Senator Ford." He had no idea if the man was in the office. Beyond the reception desk off to the right was a closed door Fitz assumed belonged to the senator. A light shone brightly behind it.

"Let me see if he'll speak to you," the young woman started to say when the door creaked open.

"I'll speak to him," Senator Ford said as she had the phone halfway up to her ear. Senator Ford, who had a thick head of dark hair, bright blue eyes, and movie-star good looks, stepped out of his office and gestured toward Fitz and Charlie to follow him. "I had a feeling I'd be seeing you. Your reputation procedes you, Fitz. I don't believe I've met your companion."

Charlie walked past the reception desk across the room to Senator Ford and extended her hand. "Charlotte Doyle. Most people call me Charlie, sir. How did you know we'd be here?"

"Senator Lane said you might be. I received quite a distressing call from him last night. That was right after I received another call impeaching Fitz's reputation. I was told not to believe a word he said because he was under FBI investigation. A call to the FBI dispelled that quickly."

Fitz extended his hand and was surprised by the strength of the senator's grip. "If you still have questions, you can reach out to Agent

CHAPTER 33

Burrows."

"No need," Ford said and yelled to his administrative assistant to hold his calls. To Fitz and Charlie, he explained, "It's a quiet day here today. Most of my staff isn't in until later. Out at meetings, reading policy, and such. You picked a good day to stop by."

"It wasn't planned," Fitz said as he followed Ford into his office. The senator went behind his desk and Fitz and Charlie pulled over chairs from the nearby table. Once they were seated, Fitz didn't waste any time. "We met with Serena this morning and she informed us of her interaction with you."

"Did she," he said, pursing his lips. "What exactly did she tell you?"

Fitz detailed what Serena had told them, leaving nothing out including that Ford had ended the relationship when she told him what she was doing.

Ford absorbed the information without a reaction. He watched Fitz carefully and nodded twice during the information to confirm accuracy.

When he was done, Fitz added, "My understanding is that even though you asked her who was behind this she refused to tell you."

"That's true. She refused to tell me. I had my suspicions but it was never confirmed. Did she disclose that information to you?"

"We knew going into the meeting with her," Charlie said, surprising him. "We went to Serena to confirm what we already suspected. We are in possession of a file that was created about you and Serena by a local private investigator who was hired to investigate you. The photos were supposed to help provide evidence. We don't believe the private investigator knew the whole thing was a setup. He was duped right along with you. He was suspicious of Serena and passed that information onto us."

Ford raised an eyebrow. "There are photos?"

"All of the photos were of the two of you in public. There's nothing...

intimate," Fitz said, finding the right word.

"Good to know my bare behind isn't going to end up on a porn site." Ford offered the sarcastic words with a shake of his head. "All of what you're saying is accurate. I know I shouldn't have engaged in any kind of relationship with a staffer, let alone one I believed to be just out of college in her first job. I…" He sighed, not finishing his thought.

"Didn't believe she was twenty-five," Charlie said, offering him the words. When Ford nodded, she went on. "To be fair, she doesn't look or act twenty-five."

Ford agreed with that. "She had the confidence of a forty-year-old woman as well as the intelligence of someone who'd been working for a long time in public relations. I was skeptical from the start."

"Did you interview her for the job?" Fitz asked.

"No. Someone else on my staff takes care of that. One of my other admins was out on maternity leave and had decided not to come back. Serena was hired shortly after." Ford brushed strands of hair off his forehead that only fell back a moment later. "Serena didn't act like a new hire either. She came in and practically ran the place overnight. She wasn't shy about taking on work or finding reasons to come into my office. She flirted with me immediately. That should have been my first red flag. I found her easy to talk to and fun to be around. She lightened up the office. Everyone liked working with her. Some of the staff were sad to see her go. I couldn't give much of an explanation. I kept our relationship out of the office, but it was hard to hide it in public."

"Serena said that you were to the point of moving in together. Is that true?" Charlie asked.

"I was in love with her. I thought, even with the office complication, I had found the woman of my dreams. She was going to be involved in my next campaign and was giving me great advice. It was hard to believe she was twenty-five. It was one of the things I was overlooking

CHAPTER 33

to be in a relationship with her. I didn't flirt back with her because she's beautiful or young. Her age and the fact she worked for me initially turned me off. It's one of the reasons I had her sign legal documents."

"That's what saved you," Fitz said, knowing it was time to move on to the part that Ford didn't know. He was sure this was going to be most difficult for him to hear. "While you're aware of the sexual harassment entrapment what you're not aware of is the other reason Serena was sent here. I'd say it was the real reason and the sexual harassment was a backup."

"Please go on. I'm all ears."

"She was here to help the nomination process for Judge Sinclair. That's Dunn & Foster's client." Ford offered no reaction. Fitz couldn't read his expression because the man's face didn't register one. "Serena was sent here to encourage you to be on board with Judge Sinclair as the pick for the Supreme Court and help his confirmation process go more smoothly. She was also here to seduce you and ensure that if you didn't get on board with Sinclair that there would be leverage to make sure you did."

Ford's mouth dropped open. He couldn't hide his reaction but recovered quickly. He shifted his eyes to the side as if trying to process the information and all its implications.

Charlie put her hand on the desk and leaned forward. "I know this might be difficult to hear. There is scandal all around us in D.C., but even I have to admit this seems to be next level. I'm not sure if it makes you feel better but you weren't the only person targeted. We have files and files on your colleagues in Congress, criminal defense attorneys, lobbyists, and other people Sinclair was going after for one reason or another. People were paying him for his influence."

Ford's head snapped sharply to the side to make direct eye contact with her. "On the bench? Are you suggesting people were paying him

MIDNIGHT JUDGE

off to make court cases go their way?"

Fitz hadn't necessarily planned to get into all of that. "We are still trying to uncover the full scope of this. We believe that's part of what Sinclair has been doing for a long time. His fiancée, Sutton, is the one who uncovered the scheme initially. She has been investigating it with a journalist."

Ford lurched forward. "The media is involved?"

"Not the part about you," Fitz assured him. "We have not and will not share that with them. Charlie and I were the ones who connected with the private investigator and he handed over the files. The journalist and Sutton are not aware of what we have uncovered in the files or your connection."

Charlie agreed with him. "I don't like the idea of the media being involved any more than you do. That said, we don't know how high this goes in government. We have no idea the level of Sinclair's reach and it might take breaking a news story for the FBI to take this seriously."

Ford held his hand up to stop them. "I'm not sure I'm following all of this. Wasn't Sutton the woman accused of kidnapping Sinclair's son who is still missing?"

Fitz explained his former relationship with Sutton. "I rescued her from her kidnappers and she has already spoken to Agent Burrows. She had nothing to do with Holden Sinclair's disappearance. The child is still missing and we aren't sure how it all connects to what Sinclair was doing. Maybe someone is getting some retribution. It's possible they are blackmailing him for the information he's found on others. I simply can't make sense of that part of it. There seem to be two factions at work here, opposing each other."

Senator Ford leveled a look at them. "And you're in the middle."

"It would seem that way," Fitz agreed.

"Do you have any leads on who took Holden Sinclair?"

CHAPTER 33

Fitz shook his head. "It's not my investigation. The FBI is handling that and hasn't shared much with me." Fitz thought better of getting into the whole sexual assault setup.

Before Fitz could say more Senator Ford asked, "Why are you coming to me with all this information?"

Fitz hadn't been ready for that question. He started to rush an answer and then slowed himself down, giving it a more thoughtful and truthful response. "I suppose I know you're not in Sinclair's pocket and you've already said publicly that you're not in favor of his confirmation. You've been toughest on him during the hearings. You're young, hungry, and want to make a name for yourself. I don't wield the kind of power you do. This will eventually hit the media and I figured I'd give you a chance to be on the right side of this. We are going to need help to bring him down. I don't trust anyone in D.C. but I'm willing to extend you a lifeline." Fitz hadn't known his answer until he spoke it aloud. But that was why he was there.

Ford rested his elbows on the table, lacing his fingers together. "You know my father was a senator for nearly forty years. I've been running around the halls of Congress since I was a child. I might be young but I'm not green. I'm also well-connected." After a few beats, he looked right at Fitz. "Whatever you're doing to bring down Sinclair, you have my full support."

CHAPTER 34

Before leaving the office, Fitz assured Senator Ford he'd be in contact with him as soon as he had more information. The senator provided Fitz with his personal cellphone number for easier access.

As they were walking toward Nancy Gibbons's office, as if reading his thought, Charlie said, "If Senator Ford truly wants to help us, he should try to set up a meeting for us with President Mitchell to see if he's been compromised."

Fitz agreed with that. "I believe Senator Lane is on our side as well." He didn't know who else he'd be able to trust. "I was serious when I told Ford I wasn't planning to tell Timothy and Sutton about the files in those boxes. Sutton does not need to know, and I don't trust what Timothy will do with the information. I feel a sense of responsibility to protect the information now that it's in our possession."

"I couldn't agree with you more. Timothy is expecting us to be researching Sinclair's background. We are going to need to get him that information if you expect to keep the ruse up."

Fitz cursed to himself. He'd forgotten all about that. "Do you want to head back to the office and start that while I speak to Nancy alone?"

"I thought you'd never ask." Charlie stopped in the middle of the sidewalk, stepping to the side as she pulled out her phone. She texted a few documents to Fitz. "This is everything you need to speak to Nancy.

CHAPTER 34

I saved the files last night in case we needed to refer to anything. What do you want to know about Sinclair's earlier life?"

"Anything that will help." Fitz saved the documents then looked up at her. "There must have been a turning point when he decided to go down this road of blackmail. He knows we are onto him, so feel free to call anyone you need to call – classmates, law professors, anyone you can find. The more ammunition we have, the better. To take down someone of Sinclair's stature, it's going to take everything and the kitchen sink. This is more than just his Supreme Court confirmation. I want him to pay for what he's done."

Charlie didn't doubt his resolve but the skepticism on her face spoke volumes.

Fitz walked the rest of the way to Nancy's office, looking over his shoulder more than once, trying to suppress the feeling of being watched. It had started after leaving Senator Ford's office, even though he hadn't seen anyone on the street who might be following him. For all he knew, Sinclair probably had a whole stable of security experts and private investigators who'd be willing to tail Fitz's every move.

As he got closer to Nancy's office, Fitz ducked inside a coffee shop, asked for the bathroom, and headed to the back. He watched to see if anyone followed him in and even though no one else came into the shop after him, he pushed open the double swinging doors marked for staff.

The room had rows and rows of supplies. He cut down one side, went to the left, and walked right into an upturned plastic crate with a young man slumped on top of it. He had his back against the wall and a cap pulled low.

The kid tipped his head back, squinting up at Fitz. "You can't be back here, man." He had the glassy-eyed look of someone who'd recently gotten high.

"I'm a private investigator," Fitz lied with ease. "I need to head out the back way to the alley. Where's the door?"

"Over there," he pointed around a tall display of paper products. As Fitz started to walk off, the kid yelled to his back. "I wanted to be a private investigator for the longest time."

Fitz glanced over his shoulder. "Get sober and get your license. It's not that hard." Then he left without sticking around to give career counseling. Fitz found the exit and pushed it open, hoping the alarm didn't sound. He was home free in the alleyway behind the building without anyone being the wiser.

Fitz kept watching behind him as he cut through the maze of alleys. He got five buildings away and then cut up an alley that ran in between two buildings that would take him back to the street. He looked in both directions and didn't see anyone. If someone had been following him, Fitz hoped he'd left them back near the coffee shop waiting for him to come out the front door. The last thing he wanted to do was bring any more trouble to Nancy Gibbons, who seemed as if she'd already been dealing with enough because of her son's addiction.

Fitz entered the twelve-story glass structure, walked past an empty concierge desk, and headed right to the elevator. He stood in front of the directory and searched for the name of Nancy's law firm. After finding it listed for the sixth floor, he hit the elevator button and rode up to the floor alone. He stepped out of the elevator expecting to be in a hallway but was smack in the middle of a bustling office. There were a few chairs not far from the elevator Fitz assumed was a waiting area, except on that day it was empty.

He walked to the reception desk and told the young woman behind it he was there to see Nancy Gibbons. "She's expecting me," he said double checking the time on his phone. He was about five minutes early.

The young woman gave him directions to her office and asked if she should walk him there. Fitz declined and went to the left of the

CHAPTER 34

desk down the long hallway. Black and white framed art of historic courthouses and monuments in D.C. hung on the walls. The office had a contemporary clean feel to it that Fitz liked.

He found the door with her name on it and knocked once. Someone shouted for him to enter. He assumed he'd come face to face with Nancy herself but it was her assistant. She rose from her desk and knocked on an inner door and opened it for Fitz to enter.

Nancy stood with her back to him as she looked out of the floor-to-ceiling windows behind her large mahogany desk. It gave Fitz a moment to assess her. She stood about five-foot-five and had short dark hair and a trim body. Her blue suit jacket was tossed over the back of her chair and the matching skirt went to her knees. Her patterned silk blouse was a nice contrast to the monotone color of the suit.

"Ms. Gibbons," Fitz said as she turned to face him. Her angular features defied her age. Fitz knew her to be fifty-five but the woman didn't look a day over forty. "Thanks for meeting with me today. I'm sorry for being so cryptic on the phone." Fitz had only told her enough to secure the meeting – that it was about her son – without going into full details about why he needed to see her.

"Has Tyler done something?" Nancy asked, telling Fitz to sit.

He realized his mistake and apologized. "I didn't mean to make you concerned. I'm in the middle of an investigation and your name and Tyler's addiction came up. I wanted to make you aware you were being targeted. I didn't think it prudent to say much over the phone."

"Of course," she said and went to her desk. "I wasn't aware there was an investigation involving me. Tyler has been in trouble with the law in the past. I was concerned he'd gotten himself into trouble again."

"I hadn't thought it through when I called you." Fitz apologized for making her worry. "Where is your son now?"

"California. I sent him to live with my sister. We had some trouble a while back. People were harassing him and it was better to change his environment. I wanted him out of D.C. I didn't know how else to keep him safe." Nancy laid her palms flat on the desk. "I thought it better to send him away and not risk the temptation he was experiencing here."

"People were trying to get him to use again," Fitz said to Nancy's surprise. "That's why I'm here. Did you ever find out what that was about?"

Nancy shook her head. "I assumed he got in with the wrong crowd. He had been doing well for several months after his last rehab stint. He assured me this time it would stick. He was doing incredibly well. He'd gone back to school and had a part-time job. He was still living at home with me and I was able to monitor his progress. I don't know if you know anyone with addiction issues."

Fitz hadn't. "I was a D.C. Metro homicide detective for much of my career. While it's never impacted my personal life, I've seen it professionally. I know that it's a disease. I've seen the damage it can do to entire families."

Nancy chewed on her bottom lip, water filling her eyes. "I'm sorry," she said wiping a tear away. "It's unprofessional of me to cry."

"No, please," Fitz said. "I can't imagine what you've gone through. I don't have children, but I know I'd do whatever I could to help or protect my child. One of the hardest things about addiction is how much out of your control it is. Your son has to want to change for it to change and even then it's a battle."

Nancy offered him a sad smile. "You do understand then." She drew into herself, growing quiet for a moment. "You said there was an investigation into my son. You know that they were trying to get him to use again. Is this connected to a big federal drug case?"

"It's not about that. It's not even technically about drugs. That was just the weakness used to target you. If it makes you feel better, you and your son weren't the only ones targeted." Fitz gave her a brief overview of the case without mentioning Sinclair. Fitz explained

CHAPTER 34

about Pete's role and the boxes of files with blackmail information they had been given. "The private investigator has files and files of people he was surveilling and those that were being set up. The goal was to make your son relapse and get evidence of that. Whether it was him using or buying drugs and committing a crime, the goal ultimately was to use the information to blackmail you."

"Why would someone want to blackmail me? Was this a former client of mine?"

"That's what I'm here to find out," Fitz said evenly. "Do you know Judge Harvey Sinclair? He's a federal—"

"I know who he is," Nancy said, interrupting him, her tone tinged with anger. "I went to law school with him and later had some odd interaction with him. How is he involved?"

Fitz wanted to answer her question with a question to find out about that *odd* interaction. He'd give information now in the hope of gaining her trust and getting the full story. "It's Sinclair who is behind all of this. I believe he's been doling out favors for payment. As a result, he's been blackmailing people and trying to set people up to have something on them. He's amassed a small fortune in offshore accounts." Fitz explained to her about his son's disappearance and Sutton's kidnapping. "I didn't know the full scope of this until I rescued my ex-wife. He was going to have her killed."

Nancy sat stone-faced through it all, not shocked by what Fitz explained. "Why haven't you gone to law enforcement with this? Surely, the FBI would be able to do something."

"For two reasons," Fitz said holding up two fingers. "First, I don't know Sinclair's reach. When we bring it to the FBI I want the case locked down so tight that Sinclair can't wiggle free. For all I know, I could end up telling someone who'd make all of this go away. Secondly, I don't fully understand the scope of the case yet. I only got the files yesterday from Sinclair's private investigator, who was severely beaten.

MIDNIGHT JUDGE

Sinclair started asking him to do things he wasn't comfortable with and so he backed out. He was sent a message so he turned the files over to me. I'm also aware of a public relations firm working with Sinclair that on at least one occasion was willing to set up a senator for sexual harassment to ensure the Supreme Court confirmation goes smoothly. The case is unfolding like peeling an onion. I pull back one layer to find more. In the meantime, Sinclair is working to discredit me before I get to everyone. Help me to understand your interaction with him. You said it was odd."

Nancy took a deep breath. "It makes more sense now. All of it. I'm not sure how I didn't see this sooner." She spun around in her chair to a filing cabinet, tugged out the middle drawer, grabbed a file, and spun back. "I can't show you what's in here because it's a client's file. I can read you my notes." Nancy flipped open the file and detailed the time and date of phone conversations she had with Sinclair. He was hinting around about helping her secure an acquittal for one of her clients, a high-profile client accused of money laundering.

"Was he mob connected?" Fitz asked, knowing she wasn't going to tell him the client's name.

"No. But I came to learn later that he's the son of one of Sinclair's friends. He never came out directly and said he could get me the acquittal, but he said enough that I understood the meaning."

"Did he want payment?"

"We never got that far." Nancy closed the file, her expression strained. "I was clear with him that under no circumstances would I risk my career with something like that. If the client wanted to find another attorney, they could. I wasn't going to do anything to risk my license. The client moved on to another attorney and was acquitted. I don't know exactly what Sinclair did. I can only assume he did something. I thought about going to that judge and the prosecutor, but I had no evidence. It was a wild accusation to make with nothing

CHAPTER 34

to back it up."

It made sense to Fitz why Tyler was targeted. "If you were to ever come forward with what you know, he'd have ammunition to keep you quiet. Tyler never gave in and you protected him by sending him away. Sinclair was thwarted in his plan."

Nancy folded her hands on top of the file. "I don't know that my statement to the FBI will amount to much given I have no proof. I'm willing to give a statement whenever you're ready."

"Thank you," Fitz said as he stood. "You'll be a big help in lending credibility to this case."

Even if the FBI never spoke to Nancy, it was confirmation enough for Fitz about what Sinclair was doing.

CHAPTER 35

Fitz had just made it back outside when his cellphone chimed alerting him to a text. He stepped out of the way of foot traffic and pulled his phone from his pocket. Fitz read the words twice, taking a moment to realize that it was from Nancy. She told him that Harriett Silva would be calling him within the hour with more information about Sinclair when they were students in law school. She informed Fitz that Harriett had some information about Sinclair's past he might find helpful.

Fitz had only just put his phone back in his pocket when a van squealed to a stop on the street. As if watching a movie he was suddenly a part of, the side door slid open, and a man with a gun pointed right at Fitz appeared. He shouted for him to get in the van.

When Fitz stalled, the man screamed, "I said now unless you want someone to die!"

Fitz glanced to his left then to the right. People had stopped in their tracks. The man could open fire at any of these people and they'd drop right where they stood. Fitz had no time to reach for his weapon. "You want money?" he asked, knowing that wasn't what they wanted.

"Get in," the man with a black ballcap pulled low over his forehead instructed through a clenched jaw. When Fitz still made no effort to step toward the van, he leaned out. "If you do what we say, we won't hurt you. We're on the same side, but you're getting in our way."

CHAPTER 35

"Okay," he said slowly. "There are people who know where I am. If I'm not back to my office within the hour they will come looking for me. And trust me, you don't want that to happen."

"Get in," he said again, gesturing with the gun.

Fitz stepped toward the van and pulled himself in as it sped off before his feet were fully inside. The man with the gun slammed the door shut as they were halfway down the block. The inside of the van had a bench seat that faced the back doors of the van. It appeared to have been retrofitted in the space as did the shades that had been pulled down on the back and side windows. The black rubber floor liner was littered with crumbled-up fast food bags.

Fitz dropped down on the bench seat, turning his head to see behind him. There was no window or anything for him to see the driver. He turned back to the lone man in the back of the van with him. Fitz had expected there to be others. "What do you want? We could have met at a coffee shop to talk. This…" Fitz gestured with his hand. "Seems a little dramatic for my taste. You said we are on the same side. Of what?"

The man dropped down to his knees, keeping the gun pointed at Fitz. The way he was crouching on his haunches was too much to withstand the sharp turns and stop-and-go of city traffic.

"Why are you investigating Harvey Sinclair?"

Fitz narrowed his gaze on the man. "Are you the ones who kidnapped Sutton?" He didn't think so, but then again, there could have been more he hadn't seen. He assumed if they were the ones, he'd have been shot on sight. Not kidnapped and questioned.

"No. She's got nothing to do with this."

"Then you are aware of her?"

"We've been watching Sinclair for a long time," the man admitted.

"Can I get a name so we can have a conversation man to man?" Fitz wanted something to call him. Even through the darkness of the van,

Fitz could see that the man was young, younger than he'd initially thought while standing on the street. Fitz wouldn't say he was any more than thirty-five years old. "It doesn't have to be your real name just something to call you while we talk."

"No," he said looking down to the floor.

Fitz made a sitting motion with his hand. "Sit down. It will be more comfortable for you. I'm not going to attack you."

The man eased himself to the floor. "Why are you investigating Harvey Sinclair? Don't tell me you're not. I want to know why and what you've found."

"I didn't start out investigating Sinclair," Fitz admitted and gave him a little background about how he ended up involved in the whole thing. "Sutton is my ex-wife. She asked a favor and I went up to Brewster Academy. It's all been a bit of a muddled mess since then. Are you one of Sinclair's henchmen trying to scare me off the trail?"

That elicited mocking laughter. "No. We are trying to take Sinclair down and have been for a while."

We meant there was more than one of them – at least two with the driver. "How many of you are working on this? I hope there's more than just you and the guy who's doing a poor job of keeping this van straight. Is he trying to make us puke?"

The man looked toward the driver's side of the van, choosing not to respond to Fitz's critique of the driving. "There's enough of us to accomplish our missions."

Plural. "There's other people you're going after?"

"It's time we take our government back."

Radicals. It was the first word that popped into Fitz's head. "Back from whom exactly?"

"Special interest. Corporations. Big oil and pharma. The gun lobby. Everyone who thinks they can squash the little people. We are going to take them down. Every last one of them."

CHAPTER 35

"That's a heady task," Fitz said with a whistle. "How did you get first clued into what Sinclair was doing?"

"I ask the questions and you still haven't fully answered me. You said Sutton had you look into Holden. You did that but you kept going. Why?"

"Someone kidnapped Sutton. I wasn't going to let someone hurt her, not on my watch." Fitz shifted in the seat to get a little more comfortable and to stall for time. "Should I assume you weren't involved in kidnapping her?"

"Not us. We'd have no need for her."

There was something about the way he said the word *need* that perked up Fitz's ears. He wasn't going to address it head-on and spook him. "Do you know who was responsible for kidnapping her?"

"We didn't have anything to do with that."

"Okay," Fitz responded, still not sure what they wanted with him. "Can I help you with something? I don't understand what it is you want."

"We want you to back off the Sinclair investigation. You got what you needed at the school. You found out Holden sexually assaulted a young woman and you rescued your ex-wife. I don't understand why you're still involved. You need to back off and let us take it from here. We saw you talking to that FBI agent."

Fitz knew then that's what this was about. He wasn't going to give himself away by telling the man he knew the assault was bogus. The man clearly thought he might also be looking into Holden's disappearance, which could only mean one thing. "I don't know what else you found out about Sinclair. He's involved in some underhanded dealings – bribes and such. That's all I'm looking into now. That's my only other role in this." Fitz averted his eyes from the man and started more carefully assessing the surroundings of the van while trying not to raise suspicion. "This is a good space you got here. A little messy but decent. I wonder if I should get this for my business."

The man ignored him. "We know all about Sinclair's bribes. We are working on bringing him down. If you get in our way, you're going to get hurt. Do you understand me?"

Fitz refocused on him. "What exactly is your mission?"

"Disruption," he said his voice tinged with hate. "We want the whole system torn down and rebuilt and we aren't going to stop until that happens. Until we can do that, we need people like Sinclair out of our way."

Anarchist. That was the second word that came to mind. Fitz assumed they were some kind of subversive group. Even though the man was young, he didn't seem to care that Fitz might get an advantage over him, he remained quietly confident. That alone made Fitz take notice.

"You want me to back off Sinclair? What if what I'm finding can help you? I've been an investigator for a lot longer than you have. I have some good resources in my pocket."

"What have you found?"

Fitz wasn't going to give away the whole farm. He'd drip a little information in the hopes of keeping the man talking. "Sinclair has gone after a lot of high ranking people. He's not only trying to dig up dirt on people but he's willing to set people up to have something on them. He's doing it to gain influence for the Supreme Court, and he's amassing great wealth from his other bribery schemes. There's a lot going on. What are you hoping to get from this? His reach is far and he's not going to be an easy man to take down."

The man didn't hesitate with his response. "We hoped he'd drop out of the running for Supreme Court. We can deal with him effectively after that."

"That's never going to happen," Fitz said, noting the doubt on the young man's face. "The word narcissist is overused but it applies to

CHAPTER 35

Sinclair. He's not going to back off from this. He's been gunning for the highest court in the land and now that he's inches from it, nothing is going to stop him. Even if you got him to back off, then what? He's still a federal judge. How do you plan to get him to stop taking bribes? Giving up power is one thing, giving up the way he is making millions is another. You're not going to take both from him."

"We have ways," the man said without elaborating. The cold detached tone in his voice is what had Fitz the most concerned. If he had said it in a vague insecure way that implied they didn't have a plan, Fitz would have been less worried. Fitz was sure they had a plan and it involved great pain and possibly death.

"I don't know what you're planning to do, but killing a federal judge isn't going to bode well for you," Fitz responded not being careful with his words. "You're going to end up throwing your whole life away and then you'll accomplish nothing." He took his focus off the man and continued to scan around the van, sure there must be some evidence.

The man wasn't going to be deterred. "You worry about yourself and let us handle it. We've done what we've had to do. Now you need to do the same – let us do this our way."

Fitz wasn't going to make any sort of promise. "Do you at least want some of the information I've uncovered?"

"We know what you know. You're coming from Nancy Gibbons's office, aren't you? We know all about her and her son, Tyler. We are about ten steps ahead of you, Fitz." The man smiled brightly showing a row of crooked teeth. "We've got this under our control. I'm warning you, if you get in our way it's not going to go well for you. Do we understand each other?"

"Sure," Fitz said, still scanning the back of the van. "Stay out of your way. I assume also don't tell anyone we had this conversation. Got it. Not a problem from me. I'm a little bored with this investigation and need to get back to my regular workload."

"I'm not sure I believe you."

Fitz turned his attention back to him. "What do you want from me? You're telling me to back off and I'm saying okay. You've kidnapped me and we've had a nice little chat. I don't agree with how you're going about things. I shouldn't have to have any more conversations with Agent Burrows or anyone else in the FBI, and I have other work that needs my attention. I've already warned you that this isn't going to go well for you. I also highly doubt Sinclair is going to step aside willingly."

"Then he'll pay the ultimate price." The man got up and slammed his fist on the wall behind Fitz, yelling for the driver to pull over.

This was going to be Fitz's only chance. He fished his hand in his pocket, found the small round metal disk that he always carried on him for cases similar to this. He kept his focus on the man, watching him carefully while he pulled his closed hand out of his pocket. He snaked his hand behind his back and tucked the object in the small crevice between the back and bottom cushion of the seat. Fitz could only hope that it remained in place and out of sight.

The man turned to him, looming over him. "You stay out of our way and you'll be fine, Fitz. We won't hurt you."

"Sure," Fitz said and waited for the van to stop before getting up. As he stood, that's when he saw it – the blue hood from a sweatshirt sticking out under the wrappers and bags of fast food. It had the distinct royal blue of the Brewster Academy logo. Fitz could only come to one conclusion -- he was in the presence of the man who had taken Holden Sinclair.

The van came to a stop and the man threw back the sliding door. "Don't make me come for you again," he said as he aimed the gun at Fitz.

At this point Fitz didn't think he'd shoot. He wasn't about to do anything other than memorize the man's face so he could recall it later.

CHAPTER 35

They were in the southeast part of the city in what appeared to be an alleyway.

"You won't have to come for me," Fitz assured as he hopped to the ground.

I'll be coming for you. Fitz didn't speak his thought aloud.

He got the make and model of the van as the man slammed the sliding door and the driver sped off.

Fitz waited to make sure they didn't return then walked out of the narrow alley to the road. He had to walk a little way to the intersection. He noted the cross streets and punched a number that was quickly becoming familiar to him into his phone.

When the call was answered, Fitz said, "You need to pick me up. I know who kidnapped Holden Sinclair."

CHAPTER 36

While Fitz waited for Agent Burrows to arrive, he logged into the app for the GPS tracker he slipped into the back of the seat of the van. Based on what the man had said, Fitz suspected they were the ones responsible for setting up the sexual assault then kidnapping Holden Sinclair when the setup didn't go as planned.

When the case didn't get any traction, they had resorted to kidnapping, assuming wrongly that it might scare or distract Sinclair into dropping out of the confirmation hearing. They didn't know Sinclair as well as they thought. An action like that would only embolden the man. Days later, even though his son was still missing, Sinclair was more determined than ever to be the next Supreme Court Justice. He had given an interview on a national news outlet that morning speaking to how important the role of justice was and how he was ready to assume the responsibility.

The reporter, if one could call him that, had gone light on Sinclair. There were no hard-hitting questions or any hint of Sinclair's shady dealings. It had been such a sympathetic piece, Fitz had started to wonder if Sinclair had kidnapped his own son to garner sympathy from the public.

Fitz watched the blinking light on the app navigate onto the Beltway heading back to northern D.C. The direction they were going

CHAPTER 36

indicated they might be passing D.C. altogether and heading farther north to Maryland. It's the way Fitz would have driven if he were heading home instead of going back to the office. He looked at the time, groaning with impatience. Agent Burrows was taking too long to get there, even though the agent had explained he was clear across town and with traffic it would take some time.

While he waited, Fitz called Charlie to let her know what was happening. She answered slightly out of breath. "Are you running a marathon?" he asked.

"I was in the conference room and my phone was on my desk upstairs. I nearly didn't make it." She paused to catch her breath. "I've been able to find some interesting information on Sinclair."

"We'll have time for that later. I was held at gunpoint by Holden's kidnapper."

Charlie cursed softly. "I leave you alone for a couple of hours and you can't keep yourself out of trouble. Are you okay?"

"I'm fine. I slipped a GPS tracker into the van. What's the shelf life of those new disk trackers we bought?"

"About ninety-six hours, approximately four days, if fully charged." It didn't surprise Charlie that Fitz had one on him. That was the reason they had made the purchase. They were small enough to carry around and easy enough to use. While there were some legal complications with their permissible use, Fitz didn't think the FBI would mind in this case.

"That should be plenty of time as long as they don't ditch the van. I assume it was theirs. The guy kept saying cryptic things that aroused my suspicion. It was a mess in the back of the van with fast food wrappers and then I saw the hoodie. It was the same royal blue color of Brewster Academy."

"What did they want with you?" Charlie asked.

"To tell us to back off the Sinclair investigation. I think they are radicals. That's the vibe I got. He was rambling about special interest groups and getting the money out of politics."

Charlie cursed softly. "That's some sick stuff."

As they talked for a few moments longer, Fitz provided Charlie the tracking ID so she could watch the van along with them. She made him promise to be in touch within the hour. When they first got the trackers, she had threatened to put one on him. Fitz was known to disappear from the office for hours on end, often caught up in one investigation or another. He had worked for so long on his own, he had forgotten what it was like to have a partner.

A blue sedan with government plates slowed to a stop at the curb. "I have to go," Fitz said to her. "Your boyfriend is here." Fitz slid that in and ended the call, listening as Charlie cursed at him before she was cut off.

He leaned down into the open window to see the smug smile of Burrows behind the wheel. "You don't look happy to see me or maybe that's a *I told you to stay out of my investigation* face."

"Get in," Burrows directed, unlocking the door. Fitz slid into the passenger seat. "What are you doing in this part of the city?"

"I told you they dropped me off here. I was coming out of a meeting and they stopped me right on K Street. I'm surprised no one called 911."

"Several people did. The D.C. cops got the reports," Agent Burrows explained as he turned his blinker on, looked over his shoulder, and pulled out into traffic. "I heard it on the radio but no one could figure out what happened. By the time a squad car got there, you were long gone. Well, we didn't know it was you. Just some big guy got taken off the street at gunpoint. Witnesses had the description of the van but not much else. No one could identify who was driving or the guy in the back. They weren't even sure there were just two men. The plates come back to some corporation."

CHAPTER 36

"Clancy Corporation?"

Burrows looked at him. "How'd you know that?"

"I got tailed coming back from Brewster Academy and the car's plates came back to some dummy corp."

"You never mentioned that."

"There were two of them," Fitz said and then corrected himself. "I don't think there was anyone in the passenger seat up front. I couldn't see the front seat from the back." They had pulled into traffic so quickly, Fitz hadn't even mentioned about the tracker. "Are you in a rush to get someplace?"

Burrows glanced across the car at him. "Taking you to the office to get your statement."

"Right. I have something more pressing." Fitz raised his screen and turned it so Burrows could see it. "I dropped a GPS tracker in the van. I know exactly where they are. I thought we could swing by there and see what we can find. I believe they are the ones who kidnapped Holden."

"Lead with that next time." Burrow's fingers tensed around the steering wheel. Before Fitz could respond, he asked, "Are you armed?"

"Always. I didn't get a chance to defend myself. I figured out quickly he wasn't there to kill me. They wanted me to stop looking into Sinclair. I figured I'd try to gather as much information as possible, so I let it play out," Fitz said, trying to figure out what Burrows was thinking. "I saw a blue hoodie among the rubbish in the back of the van. It was the same color as Brewster Academy. They are after Sinclair. But he denied any involvement with Sutton's kidnapping."

Burrows slowed for a stoplight, tapping the break until they were at a full stop. "It was a good idea to put the tracker in the van. Do you have one with you all the time?"

Fitz explained that they had recently made the purchase to have a few in the office. "I didn't know how they'd be of use to us, but I figured better to have them than not. I've been carrying one around with me ever since."

Burrows didn't comment on that. He hit the gas at the green light, still not telling Fitz if they were going after the men. Fitz didn't want to push him. Burrows definitely wasn't the kind of man who would take well to being pushed or persuaded to do anything. He fell into silence while the agent decided for himself.

It wasn't until Burrows exited onto the Beltway that he gestured over to Fitz. "Give me the location. Are they stationary or still moving?"

They had been still moving the last time Fitz had looked. He refreshed the app again. "It's stopped moving in Rockville, Maryland." He pulled up the address and dropped it into another app. "It's a residential house. Looks to be right in the middle of an upscale neighborhood. Maybe they ditched the van there. Then again, if this group is as organized as the guy made them seem, their operation might be well-funded."

"They might be keeping the kid someplace else too. Maybe it's at the house of one of the kidnappers."

That was a possibility as well. "What do you want to do?"

Burrows didn't answer right away. He asked for directions and Fitz supplied them. Burrows only needed them said once and he committed them to memory. Fitz had tried giving them as he was driving but Burrows wanted the whole route spelled out to him and then focused on driving.

After driving a few minutes down the road, Burrows explained, "I don't know what I'm going to do when we get there. If it seems like I can question someone, that's what we will do. If I get there and sense we need backup, I'm going to call in backup. The goal is retrieving Holden Sinclair alive."

Fitz said he understood. "Have there been any sightings of Holden since he went missing from the school?"

CHAPTER 36

"None and that's been frustrating," Burrows admitted, taking a right off an exit and slowing down. "We've had no calls for a ransom. No prior threats made that the school knows about or that Sinclair admitted to. We are running on zero information and Sinclair seems to be blocking us at every turn."

Fitz turned his head to look at him. "What do you mean blocking you? How can he be blocking the FBI?"

Burrows stared straight ahead as he spoke. "I'm not saying he doesn't want Holden found, but he's not acting like a man whose son has been kidnapped. We wanted to put a tap on his phones at the house in case the kidnappers called with a ransom demand, we'd be ready. He denied that request. He stonewalled us for information when the call first came in. As the news reported, Sinclair didn't make the call to the FBI."

"Who called you in?"

"Robins, the headmaster at the school. When he realized Holden was missing, he called Sinclair. Robins told us Sinclair specifically asked him not to call law enforcement and that he'd handle it on his own. Then Holden's roommate came forward and said that Holden had received a call on his cellphone late the night he went missing. Holden told his roommate he didn't know who had called him but the person wanted to meet him in the woods behind the dorm. He said he had information that could clear Holden from the alleged sexual assault. Of course, the kid went. The roommate followed him out without letting him know. That's how we know what happened. Holden got out into the woods and met with a guy who coaxed him to a waiting van much like you describe. The man pulled a gun and then threw Holden to the ground when he tried to run. The roommate immediately called Robins, who did call the local police before calling Sinclair."

"Are you saying Sinclair knew the full story and still didn't want

Robins to call the cops?"

"That's exactly what I'm saying," Burrows said, keeping pace with traffic. He slowed to a stop at a red light.

"But you said Sinclair told you Sutton was involved?"

Burrows nodded. "We didn't think she was working alone. Either way, it didn't seem like Sinclair cared all that much."

Fitz admitted that after Sinclair's interview, he considered that Sinclair had Holden kidnapped to drum up sympathy.

"Another of our agents said the same thing." Burrows navigated through the upscale neighborhood with wide tree-lined streets. The homes were a mix of brick and siding with wide front lawns that all looked like they were professionally landscaped. Mercedes, Lexus, and BMW seemed to be the cars of choice parked in newly paved driveways.

The white van that now had a painting company's name and logo splashed on the side sat parked at the curb in front of the address Fitz had identified. "There it is." He pointed. "I don't remember the logo. It might have been hidden when the door closed or it could be one of those magnetic stick on signs." Fitz noted the scratch on the back bumper and the Maryland license plate number that he had seen before but hadn't remembered. "I don't know if they changed that out. I couldn't get the plate before. They had taken off so quickly."

"You put the tracker in. You did more than enough. Besides the people on the street got the plate number," Burrows said, which would amount to all the praise he was going to give Fitz. "I'm going to circle around the block. See what we can gather as we drive by."

As they drove by, Fitz didn't notice anything unusual about the house. It was a split level home. The front windows were open but the wooden door closed. The mailbox atop a post at the end of the driveway didn't bear a name only the number of the home. Fitz didn't see any people or any signs of trouble. He relayed the information to

CHAPTER 36

Burrows as he circled the block.

Parking more than a block away, Fitz could still see the white van but not much of the house. Burrows put the car in park but didn't cut the engine. He pulled out an iPad, punched in his security code, and then the house information.

"James Cowan," he finally said and looked over at Fitz. "Does that name ring a bell?"

Fitz pulled back in surprise. "You mean House Minority Leader James Cowan?"

Burrows cursed softly as he gripped the door. "I hope not. You wait here. I'm going to knock. Keep the car running."

Fitz was going to do more than keep the car running. He reached for the gun on his hip and unclipped it from the holster.

CHAPTER 37

Fitz kept an eye on Agent Burrows, who had his gun drawn at his side, as he walked the short distance to the house, stopping to speak to a neighbor who had walked into the front yard and down their driveway to check the mail.

Burrows quickly holstered his weapon as he spoke to the elderly man. Fitz couldn't hear what they were saying. He assumed Burrows was asking him about his neighbors and trying to assess who lived in the home. While Burrows was doing that, Fitz called Charlie.

"I'm at the house with Burrows," he said when she answered. "He is going to check the house but has requested I remain in the car. We'll see how long that lasts. In the meantime, can you check what vehicles, addresses and businesses come back for James Cowan?"

"House Minority Leader?"

"The very one." Fitz explained Burrows had run the house information and came back with Cowan's name and the Clancy Corp for the plates. "I don't know Cowan well and he's not one of our clients."

Fitz remained on the line while he waited for Charlie to search the information. He kept his focus on Burrows to make sure he didn't need assistance. He was still deep in conversation with the neighbor. They were now turned toward the house and deep in conversation, leaning toward one another. Fitz couldn't hear them or see their expressions. He must be giving Burrows some good information for

CHAPTER 37

the conversation to have carried on this long.

Charlie mumbled to herself as she searched, rattling off details as she went. "Here, Fitz," she said with a trace of excitement in her voice. "This might be something you can use. Cowan is part owner of a commercial painting company. The company has a fleet of five trucks registered back to the company name and his name. He is co-owner of the business with his brother-in-law, Jay Sundell. They must have a few employees if they have that many trucks. Is the van a painting truck?"

Fitz confirmed that it currently had a painting truck name and logo on the side of it. "That must be it."

She asked him to hold on a few minutes as she further searched the information. "The house does come back to Cowan. He also has an apartment in the Adams Morgan neighborhood and then a house back in his home state of Ohio. Maybe he's just renting to his brother-in-law. There's nothing else listed for him relating to property. He drives a BMW five-series while he's in D.C. It's leased. There are other vehicles registered to him in Ohio. Do you need more information?"

"Is Sundell related specifically?"

"Looks to me like he's married to Cowan's youngest sister, Elise. They are separated though because I see another address for her back in Ohio. They have no children."

Fitz knew this was a longshot. "What can you tell me about the house? Is anyone else listed for the residence?"

"We don't have that kind of information here." Charlie asked him to hold and the clickity clack of Charlie's staccato typing came through the phone. "Sundell has a few arrests for protesting. They go back as far as the early days of the war in Iraq. I know you said the guy you saw looked young, but Sundell is forty-one. That would have put him right about eighteen after 9/11. There are quite a few arrests here in various states. He was arrested in New York City during Occupy Wall

Street. There are arrests at climate protests. The civil rights protests that happened during the summer of 2020. There's a long list, Fitz."

It tracked with the man he'd spoken to in the van. "Do you have a photo of him?"

"Yeah, I have several mugshots right here. Cases were dropped after many of the arrests. Most of the time he was let off with an appearance ticket. A couple of misdemeanor convictions but no jail time. Curiously, his last arrest was a few months before the painting business started. I texted the photo to you. You should receive it in a minute."

Fitz waited until the text came through and pulled the phone away from his face. He enlarged the photo Charlie sent and immediately recognized the man staring back. It was the man that had kidnapped him. "This is him. This is the guy in the back of the van with me. Other than wearing a hat he didn't try to conceal himself."

"That's a bit odd don't you think?"

Fitz had considered it odd at the time. After being let go without injury, he had second guessed his immediate response to it. "I think he's cocky enough to believe I had no idea he had kidnapped Holden. His intent was to get me to stop going after Sinclair. I can't actually tie him to any criminal activity other than pulling a gun on me and getting me into that van. I didn't try to fight him. I don't think he believes I'd go after him. When was the painting business started and when was the separation?"

Fitz wondered if Cowan was trying to divert his brother-in-law's time and energy into making money and the business rather than his activism.

"The painting business was nine years ago. The separation is recent. About six months ago," Charlie said, explaining she couldn't see any legal documents so she didn't know if it was a formal legal separation. But his wife had moved back to Ohio, got a mortgage in only her

CHAPTER 37

name, and a driver's license around that time. "They could have been separated before that. I'd have no way of knowing."

"What about weapons registered to him?" Fitz stared out of the front window of the car. Burrows was still in conversation with the neighbor.

It didn't take Charlie nearly as long to come back with this information. "Legally, he has three handguns and five rifles."

Fitz knew that a person had to have all guns registered within the state. It didn't mean it was every gun he had, but every gun he had legally bought and registered. He had to go through the same process when he moved from D.C. to his new house. He thanked Charlie for the information and promised he'd call when he knew more. As he ended the call with Charlie, Burrows was on his way back to the car.

He pulled open the door and leaned in. "The man has never seen James Cowan at the residence and said there's one guy who lives there full time but there's heavy traffic in and out of there. He said the man's name is Jay and he's a painter. Never been any trouble as a neighbor and he didn't know much more."

Fitz was able to fill in the rest of the information that Charlie had provided. "Based on the description Charlie provided me of Sundell's background, he's been an activist for a long time. It sounds to me like Cowan encouraged his brother-in-law to start the business, possibly to get him to focus on something other than the activism. From what I know of Cowan, and Sundell's arrest record, they are on opposite sides of the political spectrum."

"But both hate Sinclair," Burrows said, reminding Fitz of an op-ed piece Cowan had written for *The Washington Post* a few years back when Sinclair's name first got thrown around as a potential Supreme Court pick. "The neighbor just reminded me of the article. There's been rumors of bad blood between the men for a long time."

Fitz hadn't remembered the article. "Did he say who is in the house now?"

"Just Jay, he believes. He saw him come back to the house about twenty minutes before we arrived. He was outside watering the flowers. The two of them waved then Jay popped the magnetic signs back on the truck and went into the house. The neighbor said he didn't think it was odd the sign was off the truck as Jay took it on and off."

"What do you want to do?"

Burrows stood upright and looked back toward the house before crouching back down into the car. "Come with me and we can have a little chat with Jay. If you identify him as the man who pulled a gun on you today, we can take him in. With a little pressure, he might be willing to tell me who has Holden."

Fitz explained he had already identified Jay from a photo and was sure they had the right man. "I don't think he's going to tell you. He's a bit of a radical and might even lawyer up as soon as you identify yourself." Fitz wasn't sure they would get anything of value out of Jay. He didn't even think Jay would admit that he had met Fitz earlier. "We can give it a try. Expect him to be difficult."

"You don't think anything will get him to crack?"

"Not with that arrest record." Fitz stepped out of the car onto the pavement. He put his gun back in the holster but did not latch it. He didn't want to walk to the door armed but wanted it easily accessible just in case. Just like Fitz doubted Sundell would tell them anything of value, he didn't think the man would shoot at them without provocation.

They walked down the road and as they approached the van, Burrows instructed Fitz to stand on the far side of it while he went to the door alone. The goal was to come out from behind the van after Burrows had already engaged him in conversation. Fitz stood at the corner of it, trying to stand out of the way enough Sundell wouldn't

CHAPTER 37

be able to see him and still cover Burrows's back. They were going on the word of the neighbor that Sundell was in there alone. They didn't know that for sure.

Burrows knocked on the door and waited. He raised his fist as the door pulled open before his knuckles could contact the wood again. "Jay Sundell," Burrows said and identified himself. "I'm hoping to speak with you about an incident earlier today. I believe you might have been a witness."

Sundell stepped out onto the small concrete porch, pulling the door closed behind him. "I've been at a job site all day. Only got home about a half-hour ago."

"That your work van there?"

"Yeah," Sundell said without looking toward it. "I didn't witness anything today. I was at the job site alone, brought my lunch, and didn't see or speak to anyone. I think you might have the wrong person."

A sure sign of guilt was offering up far more information than asked. Burrows caught on to that too. "You didn't see anyone today? You didn't stop for coffee on the way in or grab some lunch?"

Sundell wasn't easily tricked. "No, I just told you. I brought my lunch and remained at the job site. What do you think I witnessed?"

Burrows pointed to the van. "This van was seen in D.C. earlier today. It pulled up alongside the curb on K Street, a man in the back had a gun and ordered another guy into the back. There were reports that came from several people on the street."

Sundell shook his head. He didn't appear upset or even rattled by the news. "It couldn't have been this van. As I said, it was with me all day."

"No one else has access to it?" Burrows asked, boxing him in.

"Nope. Just me. As I said, it was on the job site with me. There are a lot of vans that look like this. You sure it had my business name and logo on the side like this one?"

"Ahh," Burrows said with a little break of a smile. He walked over to the van and tugged off the magnetic sign. "This is easily removed, Jay. No, the van identified didn't have your logo. It looked remarkably like this right here."

"Wasn't me," he said, his jaw tight. Burrows was getting under his skin. "I have to get going now. I have a lot to do. As I said, I haven't been home from work long. I left something on the stove."

"Before you go, Jay. There's someone I need you to meet. He's a key witness who saw you today."

That was Fitz's cue to step out from behind the van. As he did, Jay's head turned slightly to look over and recognition took hold. Fitz took a few steps toward him as if he didn't have a care in the world. "How's it going, Jay? Good to finally know your name. It's nice to finally formally meet you. Maybe I should also call you Blaze. That's the name you used with Veronica, isn't it?" Fitz extended his hand but Jay made no move to take it. "Come on now. You weren't so shy when you had a gun on me."

Jay averted his eyes, focusing back on Burrows. "I've never seen this guy a day in my life."

"He's a mountain of a man, Jay. He's hard to confuse with someone else and he's certainly hard to miss. I think you remember him," Burrows coaxed. "This is going to be a lot easier on you if you tell me the truth."

Jay shifted his weight from one foot to the other, seemingly contemplating his options. He held firm in his position. "I don't know what this man has told you. I don't know who he is, and I've never seen him before. I want to call my lawyer."

Burrows nodded. "That's great, Jay, because you're going to need legal representation." He took a few steps toward him and began to read him his rights. He turned him around and slapped the cuffs on

CHAPTER 37

him. "Fitz was willing to let what you did earlier today go if you told us what you did with Holden Sinclair because we know you kidnapped him. That's a federal crime, Jay. You're looking at life in prison."

"Not to mention how much this will embarrass your brother-in-law," Fitz said, stepping toward him. He leaned down close to Jay's ear. "Then again, if you're the first one to talk, you could walk away from this scot free with the right deal made. We both know you weren't the one who came up with this plan. I've seen your arrest record. Setting a kid up for sexual assault then kidnapping is far from your scope of activism. Who talked you into this? We both know someone did. Why take the fall for them?"

Jay looked over his shoulder at Burrows. "Is he telling the truth?"

"You return me Holden Sinclair unharmed and I can get you that deal."

Jay chewed on his bottom lip. "I don't know that you'll believe me."

"Trust us," Fitz said, not quite expecting what Jay said next.

"My brother-in-law, Senate Minority Leader James Cowan, is holding Holden in one of the offices in the basement of the Capitol. He figured nobody would look for the kid in the most obvious place."

Burrows raised his head to look right at Fitz, the same surprised expression on both their faces.

If this was true, this would rock D.C. in a way nothing had in decades.

CHAPTER 38

The FBI descended on the United States Capitol building with a full force, accompanied by D.C. Metro Police and Capitol Police. The building was cleared of visitors and tourist groups. No official was allowed to leave either through the front doors or the tunnel system that ran under the building. The whole building was effectively locked down and those left inside were told little about what was happening – other than that they were safe but not allowed to leave.

FBI agents and cops went room to room spreading out over the floors. Agent Burrows allowed Fitz to join in the search, mostly because he wasn't going to say no to extra manpower.

They went together to the basement of the building in the area where Jay had instructed. He had only been there once, after hours with Cowan not long after he had kidnapped Holden. Jay couldn't explain exactly where the room was located, only that there was a pull-out couch for a bed and a full bathroom attached to the office. It was isolated enough down a narrow corridor that Senator Cowan assured Jay no one would ever discover their secret.

From what Jay described, Cowan had kept Holden down in the bowels of the Capitol building since the time he'd been kidnapped. Jay admitted he and a friend had tried and failed to set up Holden then resorted to kidnapping when that didn't work. Jay wasn't the

CHAPTER 38

one who had shot at Fitz though. Cowan had other men for that who descended on the school during the chaos of Holden's disappearance to look for the rumored evidence students had about the failed setup. Fitz had been caught in the crosshairs. Then part of that security team had tried and failed to tail Fitz back to D.C. Fitz, it seemed, had been a real thorn in Cowan's side.

It was hard for Fitz to understand Cowan's willingness to kill innocent high school students. But as Jay described it, sometimes sacrifices had to be made for the sake of the country. If they had not gotten in the way to protect Holden, and thereby Sinclair, then there'd be no issue.

Burrows had many questions about how they were able to get Holden into the building without being discovered. Jay had explained that he'd been bound and gagged and put into a trunk that had been carried into the building service entrance. From there, the trunk was loaded onto a wheeled cart and rolled down to Cowan's office. Jay had posed as a mover and had even passed by security without any issues. Cowan had explained he was bringing in a few things for his office and that was the end of that. Security let them pass without another question.

From everything Jay knew, Holden was still at the Capitol office. He'd spoken to Cowan only the day before but had not seen Holden again after unloading him from the trunk into the office. Holden had not fought Jay when he was taken into the van, stuffed into the trunk, or unloaded into the office. He was plenty scared and confused by what Jay wanted and what was going to happen to him. Jay explained he had assured Holden if he complied, he'd not be harmed. The young man believed him and had remained still and compliant.

Burrows inquired about Holden's current condition. Jay only knew what Cowan had told him, and the latest was that Holden was getting tired of being held. It was becoming an untenable task. Even though the office was in the farthest reaches of the basement and not near any of the other offices that lined the basement nooks, Cowan was concerned that if too much more time passed, someone would figure out what was happening. Some of his colleagues had already questioned Cowan's demeanor over the last few days.

Burrows had pressed Jay on the long-term plan for Holden. Jay had no idea what Cowan had planned to do with him but had complained Sinclair hadn't reacted in the way he expected. Cowan had grown disillusioned with the plan but hadn't developed an exit strategy.

Fitz didn't believe that for a second. Holden had seen the man's face and knew who had kidnapped him. That only left one possibility for Holden – death. He wasn't going to be leaving that office alive and both Fitz and Burrows knew that to be true. It didn't matter how Sinclair responded in the meantime. His son's fate had already been determined.

Upon hearing that, Burrows had handed Jay off to another FBI agent who finally arrived on the scene. They were already in the process of getting search warrants for the Capitol building, Jay's home, and Cowan's Adams Morgan apartment. Agents had been dispatched to find Cowan, but so far, he'd not been located. Fitz wondered if he was hiding out with Holden in the office.

It seemed unlikely when security said they hadn't seen Cowan enter the building at all that day. There would be questions for Capitol Police later about how a child could be held captive on their watch. Given the location of the office and Cowan's stellar reputation, it might have been something easily missed by even the most diligent officers.

There was no denying the office was remote. The U.S. Capitol building has one-hundred secret hideaway offices, some lavish and decorated on the upper floors, and smaller more cramped spaces in the basement. The offices were used by members of the Senate and

CHAPTER 38

a few senior members of the House of Representatives. The rooms did not appear on any official directory and only featured a simple room number. The offices were used as private spaces to prepare for sessions, conduct confidential meetings, and for other personal purposes.

Some senators were known to take naps in the secret offices, others had conducted affairs in them. Of course, that wasn't talked about publicly. Most people didn't even know the offices existed, especially not the ones in the basement like the one they were heading to.

Burrows had discovered where Cowan's was located and how to find it. They ran down staircases and through long corridors. The air grew considerably cooler the lower they went. They ran from one long hallway to another. Burrows took the lead as Fitz followed right behind. He could only hope for Holden's sake, he hadn't been moved.

They passed by the small subway car that took senators and staffers in the underground tunnels from one building to the next. The guy at the controls tipped his head back in a hello and cautioned them not to run on the platform. They were gone before they could offer any recognition at the greeting or the caution.

Burrows arrived at the closed door moments before Fitz. The barren end of the hallway was the perfect location for a secret meeting, an illicit tryst, or holding a kidnapped kid. Fitz slowed his run and stopped feet from him. They kept their voices low as they spoke. Fitz was surprised Cowan didn't have security but assumed that would only arouse more suspicion.

"Do you hear anything inside?" Fitz asked as Burrows pressed his ear to the door.

"Sounds like a television. I don't hear anyone talking."

Burrows drew his gun and banged his fist three times into the door. "FBI, open the door!" he shouted, his voice echoing in the empty narrow hall. He stood back clear of the door in case someone shot through it.

Fitz's heart beating in his ears drowned out the low hum from the hallway lights. The door remained closed with no response from inside. "Try again," Fitz coaxed.

Burrows banged his fist again on the door, the thin wood rocking. He shouted one more time for whoever was inside to step out, threatening to break down the door. Still, no one responded. He shifted his eyes to Fitz. "They aren't coming out easily."

"If anyone is in there at all. Let's break it down."

Burrows stepped back and let Fitz do the honor. He holstered his gun, stepped in front of the door, raised his leg, and stomped his foot as hard as he could against it, rattling the hinges. Fitz stepped back again and gave it one more and then another, the wood finally splintering under the pressure. The offices might have been remote and hidden in the building, but Fitz was fairly certain the flimsy doors were original. Security at the front of the building had assured them a battering ram wouldn't be needed to knock the door in.

Fitz stepped out of the way as Burrows brushed past him, stepping over the broken wood of the door, to enter the office. Fitz pulled his gun back from his holster and aimed it in front of him as he followed Burrows into the dark office.

Security had told them that the office had three separate spaces. It was one of the larger hideaway offices in the basement and not indicative of the others. In the late 1960s, a senator had taken over three of the offices at the empty end of the hallway where no one else wanted to be. He had brought in contractors to make the three offices into one big office space. It included a reception room, main office, and sleeping quarters. The bathroom was off the sleeping quarters in the back. He had set himself up a private suite. The office would have been prime picking for any senator but so far away from everything else in the building no one wanted it.

CHAPTER 38

As minority leader, Cowan would have had his pick without a fight. Fitz followed a few steps behind Burrows who made his way from the reception room to the inner office. The door between them was left open. "You can hear the television, right?" Burrows asked, glancing over his shoulder.

Once they were inside the office, Fitz's racing heartbeat finally began to steady, though his senses remained on high alert. The relentless hum filled the room. "There's definitely the buzz of something—a television or radio," he murmured, his voice taut.

Burrows made his way to the farthest door, right next to the senator's desk. A faint, erratic flicker of light seeped from beneath it. Burrows hesitated for a split second, then placed his hand on the doorknob, turning it with agonizing slowness. His voice rang out, strained and urgent. "FBI! Come out with your hands up!"

Fitz's mind raced with a grim realization. The shout seemed futile now, like a cry into a void. For the first time, Fitz allowed the chilling possibility to seep in – this might not be a rescue operation at all but a recovery. His breath hitched as the door creaked open, and his heart pounded with a fierce intensity.

The first sight that met him was the socked feet of someone lying on what Fitz assumed was a bed. The figure remained still despite their noisy presence. Burrows's face tightened with urgency as he darted into the room, which was only half the size of the outer offices. He dropped to his knees beside the prone figure.

"It's Holden!" he shouted as he pulled the covers down from the face. "Find a light."

Fitz turned quickly, searching for a switch on the wall. He found one inches from the door and flipped it upright. A small table lamp on a black end table next to the head of the bed brightened the space. "Is he breathing?" Fitz asked as he took the few steps toward Burrows.

Burrows checked for a pulse and offered a curt nod. He tipped

Holden's head back and checked his airways. "He's breathing but it's faint. Pulse is faint too." He pushed himself upright and radioed in for help.

Fitz scanned around the room for any signs of what might have put Holden into that state. With nothing jumping out to him he moved into the small bathroom. Right there on the counter was the answer. A small prescription pill bottle with the cap crooked on top. Fitz leaned down to read the label, careful not to touch it. A valium prescription for James Cowan. "It's prescription valium, Burrows. He's been giving the kid something to knock him out." Fitz stepped out of the bathroom. "I don't know how much he gave him but the dosage is high."

"Enough to overdose him?"

"Not from the valium, at least," Fitz explained. "We don't know what else he might have given him."

"What is the meaning of this?" a voice shouted from the outer office. "Whoever did this is going to pay!"

Fitz reacted first, pointing his gun at the sound of the threat. "Don't move," he said as he took a few steps through the doorway to the inner office.

James Cowan locked his gaze on Fitz and hesitated. "What are you doing in my office?" The man had the audacity to sound affronted. "I asked you a question. What are you doing in my office?"

"I think the bigger question is what is Holden Sinclair doing in your office?" Fitz asked as Burrows moved past him and told Cowan to keep his hands where they could see them.

Cowan's eyes grew wide. He held his hands out in front as if to stop them from advancing. "There's got to be some mistake. There shouldn't be anyone in this office. I was just notified that the FBI was here searching the building and I came over to unlock it so you could search. What are you talking about? How is Holden Sinclair in here?"

Burrows jerked his thumb over his shoulder. "Come see for

CHAPTER 38

yourself."

Fitz stood back and allowed Cowan to enter.

He gasped as his hand flew to his mouth. "I haven't been down in this office in weeks. I..." He squeaked, stumped to find the right words.

Either Cowan was a sociopathic liar or he really had no idea. It was impossible for Fitz to tell.

CHAPTER 39

The next morning Fitz sat at his dining room table with his head hung low over a cup of coffee. He breathed in the aroma as he struggled to keep his eyelids up. He replayed the events of the previous evening like a reel he watched over and over again.

After paramedics arrived in the Capitol building and took Holden away on a stretcher, Burrows handcuffed Cowan and took him into custody. The man didn't remain silent but kept protesting his innocence, trying desperately to assure Burrows that he had nothing to do with Holden's kidnapping.

Burrows had told Fitz he didn't know what to believe. But given it was Cowan's office, he had no choice but to bring the man into custody. As much as Fitz would have liked to be there when Cowan was questioned, Burrows wouldn't allow it. He had asked Fitz to go with Holden and another agent to the hospital to make sure Holden was okay.

The doctor in the emergency room took the young man's vitals and assessed him. They had debated back and forth about whether they should pump his stomach, not knowing for sure what he had ingested. Fitz brought the bagged pill bottle with them to the hospital so the doctor could see what they assumed was evidence. The doctors had opted not to put Holden through the trauma of pumping his stomach and instead decided to watch him closely through the night until he

CHAPTER 39

woke.

Burrows had notified Sinclair that his son had been found. He rushed to the hospital where Fitz and the other agent met him. Fitz would have thought he'd be so overjoyed that Holden had been rescued that Sinclair might have thanked him for helping to find his son, or at the very least, ignored his presence. Instead, Sinclair had made a big deal about Fitz being there and had asked the doctor to remove him.

Fitz left without a fight or making the doctor have an awkward confrontation. Burrows had already told him that once Sinclair arrived, he was free to call the media to let them know Holden had been found. If it was leaked to the media where he'd been found, Burrows was hoping it would put some pressure on Senator Cowan.

Fitz didn't think he had a choice but to give the tip to Tim. The story was already running online, and it would make the cover of *The Washington Post* that morning.

Fitz arrived home exhausted but thankful Holden would be fine. He had peeled off his clothes, taken the hottest shower his skin could tolerate, and crawled naked into bed. He half-expected Sutton to be at his door but he had slept uninterrupted for a couple of hours.

He had set the alarm on his phone for five-forty-five. When it went off, he had dragged himself from his bed, threw on a pair of boxers and ratty band tee-shirt, and ambled to the kitchen for the first of what would probably be several cups of coffee. He had a meeting scheduled with Agent Burrows at nine that morning, a few phone calls that he had missed to follow up on, and then a plan to make about bringing Sinclair to justice. It was time, well past time.

The first call Fitz had received that morning was from the agent at the hospital with him the night before. He let Fitz know Holden had woken up and was talking about the ordeal. Unfortunately, the young man was not able to identify anyone other than Jay Sundell. The man who had given him food, checked on him, and drugged him at night was wearing a mask and thick black gloves. Holden believed it was the same man each time.

For all of the time he'd been kidnapped, Holden remained in that one room with access to the bathroom. A few times during the day, he had tried to call for help but was never able to make it out of the bedroom area. The door had been locked from the outside. If Holden got too noisy, he was drugged. After a while, he got tired of being drugged, realized his efforts were of no use, and spent the time watching television. He was able to shower, had been fed well enough, and the kidnapper dropped off fresh clothing. The man's voice was deep, gravelly almost and sounded fake as if the person were intentionally doing that with his voice.

The kidnapper didn't explain why Holden had been taken. Didn't mention his father. He hadn't asked Holden anything and wouldn't answer any of his questions. Holden was surprised to learn that he'd been held in the Capitol building. He had suspected it was some kind of underground bunker or warehouse given how cold and stale it seemed. He wasn't far off in his reasoning. There was nothing gleaned from the interview that was helpful in uncovering more than they knew.

Fitz had only just ended that call when Burrows called to update Fitz that Cowan was still professing his innocence. They found nothing in his apartment or in a thorough search of the office. The two laptops they took were wiped clean. FBI tech was working to see if anything could be recovered. It might take some time. The other computer taken from Cowan's main office in the Russell Senate Office Building was being held. There were some concerns about searching it given the agents might not have the security clearances to view it. A judge would make the call later that day.

After hanging up with Burrows, Fitz cycled through his voicemails. There was one from Harriett Silva. She had called within the hour of

CHAPTER 39

Fitz's meeting with Nancy as she had promised and then called again later in the evening.

In her last message, Harriett indicated she was up before the crack of dawn and to call whenever he could – no time was too early unless it was still the middle of the night.

Fitz punched in the number she provided. It rang twice before an older woman with a crisp, clear voice answered. Her voice was strong as if she'd been awake for hours. "Harriett, this is Fitz. You called me yesterday." He apologized for not answering or calling her back. "It was a hectic day but as you might have seen on the news, we recovered Holden Sinclair."

"I saw that. I'm glad the young man was found alive. As much as I despise Harvey, I wouldn't want to see anything happen to an innocent child."

Fitz hadn't heard anyone call Sinclair by his first name. "Nancy Gibbons said you were in law school with them. She also said you might have some information to share with me."

"Absolutely. I've known him a long time. I was the one who turned him into Georgetown for cheating. His father bought his way out of that scandal. It seems the lesson was never learned and he's continued his despicable behavior. I guess that was bound to happen if he never learned his lesson."

None of what she said surprised Fitz. He listened without saying a word as she described how Sinclair not only stole tests from his professors ahead of the exam but also used cheat sheets. Harriett explained how she went directly to the ethics board with her complaints. Sinclair went after her more than once, trying to sabotage her to keep her quiet. He broke into her apartment and stole books and notebooks with her notes. A mutual friend of theirs took pity on her and retrieved them from Sinclair. After that, she started keeping duplicates, purposefully leaving one copy for him to steal. The ethics

297

committee listened to her, seemingly ready to rule in favor of kicking Sinclair out of Georgetown only to backtrack after a sizeable donation was made in the Sinclair family name.

Fitz was so engrossed in her story he didn't notice Sutton had come into the kitchen. He caught movement out of the corner of his eyes and spotted her pouring coffee. "I believe everything you're saying. Do you have anything to corroborate all of this occurred?"

"Oh," she said with an evil chuckle. "I have all the proof you need including all the notes from the ethics committee meetings, signed affidavits from ethics committee members who I spoke with after I graduated, and even a couple of law professors who were told that if they wanted to keep their jobs they'd keep the chatter about Sinclair's cheating under wraps. Not to mention signed affidavits from classmates including the one who knew Sinclair stole my work."

Fitz's mouth hung slightly open, not sure how or why Harriett had gathered all of this information. He pulled himself together. "Is this something you're willing to share with me?"

"Come by anytime and pick it up." She paused for only a moment before adding, "You're wondering why I have this and you're either too stunned or polite to ask."

"You read me well," Fitz admitted. "It does seem strange that you'd have it."

"Sinclair got a high-profile job right out of law school and I heard he was up to his old tricks, harassing people and trying to use his power for personal gain. I figured I might need this information at some point. I promised those who gave me statements I'd never use them unless absolutely necessary. I tried to get them to the Senate Judiciary Committee. They refused the information. It's been long enough, Fitz. It's time someone brought him down."

Fitz thanked her and promised he'd be to her house before his nine o'clock meeting with Burrows. He ended the call and looked over

CHAPTER 39

at Sutton who was leaning against the kitchen counter sipping her coffee. She was watching him over the rim of the cup.

"You got in late last night," she said with a slight accusatory tone when he ended the call.

"Are you jealous that I was out working to bring Sinclair down without you or do you think I was with a woman?" Fitz wasn't sure why he was getting attitude so early in the morning. When Sutton remained tightlipped, he explained the events of the evening before. He had not been keeping her up-to-date on what was happening and he had instructed Charlie not to do so either. The last thing he needed was Sutton getting in the middle of it.

He pushed his chair out and stood. "You might want to check the news to see we recovered Holden last night. He's in the hospital but doing well. I spoke to Tim in the wee hours of the morning and gave him the story to break. We have a lot more work to do to bring Sinclair to justice. I'm going to shower, then I have a full day ahead."

"I want to come with you."

Fitz shook his head. "It's not safe for you, Sutton. Call Tim and help him work on the story. Tell him to come here and the two of you can work on the article. Let him know I'll be in touch later today with information. This is going down today so you two better be prepared."

As Fitz left the room, Sutton called to him. "Who were you on the phone with?"

Fitz wasn't going to give up that information. Not yet anyway. If Harriett had the documents she claimed, Tim and Sutton would know soon enough. He did something he was never known to do – he outright ignored the question. She cursed at him as he ascended the stairs. She'd get over it or not. Fitz really didn't care anymore.

Thirty minutes later, when Fitz was showered and dressed, he called out to Sutton to let her know he was leaving. When she didn't respond, he knocked once on the door and pushed it open to find her sulking.

"I said I'm leaving and will engage the alarm system. Did you call Tim and tell him to get writing?"

Sutton raised her eyes to him. "A little hard to start writing when he doesn't have all the information."

"He has enough to get started, Sutton." He could see she wasn't happy with him. "You both did a terrific job starting this investigation. It's time to let Agent Burrows handle the rest. Tim will have this story and I'll make sure to give you both credit. I know you don't like being left out of something you started."

Sutton didn't say a word as she got up from the chair and crossed the room to her suitcase. She pulled out a manilla envelope and walked it over to him. "There is more evidence in there."

Fitz took it without checking the contents. "What's in here?"

"The offshore documents. I called about them, pretended to be Sinclair's financial advisor, and gave all the information needed to get access."

Fitz knew that wasn't possible. "Was his financial advisor listed on the account?"

Sutton nodded. "I pretended to be her. Sometimes you have to do what is right even if there's no good way to go about it."

"It's illegal," Fitz reminded her but was proud of her for getting the information. He didn't want to encourage it because she was risking not only her reputation but her life. He reached out and squeezed her shoulder, but resisted pulling her in for a hug. "I'm sure Agent Burrows will be able to figure out how to access this legally to use in court. As soon as I know more, I'll call you."

An hour later, Fitz showed up at FBI Headquarters armed with as much information as possible. He had the evidence, including a list of witnesses willing to be interviewed about Sinclair's blackmail scheme including Pete, the evidence from Sutton, all the signed affidavits from Harriett, and what Charlie had gathered about Sinclair's past.

CHAPTER 39

It would show a lifelong systematic theme of cheating, bribery and blackmail. If this wasn't proof of Sinclair's wrongdoing, then nothing would be.

CHAPTER 40

Fitz was armed with every argument possible to convince Burrows to go after Sinclair. That's why he was so confused when Burrows leapt from his chair and ushered Fitz into his office with the haste of a man who had no time to spare. His flushed face was pinched in at the forehead and his eyes were narrow.

"What's going on?" Fitz asked as he put his knapsack, which held all the evidence, down on the chair in front of Burrows's desk. He turned to face the agent who was closing and locking the door. He drew the shade down on the window that overlooked the hall. "You're freaking me out right now. What is going on?"

"Cowan finally confessed to everything. He set up Clancy Corp as a front for the whole operation from setting up Holden to shooting at you, trashing the student's room, and the kidnapping. They set up the website where they posted that fake video, claiming it was Holden sexually assaulting the girl. He admitted everything. He gave me the names of everyone who helped him."

"That's a good thing, right? We already knew he did it. If he confesses, the country can move on and we don't have to go through the pains of a long drawn-out trial." The look on Burrows's face didn't match what Fitz considered good news.

"You don't understand." Burrows gestured toward the chair for Fitz to sit. "This has to stay between us right now. I don't know exactly

CHAPTER 40

what I'm going to do with the information."

Fitz eased himself into the chair and waited for Burrows to go around his desk and sit. The man took a few moments to gather his thoughts. "Judge Harvey Sinclair has been blackmailing and bribing people for a long time. Cowan said he took Holden to force Sinclair to drop out of the confirmation hearings. He was hoping that in doing that he could protect the country from Sinclair. He went to Sinclair to tell him to back out of the confirmation hearing and the man refused. He went to the president and he refused to rescind the nomination. He tried going to his colleagues but Sinclair has the votes. He didn't know what else to do. I don't have evidence of all of this. Cowan said he's been in the process of collecting it but he thinks Sinclair's reach goes high up. He cautioned me about who to speak to and warned that if I started an investigation it could get shut down."

Burrows said all of that in nearly one breath and by the time he was done, he sucked in air. "If that's not enough, Cowan thinks the president is compromised. There's no other reason Cowan can come up with as to why Sinclair would be nominated."

Before Fitz could react or respond, Burrows continued. "I don't know what to do, Fitz. I don't know if this is a desperate man trying to convince me he had a good motive for kidnapping a kid or what? The FBI investigation into Sinclair didn't show any of this. Of course, Cowan assured me that this wasn't information readily available and the FBI would have no idea to even look into this. Cowan has a stellar reputation. He always has had. I've never known the man to be anything other than an upright citizen and forthright – even for a politician!" He stared over at Fitz and waved his hand at him. "You don't seem to be panicking at all about this. Did you hear me? Do you understand what this means?"

Fitz patted the knapsack and assured Burrows that everything was going to be okay. "Cowan was telling you the truth. I brought you

303

evidence going all the way back to Sinclair cheating his way through law school. Signed affidavits of professors and people on the ethics committee and other students taken by an attorney. I have Sinclair's offshore accounts where you can see large sums of money going in from interesting sources. Then I have a list of people who are willing to speak to the FBI and make statements about how Sinclair was either trying to blackmail them or was blackmailing them. Not to mention the private investigator who was tasked with gathering incriminating and embarrassing information on these people and is willing to give you a statement and turn on Sinclair. It's a wrap for him if the FBI is willing to get involved."

Burrows shifted his eyes to the knapsack. What should have been relief on his face wasn't.

Fitz didn't understand the reaction. "I'm handing you everything on a silver platter. What more could you possibly want? All the evidence you need is right there. You'll have to get warrants and get the information legally and take some statements. It's going to be a lot of work, but you have everything you need. Surely, there is someone here you trust to help you."

Burrows shook his head. "You don't understand, Fitz. This might all be too late. The confirmation vote was pushed up. They were in the middle of the hearing and then all of a sudden they called for the vote today. It's happening right now."

Fitz lurched forward until his arms were resting on Burrows's desk. He'd had no idea the vote had been pushed up. Fitz took a few deep breaths as his mind reeled with the inevitable outcome of having Sinclair on the highest and most powerful court in the land.

"No," Fitz said as he turned over the possibilities. He slammed his fist down on the table. "No! We aren't going out like this. Get up!" Fitz rose as he said the words and reached for the knapsack. "Let's go! We are going down to the Capitol building to the Senate floor and

CHAPTER 40

bring this to their attention."

"Fitz, we can't bust in on a Senate confirmation vote. Have you lost your mind?"

Fitz shook the knapsack. "Consider the possibilities if we don't do everything in our power to stop this from happening. Think about how compromised our legal system would become. Get up!" Fitz watched Burrows whose mouth fell open and he nervously licked his lips. He had gone from a confident FBI agent to a man who was scared to risk it all. Fitz cursed at him. "If you're out of a job, I'll hire you. Trust me I'll have plenty of work if we break this. If you don't help me, I'm calling Tim Dalton with *The Washington Post*."

Burrows rose from his chair. "What does he have to do with any of this?"

"He's the one who has been working on this investigation with Sutton for months!"

"Why didn't he bring it to the FBI's attention?"

Fitz didn't have time for this. "The same reason Cowan told you to watch your back." He raked a hand through his hair, frustration spilling over. "Look, we don't have time for this. We have a confirmation to stop. Just trust me. Get me onto the Senate floor and let me handle this. I'll protect you. If not, come work for me. You'll make a heck of a lot more money working for me than the feds." Fitz tried to lighten the mood. He smiled over at him. "I have better health insurance plans too."

"Let's go," Burrows said finally relaxing the muscles in his face. "I don't know that the Capitol Police are going to let us in."

Fitz wasn't going to let them deny them entry. He didn't know what exactly he was going to do, but he was going to get the information to those who needed it most. As they left the FBI Headquarters and rushed to the Capitol building, Fitz called Tim, directing him to come to the Capitol building with a photographer. He also told him to call anyone else in the television press who might also break the story if needed. Either way, the story was going live now.

Tim protested until Fitz shouted into the phone that the vote was happening now. The reporter changed his tune quickly, understanding the gravity of the situation. Fitz ended the call and shoved his phone back in his pocket as they reached the Capitol building steps. They rushed up the steps to the front door, slowing down long enough not to blast through them and startle the Capitol Police.

Fitz, not the young man he used to be, gulped in breaths of air, filling his burning lungs enough to speak. "We need to get into the Senate chamber. We have some information that the senators need."

Burrows shouted at the cops standing guard. He flashed his badge and went through the metal detectors.

Fitz did the same and had to hand over his knapsack. "There is evidence in there. Please be careful with it," he shouted as he stepped through then was wanded by one of the other guards.

"We can't let you in the chamber, Agent Burrows. The vote is happening right now."

Agent Burrows seemed to have recovered from the shock. He stepped forward toward the Capitol Police officer, his hands stopping short of grabbing the man by the front of the shirt. "You need to let me in that chamber. This is a grave matter of—"

He didn't get the rest of the sentence out because Fitz grabbed the knapsack from the counter after it had been searched, threw it over his shoulders, and took off in a sprint. It was a move that could have gotten him shot, but he didn't have time to debate the merits of appropriate decorum for the Capitol building. Before he got too far he watched over his shoulder as Burrows had his back.

"Stand down!" Burrows yelled to the one Capitol Police officer who had drawn his gun. "This is a matter of national security," he shouted again taking off after Fitz. He looked over his shoulder and

CHAPTER 40

called to the officers. "This is going to lead to the arrest of Harvey Sinclair." One officer shared a look with the other and then radioed to his colleagues.

Fitz was too far into the building at that point to hear what was said. He ran down one corridor but no one stopped him. An officer stepped out of his way, shouting something to Fitz he didn't hear. He zigged and zagged through the hallways and then ran up steps. He knew the doors would be locked at the lower level but he hoped where he was headed would provide him access.

His shoes squeaked against the floor and his breath heaved as he took the stairs as quickly as he could. Two Capitol Police officers stood at the doors Fitz needed to breach. He had no choice but to come to a halt in front of them. He expected resistance but was met with none.

One officer pulled open one door and the other stepped aside to let Fitz through. At the end of the day, they might all be hailed national heroes or they might all be unemployed. All Fitz knew was that the people who could do something to make things right were stepping up to do it.

As soon as Fitz entered the balcony overlooking the Senate floor, all the staffers who were watching the vote turned to look at him. He was sure his face was flushed and his eyes crazy. "Stop the vote!" he shouted at the top of his lungs. "Stop the vote! Stop the vote!" He shouted it three more times as he jogged down the steps to the balcony ledge. He leaned over and shouted it one more time for good measure. At that point, all eyes were on him.

Senate Majority Leader Lucy Gladstone turned to the balcony. "What is the meaning of this?" she shouted from the floor.

Fitz held up the knapsack. "I have evidence that Judge Harvey Sinclair has been blackmailing many of you for your votes. He employed Dunn & Foster and a local private investigator to buy your votes. This entire proceeding is compromised! It's compromised! Stop the vote!"

A collective gasp reverberated around the room. They all looked at one another in stunned silence and then a rush of voices consumed the floor, echoing in the chamber.

Senator Gladstone banged the gavel over and over again to get people to quiet down. As the din of noise hushed, she angled her head to look up at Fitz. Her words died on her lips as Agent Burrows entered the floor before Fitz was questioned about anything.

His badge held more power than Fitz with the bag of evidence. "Fitz is with me," Agent Burrows started, tucking his badge back in its holder. He went on to explain the evidence that Fitz was holding – even though Fitz realized he'd never seen one stitch of it. He had taken Fitz fully at his word and never asked to see the documents. Fitz stepped back from the ledge and sat in one of the seats, listening to how eloquently Burrows laid out the case.

When he was done, Senator Gladstone summoned Fitz down from the balcony to the Senate floor with the evidence. When it was time to hand it over, he struggled to let go of the bag – a clear sign that he still wasn't sure who to trust.

"Please," she said, meeting his eyes. "You can trust me with it." When it was in her hands, she instructed both Fitz and Burrows to leave the Senate chamber, promising them word would come soon enough about their decision.

All they could do was wait. Burrows put his hand on Fitz's back as they walked out of the Senate chamber. "We did all we could. It's in their hands now."

"It doesn't matter what they vote, you have to investigate him and bring him to justice," Fitz said with hope in his voice.

"Agents are headed to his house now. They are working on search warrants."

CHAPTER 40

Fitz breathed a sigh of relief. They got to the doors of the Capitol building just as Tim, Sutton, and a local news crew arrived. Fitz stuck out his hand and explained what transpired. "You have your story. The Senate is deciding what to do with the evidence and the FBI is headed to Sinclair. I know this didn't go down as neatly as you two would have hoped."

Timothy nodded. "It doesn't matter at this point. As long as Sinclair ends up behind bars instead of behind the Supreme Court bench. Sutton is willing to go on the record about her kidnapping."

He was glad Sutton was there and willing to finally speak freely. He offered her a smile and told her he was proud of her. Fitz hitched his thumb over his shoulder. "Let's hope they make the right call."

He knew no matter what happened Tim would be there to break the story. There was nothing more for Fitz to do and going back to his office was the only thing he wanted.

Burrows and Fitz parted at the Capitol steps with a handshake that turned into a hug.

"It will all work out, Fitz," Burrows called after him when they were feet apart and headed in opposite directions.

Fitz didn't turn back to him. He raised one hand in the air and gave him a wave.

All Fitz wanted was to walk the streets of D.C. in quiet contemplation.

The weight of the last few days was finally taking its toll.

CHAPTER 41

The news of the Senate's decision didn't come down for hours. Fitz and Charlie had remained holed up in the office with the television on. They had ordered food, neither one of them wanting to leave for fear of missing the announcement.

Charlie hadn't been surprised by the rush to the vote. President Mitchell was in his final term with only months of his presidency remaining. He was ramming the confirmation through with considerable pushback.

"It's a Midnight Judge situation," Charlie had said through bites of her salad.

Fitz hadn't heard the term before now. "What does that mean?"

Charlie finished chewing and wiped her mouth with her napkin. "It's what they called the many appointments outgoing President John Adams made in the last days of his presidency. They were approved by the Federalist-controlled Senate in February and March of 1801. Some say he was busy right up until midnight of his last night in office."

It didn't surprise him Charlie knew more about American history than he could have ever hoped to know. She had a knack for information like that and once she filed it away in her memory, it was locked in there forever. "It certainly sounds like what Mitchell was doing. I assume he was pushing so hard because Sinclair has

CHAPTER 41

something on him. We can only assume he found someone to go after his daughter as Pete described. We probably won't ever know for sure."

Charlie looked at her phone then raised her eyes to Fitz. "Have you spoken to Sutton?"

Fitz offered a slight nod of his head. "After Tim and Sutton were interviewed on the local news, the story was picked up by all the major networks. It would have taken too long to get something to print so he decided just to break the story on the news – *The Washington Post*, of course, being credited with first uncovering the scandal. The two of them are preparing for a media blitz. All the major news stations are clamoring to speak to them."

"What about you? They might have been the first on the story, but if you hadn't dropped that tracker, the whole thing wouldn't have cracked open the way it did. Plus, you saved a kid. Surely you deserve some credit, Fitz."

"No, not me," Fitz said with a laugh. "I know better than anyone what media attention brings. I'm happy to work in the shadows."

"I knew that's why I liked you," Senator Austin Ford said from the doorway to the conference room.

"I'm sorry, sir," Fitz said, wiping his hands and standing. He extended his hand to Senator Ford. He thought he had locked the front door after the dinner delivery. He must have been so distracted he hadn't. "Can I help you with something?"

"I spoke to Senator Tom Wilson. He wanted to let you know Trevor is doing well. He said the whole country owes you a debt of gratitude. I agree."

Given the senator's presence, Fitz could only assume the vote had been completed. "What happened with the vote?"

A slow smile spread across Ford's face. "I came to deliver the news in person. It was a no vote. We also heard from Agent Burrows that

Harvey Sinclair has been arrested. The FBI found a treasure trove of evidence in the man's home and office including the plot to kill Sutton as well as some of the people working for him. The extent of his crimes will be coming out in the days, weeks, and months to follow. We were assured the House will have the votes for impeachment after the Judicial Conference submits a report. He'll be disbarred as well. All in good time. As I said, we owe you our gratitude."

Fitz felt the hot burn of embarrassment creep up his neck and settle into his cheeks. "Just doing my job."

"It wasn't your job though," Ford countered, gesturing toward the table. Fitz stepped back and offered him something to drink, which he declined. "We know how this all got started. It was your ex who pulled you in and I'm glad she did. This wasn't a case where you got paid. You did this because you saw a wrong and you wanted to right it. Maybe that's something innate in your character. It's certainly your reputation with this business. There were things I couldn't tell you before. While Serena thought she was playing me, I was playing her. I knew all along what she was sent to do. I let her play her game in the hopes of finding out information. In some ways, I fell in love too. It clouded my judgment."

Fitz was so surprised by the declaration, he didn't know what to say. He wasn't sure if Ford was saving face or if Fitz believed him. Fitz didn't think it mattered now.

"Do you have a political affiliation?" Ford asked.

It was a bold question and one many of his clients had asked. "I don't. You could say I hate both parties and see value in them both. I believe that as much as people should know the positions a politician holds, they should also know their character. I think that might be even more important and the most overlooked."

"I agree with you wholeheartedly." Ford looked over at Charlie. "I know your reputation as well. I don't know much more about you,

CHAPTER 41

but I suspect that's by design."

He shouldn't have known Charlie was retired CIA but his statement implied he did. Fitz leaned back in his chair, assessing the man. He had come for more than to thank them for their hard work. There was something different about him from earlier when they had met that was starting to put Fitz on edge. "Is there something you wanted, Senator Ford?"

Fitz glanced over at Charlie. She had stopped eating and had one hand down by her side, probably resting on top of her gun. A clear sign she was uneasy about the man's intention.

Senator Ford glanced between them. "You both can relax. I'm here to make you an offer. We recently lost one of the good ones. He had been doing this for so long that he lost perspective. Took risks and did things he shouldn't have done. He went further than we are comfortable going."

Fitz wasn't sure he was following. "Are you talking about House Minority Leader Cowan?"

"It's a shame he went the direction he did. It wasn't sanctioned. He'll take full responsibility for it as he must do to protect us."

"We. Us. What are you talking about, Senator?" Charlie asked from across the table. She still had her hand on her gun. "I'm not following here."

"Well, you're not supposed to yet."

Fitz didn't like all the double-speak. He wanted Ford to get straight to the point. He expressed as much. "If you have something to say, we'd appreciate you getting to the point in clear language we understand."

"I appreciate your candor, Fitz. We've been watching you since you took over the business and partnering with Charlie, we saw two real assets here." Ford held up his hand to stop Fitz. "I know, speak more clearly. I need your confidentiality. Both of you."

Fitz glanced over at Charlie and she nodded. He turned back. "You can be assured nothing you say leaves this room unless you admit to a crime."

"Fair enough. As I said, we try to keep on the straight and narrow and not break the law. Sometimes we bend it. Cowan went several steps too far." Senator Ford could see that the pair of them were growing annoyed. "We are part of a secret order that goes back to the founding of this country. It was started by Dr. Joseph Warren. You might have heard of him."

Fitz would have to brush up on his history. The little he knew would get him by for now. Warren was a skilled doctor heavily involved in the Revolutionary War who did much for the Patriots' cause, including paying the ultimate sacrifice. He was brutally killed during battle.

"Warren was a man of skill and precision," Ford explained. "He wasn't afraid to get his hands dirty. Above all, he used his talents and leadership as a doctor and revolutionary. Warren had a unique talent of being respected and trusted by the intellectuals of the time and the common citizen. He was a good bridge between the two. But above all, he fought for what was right."

"And that's what you do?" Charlie asked, the skepticism clear in her tone. "Who else are members?"

"You know I can't tell you that. Not yet anyway." Senator Ford pulled out his wallet and tugged a white business card embossed with a gold capital W with a circle around it. He slid it over to Fitz and explained, "The Warren Circle. This is your official invitation to join. If you choose not to, and almost no one turns us down, you still have our gratitude. This is your chance to be a part of history. We've been around since the founding, passing the torch from one generation to the next. Just like my father passed the torch to me."

Senator Ford stood and extended his hand to Charlie. "I'll give you time to decide. Call the number on the card when you're ready and tell them *Dr. Warren sent you*. Information will be provided after that."

CHAPTER 41

Ford shook Fitz's hand and then left as quietly as he had arrived.

Fitz followed him out, ensuring the door was shut and locked behind him. He even double-checked it before returning to the conference room.

Fitz leaned against the doorjamb holding the small card in his hands, knowing there wasn't any way he was going to turn down the offer. He raised his eyes to Charlie. "What do you think?"

Charlie chuffed. "I've given enough for this country."

"You're in though, right?" Fitz said with a teasing smile.

Charlie hesitated for only a second. She rolled her eyes as a smile appeared on her lips too. "Of course, I'm in."

Fitz knew life for both of them was about to get interesting. Maybe being fired from the police force wasn't the worst thing that had happened to him.

It might have finally been the thing that pushed him onto the right path.

About the Author

Stacy M. Jones was born and raised in Troy, New York, and currently lives in Little Rock, Arkansas. She is a full-time writer and holds masters' degrees in journalism and in forensic psychology. She currently has four series available for readers: the completed cozy paranormal Harper & Hattie Magical Mystery Series, the hard-boiled PI Riley Sullivan Mystery Series, the FBI Agent Kate Walsh Thriller Series and the new Connor Fitzgerald Thriller series. To access Stacy's Mystery Readers Club with free novellas, visit StacyMJones.com.

You can connect with me on:
- http://www.stacymjones.com
- https://www.facebook.com/StacyMJonesWriter
- https://www.bookbub.com/profile/stacy-m-jones
- https://www.goodreads.com/StacyMJonesWriter

Subscribe to my newsletter:

✉ http://www.stacymjones.com

Also by Stacy M. Jones

Watch for the next Connor Fitzgerald Thriller in Spring 2025

Access the Free Mystery Readers' Club Starter Library
PI Riley Sullivan Mystery Series novella "The 1922 Club Murder"
FBI Agent Kate Walsh Thriller Series novella "The Curators"
Harper & Hattie Mystery Series novella "Harper's Folly"

Sign up for the starter library along with launch-day pricing and special behind-the-scenes access. Hit subscribe at http://www.stacymjones.com/

Please leave a review for Midnight Judge. Reviews help more readers find my books. Thank you!

Other books by Stacy M. Jones by series and order to date

FBI Agent Kate Walsh Thriller Series
The Curators
The Founders
Miami Ripper
Mad Jack
The Fuse
Dead Senate
Close Killer
Diamond King
The Magician
Helix Syndicate

PI Riley Sullivan Mystery Series
The 1922 Club Murder
Deadly Sins
The Bone Harvest
Missing Time Murders
We Last Saw Jane
Boston Underground
The Night Game
Harbor Cove Murders
The Drowned Boys
What He Saw
Fear City
What Stays Buried

Harper & Hattie Magical Mystery Series
Harper's Folly
Saints & Sinners Ball
Secrets to Tell
Rule of Three
The Forever Curse
The Witches Code
The Sinister Sisters
Scandal Knocks Twice
A Treasure Most Deadly

Made in United States
North Haven, CT
06 May 2025